THE NEW MIDDLE AGES

BONNIE WHEELER, *Series Editor*

The New Middle Ages is a series dedicated to pluridisciplinary studies of medieval cultures, with particular emphasis on recuperating women's history and on feminist and gender analyses. This peer-reviewed series includes both scholarly monographs and essay collections.

PUBLISHED BY PALGRAVE:

Women in the Medieval Islamic World
edited by Gavin R. G. Hambly

The Ethics of Nature in the Middle Ages: On Boccaccio's Poetaphysics
by Gregory B. Stone

Presence and Presentation: Women in the Chinese Literati Tradition
by Sherry J. Mou

The Lost Letters of Heloise and Abelard: Perceptions of Dialogue in Twelfth-Century France
by Constant J. Mews

Understanding Scholastic Thought with Foucault
by Philipp W. Rosemann

For Her Good Estate: The Life of Elizabeth de Burgh
by Frances A. Underhill

Constructions of Widowhood and Virginity in the Middle Ages
edited by Cindy L. Carlson and Angela Jane Weisl

Motherhood and Mothering in Anglo-Saxon England
by Mary Dockray-Miller

Listening to Heloise: The Voice of a Twelfth-Century Woman
edited by Bonnie Wheeler

The Postcolonial Middle Ages
edited by Jeffrey Jerome Cohen

Chaucer's Pardoner and Gender Theory: Bodies of Discourse
by Robert S. Sturges

Crossing the Bridge: Comparative Essays on Medieval European and Heian Japanese Women Writers
edited by Barbara Stevenson and Cynthia Ho

Engaging Words: The Culture of Reading in the Later Middle Ages
by Laurel Amtower

Robes and Honor: The Medieval World of Investiture
edited by Stewart Gordon

Representing Rape in Medieval and Early Modern Literature
edited by Elizabeth Robertson and Christine M. Rose

Same Sex Love and Desire among Women in the Middle Ages
edited by Francesca Canadé Sautman and Pamela Sheingorn

Sight and Embodiment in the Middle Ages: Ocular Desires
by Suzannah Biernoff

Listen, Daughter: The Speculum Virginum *and the Formation of Religious Women in the Middle Ages*
edited by Constant J. Mews

Science, the Singular, and the Question of Theology
by Richard A. Lee, Jr.

Gender in Debate from the Early Middle Ages to the Renaissance
edited by Thelma S. Fenster and Clare A. Lees

Malory's Morte Darthur: *Remaking Arthurian Tradition*
by Catherine Batt

The Vernacular Spirit: Essays on Medieval Religious Literature
edited by Renate Blumenfeld-Kosinski, Duncan Robertson, and Nancy Warren

Popular Piety and Art in the Late Middle Ages: Image Worship and Idolatry in England 1350–1500
by Kathleen Kamerick

Absent Narratives, Manuscript Textuality, and Literary Structure in Late Medieval England
by Elizabeth Scala

Creating Community with Food and Drink in Merovingian Gaul
by Bonnie Effros

Representations of Early Byzantine Empresses: Image and Empire
by Anne McClanan

Encountering Medieval Textiles and Dress: Objects, Texts, Images
edited by Désirée G. Koslin and Janet Snyder

Eleanor of Aquitaine: Lord and Lady
edited by Bonnie Wheeler and John Carmi Parsons

THE FLIGHT FROM DESIRE

AUGUSTINE AND OVID TO CHAUCER

Robert R. Edwards

First published in 2006 by
PALGRAVE MACMILLAN™
175 Fifth Avenue, New York, N.Y. 10010 and
Houndmills, Basingstoke, Hampshire, England RG21 6XS
Companies and representatives throughout the world.

PALGRAVE MACMILLAN is the global academic imprint of the Palgrave Macmillan division of St. Martin's Press, LLC and of Palgrave Macmillan Ltd. Macmillan® is a registered trademark in the United States, United Kingdom and other countries. Palgrave is a registered trademark in the European Union and other countries.

ISBN-13: 978–1–4039–6411–3
ISBN-10: 1–4039–6411–4

Library of Congress Cataloging-in-Publication Data is available from the Library of Congress.

A catalogue record for this book is available from the British Library.

Design by Newgen Imaging Systems (P) Ltd., Chennai, India.

First edition: May 2006

10 9 8 7 6 5 4 3 2 1

Printed in the United States of America.

For Dick, Anne, Mili, and Vic

CONTENTS

PREFACE

This book argues the need to revise part of our critical understanding of love and desire in medieval literature. Medieval writers recognized that love was a defining element of human experience and that it was central to ideas of selfhood, to the formation of knowledge, to moral judgments, social theorizing, and spiritual reality. Over the last century, an impressive body of historical and interpretive scholarship sought to give coherent definition to love in these various spheres and to trace connections and conceptual unities between them. In recent decades, focus has shifted to more specific topics and themes—misogyny and idealization (R. Howard Bloch), love and hermeneutics (Toril Moi), readership and poetic self-reflexivity (Peter Allen), friendship and virtue (C. Stephen Jaeger), the couple (Jean Hagstrum), the loving subject (Gerald Bond), and objects and contradiction (Sarah Kay). My focus on desire is inevitably part of this shift, but it is also a move away from what I take to be a governing but unexamined assumption that persists in criticism, theory, and literary history.

The significant contributions of recent scholarship (my list above is illustrative, not exhaustive) largely share the assumption of earlier work that doctrines and theories of love can be formulated systematically within literary representation. These formulations quite properly reflect the need to establish conditions of intelligibility across time and cultural differences. Medieval writers and commentators registered a similar need when they drafted the manuscript rubric "Quid sit amor"—a phrase that hovers enticingly between question and definition. The position I argue in this book is that our understanding of love in medieval literary texts requires a complementary dimension, which is some account of the workings of desire. Desire invests love with urgency and unruly, ambivalent demands, chief among them sensation and pleasure. It unsettles explanatory doctrines and theories, even as it depends on them as a framework for expression. It is also a form of knowledge that reveals facets of the self, the attachments we make and ask for with others, the social roles we play as agents moved by passion, will, and affect.

The account of desire I offer in this book traces out sets of relations structured dialectically within language, representation, and performance. It emerges from the study and interpretation of texts and of the discursive formations these texts both drew upon and helped constitute within medieval literary culture. What I try to describe, then, is a process and a hermeneutic rather than a fixed meaning or structure. For that reason I am as much concerned with the oblique ways in which desire speaks as in the formulations that love offers for what it is or ought to be. My account focuses on an interplay that extends through representation, authorship, and reading. It follows textual dialectics of love and desire whose syntheses, if any, are occasions for further revision, amendment, and reinscription. The claims I make are finally those of persuasion and of literary and historical understanding. If my account is provisional and partial, as it must be, it remains, I hope, true to the texts, to their varied rhetorical, conceptual, and poetic frameworks, and to the qualities that mark their historical reception and our continuing fascination with them.

I thank the friends and colleagues who shared their learning and good counsel and challenged me to rethink my own assumptions as this book took shape: Rémi Brague, Carolyn Collette, John Fyler, Warren Ginsberg, Norris Lacy, Sherry Roush, Winthrop Wetherbee, and the late Carl Vaught. I thank Patrick Cheney in particular for his generosity and unfailing care in reading successive drafts of my chapters and for his patient insistence that this was the book for me to write, even if it took longer than either of us expected. The anonymous reader of my final manuscript offered wise and welcome advice for clarifying my aims. It is a sadness that Jean Hagstrum is not with us, for the origins of this book lie in a Fellows' seminar he organized at the National Humanities Center two decades ago and in the conversations the seminar generated with David Halperin, Stephen Spector, and other Fellows and visitors. Over the course of this project Tim Arner, Colin Fewer, Jennifer Merriman, and Steele Nowlin contributed splendid research assistance as they mapped out their own exciting projects of research. Other students, particularly Craig Bertolet, Laura Getty, Heather Hayton, Danielle Smith, and Dustin Stegner, worked through the texts with me in seminars and courses, showing me so often where the questions had to lead.

This project had strong support from my home institution. Don Bialostosky and Robert Caserio, my department heads in English at Penn State, and Caroline Eckhardt, my department head in Comparative Literature, understood what I was trying to do and generously gave me their backing. I gratefully acknowledge the College of the Liberal Arts and the Institute for the Arts and Humanities at Penn State for research funding and the College for a sabbatical leave to finish research and writing. Pattee

Library, Cambridge University Library, and the Bibliothèque nationale Française have made materials available and concentrated work possible. I thank Bonnie Wheeler for her warm reception of this book and her inclusion of it in the New Middle Ages Series under her direction and editorship. An earlier version of chapter 7 appeared in *Studies in Philology* 94 (1999): 394–416, and a version of chapter 4 is forthcoming in a special issue of *Mediaevalia*. Warm thanks are due the editors of both journals, Don Kennedy and Sandro Sticca, for permission to reprint the materials.

I have two other debts, one long-standing and the other happily continuing. My dedication records the first. Richard Fly, F. Anne Payne, Mili Clark, and Victor Doyno were extraordinary colleagues and loyal friends in the English Department at SUNY-Buffalo, where I had the remarkable good fortune to begin my career. Their commitment to literary scholarship, the intensity of intellectual life, and the worth of teaching shaped much of what I hoped to become. My other debt is to Emily Grosholz, whose achievements as a philosopher, poet, and woman of letters—at once distinct and wholly inseparable—sustain a life of discovery and ideas for the two of us and for our family. Holding together those worlds, she makes a better one for me, Benjamin, Robert, William, and Mary-Frances.

INTRODUCTION

In his *De vulgari eloquentia*, Dante identifies passionate love as one of three *magnalia*, or preeminent topics in his literary tradition. Love offered medieval writers perhaps their most interesting and compelling subject, one fit for nuanced thematic treatment, complex philosophical reflection, and serious artistic expression in an elevated style. By love Dante means erotic attachment to an object of compelling physical attraction: "dicimus illud esse maxime delectabile quod per pretiosissimum obiectum appetitus delectat: hoc autem venus est" ("here I say that what is most pleasurable is what is the most highly valued object of our desires; and this is love" [2.2.7]).[1] He situates love in the middle of a hierarchy of topics, above arms and below moral virtue. The hierarchy corresponds to man's vegetative, animal, and rational souls.[2] In this scheme, love reflects our creaturely condition: it is what we seek because we are animate and conscious, alive to sensation and pleasure and able to make judgments about them. For Dante, it is the middle track in mankind's three-fold path ("triplex iter") between brute necessity, which compels survival through prowess in arms (the topic of epic), and reason, which controls the direction of the will (the topic of a poetry concerned with virtue).

Dante's alignment of passionate love with philosophical reflection and elevated style acknowledges a key formulation in Western literary and cultural history. Such a connection had no significant place earlier within the classical hierarchy of literary styles, where love is associated with comedy, yet it is largely inescapable after the Middle Ages and Renaissance in the ways we think about love as a central feature of experience and identity. As Dante describes love, he treats it as a stable topic, fully established in literary tradition and already given exemplary treatment in poems by Arnaut Daniel and Cino da Pistoia. The poems he cites, however, belie the impression of stability and settled literary decorum. They are works that give voice to anxiety and profound contradictions as well as the affirmation of love. Arnaut, for instance, acknowledges that love is the veil for other things: "ma·l cors ferms, fortz, / mi fai cobrir / mains vers" ("But my firm, unflinching heart / Makes me cover up / Many true things" (9.45–48).[3]

This book investigates the literary dynamic implied by Dante's formulation and made fleetingly visible here in Arnaut's poem. My governing premise is that within the literary system Dante describes for high culture in the Middle Ages love and desire operate dialectically. My title expresses this complex relation through the figure of a flight from desire. In ascetic literature, withdrawal from the world constitutes what Saint Ambrose calls a "fuga saeculi" ("flight from the world").[4] In Abelard's *Historia calamitatum*, Heloise extends Ambrose's notion from ascetics to philosophers, who do not abandon the world so much as flee it ("nec tam relinquentes seculum quam fugientes").[5] For Ambrose and Heloise those flights lead nonetheless to disciplines at the service of erotic attachments—for Ambrose the soul's salvation in God and for Heloise the singular, passionate embrace of philosophy as a way of living and being.[6] The flight from desire, in other words, is a movement toward forms that already contain desire.

In the texts I shall examine, this dialectic unfolds between love as an informing theme and erotic demands that remain irreducibly different from overt formulations of love, such as charity, affection, and devotion. Writing about the pleasures and values involved in love typically reveals a project for defining selfhood, shaping subjectivity, and understanding vital dimensions of moral, social, and spiritual life. As one of the *magnalia*, love provides a discursive form that contains demands which (as modern interpreters after Freud and Lacan argue) can be neither adequately controlled nor fully possessed. My point is not, however, that all passionate attachments are erotic displacements or sublimations, nor do I propose that love can be reduced merely to desire. Desire is not at the far end of love; more often, it is located somewhere sideways within it. In the *Vita nuova* and the *Commedia*, one of Beatrice's functions is to remind Dante that his professed love for her serves to mask the presence of other erotic demands, of which he is not fully or adequately aware.

Love as a poetic topic, then, complements desire by providing a formalized discourse within which erotic demands emerge. The literary discourse of love presents itself as a universal that structures understanding and practice, as if the universal had taken a concrete, particular form.[7] Love thereby offers a framework of conventions for expression and reception, for coding and uncoding, within which desire speaks obliquely, as by definition it must. What I want to explore in this book might be illustrated by an example from Dante's early literary career in which he reflects on the twin projects of love and writing about love. His formulation deserves our particular attention for its discovery of desire simultaneously within love and writing.

Dire d'amore

E lo primo che cominciò a dire sì come poeta volgare, si mosse però che
volle fare intendere le sue parole a donna, a la quale era malagevole d'intendere li versi latini. E questo è contra coloro che rimano sopra altra matera che
amorosa, con ciò sia cosa che cotale modo di parlare fosse dal principio
trovato per dire d'amore.

[And the first who began writing as a poet of the vernacular was prompted
by the desire to make his words understandable to ladies, to whom it was difficult to understand Latin verses. And this counters those who rhyme on
other matters than the amorous, for that mode of versification was developed
from the beginning in order to write of love.][8]

In this passage from the *Vita nuova* (25.6), Dante imagines a founding
moment for vernacular lyric with an originary first poet. This poet invents
himself by inventing his role as one who writes as if he were a vernacular
poet ("sì come poeta volgare"). He creates his role, that is, by imagining it
as already constituted by love. Writing about love depends here on two
different aims. In philosophical terms, love, says Dante, is an accident in
substance that originates outside language; and so, rhetorically, it requires a
parallel invention of ideas and linguistic adornment. As in medieval
allegory, rhetorical colors and figures of thought and speech lend a covering
for what exists and can be understood in some other discursive field. Hence
poets must always be able to furnish a prose equivalent for what they want
to say. Dante's image for poetic composition insists on devestiture, exposure, and exhibition—"denudare le sue parole da cotale vesta, in guisa che
avessero verace intendimento" ("unveil their words in a way that would
show their true reasoning" [25.10]). Poets adopt the vernacular, however,
for altogether different rhetorical aims. Vernacular writing circumvents the
exclusions of Latin, which separates men from women and thereby forestalls their conversations about love. The vernacular is thus performative as
well as mimetic. It requires symbolic terms that operate within an eroticized medium, a "modo di parlare" that simultaneously links poets and
their audience, lovers and their beloveds.

To this point, what Dante says about love and writing might be formulated
as merely a choice of expression: love can be adorned by poetic figures or
translated to prose and rendered transparent in its meaning. Divested of
rhetorical adornment, love can presumably be seen for what it is. If we look
closely, however, the motive that originally drives writing remains
stubbornly beyond the transpositions of poetry and prose, rhetorical covering and true meaning. As Dante also makes clear in this passage, some form
of desire exists even before love is put into language. Indeed, desire is a
necessary condition of language. His originary poet is moved initially to

present his will and his intent to force understanding ("che volle fare intendere le sue parole a donna"). Beneath his rational alignment of figures and
meaning lies an erotic negotiation through language. He addresses not just
a concept or personified figure of love—the abstraction made seemingly
concrete and particular, like the God of Love who appears to Dante in his
dream visions—but the specific object of his desire, the interlocutor sought
for conversation. For her part, she can speak back in the same language
or—as Beatrice chooses in the *Vita nuova*—decide not to. And while her
silence may cancel out or deflect the expression of love into new projects
and poetic formulations, as it ostensibly does in Dante's *libello*, it does not
affect the movement of desire, which remains precisely as Dante formulates
it: the emphatic wish to make the words understood by someone else, to
reveal and disclose their *verace intendimento*—their true meaning, intent, and
purpose—to another as a form of erotic demand.[9] Dante's founding moment
for writing about love reveals the deep structure of his topic, for the project
of writing about love is radically connected to desire. As we shall see in the
letters of Heloise and the *Lais* of Marie de France, the same structure holds
when the intending agent is female and authorial, writing against male
structures of intellectual and political power.

The Erotic Field

Dante's work as a poet-theorist teaches us that desire resides uncertainly
but somehow necessarily within the great poetic topic of love; it can function as immediate erotic attraction ("hoc autem venus est") and ultimately
as the will's intent to disclose itself, as demand itself. These shifting modes
remind us that for medieval writers desire exists within a large conceptual
and discursive field. The chapters that follow are especially concerned with
desire as absence, substitution, mutability, and disclosure. It may be useful
therefore to look briefly at how these particular features operate within the
broad tradition of speculating on the nature of eros. My purpose is not to
suggest direct sources or systems of thought that explain literary texts but to
describe provisionally how the problem of desire can be formulated within
a multiform tradition.[10]

In classical and medieval descriptions, desire is a movement of the soul
toward an object perceived as good and beautiful. It differs from other
forms of affection like friendship and divine love by its self-interest, intensity,
and undercurrent of sexuality. Most accounts of desire characterize it as a
passionate yearning based on absence. Aristotle, in a passage cited by Aquinas,
defines desire as wanting the pleasurable.[11] Aquinas uses Aristotle's model
of physical movement and local motion to describe the attraction exerted
by pleasure not as absolute but as a form of absence: "bonum delectabile

non est absolute objectum concupiscentiae, sed sub ratione absentis" ("The pleasurable is the object of desire, not *qua* pleasurable, but *qua* absent").[12] Absence also locates desire in time. And desire is thus a structure of finitude. In Plato's *Phaedrus*, the erotic quest is tied to memory and recovery; in the *Symposium*, it looks forward toward possession of the good. For Cicero, who follows the Stoic belief that desire is a *pathos* or *perturbatio* afflicting the self, yearning is thrust into the future because lust (*libido*) depends on anticipation, even though physical delight is experienced in the present.[13] Saint Augustine accepts Cicero's temporal mapping of the passions,[14] and he distinguishes *desiderium* from *concupiscentia* in both concept and usage: all desire is concupiscence but not all concupiscence is desire because desire is for something wished for but not possessed.[15]

An important, if problematic, formulation of desire as absence comes at the very beginning of Andreas Capellanus's *De amore* (1.1), a work that proposes both to teach and repudiate passionate love. Andreas gives a formal definition of love according to its genus and specific differentia, and he identifies the final cause of love:

> Amor est passio quaedam innata procedens ex visione et immoderata cogitatione formae alterius sexu, ob quam aliquis super omnia cupit alterius potiri amplexibus et omnia de utriusque voluntate in ipsius amplexu amoris praecepta compleri.
>
> [Love is an inborn suffering which results from the sight of, and uncontrolled thinking about, the beauty of the other sex. This feeling makes a man desire before all else the embraces of the other sex, and to achieve the utter fulfilment of the commands of love in the other's embrace by their common desire.]

In this definition, the genus of love is a somatic disturbance (*passio*), and the specific differentia is the sequence of sight and imagination. Love follows from the sensuous apprehension of beauty, and it is preserved internally by obsessive reflection. The object desired by the lover is real and separate from him, but it operates here within his imagination. The immediate effect of sight and inner contemplation is to pose the lover's absolute demand for erotic possession. The final cause or purpose is to achieve sexual gratification, which is sought by lover and beloved alike.

The full significance of love remains, however, only partially conveyed by Andreas's definition. As Toril Moi remarks, Andreas represents love as naturalized, impossible, and displaced or concealed.[16] In addition, he passes over the central mystery by which love transforms from the lover's internal excess, from his *immoderata cogitatio* and demand for consummation "super omnia," to the reciprocity of two lovers who share each other's intention (*utraque voluntas*) of achieving physical satisfaction. In one sense, of course, this reciprocity may itself be nothing more than a disguised erotic demand, for the disturbed lover pondering the image of his beloved is perhaps merely seeing his own will mirrored back to him in the imagined will of his beloved.

Andreas composes an eclectic definition. He draws on the Stoic vocabulary of perturbation and pathology to express the unbalancing of emotions in a well-regulated agent. His ideal of erotic reciprocity is an eroticized form of Cicero's *consensio animarum* in virtuous friendship and a reminder of Ovid's goal of mutual pleasure.[17] Still, the interiority of desire and the absence that is its defining condition pose continuing challenges to understanding and erotic life. Some medieval writers register this problem directly by offering a shortened form of Andreas's definition: "Amor est passio quedam innata, ex visione et immoderata cogitatione forme alterius sexus procedens."[18] This truncated version fully expresses the solipsism of eros—its complete interiority, as the sight of the sensuous form of the other leads to an excessive contemplation that has no stated purpose outside itself: love is a self-sustaining internal pathology.[19] Andreas's lover, on these terms, experiences desire guaranteed by absence.

Capellanus's definition is one among several in a large discursive field of erotics. It generated not just variants like the shortened form above but textual reworkings and translations, such as in Jean de Meun's continuation of the *Roman de la Rose*. Patrick Boyde describes a more systematic formulation drawn from Aristotle and Aquinas and applied in Dante's *Commedia*. Love moves, in this analysis, from inclination through desire to fulfilment:

> "Inclination" relates to the *principium*. It is the innate capacity for loving certain kinds of "good," which is an inalienable property of every living form. "Desire" is the phase in which this potential for love is actualised by the perception of a good; and it refers to a particular "movement of the soul" towards that particular good. Desire is not, or should not be, permanent (the souls in Limbo suffer because they must "live in desire without hope"). It ceases in the phase called "fruition," when the movement has come to its "end." *Fruitio* is a state of stillness, characterised by a feeling of delight or pleasure, in which the "amante" is united with and lovingly enjoys the "cosa amata." It is the "final cause" of love. When it is long lasting and only slightly disturbed, it is known as "happiness" (*felicitas*). When it is eternal and complete in every way, it is called "blessedness" (*beatitudo*).[20]

We can see immediately that this account gives a different place to eros from the one it holds in Andreas's definition. Desire is not pathology but a condition of being. It acts as an efficient cause to move inclination from potency to act. Where it diverges still further from Andreas is in the dimensions of time and finitude. Fruition, for Andreas, is a complete and bounded act of mutual sexual possession, a reciprocal (if mystified) interchange of wills. Boyde's scholastic account pushes fruition further ahead in time past the bounded act to long-lasting happiness or eternal blessedness. Love, in this analysis, looks resolutely beyond the immediacy of delight and pleasure, while desire remains instrumental within time and finitude.

The pleasurable object sought by desire, whether bounded or projected in time, proves in fact to be doubly elusive. First, it is absent, lost in the past or deferred to the future. Second, it is a substitute for something else. Desire reaches beyond the objects that set it in motion. While we cannot possess what we wish, what we wish is not what we actually desire. Plato offers a structural model of erotic substitution that will recur in various permutations in the medieval texts we shall study. Gregory Vlastos points out that Plato's theory of love is not about love for persons as such: "What it is really about is love for place-holders of the predicates 'useful' and 'beautiful'—of the former when it is only *philia*, of the latter, when it is *eros*."[21] Plato's discussion of *eros* resituates the finitude of desire past need, possession, and gratification in an attraction for what lies beyond and apart from desire's immediate object. David Halperin rightly points out, "Erotics is not a science but a mystery."[22] For Christian writers, the objects of erotic investment are, at least from the retrospect of grace, signs of a divine providence that subsumes all desire. Thus Augustine can classify desire according to the lusts of the flesh, eyes, and world (1 John 2:16) while speaking of Christian life as a *sanctum desiderium*.[23]

Operating through proxies and substitutes, desire is crucially different from appetite. Aristotle explains the difference by saying that appetite can operate contrary to wish and calculation.[24] Aquinas's discussion of *concupiscentia* builds on Aristotle's distinction between nonreflective, common appetites for food and drink and desires for things perceived as good and fitting (*bonum et conveniens*), hence pleasurable.[25] Halperin illustrates the difference thus: "the objects of appetite are *samples*, whereas the objects of erotic desire are *instances* or *manifestations*."[26] Common and necessary appetites recur periodically and can be satisfied, whereas desire persists in time and represents a demand beyond its immediate objects of pleasure. Desire is open to deliberation and moral reflection in a way that simple appetite such as natural love is not.

Absence and substitution are features that link traditional and modern theorizing, however much the historical periods may differ in their valuations of erotic experience. In modern theories, the immediate objects of desire emerge from deeper demands, wishes, and instincts, and so they are inevitably substitutes or symptoms. What they replace eludes direct, conscious understanding, for it resides in the human unconscious or as the

residue of demands after the appetite of satisfaction is subtracted.[27]
R. Howard Bloch proposes that modern theorizing about eroticism and
death is woven into our master narratives of love in the Middle Ages as
promulgated by figures like Denis de Rougemont. De Rougemont's *Love
in the Western World* construes the continual obstacles to lovers' fulfilment
as signifying a more powerful wish for death and transcendence.[28] Bloch's
own argument—that misogyny is the obverse, not the opposite, of elevated
expressions of love—tacitly builds on another master narrative of medieval
love: Irving Singer's contention that love depends on idealization, on
imbuing love objects with value.[29] Bloch connects misogyny with the
ascetic discourse of virginity in a shared effort to make women abstractions;
desire thus directed has an absolute and impossible object, and as soon as
such desire is put into language, it is disclosed, betrayed, and transformed
into an obstacle. To desire another is to demand what by definition can
never be possessed, to demand impossibility itself.

Absence and substitution also reflect the mutability of desire. Replacing
one object with another does not carry us closer to whatever it is that desire
signifies any more than the gratifications of appetite satisfy desire. One
consequence of moving between objects in time is to reveal desire as a
paradox—an attachment constructed out of its own finitude and frustration. Jonathan Dollimore points out, "On the one hand, mutability is the
ineluctable enemy of desire because it ceaselessly thwarts it. . . .On the
other hand, movement, motion, change, inconstancy are the very stuff not
just of life but also of desire; that is to say, *mutability is also the inner dynamic
of desire.*"[30] Another consequence is to enable the ambivalent discoveries of
desire. If desire cannot disclose itself completely, it uncovers the presence
of demands that cannot be acknowledged or processed as they intrude into
consciousness. To act on desire is simultaneously to submit to desire, and
in this way to enter a domain of contingency whose shape and constraints
cannot be known fully beforehand. Kenelm Foster, explaining the link
between erotic appetition and cognition in Dante, remarks, "desire always
tends to outrun knowledge."[31] The intending subject is both the agent and
victim of his desire. What Froma Zeitlin observes of classical texts also
applies to medieval erotic discourse: "the beauty of sexual allure also proves
more often to be a snare and delusion rather than an unmixed joy."[32]

The discoveries enabled by desire bear equally on the objects and modes
of representation. For Dante to find that love and writing about love depend
on a desire already in place is to encounter something that revises his system
of thought and its conditions of intelligibility. It is an aesthetic discovery and
recognition of new imaginative possibilities. These possibilities may not be
entirely welcome—the *Vita nuova* is nothing if not a virtuoso act of
revision, censorship, and self-policing, as are other texts we shall

examine—but erotic discovery and recognition persist as challenges to ideological and textual systems, to love as a stable and settled topic. Moreover, representation itself is a form of desire, as medieval writers fully recognized, feared, and exploited. Texts not only convey movements of the soul toward objects invested with beauty and value; they can also constitute such objects themselves in the pleasures of reading and imagination. If Beatrice can figuratively become Christ in the *Vita nuova*, Paolo and Francesca can literally become Lancelot and Guenevere in the *Inferno*. And if Guillaume de Lorris can enclose all the art of love in the *Roman de la Rose*, Jean de Meun can rewrite his story in drastically changed terms. In the process of rhetorical invention that underlies writing in medieval literary culture, desire serves the ambitions of authorship no less than the practical aims of composing texts.

Exemplary Desire

A comprehensive treatment of love and desire in medieval literature is beyond the scope and objective of this book. My project might be described instead as the study of exemplary desire. By that I mean the study of texts that present us with significant interpretive issues in the workings of love and desire. Though each is a major, canonical text, these works are not intended to stand as representatives of a particular genre or theme or as consummate expressions of a historical moment. They command our attention, rather, because they make us rethink the issues. Exemplarity in this sense locates critical and historical understanding in the problems of desire. As a method of inquiry, it directs our reading to particular formulations and forces us to interpret against the criteria of textual evidence. If desire entails forms of signification that cannot be tabulated or inventoried completely, it follows that, to the extent that we can understand desire at all, we must understand it in the textual form it takes. In classical, modern, and medieval theories, desire may have a single source or unitary structure, but we always see its workings in particular texts.

The approach I take risks, of course, merely reproducing what modern readers have been conditioned to see and understand. In practice, though, interpretation requires us to set our understanding of exemplary texts against language and history. If what we understand about desire after Freud and Lacan is something different from what was meant in antiquity and the Middle Ages, desire functions nonetheless within language that we can situate in textual systems, discursive contexts, and communities of writers and readers. These provide not only the measure of alterity but also criteria of corrigibility: they rule out readings that have lesser or no persuasive support. On these terms, interpretation is a contingent historical act, embedded in practice and context. Whatever else it brings by way of modern suppositions, such reading is inescapably an engagement with a literary tradition that has already shaped important dimensions of our understanding.

The structure of this book draws on what I take to be the interpretive power of exemplary desire. I focus on works connected to each other intertextually and grounded in two earlier sources for analyzing desire that proved widely influential in the Middle Ages. Augustine in his *Confessions* (chapter 1) sets out a theory that radically integrates facets of desire and holds out the promise of plenitude by identifying the source of all desire. To do so, he exploits the retrospect offered by conversion narrative to chart a forward movement (provisionally completed) through carnality, worldly attachment, ambition, and false, partial conversions. Writing for an ecclesiastical elite of provincial churchmen experienced in the literature of philosophical and religious conversion, he traces the diverse manifestations of desire back to the love of God that is the forward destination of his story. For modern readers at least, his narrative presents two related problems. One is the impoverishment of desire as a reality of human experience, imaginative sympathy, and moral reflection. The other is the relocation of divine plenitude as a form of demand for erotic presence in narratives of abandonment. Both problems will surface repeatedly in the medieval texts we investigate.

The writer I pair with Augustine in my interpretive framework is Ovid (chapter 2). A great deal of criticial interest has developed in Ovid's reception in the Middle Ages, especially as an author in the school curriculum from the twelfth century onwards, for which we have academic introductions and commentaries. My focus lies not in Ovid the moralist as portrayed by this tradition but in the magisterial role Ovid fictionally claims for himself in the *Ars amatoria* and *Remedia amoris*. Ovid offers just the opposite from Augustine's integration of desire and demand for plenitude. His pseudo-didactic teaching, directed to and satirizing a class of leisured, sophisticated readers, is centrifugal and seemingly promiscuous; it ostensibly describes techniques for finding, capturing, keeping, and, when necessary, removing or fleeing objects of pleasure. Technique (*ars*) presumably confers mastery over love objects and mastery over oneself in servicing appetite. Yet desire lies beyond this view of love as a craft and practical skill. The Ovidian *praeceptor* expounds his tactical lessons only to discover himself snared by the desire that appetite disguises and amatory craft seeks to control.

In the chapters that follow my readings of Augustine and Ovid, I examine representations of desire that emerge from these models and from the intertextuality and rewriting of desire that connect medieval writers in diverse genres and literary communities. Within the conventions of medieval letter-writing, Abelard begins an Ovidian career that turns to

Augustinian conversion, while Heloise devises strategies of reading and writing that resist the integration Abelard seeks to impose on her (chapter 3). She claims unaccommodated desire as a basis for subjectivity and selfhood. The *Lais* of Marie de France (chapter 4), I argue, concentrate on a particular phase of Ovid's erotic program—keeping a lover and prolonging pleasure. They engage the problem of sustaining erotic attachment largely outside marriage but within the regulatory violence of medieval baronial culture.

In some measure, Heloise and Marie recognize that writing about desire means rewriting previous narratives and resituating their contexts and frames of reference. My next three chapters study texts where reinscription is the problem of desire. In the *Roman de la Rose* (chapter 5), Guillaume de Lorris rewrites Ovidian craft as desire and locates it within medieval courtly culture. His courtly invention is the poetic material that both permits and constrains Jean de Meun's elaborately staged satiric continuation of his dream vision. Jean's rewriting depends on relocating Guillaume's formulation of desire within the linear retrospect of Augustinian narrative. What we discover at the end of the *Rose*, I contend, is not a conversion narrative but a posthistory of eros. Dante, who may have translated the *Rose* into the sonnet sequence of the *Fiore*, uses Augustinian retrospect more directly than Jean to shape the narrative of the *Vita nuova* (chapter 6). Conversion narrative redirects the power of desire in memory and in earlier lyrics that he chooses to include in the prosimetrum of his *libello*. He constructs a work of erotic and poetic revision that does not fully resolve the problem of desire but instead defers it until another work can be written. In other words, he flees desire by making a new project of writing the object of desire's anticipation.

My final chapter traces a sequence of poetic revision grounded in Augustinian and Ovidian models of desire but drawing as well on a tradition of biblical exegesis. I focus here on a scene from Chaucer's *Troilus and Criseyde* in which Troilus revisits the sites of his earlier pleasures with Criseyde as he waits in vain for her promised return to Troy. On the one hand, Chaucer rewrites the scene from his immediate source, Boccaccio's *Filostrato*. On the other, he evokes the imaginative power of Boccaccio's own intertext, Dante's citation of the Book of Lamentations to signify Beatrice's death in the *Vita nuova*. In this way, Chaucer's poem reframes part of Ovid's erotic doctrine within the poetics of loss expressed by Lamentations and expounded by medieval commentaries on the text. For medieval readers, loss is balanced by the promise of restoration. Evoking this interpretive context, Chaucer uncovers the problem of his revisionary narrative, which is the demand for plenitude within a history that has no future.

What emerges from these exemplary texts is, I hope, a heightened understanding of the imaginative power and conceptual refinement that the interplay of love and desire makes possible. The dialectic I trace reaches no syntheses, either within the texts or in their successive reinscriptions, but this inconclusiveness does not mean that each text somehow produces the same aporia. Abelard and Heloise negotiate desire differently from each other and from the aristocratic couples in Marie's *Lais*. Guillaume's thwarted lover is different from the disenchanted narrator at the end of Jean's reworking of the *Rose*. Dante finds a strategy of deferral and substitution that does not work for Boccaccio or Chaucer. If my readings show love doctrines at risk from desire within, they also demonstrate the necessity of doctrines and amatory theories as the structures through which desire reveals itself in language. Such disclosure is always partial and inferred, and the continuing work of interpreting it testifies to the centrality of erotic discourse in medieval culture and modern understanding. Desire works through language, doctrine, and ideology to make itself both knowable as a demand and known to others. It thus serves as a way of negotiating attachments and identity in the social world and of appraising the moral claims of what we do and what we want. As they show by their continual effort to invent and revise, medieval writers recognized that this work of imagination and understanding is a condition of aesthetic, emotional, and historical experience.

CHAPTER 1

DESIRE IN SAINT AUGUSTINE'S *CONFESSIONS*

Saint Augustine's *Confessions* presents a story of spiritual conversion structured by providence yet working through desire. Desire is the path that leads Augustine from carnal indulgence and worldly ambition through his partial conversions to Manicheism and philosophy, thence toward a full conversion to orthodox Catholicism and a final beatific vision shared with Monica shortly before her death at Ostia. It serves rhetorically to lend conceptual and thematic unity to what Henry Chadwick calls "a prose-poem in thirteen books" and Jean Hagstrum sees as "supremely a love poem."[1] Desire connects the autobiographical and speculative dimensions of the *Confessions*, linking the story of Augustine's life to age thirty-three (books 1–9) with the topics of memory, time, and creation (books 10–13). It has a structure and development, evolving from an originary model associated with infancy and the acquisition of language to a refined model that emerges in Augustine's account of adolescence and early adulthood.

Augustine's portrayal of desire in the *Confessions* represents a decisive historical formation. Jacques Le Goff observes, "Saint Augustine was the first to give prominence to the concept of concupiscence, sexual desire."[2] Le Goff places a special emphasis on the shift from the multiple lusts mentioned by Saint Paul to Augustine's single, unitary lust. As Augustine's conversion story progresses, desire becomes a means of integrating domains of human experience beyond carnality and spirituality. Augustine's deep ambivalence toward the beautiful lies of art, for example, situates poetry under the rubric of desire and carnality. Friendship, another cognate of desire, develops from a classical ideal of reciprocity to a metaphor of the soul's union with God. The erotic, as Hagstrum remarks, is "on a continuum," but the manifestations lead back to their source and final referent in God.[3] This capacity for integration nonetheless proves deeply problematic. If the erotic history related in the *Confessions* tells a story that powerfully integrates different forms of affect, it also impoverishes desire as a domain of experience and moral deliberation in its own right; the sensual, particular, and concrete lose their claims on our attention and moral sympathy.

Augustine plots a trajectory from carnal appetite and absence to spiritual repletion, and he thereby generates what we might call a romance of plenitude. Moving through the temporal embodiments of desire, he approaches the spiritual fulfillment that worldly attachments finally signify. In principle, erotic plenitude is available at any step if he recognizes and acts on the signs that mark its presence. An important strand of his story is the willed, even indulgent deferral of such recognition and action. At the same time, the plenitude of divine love explains the disparity between events and meaning in the *Confessions*—famously in the pear-tree episode but also in his unnamed loses (his concubine, his friend, the lost treatise by Cicero that sets him on the path of philosophy). In this sense, plenitude is the integration of desire read backwards. If the episodes of desire that Augustine recounts are substitutes for divine love, their final meaning invests them as impossible demands.

The integration and plenitude of desire, then, are different aspects of the same thing in the *Confessions*. As we shall see in later chapters, Augustine's formulation opens up possibilities of literary imagination and moral insight for medieval writers. Augustine shows a way of going beyond the substitutions and mutability of desire or, alternatively, of locating tragic absence and loss within the promise of attachments. Equally important, he devises a narrative structure for his story of demand and repletion. The retrospect of Augustine's conversion narrative at once traces the forward movement of erotic life and looks back from its discovery of desire's final meaning. The narrative form of the *Confessions* emerges from both a philosophical and a literary context.

Desire and Narrative Form

Augustine's representation of desire in the *Confessions* has its grounding in late classical debates on the nature and morality of concupiscence. As a passion of the soul, concupiscence is rejected in Stoic ethics but accepted by the Peripatetics, at least for those who can moderate its demands. As François-Joseph Thonnard points out, within Augustine's work, concupiscence is a theme rather than a precise concept.[4] It carries both the pejorative meaning of carnal appetite and a positive sense of orientation toward a good that can satisfy us. Some two decades after composing the *Confessions*, Augustine provides an extensive discussion of concupiscence in book 14 of the *The City of God*. There he accepts the Stoic assertion that desire has its origin in the soul and rejects the materialist explanation of the Epicureans, the radical dualism of matter and spirit among the Manicheans, and even the Platonists' view that the flesh is the cause of all vices.[5] His account distinguishes the moral dimensions of concupiscence according to whether men choose to live by the flesh or the spirit (14.1). Throughout his writings, Augustine's usage seems to propose a rough approximation among terms like *voluntas*, *appetitus*, *cupiditas*, and *amor*, which scholastic philosophers will try to delineate precisely.[6]

Desire can be distinguished from concupiscence in the sense that concupiscence applies to both what we have and what we do not have, whereas desire is for something absent.[7] Like concupiscence, desire is strongly associated with will and love (here meaning love taken in the sense of its final goal, *delectatio*). In the act of the soul's movement (*animi motus*), desire can be defined practically as will joined to an object.[8] Repeated over time and thereby reinforced, the desiring will becomes habit, and habit functions as a complement to original sin, the individual soul's microcosmic repetition of the fall of mankind.[9] Like the other Stoic passions (happiness, fear, and sadness), desire constitutes the lowest level of knowledge; it is sensation rather than reason and intellect, and it remains the source of affective life. All the passions nonetheless are violent perturbations, upsetting order and reason while promoting false judgments.[10] Aimé Solignac proposes that Augustine worked out an understanding of desire in treatises that antedate the *Confessions*: "appetitus animi quo aeternis bonis quaelibet temporalia bona praeponuntur" ("an appetite of the soul by which any temporal goods are preferred to eternal goods").[11]

Augustine's philosophical reflections on desire are, of course, ultimately theological. Early and late, his definitions seek to integrate the psychological, moral, and metaphysical dimensions of desire. In the *Confessions*, Augustine gives these dimensions concrete expression within a rhetorical form that combines earlier literary conventions to produce a distinctive narrative structure. The *Confessions* draws on the tradition of pagan philosophical autobiography as well as Christian sources. The *libri Platonicorum* ("books of the Platonists") that Augustine mentions in book 7 set out a model of confessional writing that portrays a quest for truth. Pagan and Christian conversion literature furnish characteristic narrative elements such as a decisive moment of divine revelation—in Augustine's case, the intrusion of grace rather than the late-classical philosopher's turn to either skepticism or mystery cults. Pierre Courcelle has argued, "The distinguishing characteristic of the *Confessions* is that Augustine presents in them his quest for truth in the form of an avowal of sins."[12] Courcelle properly identifies quest and confession as the key elements of narrative structure, but he does not, I believe, give adequate attention to Augustine's artistic transposition of these elements. Augustine inverts the temporal extensions of quest and confession in order to create a dual framework for representing desire in all its resonant and evocative power. The forward temporal movement of the quest corresponds not to the future but to Augustine's past. The retrospect of confession, a term that encompasses the recounting of past sins, praise of God, and assertions of faith, is the narrative present from which Augustine looks back on the progress of his quest.[13]

The explanatory and emotional power of this narrative structure cannot be understood fully without some consideration of the rigorous analysis of time that appears in book 11 of the *Confessions*. Augustine denies ontological status to time and presents a phenomenological account of it instead.[14] He perceives that time is an extension of some sort, but it is not the motion of an astral body (11.23.30; cf. 11.26.33).[15] Time exists in the mind, in order to measure impressions and thereby distinguish past, present, and future. He explains, "Affectionem, quam res praetereuntes in te faciunt et, cum illae praeterierint, manet, ipsam metior praesentem, non ea quae praeterierunt, ut fieret; ipsam metior, cum tempora metior" ("As things pass by they leave an impression in you [my mind]; this impression remains after the things have gone into the past, and it is this impression which I measure in the present, not the things which, in their passage, caused the impression. It is this impression which I measure when I measure time" [11.27.36]).[16]

What proves as important for Augustine's narrative as for his theology is the direction in which time moves. Unlike moderns who see themselves moving forward in time, Augustine envisions time moving toward him. He asks where time comes from ("unde et qua et quo praeterit") and answers, "Vnde nisi ex futuro? Qua nisi per praesens? Quo nisi in praeteritum?" ("It can only come from the future, it can only pass by way of the present, and it can only go into the past" [11.21.27]). He thus situates the mind at a juncture where the future converges on the present and the past falls away. There the mind exercises its twin powers of anticipation and memory; it can read the future as causes and signs (11.18.24) and the past as feelings contained in memory (10.14.21).[17] The literary framework of the *Confessions* is thus continuous with its metaphysics; medieval writers will exploit this convergence as a key feature of rhetorical and narrative technique.

Anticipation and retrospect are, of course, general features of conversion narrative, for in such stories we witness a determinate, if still unrecognized, future working its way surely toward a fully realized present. John Freccero, who has taught us to read the *Confessions* as the master text of a poetics of conversion that makes possible Dante's journey in the *Commedia*, contends that its distinguishing characteristic is the fusion of the personal and the exemplary demarcated in time:

> The point is that in the "then" of experience, grace came in intensely personal form, whereas in the "now" of witness, the particular event is read

retrospectively as a repetition in one's own history of the entire history of the Redemption. For both Dante and Augustine the exegetical language seems to structure experience, identifying it as part of the redemptive process, while the irreducibly personal elements lend to the *exemplum* the force of personal witness. Together, *exemplum* and experience, allegory and biography, form a confession of faith for other men.[18]

Augustine maps these positions from the perspective of lived experience rather than secure retrospect.[19] "Now" is as open and fiercely contested as "then," and Peter Brown has rightly called the narrative of the *Confessions* "the story of Augustine's 'heart,' or of his 'feelings'—his *affectus*."[20] The story of feelings provides a dynamic context of self-understanding, framed by the retrospect of faith and understanding. If Plato and Aristotle see desire moving forwards and even upwards in a quest for transcendence, Augustine looks backwards from a knowledge of the final referent of desire, which he identifies as God. This knowledge does not, however, abstract him from history and experience. As James J. O'Donnell points out, "The *Confessions* are not to be read merely as a look back at Augustine's spiritual development; rather the text itself is an essential stage in that development, and a work aware both of what had already passed into history and of what lay ahead."[21] In positing an endpoint of desire, then, Augustine proposes a radical alternative that remained inaccessible through either Platonic recollection or Aristotelian deliberation. His *Confessions* argue nothing less than that desire can be satisfied. But they do so from the vantagepoint of history and experience that continue to unfold.

Models of Desire

Within the temporal framework of anticipation and retrospect, Augustine's analysis of desire suffuses the *Confessions*. Infancy and childhood take shape around instinctual demands and gratification. In early manhood, "wandering desire" leads Augustine to take a concubine. After he turns to philosophy, he remains trapped in "omnes uanarum cupiditatum spes inanes et insanias mendaces" ("the empty hopes and deceitful frenzies of vain desires" [6.11.18]). Later, at the point of his conversion, he still oscillates between charity and "the bondage of my desire for sex" ("de uinculo quidem desiderii concubitus, quo artissimo tenebar" [8.6.13]). Under the rubric of desire, Augustine groups love, friendship, concupiscence, and physical appetite; and he associates them thematically with memory, curiosity, beauty, and language. His analysis of desire concentrates on the autobiographical portions of the book, particularly books 2–5, but the formulation he gives it extends as well to the discussions of memory and time (books 10 and 11) and even to the interpretation of Genesis that occupies books 12 and 13 of the *Confessions*.[22]

We can distinguish two models in Augustine's reflections on desire. Augustine sets forth an originary model of desire in his account of "the food of my infancy." Speaking here of God's mercy, he achieves the multiple goals of confession, revealing his own desires while framing them in an order seen in this recounting from the retrospect of his conversion.

> Exceperunt ergo me consolationes lactis humani, nec mater mea uel nutrices meae sibi ubera implebant, sed tu mihi per eas dabas alimentum infantiae secundum institutionem tuam et diuitias usque ad fundum rerum dispositas. Tu etiam mihi dabas nolle amplius, quam dabas, et nutrientibus me dare mihi uelle quod eis dabas.(1.6.7)

> [I was welcomed then with the comfort of woman's milk; but neither my mother nor my nurses filled their own breasts with milk; it was you who, through them, gave me the food of my infancy, according to your own ordinance and according to the way in which your riches are spread throughout the length and depth of things. You also granted me not to desire more than you supplied; and on those who suckled me you bestowed a desire to give me what you gave to them.]

The constitutive elements of this first model are appetite, constraint, and convergence, and they exist in a dynamic relation. Desire serves the biological, appetitive need of sustenance and produces the psychological effect of comfort. Both facets are expressed in the term *consolationes*. As mere physical appetite, desire can be fulfilled in more than one way ("mater mea uel nutrices meae"). And since it can be satisfied, desire is limited. Augustine traces the source of this constraint not to the structure of appetite itself but to a divine gift—namely, the paradox of God's giving him the desire not to want more: "Tu etiam mihi dabas nolle amplius, quam dabas." Moreover, desire is social, for satisfaction requires an unforeseen reciprocity of motives. The infant seeking nourishment and nurture is satisfied by others who participate in a preexisting harmony unknown to them.[23] This convergence of mutual desires Augustine terms *ordinatus affectus* ("ordered feelings").[24]

Augustine elaborates on this first model of desire in his account of how he acquired language, which immediately follows the description of infant appetite. Wanting to express "uoluntates meas" ("my desires") to those who might satisfy them (1.6.7), he discovers that desire is internal ("intus") while the agents of satisfaction remain exterior ("foris"), isolated from direct perception of his wants and needs because they cannot penetrate his mind ("introire in animam meam"). The image of entering looks forward to the conversion in the garden at Milan and to the entry of grace. It is resolved rhetorically in the lyric passage "Sero te amaui," especially in the lines that express the seriousness of Augustine's former estragement from God, which is an alienation from himself: "Et ecce intus eras et ego foris" ("And, look, you were within me and I was outside" [10.27.38]). In infancy, the dissonance of inside and outside is mediated only imperfectly. The infant's gestures and sounds are signs of his desire but not of the objects of his desire: "signa similia uoluntatibus meis. . .non enim erant ueresimilia" (1.6.8).

As he grows past infancy and its speechlessness ("infans, qui non farer" [1.8.13]), Augustine acquires language by natural reason ("mente") rather than training. His experiments in a domain of signs composed of cries, noises, and gestures reproduce, however, the essential problem of infancy—to express inner feelings ("sensa cordis mei" [1.8.13]) to those who will satisfy his demands. The power of natural memory allows him to associate names and objects in what he describes as a "universal language" ("tamquam uerbis naturalibus") of gestures that registers the feelings ("affectionem animi") associated with objects. Repetition of the signs in proper grammatical utterances lets him connect desire, things, and signs in the realm of spoken language: "measque iam uoluntates edomito in eis signis ore per haec enuntiabam" (1.8.13).[25] Furthermore, as Eugene Vance points out, "It is through the acquisition of language. . .that Augustine becomes ensnared in the external, temporal Law" which is literally the positive law of human society and figuratively the Mosaic Law that the New Man must supersede.[26] Thus he shares with others "uoluntatum enuntiandarum signa" ("the language for the communication of our desires") and sets forth into the stormy fellowship of human life ("uitae humanae procellosam societatem" [1.8.13]).

Margaret R. Miles has argued that Augustine's account of desire can be reduced to concupiscence and repetition compulsion and that "his paradigm of concupiscence was the newborn infant."[27] It is clear from the resonant language of the *Confessions*, however, that desire is the topic of a complex reflection and that the trope "small child, great sinner" speaks only of the surface of a powerful thematic structure. If it reduces to mere blind appetite, desire also extends in a vast, connecting metaphor to the desire for God. For instance, in the beatific vision of transcending the pleasure of bodily senses (9.10.24) that he shares with Monica shortly before her death and that serves as the narrative climax of his conversion story, Augustine describes his mother and himself in the same language he uses earlier for carnal desires. The two of them rise up "ardentiore affectu" ("with our affections burning"), their ascent combines the interior silence of infancy ("interius cogitando") with the sociability of speech ("loquendo"), and they reach "regionem ubertatis indeficientis, ubi pascis Israhel in aeternum ueritate pabulo" ("that region of never-failing plenty where *Thou feedest Israel*"). The concupiscence of the infant finds its ultimate referent in the Psalmist's image of God's feeding his chosen people (Psalms 79.2).[28]

In works such as the *De trinitate* and *De libero arbitrio*, Augustine will distinguish the components of sensory and psychological experience, but here in the *Confessions* they stand conceptually and rhetorically as analogues to one another. *Sensa mea*, *affectus*, and *uoluntates meas* identify separate facets of the same thing in Augustine's analysis of desire. The first designates a cause originating in appetite, while feeling (*affectus*) is the effect produced by sensory appetite. The mechanism of cause and effect implies a set of intentions (*uoluntates meas*) projected by a desiring subject, for even if the senses are moved by external stimuli, one nonetheless anticipates and therefore has intentions toward the effects. For all these distinctions, however, Augustine's originary model of desire remains cohesive and integrated: in experience, cause and effect refer to the same desire; it is only from retrospect that one recognizes them as acts of will and from the perspective of the convert that one sees them clearly as adumbrations of divine pleni-tude. At the end of the *Confessions*, reflecting on the oppressive weight of desire ("pondus cupiditatis"), Augustine fashions cupidity and charity as movements of desire heading in opposite directions: "Affectus sunt, amores sunt, immuniditia spiritus nostri defluens inferius amore curarum et sancti-tas tui attollens nos superius amore securitatis" ("There are affections, there are loves, there is the uncleanness of our spirit flowing away downward in love of care and distraction, and there is your sanctity raising us upward in the love of freedom from care" [13.7.8]). The difference lies not in the workings but in the objects of desire, in the capacity to see through signs and manifestations to the supreme peace they finally signify: "et ueniamus ad supereminentem requiem."

Augustine offers a second model of desire in books 2–4 of the *Confessions*. These books cover the period from age sixteen to twenty nine and constitute an extended autobiography of desire. He connects all three books rhetorically by repeating the trope of the circularity of desire. What delights him, he tells us early in book 2, is "amare et amari" ("to love and be loved" [2.2.2]). At the beginning of book 3, he goes to Carthage, not yet in love ("nondum amabam"), but he loves to love ("amare amabam" [3.1.1]). At the start of book 4, he looks back on nine years of seducing and being seduced: "seducebamur et seducebamus falsi atque fallentes in uariis cupiditatibus" (4.1.1). The fundamental point made throughout this sequence is that desire precedes the objects of desire. As he explains in book 3, "Quaerebam quid amarem, amans amare" ("Being in love with love I looked for something to love" [3.1.1]). From retrospect he recog-nizes that he turned from the One to the many (2.1.1), but the immediate experience presents itself sensuously as the madness of unbridled lust ("uesania libidinis licentiosae" [2.2.4]). Marriage, a conventional regulator of desires of the flesh for men of Augustine's social class, runs counter to his family's ambition for worldly achievement in a career advanced by oratory. The demands of desire only intensify during the period of leisure (*otium*) between his grammatical study in Madaura and his departure for advanced studies in Carthage. The retirement from worldly cares that *otium* will permit later at Cassiciacum, as Augustine enters the final stages of preparing for conversion, is prefigured by its antitype during the interval in which he returns home to Tagaste. The thorns of worldly lusts ("uepres libidinum" [2.3.6]) overgrow him, and his native city is transformed into a figurative Babylon (2.3.8).

Augustine demonstrates the priority, hence the apparent autonomy, of desire over the objects of desire in the episode of the pear tree, which serves as the most compelling symbol of the confusions of this period of leisure. Wandering the streets late at night, Augustine and his friends steal fruit from a neighbor's pear tree, though they have no apparent attraction to the fruit itself and later throw it to pigs. Augustine is interested not in the event but in its meaning. He presents the episode as a paradigm of evil.[29] He explains, "Dicat tibi nunc ecce cor meum, quid ibi quaerebat, ut essem gratis malus et malitiae meae causa nulla esset nisi malitia" ("now let my heart tell you what it was looking for there, that I became evil for nothing, with no reason for wrongdoing except the wrongdoing itself" [2.4.9]). At an ethical level, the episode represents the misdirection of will, but Augustine finds even more profound lessons in the experience of arbitrary theft. The episode directs his attention to desire in absolute terms and then to the significance of desire. Crime is usually motivated, he says, by an *appetitus* for obtaining lower goods (things of the world) or by fear (2.5.11). His motive, by contrast, had no object beyond itself: "amaui defectum meum, non illud, ad quod deficiebam, sed defectum meum ipsum amaui" ("I loved my sin—not the thing for which I had committed the sin, but the sin itself" [2.4.9]). He emphasizes the point through elaborate wordplay on the verb *deficere* ("to fail"). This is at once a rhetorical tour de force and a demonstration of how language reproduces the paradoxes of desire. For the supine form of the verb gives the noun for sin (*defectum*), while the inflected forms designate the lack of lower goods that motivates crime. In this way sin defined absolutely ("defectum meum") is derived from the appetitive cause of lacking ("non illud, ad quod deficiebam") in order to identify the essential claims of desire: I loved the sin itself, which has no object in its own right ("defectum meum ipsum amaui").[30]

This formulation of desire as lack anticipates Augustine's definition that evil is the privation of the good (3.7.12). The pears, unattractive as they are, stand as a reminder of the beauty of divine creation. They are a creaturely sign of God's providence, ultimately of God himself. On this view, Augustine's desire for them is an awkward imitation of his desire for God: "Peruerse te imitantur omnes" (2.6.14). This is the perspective Augustine adopts from the retrospect of confession. The immediate experience, however, is of desiring unqualified absence, a quest for that which can be defined only to the extent that it does not come into being (*deficere*). Thus, when Augustine announces, "defectum meum amaui," he identifies the ground of desire. In the progress of his spiritual quest, he also, of course, establishes the conditions by which he will come to know the final referent of desire. Just as God stands for Augustine at the core of all memory, so, too, is he the object of Augustine's desire and the promise of its satisfaction: "Te uolo. . .insatiabili satietate" (2.10.18). At this point in the quest, though, the emphasis falls on the desperate, ungoverned, arbitrary craving that moves him.

Seen from another viewpoint, the pear-tree episode is a negative account of friendship, a monitory example of "perverse imitation" in social relations. Friendship is a theme that will decisively shape the affections of Augustine's adult life. At various stages he will mislead his friends, pointing Romanianus toward Manicheism and nearly inducing Alypius to marry. Augustine prefaces the episode by a definition of friendship as the measure or means ("modus") connecting one soul to another, the bright path ("luminosus limes") linking them (2.2.2). His final reflection in book 2 addresses the role of friendship in leading him toward his crime. He reasons that he did not commit the theft alone but loved the fellowship and association ("consortium") of those with whom he acted. Had he merely desired the fruit, he would have consumed it himself, without exciting his accomplices to share his guilt. Yet friendship is accidental rather than constitutive of the crime. His pleasure lies in the desire that leads him to his crime—"ea [uoluptas] erat in ipso facinore" (2.8.16). Though his companions share in the effects of pleasure and sin, the source remains Augustine's desire itself.

Augustine's residence in Carthage as a student (371–74) and later a teacher (376–83) shares many features with his earlier descriptions of erotic experience. These features move his narrative toward decisive, if as yet inadequate, moments of recognition. Carthage is the frying pan of shameful loves ("sartago flagitiosorum amorum"). There as in Tagaste, desire precedes the objects of desire: "Quaerebam quid amarem, amans amare." In this circularity, desire discovers its objects as the accidents rather than constitutive elements of gratification: "Amare et amari dulce mihi erat magis, si et amantis corpore fruerer" ("It was a sweet thing to me both to love and to be loved, and more sweet still when I was able to enjoy the body of my lover" [3.1.1]). In an enticingly cryptic passage, he reports that he was once moved by desire and found gratification ("concupiscere et agere negotium") during the celebration of services at church (3.3.5).[31] He also finds a perverse ideal of friendship, like the fellowship of crime in the pear-tree episode, among the Eversores (the Overturners or Destroyers), a group of students whose behavior is intended to outrage modesty and decorum with no other object than the enjoyment of its own malevolence. Augustine's language for their antics ironically invokes the imagery that expresses the satisfaction of desire. If God feeds Israel with "ueritate pabulo" (9.10.24), the Eversores consume the empty fodder of their own vain pleasures: "inde pascendo maliuolas laetitias suas" (3.3.6).

Augustine's description of the unnamed concubine whom he takes at Carthage offers an important perspective on the formulation of desire in the *Confessions*. Unlike the descriptions of infancy, childhood, or the pear-tree episode, the account here is rhetorically spare and devoid of emotion. Uneducated and socially subordinate, the woman will prove to be an obstacle to the social advancement into high administrative circles that Augustine pursues as the parallel track of his quest for truth. She will tactfully withdraw to North Africa, promising never to take another man (6.15.25) and presumably entering religious life, while Augustine waits to marry a well-placed, though still underage, bride in Milan. The account of his life with the concubine is compressed into a brief report:

> In illis annis unam habebam non eo quod legitimum uocatur coniugio cognitam, sed quam indagauerat uagus ardor inops prudentiae, sed unam tamen, ei quoque seruans tori fidem; in qua sane experirer exemplo meo, quid distaret inter coniugalis placiti modum, quod foederatum esset generandi gratia, et pactum libidinosi amoris, ubi proles etiam contra uotum nascitur, quamuis iam nata cogat se deligi. (4.2.2)

> [In those years I lived with a woman who was not bound to me by lawful marriage; she was one who had come my way because of my wandering desires and my lack of considered judgment; nevertheless, I had only this one woman and I was faithful to her. And with her I learned by my own experience how great a difference there is between the self-restraint of the marriage covenant which is entered into for the sake of having children, and the mere pact made between two people whose love is lustful and who do not want to have children—even though, if children are born, they compel us to love them.]

The passage portrays Augustine's lover as the accident of his desire. His "uagus ardor" happens to find her as its object. The Latin verb Augustine uses for this discovery ("indagauerat") has the primary sense of "tracking down," and its common meaning is to hunt game with dogs; only in a secondary sense does it mean to investigate, search for, or try to obtain something. His lover is the quarry tracked down by his desire; like quarry flushed from cover, she is the individual randomly made the concrete object of the hunt. Furthermore, Augustine represents his desire here as the consequence of a moral and social defect—the failure of prudence. By prudence he means not only an ethical virtue but also the self-discipline expected of a Roman citizen in late antiquity.[32] In place of prudence, he offers a kind of fidelity as a substitute, asserting the ironic chastity of his devotion to a single mistress and the natural affection he feels toward the child she subsequently bears him. Nonetheless, the relationship is not *coniugalis modus*, a proper measure of conduct between husband and wife which shares in common the sense of boundary that also characterizes friendship; it is an agreement ("pactum") founded on carnal appetite.

Besides his language, Augustine's technique of narrative disposition helps define the nature of desire in this episode. The passage about his mistress appears as the middle section of a carefully structured chapter, and a significant pattern shapes the three sections. The theme uniting all three sections is Augustine's latent probity. In the first section, he describes his profession as a teacher of rhetoric. Overcome by greed, he sells the art of rhetoric and successful speech-making: "artem rhetoricam et uictoriosam loquacitatem uictus cupiditate uendebam" (4.2.2). Though he shares in his students' love of vanity and their search for lies, he seeks to act honorably toward them and retains the smallest flicker of faith ("scintillantem fidem meam"). In the third section, he remembers rejecting a magician's offer to intercede on his behalf and guarantee him victory in a poetry competition by offering sacrifice. Revolted by the proposal, Augustine properly sees it as sacrifice to demons, though he still finds himself hampered by being unable to imagine God in anything other than corporeal terms, as a figment of imagination.

In its arrangement, then, the chapter is structured according to the schema that Augustine analyzes later in the *Confessions*: lust of the flesh, lust of the eyes, and ambition of the world ("Iubes certe, ut contineam a concupiscentia carnis et concupiscentia oculorum et ambitione saeculi" [10.30.41]).[33] Augustine's teaching career corresponds to worldly ambition and the magician's art to the lust of the eyes. He expresses both species of lust through motifs that stress their insubstantiality. His latent faith shines through the slipperiness and smoke of worldly ambitions ("in lubrico et in multo fumo"); dealing with magicians is like feeding the wind ("uentos pascere"). Bounded on each side by these images of insubstantiality, the lust of the flesh is thus central and strikingly concrete: a hunt for carnal gratification. It is only later, after Augustine accepts the command to abandon concubines and forego marriage, that desire is banished to the domain of insubstantial images, where it lives in memory and returns through sleep to work its power on the soul (10.30.41).

The *Confessions* reaches one point of provisional closure in its narrative of desire with the scene in which Augustine abandons Carthage to flee to Rome. His motive for leaving depends, as in the earlier passage, on ambitions of the world—here the prospect of higher fees, advancement, and better-disciplined students. These reasons only mask a deeper motive. The journey to Rome is a flight from Monica. Augustine recalls that she bitterly laments his leaving and follows him to the coast, clinging to him violently and in a sense forcing him to deceive her. The episode of Augustine's flight from Carthage is doubly framed, for he sees it from the retrospect of God's completed intention and through a Christianized reading of Vergil. In retrospect, Augustine discerns the workings of providence at the very opening of the episode: "Egisti ergo mecum, ut mihi persuaderetur Romam pergere et potius ibi docere quod docebam Carthagini" ("You acted upon me in such a way that I was persuaded to set out for Rome to teach there the same subjects as I had been teaching in Carthage" [5.8.14]).

The literary model for this removal is Aeneas's abandonment of Carthage in book 4 of the *Aeneid*. The evocative prose of Augustine's departure scene captures, for example, the same poetic effect of a shoreline withdrawn from sight that Vergil achieves in Aeneas's hasty retreat after Mercury's second warning in *Aeneid* 4. Augustine says, "Flauit uentus et impleuit uela nostra et litus subtraxit aspectibus nostris" ("The wind blew and filled our sails; we lost sight of the land" [5.8.15]). He tropes Vergil's description: "litora deseruere; latet sub classibus aequor" ("they have quitted the shore; the sea is hidden under their fleets" [4.582]). In adapting Vergil, Augustine implicitly construes the *Aeneid* in a way that points toward his own story of conversion. Aeneas's wandering is a figure for the wandering desire before Augustine's conversion. The full realization of each story lies in a future that can be rendered intelligible only from perspectives expressed respectively as destiny and faith. But in Augustine's evocation of the *Aeneid*, the structural parallels become artistic transpositions. That is to say, the parallels are not simple points of correspondence but figures of analogy that point toward spiritual completion.

Within the structure of analogy, Fate, which hovers over Aeneas even as he enjoys the erotic interval at Carthage, is to be recognized as an adumbration in Vergil's poem of the divine providence that shapes Augustine's journey toward truth through its own interludes and successive moments of premature closure. Vergil calls Jupiter by the honorific title "Omnipotens" (4.220), but the full meaning of that title resides for Augustine in the Christian God who oversees mankind much as Jupiter superintends Aeneas's heroic quest ("tu alte consulens" [5.8.15]). Jupiter turns his eyes toward Carthage and sees Dido and Aeneas forgetful of their better fame ("oblitos famae melioris amantis" [4.221]), then sends Mercury to remind

Aeneas of his duty to destiny (4.223–37). Vergil's depiction of Jupiter's knowledge ("oculosque ad moenia torsit / regia" [4.220–21]) is concrete; Mercury's embassy is a practical device to convey Jupiter's knowledge and intent. They serve, in the retrospect of Augustine the convert, as examples of precisely the fleshly images of God's omniscience and grace that he wrongly perceived with the senses rather than the intellect (3.6.11). Aeneas's duty, deferred and misdirected by desire during the Carthaginian interval, drives him to fulfill a historical design (4.229–31). Augustine inhabits the erotic interval that Aeneas must abandon for duty, and his duty is to discover the source and referent of desire. If empire, dynasty, and the rule of law lie before Aeneas, it is salvation that awaits Augustine.

In the allusions to the *Aeneid*, Monica plays perhaps the most complex role. John O'Meara finds it no surprise "if at times we feel that Monnica is thought of not only as Dido but, perhaps, more suitably as Aeneas's mother Venus, who had taken an active part in helping her son to fulfill, however reluctantly at times, his destiny." O'Meara views the resemblance as an example of Augustine's artistic power "to combine, to assimilate, things that might seem to have no apparent connection—and even things that were clearly contraries."[34] But Augustine's narrative strategy here is to employ the logic of analogy rather than random assimilation. Though Venus is one case in point, the strategy is most effective in elaborating analogies with Dido as she bewails Aeneas's leaving. Like the abandoned queen of Carthage, Monica remains behind lamenting as Augustine sails off ("mansit orando et flendo" [5.8.15]). Her sickening grief ("illa insaniebat dolore") is the analogue to Dido's surging passion (*irarum aestus*), an image used twice in Vergil's poem with small variation.[35] Augustine's language describes Monica in terms borrowed from the portrayal of Dido's frenzy. Monica fills God's ears with complaints and groans ("querellis et gemitu") that recall the protests Aeneas wants to dismiss in his final speech to Dido: "desine meque tuis incendere teque querellis" (4.360). Monica laments and wails ("flebat et eiulabat"), and so recalls both Dido's raving through the city ("totamque incensa per urbem / bacchatur" [4.300–301]) and the answering wails after her death ("lamentis gemituque et femineo ululatu / tecta fremunt" [4.667–68]).

In sketching these parallels, Augustine reads Vergil differently from his near contemporaries and medieval successors. Fulgentius proposes that the *Aeneid* is organized according to the ages of man, and he allegorizes book 4 as a period of adolescent excess, unchecked by discipline. The figure is reminiscent of Augustine's description of the interval before his setting out for Carthage: "Feriatus ergo animus a paterno iudicio in quarto libro et uenatu progreditur et amore torretur, et tempestate ac nubilo, uelut in mentis conturbatione, coactus adulterium perficit" ("In book 4 the spirit of adolescence, on holiday from paternal control, goes off hunting, is inflamed by passion and, driven on by storm and cloud, that is, by confusion of mind, commits adultery").[36] The twelfth-century commentary attributed to Bernardus Silvestris regards book 4 as a literal and allegorical demonstration of the nature of youth.[37] Carthage is the "new city of the world" and Dido is glossed as *libido*.[38] Augustine's interest is not in moralization but in witnessing the unfolding of providence. For him the resemblance between Monica and Dido is one not of kind but of analogy, and its strongest point of correspondence lies in the representation of incomplete and misdirected love. Like Dido, Monica does not see the providential design motivating Augustine's flight, and sorrow is the punishment for her mistake. Augustine's final comment on the Carthaginian period makes it clear that the essential issue is to discover the proper ends of desire: "me cupiditatibus meis raperes ad finiendas ipsas cupiditates et illius carnale desiderium iusto dolorum flagello uapularet" ("all the time you were dragging me away by the force of my own desires in order that these desires might be brought to an end, and you were justly punishing her with the whip of sorrow for an affection that was too much of the flesh" [5.8.15]).

Imagination and Friendship

Desire not only establishes the thematic unity of Augustine's narrative; it serves, at the same time, as a means for analyzing and connecting domains of experience beyond carnal pleasure. The discovery of philosophy, for instance, is the first of several proleptic conversions, and Augustine describes it in the same language that elsewhere conveys the demands of lust. Cicero's *Hortensius*, like the episodes of erotic life, exhibits again for Augustine the existence of a compelling impulse toward an object still only imperfectly imagined. He recounts that he did not know Scripture, but one aspect of Cicero's treatise nonetheless delighted him: "sed ipsam quaecumque esset sapientiam ut diligerem et quaererem et assequerer et tenerem atque amplexarem fortiter, excitabar sermone illo et accendebar et ardebam" ("I was urged on and inflamed with a passionate zeal to love and seek and obtain and embrace and hold fast wisdom itself, whatever it might be" [3.4.8]). Such associations with erotic life occur throughout the *Confessions*; they contain the centrifugal exuberance of recollection and praise. Perhaps the most revealing of these associations are those that connect desire to the literary imagination and to friendship.

Throughout the *Confessions* Augustine presents literature, poetry, and the theater as cognates to the desiring subject's vain search for satisfaction. He recalls the pleasure fiction held for him as a young student, using a metaphor that applies traditionally to sexual appetite: "amans. . .scalpi aures

meas falsis fabellis, quo prurirent ardentius" ("I loved having my ears tick-
led by false stories, so that they might itch all the more" [1.10.16]). Fiction
is a lust of the eyes and a source for curiosity. Curiosity leads in turn to the
pleasure of spectacles for adults, the "ludos maiorum." Liberal education
gives Augustine command over language and writing, but he is able to recognize, in retrospect, that his empathy for Aeneas and Dido was false and
misplaced. He is not able to read them in their full sense as signs of his spiritual condition: "tenere cogebar Aeneae nescio cuius errores oblitus erro-
rum meorum et plorare Didonem mortuam, quia se occidit ab amore, cum
interea me ipsum in his a te morientem, deus, uita mea, siccis oculis ferrem
miserrimus" ("I was forced to learn about the wanderings of a man called
Aeneas, while quite oblivious of my own wanderings, and to weep for the
death of Dido, because she killed herself for love, while all the time I could
bear with dry eyes, O God my life, the fact that I myself, poor wretch, was,
among these things, dying far away from you" [1.13.20]). As in the analogy
with Monica, Dido represents misdirected love for the world, which
Augustine defines as fornication ("Amicitia enim mundi huius fornicatio
est abs te" [1.13.21]). He appropriates the Vergilian language of her death
(*Aeneid* 6.456–57) to his own spiritual entropy: "flebam Didonem extinc-
tam ferroque extrema secutam, sequens ipse extrema condita tua relicto te
et terra iens in terram" ("I wept for dead Dido 'who by the sword pursued
a way extreme,' meanwhile myself following a more extreme way, that of
the most extremely low of your creatures, having forsaken you, and being
earth going back to earth" [1.13.21]).

The curtain hung over the entrance to the grammar schools serves for
Augustine as a figure for the obscurity and mystification of literary study
rather than as a divide that separates its exclusive learning from common
knowledge. Like other educated Christians of his age and social background,
he is troubled by the corrupt moral examples offered in classical mythology,
especially Jupiter's adulteries (1.16.26). Yet it is poetry's sensuous appeal to
the imagination that proves more dangerous than obscurity. Augustine is
attracted as a student by the alluring "spectaculum uanitatis" ("spectacles of
vanity" [1.13.22]) offered in Homer and Vergil; poetry creates compelling
figures in the imagination that pose the gravest moral danger. The rhetorical
discipline he practices is a counterpart to his wandering in the land of unlikeness, for the poets' texts which he converts into verse as exercises are in reality the site of his exile: "figmentorum poeticorum uestigia errantes sequi
cogebamur" (1.17.27). The models of action and probity offered him are
only exemplars of style covering a narrative of lust (1.18.28).

Augustine's arrival at Carthage amplifies the equation of desire and literary works, for the public spectacle of theater replaces the interior images
produced by reading epic. Augustine gives a striking description of the

effects of theater: "Rapiebant me spectacula theatrica plena imaginibus mis-eriarum mearum et fomitibus ignis mei" ("I was carried away too by plays on the stage in which I found plenty of examples of my own miseries and plenty of fuel for my own fire" [3.2.2]). His famous critique of the theater arises from the discrepancy of tragic effects: ludic images represent scenes that arouse compassion on stage yet correspond to misery in life. He asks, "Quid est, quid ibi homo uult dolere cum spectat luctuosa et tragica, quae tamen pati ipse nollet" ("Why is it that people want to feel sad at miserable and tragic happenings which they certainly would not like to suffer them-selves?" [3.2.2]). From this discrepancy there follows a perverse shuffling of expectations so that spectators require sadness and castigate performers who do not provide it. Augustine's critique initiates a line of reasoning that reaches culmination later in the *Confessions* when Alypius misjudges his power to withstand the effects of sensory images of gladiatorial games at the amphitheater and temporarily gives himself over to the frenzy of the crowd (4.4.11–8.13). In addition, the emptiness of poetic images serves as a means to characterize the delusion of Manichean doctrine. Augustine finds more substance in verses, songs, and even Medea in her chariot than in articles of Manichean belief (3.6.11); and he describes his time in Carthage as a life divided between a false religion observed secretly ("occulte") and a public career in the liberal arts devoted to pursuing the emptiness of public renown ("popularis gloriae sectantes inanitatem" [4.1.1]). The latter he identifies specifically with insubstantial images of theater: "usque ad theatricos plausus et contentiosa carmina et agonem coronarum faenearum et spectaculorum nugas et intemperantiam libidinum" ("theatrical applause from the audi-ence, verse competitions, contests for crowns of straw, the vanity of the stage, immoderate lusts" [4.1.1]).

In some measure, Augustine's rejection of poetry and theater follows a tradition of Christian iconoclasm that associates spectacle with lust, concu-piscence, and moral decay. Tertullian's *De spectaculis* makes perhaps the strongest case against artistic representation, denying any possibility of aesthetic distance and warning of the moral perils of the theater for actors. Augustine's own reflections on poetry in the *De musica* register his profound ambivalence about the effects of images, which he locates at "the very entrance of error" where opinion can replace knowledge and percep-tion mimics reality.[39] Yet this rejection, like Augustine's treatment of other facets of desire, heralds an eventual fulfillment. In the story of Ponticianus's visit which precedes Augustine's conversion in the garden at Milan (8.6.14–15), what had repelled Augustine in the stories of the poets and in the spectacle of theater achieves its full and proper embodiment in the narrative of conversion.

The story is presented through a succession of figural analogies. Seeing a book of Saint Paul's epistles lying open on the table as he visits Augustine and Alypius, Ponticianus is prompted to talk first about Saint Anthony, then about monastic communities, and finally about the conversion of two imperial courtiers of his acquaintance who read Anthony's life. Courcelle and Brown have remarked on the power and popularity of conversion narratives within aristocratic circles in late antiquity. In the literary structure of the *Confessions*, Anthony's narrative demonstrates the proper use of literary texts and the proper set of readerly responses. Ponticianus's story begins as he and the other courtiers walk through gardens near the city walls of Treves while the emperor attends the spectacle of races at the circus (8.6.15), and so it recalls and corrects Alypius's attendance at the games in the amphitheater. The language describing the first courtier's conversion is the language of desire and sensuous response: "repletus amore sancto et sobrio pudore iratus" (8.6.15). The passions of love and anger are redirected to spiritual ends. Ponticianus and another companion, learning of the converts' resolve to remain as ascetics, weep for themselves while holding to their secular lives ("nihilo mutati a pristinis fleuerunt se tamen"). In other words, they achieve the self-recognition and appropriate compassion that pagan tragic spectacle hides from the spectator's consciousness. And for Augustine the story of Ponticianus's response forces the moment when he confronts himself. The parataxis of his account makes it clear that this moment occurs in consequence of the narrative:

> Narrabat haec Ponticianus. Tu autem, domine, inter uerba eius retorquebas me ad me ipsum, auferens me a dorso meo, ubi me posueram, dum nollem me attendere, et constituebas me ante faciem meam, ut uiderem, quam turpis essem, quam distortus et sordidus, maculosus et ulcerosus. Et uidebam et horrebam, et quo a me fugerem non erat. (8.7.16)

> [This was what Ponticianus told us. But you, Lord, while he was speaking, were turning me around so that I could see myself; you took me from behind my own back, which was where I had put myself during the time when I did not want to be observed by myself, and you set me in front of my own face so that I could see how foul a sight I was—crooked, filthy, spotted, and ulcerous. I saw and I was horrified, and I had nowhere to go to escape from myself.]

Here at last Augustine answers his earlier question, why would someone want to see misery onstage that he would lament in his own life? The conversion story brings into alignment tragic emotion and the imagination's capacity to picture events. Like the converts and Ponticianus, Augustine responds to the scene in terms relocated from the language of desire: "ardentius amabam illos" ("the more ardent was the love I felt for those two men" [8.6.17]).

The recuperation of poetic images in this scene is closely related to a second association of desire in the *Confessions*. Augustine consistently treats friendship as the locus of his most intense affective relations. Marie Aquinas McNamara writes, "Saint Augustine's attitude toward his friends was penetrated with the notions of classical friendship."[40] Cicero's *De amicitia* offers the fullest articulation of those notions, particularly of their foundation in virtue and altruism rather than advantage. Arguing from a social and cultural perspective, Brown contends that friendship enjoyed a value over physical desire: "For a young intellectual of the fourth century, male friendship opened the door to deeper satisfactions" than sex, chief among them sociability, mutual affection, and a sense of unity.[41] Augustine's treatment of friendship in the *Confessions* builds through a sequence of contrasts and incomplete formations to a final realization of friendship with God based on the model of charity.

The early books of the *Confessions* repeatedly contrast desire and friendship. Augustine's need to love and be loved leads him to obscure the nature of friendship, which is based on an ideal of moderation and reciprocity. He reflects near the beginning of book 2: "Sed non tenebatur modus ab animo usque ad animum, quatenus est luminosus limes amicitiae, sed exhalabantur nebulae de limosa concupiscentia carnis et scatebra pubertatis et obnubilabant atque obfuscabant cor meum, ut non discerneretur serenitas dilectionis a caligine libidinis" ("But I could not keep that true measure of love, from one mind to another mind, which marks the bright and glad area of friendship. Instead I was among the foggy exhalations which proceed from the muddy cravings of the flesh and the bubblings of first manhood. These so clouded over my heart and darkened it that I was unable to distinguish between the clear calm of love and the swirling mists of lust" [2.2.2]). Light and darkness, spirit and matter mark the opposition between desire and friendship. The same images recur in the description of his arrival at Carthage: "Venam igitur amicitiae coinquinabam sordibus concupiscentiae candoremque eius obnubilabam de tartaro libidinis" ("And so I muddied the clear spring of friendship with the dirt of physical desire and clouded over its brightness with the dark hell of lust" [3.1.1]).

The sharpness of these distinctions recedes at significant points to a more complicated view of friendship and of the place desire holds within it. The incident of the pear tree, as we have seen, is an example of perverse friendship, in which reciprocity depends on the mutual desire to commit gratuitous evil. In the same way, Augustine's admiration for the Syrian orator Hierus develops out of mediated desire and ambition. He dedicates a treatise on aesthetics (now lost) to Hierus on the strength of reputation ("Laudatur homo et amatur absens" [4.14.21]), following the judgment of others. His motive shows, however, that the gesture of homage remains within the circularity of his own desire, because Hierus as an orator represents what Augustine aspires to become ("sic amabam, ut uellem esse me talem" [4.14.23]). Just as he cannot see theologically beyond corporeal forms and concrete embodiments of abstractions like evil, so he cannot judge morally beyond style and reputation. Augustine's portrayal of flawed friendship is balanced nonetheless by Nebridius and Alypius. When Augustine is drawn toward astrology and divination, Nebridius tries to prevail on him to reject false doctrine (4.3.6). Alypius comes close to catastrophe in being carried away by the spectacle of the games and later by wanting to marry, yet his peril serves as a monitory example to Augustine. Before conversion, Augustine's friendship for both of them demonstrates the limits of classical friendship and virtue.

The most exhaustive inquiry into friendship and desire occurs in Augustine's account of an unnamed friend who dies at Tagaste before Augustine decides to leave for Carthage. The two friends are bound by age, upbringing, and their shared enthusiasm for literary studies. Augustine leads his friend into Manicheism, much as he elsewhere influences others to err. He describes his friendship as superabundant: "suaui mihi super omnes suauitates illius uitae meae" ("sweeter to me than all sweetnesses that in this life I had ever known" [4.4.7]). When his friend takes ill, recovers briefly, and then finally dies, Augustine undergoes the first profound shock of his life. It is not the death alone that disturbs him but estrangement and a realization of his mixed motives. In the short interval of his recovery, Augustine's friend, who has meanwhile been baptized as he lay unconscious, rejects the blasphemies of his former life and admonishes Augustine not to joke with him about his baptism. When the friend dies a few days later, Augustine's grief carries him into mourning and then to an understanding of the false grounding of friendship. In his misery, he reflects that he nonetheless holds his miserable life dearer than his dead friend. He specifically rejects the classical model of friendship in Orestes and Pylades and confronts his over-riding fear of death. Rejection and fear work paradoxically to affirm a basis for friendship in identification and unity. Echoing Horace and Ovid, Augustine reasons, "Nam ego sensi animam meam et animam illius unam fuisse animam in duobus corporibus, et ideo mihi horrori erat uita, quia nolebam dimidius uiuere, et ideo forte mori metuebam, ne totus ille moreretur, quem multum amaueram" ("I felt that my soul and my friend's had been one soul in two bodies, and that was why I had a horror of living, because I did not want to live as a half being, and perhaps too that was why I feared to die, because I did not want him, whom I had loved so much, to die wholly and completely" [4.6.11]).[42]

In this episode, friendship emerges as a plausible, if temporary, ground of moral action and erotic attachment. Augustine's friend is converted by his baptism, even though unconscious, and his rejection of his former life as a Manichee anticipates Augustine's own rejection of the sect. Moreover, it is in this friendship that Augustine discovers a framework that offers a kind of completion for the desiring subject. The Horatian trope of the soul's other half ("dimidium animae suae") relocates the object of desire within the self. No longer external and accidental, as in the erotic hunt that yields his concubine as its prize, desire operates within a newly defined circularity, in which the identification of self with other replaces possession and gratification and the other proves to be a complement of the self. The logic of this identification rather than casuistry or self-serving leads Augustine to realize that his fear of death involves not just himself but his friend as well. Friendship offers unity—one soul in two bodies—and unity promises the fulfillment of desire. It supersedes the dialectic of inside and outside by making the external object of desire interior, domesticating it to the heart. It removes autonomous desire from accident and renders it a mechanism of selfhood.

Augustine's extended meditation on this friendship marks at the same time the limits of the classical ideal. Augustine reflects on the episode from the dual perspective of his conversion history. Viewing it from retrospect, he recognizes that his sorrow had its origin in mistaking temporal for spiritual goods. He says, "fuderam in harenam animam meam diligendo moriturum acsi non moriturum" ("I had poured out my soul like water onto sand by loving a man who was bound to die just as if he were an immortal" [4.8.13]). As his mourning abates, he finds comfort in other friends, but as he looks back, he realizes, "hoc erat ingens fabula et longum mendacium" ("this was one huge fable, one long lie" [4.8.13]). Yet in the forward movement of his quest, he is able to characterize friendship in terms that point beyond its limits toward a full realization. He describes a life of easy intimacy, much of it founded on conversation:

> conloqui et conridere et uicissim beniuole obsequi, simul legere libros dulciloquos, simul nugari et simul honestari, dissentire interdum sine odio tamquam ipse homo secum atque ipsa rarissima dissensione condire consensiones plurimas, docere aliquid inuicem aut discere ab inuicem, desiderare absentes cum molestia, suscipere uenientes cum laetitia: his atque huius modi signis a corde amantium et redamantium procedentibus per os, per linguam, per oculos et mille motus gratissimos quasi fomitibus conflare animos et ex pluribus unum facere. (4.8.13)

> [to talk and laugh and do kindnesses to each other; to read pleasant books together; to make jokes together and then talk seriously together; sometimes to disagree, but without any ill feeling, just as one may disagree with oneself, and to find that these very rare disagreements made our general agreement all the sweeter; to be sometimes teaching and sometimes learning; to long

impatiently for the absent and to welcome them with joy when they
returned to us. These and other similar expressions of feeling, which proceed
from the hearts of those who love and are loved in return, and are revealed
in the face, the voice, the eyes, and in a thousand charming ways, were like
a kindling fire to melt our souls together and out of many to make us one.]

The familiar elements of Augustinian desire are present here, embedded in
the language and themes of the passage. The formula of circularity reappears
to describe those who love and are loved in return. Absence and repletion
are the emotional trajectory. The imagery of fire and heat is the symbolism
of affect. The crucial difference lies in the setting and aim. Augustine
relocates the language of desire from the individual to a community, and
the objective is to create one from many by a commonality of reciprocal
desire.

As it reaches its perfection, this ideal finds a limit in the way it imagines
the goals of desire. Augustine makes it clear, from retrospect, that the community of friends achieves a false unity. Its objective is a sublimation of the
desiring subject. The subject finds himself in others, but it is always and
only himself that he finds. Such friendship is "amicitia rerum mortalium"
("love for mortal things" [4.6.11]), of which the most prominent mortal
thing is oneself. In these terms, the aim of melting souls and making one
from many can only reproduce the dilemma of mortality and loss. For this
reason, Augustine must abandon the "huge fable" of classical friendship for
an attachment that is both objectified and permanent. The full realization
of what a circle of friends could mean, Augustine says, lies in the notion of
friendship with God. In that notion, the mechanism of charity displaces
both the reciprocity of idealized friendship and the circularity of individual
demands for gratification. The final comment Augustine offers on these
passages portrays human friendship as an instrumentality of friendship with
God: "Beatus qui amat te et amicum in te et inimicum propter te"
("Blessed is the man who loves you, who loves his friend in you, and his
enemy because of you" [4.9.14]). The decisive example of such friendship
occurs later, in the conversion story, which Ponticianus recounts to
Augustine and Alypius. At the moment when the imperial courtiers are
filled with *amore sancto*, they reflect on the final cause of their lives. Their
goal ("spes nostra") has been to advance in the palace so that they might
become friends of the emperor ("ut amici imperatoris simus"). It is, they
now realize, a fragile goal, full of dangers leading to other dangers and
uncertain of fulfillment. Thus they choose the alternative of friendship with
God: "Amicus autem dei, si uoluero, ecce nunc fio" (8.6.15).[43]

This transformation of friendship frames and thereby helps to explain
the scene of Augustine's definitive conversion in the garden at Milan.

Ponticianus's story of friends abandoning the world and inspiring a similar renunciation in their fiancées forces Augustine to see himself face to face, and in the experience of recognition he sees that his deferrals are at an end. Time has run out on his prayer, "Da mihi castitatem et continentiam, sed noli modo" ("Make me chaste and continent, but not yet" [8.7.17]). The convergence of present and future prophesied in Monica's dream of the ruler (3.11.19) finally occurs, as he confronts a will hindered by its own habits of sensual pleasure. Desire and sexuality are the "antiquae amicae meae" (8.11.26) that seek to hold him back by insinuating themselves. These temptations speak directly to him in the murmurs of personified voices in the garden scene: " 'Dimittisne nos?' et 'A momento isto non erimus tecum ultra in aeternum' et 'A momento isto non tibi licebit hoc et illud ultra in aeternum' " (" 'Are you getting rid of us?' and 'From this moment shall we never be with you again for all eternity?' and 'From this moment will you never for all eternity be allowed to do this or to do that?' " [8.11.26]). The voices are the final embodiment of false friendship and the other half of the self which is the desiring subject all along. In coming to terms with a will constrained by its habit, Augustine acknowledges the solipsism of his desire.

In this context, the external voice that intervenes in the scene shows the way to escape circularity. The historicity of the garden scene and the overlay of biblical parallels and autobiography are recurrent topics in interpretation.[44] Regardless of how much Augustine may recast experience in the light of faith, it is clear that within the literary structure of the *Confessions* the narrative has elaborated the themes of desire and friendship to the point where resolution must take place. The indeterminate child's voice that tells him in singsong, "Tolle lege, tolle lege" ("Take it and read it" [8.12.29]) represents a device to transcend the self once the will has acceded to being surpassed. Augustine may be uncertain whether the speaker is a boy or girl ("quasi pueri an puellae, nescio") and whether he can identify the game from their words. He has no doubt, however, that the admonition is a divine command ("nihil aliud interpretans diuinitus mihi iuberi"). His response is consciously an imitation of Saint Anthony's use of the biblical *sortes* and tacitly a repetition of the courtiers' conversion. The passage from Saint Paul to which he opens (Romans 13:13–14) is an exhortation to abandon carnal desires, just as the passage from Matthew 19:21 was a commandment to Anthony to abandon worldly goods. The Pauline text orders the abandonment of lusts of the flesh and the world: "Not in rioting and drunkenness, not in chambering and wantonness, not in strife and envying; but put ye on the Lord Jesus Christ, and make not provision for the flesh in concupiscence." When Alypius takes the book, reads further, and discovers the appropriate passage for him, the repetition of the courtiers' narrative is essentially complete. The disclosure of their conversion to Monica is the final parallel, reenacting the courtiers' announcement to Ponticianus of their resolve to quit the world.

Integration and Plenitude

The representation of desire in the *Confessions* marks a significant achievement in narrative art, yet it also proves to be deeply problematic for reasons I suggested at the beginning of this chapter. Augustine goes beyond the formulations of Plato and Aristotle and beyond the ethics of the Stoics to devise a theory of erotic attachment that connects appetite and desire. He elevates these passions past the lower goods of the world by making them signs and markers of the soul's love for God. They are often, as his exemplary history demonstrates, misdirected to temporal things, but the capacity to understand them properly remains open to reflection and the workings of grace. Seen in the light of faith, desire serves as an encompassing metaphor for what lies outside the immediate realm of erotic attachments; it explains important features of imagination and memory, of aesthetic response, of social relations in the human community. The resolution Augustine effects between body and spirit is so thorough and his extensions to other areas of experience so compelling that he paradoxically generates a new order of problems.

The first problem is the radical integration of desire. Because he portrays desire for temporal goods not merely as cupidity but also as an adumbration of the proper desire for God, Augustine impoverishes the particulars of experience as topics of moral deliberation. He may retain the intensity of affect—how else to explain the emotional texture of the pear-tree episode?—but the substance disappears. Saint Paul's admonition that the letter kills and the spirit gives life offers a warrant for reading experience only in the fullness of its spiritual meaning. Nonetheless, the effect is to empty experience of heterogeneity and particularity. The reality of lived experience recedes before the transcendent. No name attaches to Augustine's lover or to his male friend who dies in Tagaste. As the inner life of the soul opens up, domestic and private life fall from sight; the details that give them a specific definition disappear before the divine referent that gives them significance. It is not simply that in the *Confessions* the literal gives way to the figurative; in the dual framework of Augustine's narrative, the figurative precedes the literal and awaits it. Augustine's integration of desire finally effaces the objects of desire, rendering them all a species of equivalent signs.

A second problem resides in what I called earlier the romance of plenitude. Desire signifies the incommensurate gift of divine love. Even when misdirected by the will as "perverse imitation," it eventually leads to God's plenitude, for the objects of desire serve as signs of their maker. The tragic possibility that Augustine holds open, especially in the episodes about loss, arises from misreading the signs of plenitude. The disparity between objects and affect uncovers the demand for a full presence immediately available to the desiring subject in the life of pleasure, friendship, or philosophical understanding. Taken out of the dual framework of anticipation and retrospect, the narrative of desire threatens to collapse into a mechanism for forcing plenitude out of embodiment, immanence out of presence. In medieval writers who restage Augustine's flight from desire and adapt his conversion narrative, we will see the reformulation of Augustine's transcendence as impossible and implacable demand under the guise of love.

CHAPTER 2

"NULLUM CRIMEN ERIT": OVIDIAN CRAFT AND THE ILLUSION OF MASTERY

O vid's satirical writings on love offered medieval readers a sophisticated and canonical alternative to Augustine's integration of desire in
the narrative of conversion. In one sense, of course, Augustine's story of
his wandering desires and quest for plenitude replicates the underlying
narrative of Roman love elegy. In Catullus, Tibullus, and Propertius, the
erotic subject is driven by incessant desire for a mistress who is an object of
impossible demand, continually evoked but never fully present and available.
Ovid claims the erotic stasis of the poet-lover as his literary heritage. In his
erotodidactic poems, he addresses what Joy Connolly describes as the "project" within each love elegy: "the search for ways to defer bliss and thus its
own ending."[1] Recent scholarship reminds us that medieval readers
encountered Ovid in the school curriculum as an ethical writer, treating
the behavior of lovers.[2] But as Warren Ginsberg notes, poets within that
tradition acknowledged and responded to the literary qualities that inform
Ovid's erotodidacticism.[3] My focus in this chapter is on the formulation
Ovid gives to love and desire within a discipline of craft and mastery. This
formulation provided an extraordinary thematic and structural resource for
medieval writers, and it posed a continuing literary problem for them to
resolve.

Ovid's strategy is not to transcend or integrate desire, as Augustine
hopes to do, to regulate and transform it. He accepts the dispersal of
erotic attachments and seeks to navigate among them. In the *Ars amatoria*
and *Remedia amoris*, he sets out a technology that promises to deliver the
objects of these attachments while freeing the self from the constraints of its
own desire. Within this program, mastery and discipline hold out the
prospect of control, but they never succeed in fully transforming and
directing desire. Ovidian craft provides a means for servicing appetite,

while desire remains beyond the technology of control. Indeed, at various points in Ovid's erotodidactic poems, desire surfaces as a form of resistance and a challenge to his precepts for managing love. Seen in its full dimensions, the Ovidian program of mastery represents a flight from desire, an evasion through art that displaces desire and offers appetite as a substitute for it under the rubric of love.

Ovidian Craft

The key to Ovid's strategy lies in the ambitious claim made at the start of the *Ars amatoria* that love can be regulated by art: "arte regendus amor" (1.4).[4] Art, in the sense of craft and technique, operates through each of the four phases that Ovid goes on to outline. It makes possible the lover's search for a mistress and his capture of her. It allows him to maintain a love affair over time. It also underwrites a final stage implicit in the *Ars amatoria* and expounded directly in the *Remedia amoris*—a retreat from love when it grows oppressive and the mistress takes on a strong resemblance to the figures who torment the earlier elegiac poets.[5] The nature of this craft is practical rather than theoretical: "usus opus movet hoc" (1.29). Ovid places it explicitly beyond the vatic powers of Apollo and so beyond transcendence (1.25). Ovid's claim—"vera canam" ("true will be my song" [1.30])—is about accuracy and utility rather than truth in a larger sense: his precepts fit the facts of experience. Early in the *Ars amatoria*, Ovid seems to obscure the sharp distinction between divine inspiration and mundane human practice by paradoxically describing himself as a *vates peritus* ("an experienced bard" [1.29]). But the term *vates* means a poet and an interpreter of signs, and the seeming paradox of inspiration and experience allows him to establish a complex persona rather than assert divinatory powers.[6] When Apollo reenters the poem in book 2, his prophetic injunction of self-knowledge is absorbed within Ovid's teaching (2.493–510) and made practical. To love *sapienter* (2.501), as Apollo now explains, means using one's endowments to good effect.

Pragmatic and profoundly indifferent with respect to its objects, the Ovidian craft of love operates simultaneously on two planes. It allows the lover guided by its techniques to find, capture, and control his quarry. At the same time, it establishes a regimen of internal control. The former depends on the latter. The lover is able to move through the sequential phases of his career by training himself to stand apart from the constraints of love. As Alison Sharrock points out, there is a significant parallel between the love object sought by the trained (*doctus*) lover and the lover trained by the Ovidian master (*praeceptor amoris*), for each is subjugated and transformed, though in different ways.[7] Moreover, these two planes are connected in a logic of erotic appropriation: the *praeceptor* trains the lover; the lover captures his prey; the spoils are finally claimed for the master. Consequently, the same assertion of proprietary interest can be made for male and female prey in the first and second endings of the *Ars amatoria*, where teaching has been directed to men and women respectively: "Naso magister erat" ("Naso was my master" [2.744, 3.812]).

The power that Ovid claims for his art is mediated, of course, by his comic tone, his inversion of genre, and the figure of the *praeceptor amoris* who ostensibly furnishes the principles and practical illustrations of erotic control to his student. The *Ars amatoria* and *Remedia amoris* extol their craft but maintain an ironic distance on their topic. Their topic (*erototechne*) is consciously discordant with the seriousness of Lucretian and Vergilian didactic poetry.[8] The *praeceptor* is and is not the poet. John Fyler calls him "a pedantic fool," adding, "we err greatly if we identify him with Ovid or take his self-characterization seriously."[9] We thus share the *praeceptor*'s vantage point yet see its ironies and contradictions in a fuller perspective. We do not believe him, but, as Peter Allen suggests, we see what he can imagine.[10] When he speaks as a lover, he is speaking often as a poet committed to writing love elegy as much as a teacher explaining the art of love.[11] Over the course of the *Ars amatoria*, the *praeceptor*'s role devolves as he expounds his doctrine. He is at first a master teaching love as Chiron once taught Achilles (1.17). Later, he is a teacher only to the poor (2.161–65). When Apollo reappears, the teacher is "Lascivi. . .praeceptor Amoris" ("Preceptor of wanton love" [2.497]). This description is then fully accommodated at the beginning of book 3: "Nil nisi lascivi per me discuntur amores" ("Naught save wanton loves are learned through me" [3.27]). Even the *praeceptor*'s dependence on experience (*usus*) as the foundation of his teaching is, in Richard J. Tarrant's phrase, "a ruse," for his lessons are taken from poetry, including his own *Amores*, and not from life.[12] The *Ars amatoria*, as Alexander Dalzell points out, "is a text written upon a text."[13] When the *magister* extolls his craft in the *Remedia* to save classical heroines from their tragic fates (55–63), his text unwrites the text of mythology and much of his own *Heroides*, the epistolary complaints of women victimized by men who have intuitively known what Ovid now purports to systematize and teach.

Traditionally, these contradictory features have been taken as evidence of Ovid's superlative wit, his commitment to the lighter topics of elegy over the seriousness of epic and tragedy, and his preference for style over substance. More recent critics explain them as discursive features that artfully or profoundly (or both) deconstruct erotic doctrine while subverting Augustan social norms and their consummate expression in Vergil. Along those lines, we might argue, with Duncan F. Kennedy, that the Ovidian instructional project reverses the polarity of subject matter and learning in order to create rather than simply convey knowledge. That is, the poems model more than teach, and their pedagogical aim is to lead the erotic subject to act so that he or she becomes a topic of literary discourse. If we look beyond Ovid's comic strategies, then, something besides wit and style is at stake, though wit and style never disappear. In particular, we can see that Ovid's endorsement of art and technique rests on two serious propositions that his poems exploit yet finally undermine. The first is the illusion of control, and the second is the innocence of love.

Ovidian Mastery

Ovid's initial similes in the *Ars amatoria* define the structure of control. Like the motion of ships and chariots, love operates through a dynamic power, and this power can be restrained and redirected to an end—most immediately to the gratification of the lover and finally to the interest and renown of the poet. The key metaphor for erotic control is hunting. C. M. C. Green notes that hunting is a metaphor "for all human arts" and that Ovid follows poetic tradition by equating love with the hunt.[14] But Ovid goes significantly beyond the immediate simile by insisting that the erotic huntsman is not simply pursuing his quarry but also locating himself, consciously or not, within a predatory landscape.

> Scit bene venator, cervis ubi retia tendat,
>   Scit bene, qua frendens valle moretur aper;
> Aucupibus noti frutices; qui sustinet hamos,
>   Novit quae multo pisce natentur aquae:
> Tu quoque, materiam longo qui quaeris amori,
>   Ante frequens quo sit disce puella loco.
>   (1.45–50)

[Well knows the hunter where to spread his nets for the stag, well knows he in what glen the boar with gnashing teeth abides; familiar are the copses to fowlers, and he who holds the hook is aware in what water many fish are swimming; you too, who seek the objects of a lasting passion, learn first what places the maidens haunt.]

Part of Ovid's wit is to recast the hunter's terrain as a cityscape, in which public locales, theatres, and the circus become a ground for stalking prey for capture. Green points out that the Ovidian hunt has a specific recreational form, a closed pursuit rather than a chase through forests and woodlands: "Rome abounds with women because Rome is Venus' game preserve."[15] This artificial, stylized pursuit occurs in a domain already occupied and coded with political, dynastic, and mythological meaning. Ovid redefines the existing significance of these places and remaps the city. The porticoes associated in civic memory with Pompey and the imperial family become sites in an erotic topography (1.67–72).[16] The rape of the Sabine women by Romulus and his men, staged within the space of a primitive theater, is transformed from a city-founding crime to a quotidian model of distribution and patronage repeated now in ordinary experience: "Romule, militibus scisti dare commoda solus: / Haec mihi si dederis commoda, miles ero" ("Ah, Romulus, thou only didst know how to bestow bounty on thy warriors; so thou but bestow such bounty upon me, I will be a warrior" [1.131–32]). The "commoda" dispensed to love's soldiers are not the spoils of heroic endeavors but "fringe-benefits" for journeyman's work.[17]

The external control that Ovid's hunter-lover exercises is based on an internal disparity of appetite that generates a profound and unresolvable anxiety. The *praeceptor* assures his disciple that women can be captured and that they share the same pleasure in stolen love ("furtiva venus" [1.275]) as men. Women differ by concealing appetite better than men, but the most profound difference is their failure or inability to regulate themselves: "Parcior in nobis nec tam furiosa libido: / Legitimum finem flamma virilis habet" ("In us desire is weaker and not so frantic: the manly flame knows a lawful bound" [1.281–82]). The contrast is quantitative, qualitative, and structural. Male passion is less, measured in absolute terms; different in kind, because less consuming; and differently constructed. The anxiety here is that male passion might be taken as a defective, if more highly socialized, version of a stronger female sexuality. For that reason, the *praeceptor* chooses the image of a "flamma virilis" to represent a form of appetite that can burn without excess and so without falling into the madness ("furiosa libido") that designates the loss of self as a social being. To be *furiosus* is to join the deaf, mute, and profligate who are incapable of conducting business or giving credible testimony in court.[18] Male passion, according to the *praeceptor*'s formulation, has a shape that brings it under control. It accepts and imposes limits (*modus*). Its indwelling sense of a proper aim and direction ("legitimum finem") makes self-regulation possible.

Masculine erotic selfhood depends on a two-fold contrast with women's appetites that presumably makes it a mean between excess and defect. The *praeceptor* appends a list of exempla (1.283–340) that illustrate the violent qualities of women as lovers. In the cases that head his list, Byblis, Myrrha, and Pasiphaë represent not just the excess and intensity of women but the bestial, destructive passions that potentially hover in the background of their sexuality. In all his examples, bonds within the patriarchal family fall victim to women's unbridled passion: "Omnia feminea sunt ista libidine mota; / Acrior est nostra, plusque furoris habet" ("All those crimes were prompted by women's lust; keener it is than ours, and has more of madness" [1.341–42]).[19] Eleanor Leach points out that this equation of nature, animals, and women is paralleled by a second comparison, which completes Ovid's mock-georgic theme. Like fields and crops, women can be guided by the craft of husbandry.[20] The trained lover, like the Vergilian farmer of the *Georgics*, harvests the bounty that nature variously bestows and that tests his knowledge, ingenuity, and skill at improvisation. Allied with animal and vegetative nature, women are paradoxically aggressive and compliant to the self-regulating men who can control them through art. In this way, they remain foils, unconscious of themselves as objects, while men stand fully in possession of themselves as subjects.

As Ovid's poem moves to other phases in the erotic project, the structure of control remains in place. Book 2 opens with the suggestion that maintaining love can require even more art than capturing the prey. Chance may figure in the initial capture, but craft is required to retain the prey ("Casus inest illic; hoc erit artis opus" [2.14]). The task of restraining Cupid's symbolic flight ("imposuisse modum" [2.20]) is not external but internal and repetitive ("Ipse deum volucrem detinuisse paro" [2.98]). The Ovidian disciple consciously refines his qualities of character to shape a self pleasing, ingratiating, and alert. Even his language in love-making is regulated by the demands of craft. The *praeceptor* warns: "Tantum, ne pateas verbis simulator in illis, / Effice, nec vultu destrue dicta tuo. / Si latet, ars prodest" ("Only while so talking take care not to show you are feigning, nor let your looks undo your words. Art, if hidden, avails" [2.311–313]). The threat here is unconscious revelation. If the adept seeks occasional novelty and variety with other partners, pleasure still remains under the veil of discretion: "Ludite, sed furto celetur culpa modesto" ("Have your sport, but let modest deception veil the fault" [2.389]).

Modern readers of the *Ars amatoria* have recognized that the control exercised over the Ovidian lover by the teacher and by the student over himself is a form of mechanization. Eric Downing usefully summarizes this view: "The male student is engaged in a process of self-automatization and self-impersonation from within: he is to suppress, regulate, even eliminate his 'natural' self and *amor* and to govern or replace them with a system of interceding literary citation and re-presentation." The difference between men and women, Downing goes on to say, is that "Men mechanize (and replace) their inner lives; women mechanize (and replace) their superfical, surface appearance."[21] Ralph Hexter says, "Just as 'love' is an object of technique and technologization, so there is nothing 'natural' about the body."[22] The means to this artificial, confected self is *cultus*—a term whose semantic range includes traditional agriculture, styles of dress, education, refinement, civilization, and even dissipation. Vergil uses it to denote aspects of husbandry (*Aeneid* 8.316; *Georgics* 1.3, 1.52, 2.1, 2.35). In the *Ars amatoria*, Ovid applies it specifically to hygiene (1.514) and grooming (3.101) and broadly to a civilization marked by elegance and refinement (3.127)—the modernity he enthusiastically sets against ideals of a Golden Age, the imagined past of Roman rustic virtue, and thus implicitly against Augustan social moralizing. In the *Remedia*, cultivation is what the lover must see through in order to disconnect himself from his overbearing mistress: "pars minima est ipsa puella sui" ("a woman is the least part of herself" [344]).

The defining quality of Ovidian *cultus* lies not just in the actual presentation of self but in the self-mastery (and self-alienation) that permits a lover to shape himself or herself. Sharrock connects this mastery to a broad concern with male autarky—the regimens of internal and external control—within Roman culture.[23] The *praeceptor* advises his male disciple in book 1 to cultivate a natural look: "Forma viros neglecta decet" ("An uncared-for beauty is becoming to men" [1.509]).[24] His social bearing, too, is a product of calculation: "Qui fuerat cultor, factus amator erat" ("he who had been an admirer became a lover" [1.722]). Meanwhile, women work to highlight the advantages nature gives them and to minimize or obscure their physical defects. Ovid's instructions to them begin with advice on physical appearance: "Ordior a cultu" ("I begin with the body's care" [3.101]). Patricia Watson has proposed that *cultus* in this context refers only to women's adornment and that Ovid not only juxtaposes the expected contrast of now and then but deflates the moralizing opposition by celebrating an age notable for good grooming. But for the specific advice to produce its effects, lovers of either sex must first know and regulate themselves.

Cultus follows, then, from a highly restrictive form of self-knowledge that underwrites control. This is what Apollo means when he exhorts men to love *sapienter*. And it is what the *praeceptor* means when he applies the Delphic injunction to women with the same overt intent: "Nota sibi sit quaeque: modos a corpore certos / Sumite: non omnes una figura decet" ("Let each woman know herself; from your own bodies fix your methods; one fashion does not suit all alike" [3.771–72]). Using the metaphor of parlor games, Ovid advises women what the larger objective of cultural production really is: "Maius opus mores composuisse suos" ("more important is it to control one's own behavior" [3.370]). The self artfully constructed in its behavior (*mos compositus*) is an artifact on display rather than a moral being; other facets of character must be cancelled out, redirected, or replaced. The same process attaches to men in the final stage of the Ovidian career. The *Remedia amoris* announces a project of discipline that returns the erotic subject to control of itself: "saevas extinguere flammas, / Nec servum vitii pectus habere sui" ("to extinguish savage flames, and have a heart not enslaved to its own frailty" [53–54]). This apparent call for freedom and autonomy comes at the cost of internalized oppression. The "saevas flammas" extinguished by *cultus* are passions that presumably stand outside and apart from the "flamma virilis" of *Ars amatoria* 1.

The dialectic of nature and culture in erotic life generates two different formulations. The "furiosa libido" (1.281) of women is always in motion (1.341). As Downing points out, the counsel of book 3, which leads progressively away from nature toward culture and artifice, has as its goal the transformation of a naturally mobile self into statuary—"an enslavement of immobility, a depriving women of their natural desire to move."[25] By contrast, the male lover operates through calculated motion. His model at the end of book 1 is Proteus. He moves within the varied landscape of female sexuality, adapting himself and his metaphorical shape as different pleasures offer themselves: "Qui sapit, innumeris moribus aptus erit, / Utque leves Proteus modo se tenuabit in undas, / Nunc leo, nunc arbor, nunc erit hirtus aper" ("the wise man will suit himself to countless fashions, and like Proteus will now resolve himself into light waves, and now will be a lion, now a tree, now a shaggy boar" [1.760–62]). "Qui sapit" is the important qualification for understanding this passage, for it refers not just to a mastery of erotic technology but first and foremost to a kind of self-possession that allows external change without losing the internal self who seemingly orchestrates change as needed. It makes possible self-alienation in the service of gratification, for which mechanization is the means. In book 2, the model of shifting erotics is Ulysses, whose eloquent digressions create and reproduce the extended interim of love (2.123–42). In the *Remedia amoris*, Ovid will return to the model of Proteus, when he describes himself as a physician varying his therapy according to the disease (525–26). The physician knows his art because he is a recovered lover.

By setting forth the Protean lover as a model of control and adaptation, Ovid ironically undermines the doctrine that the *praeceptor* expounds. In book 3, we see that the games women play as pasttimes carry the potential to reveal something besides the artifice of self. The *mos compositus* polices anger and rivalry so that an indwelling disorder does not show itself openly: "Tum sumus incauti, studioque aperimur in ipso, / Nudaque per lusus pectora nostra patent" ("Then are we incautious and reveal ourselves in our very zest, and in our games our hearts show clear to see" [3.371–72]). The male lover who has internalized Ovid's teaching theoretically escapes this disclosure through his discipline. Yet Ovid gives us abundant examples of the failures of control. Lawyers find themselves trapped by love in the law courts where they usually hold sway (1.83–88). Spectators at gladiatorial games are wounded by Cupid (1.165–70). At times, even the *praeceptor* himself fails his doctrine: "Hac ego, confiteor, non sum perfectus in arte; / Quid faciam? monitis sum minor ipse meis" ("In this art, I confess, I am not perfect; what am I to do? I fall short of my own counsels" [2.547–48]). Poets, as the masters of invention and fictional construction, shun public life for erotic topics that soon control them: "Sed facile haeremus" ("But we are easily caught" [3.543]). As Ovid's irony demonstrates, control is an illusion for disciple and teacher alike. The self brought under discipline remains vulnerable to what control would superintend and regulate. I shall argue later that the threat always present in the Ovidian program is desire. But first I want to examine the assertion that the *praeceptor* makes as a parallel to control: the claim that love, within the scope of his teaching at least, is safe and harmless.

Harmless Love

Love has a wide semantic range but a fairly determinate poetic usage in the *Ars amatoria* and *Remedia amoris*. Ovid uses terms such as *libido, cupido*, and *ardor* in concrete senses to describe passion experienced in an exemplary way. *Libido* is applied exclusively to women. Women have a "furiosa libido" (1.281), and the crimes of Byblis, Myrrha, and other women in mythology are driven by a particular passion: "Omnia feminea sunt ista libidine mota" ("All those crimes were prompted by women's lust" [1.341]). In the social sphere, feminine rivalry in games and pasttimes threatens to reveal a deeper, acquisitive drive—*cupido*, a love of advantage or profit ("lucrique cupido" [3.373]). Romulus's men carry off the Sabine women on their eager breasts (*cupido sinu* [1.128]). Procris feels "pectoris ardor" (3.714) when she mistakenly believes that Aura is her rival for Cephalus's affection. But she is only the mythological figure who stands generally for every woman who has been displaced by a rival. This paradigmatic woman reacts to challenges with beastial rage: "Ardet et in vultu pignora mentis habet" ("she is aflame and on her face she bears the tokens of her feelings" [2.378]). Pleasure (*voluptas*) is the continual, egoistic goal of Ovidian lovers: "curae sua cuique voluptas" ("none cares but for his own pleasure" [1.749]). The term that carries the greatest resonance in the erotic lexicon of these poems, however, is *amor*. In classical authors, *amor* signifies a bond of affection, the object of affection itself, the personified god of love, a passionate longing for something, and even a love charm (the *hippomanes*). Cicero distinguishes *caritas* from *amor* by their objects. The former is directed to parents, homeland, or men renowned for wisdom and deeds. The latter concentrates on attachments associated with domesticity and familiarity—wives, children, brothers, and others.[26] Thus, while charity, benevolence, and love can be shown to other humans, love can also apply to beasts.

In the *Ars amatoria*, as Katharina Volk argues, *amor* vacillates grammatically between the god of love and the experience of loving and conceptually between an emotion (erotic attraction) and a social practice (seduction and love-making).[27] Ovid's narrator sets himself as a master over a personified god of love (1.7–8), with whom he shares an ongoing struggle for dominance: "Quo me fixit Amor, quo me violentius ussit, / Hoc melior facti vulneris ultor ero" ("The more violently Love has pierced and branded me, the better shall I avenge the wound that he has made" [1.23–24]). His struggle here cancels out his earlier submission to love at the beginning of the *Amores* and to the elegiac tradition as a whole: "omnia uincit Amor: et nos cedamus Amori" (Vergil, *Eclogues* 10.69). The violence of love is expressed, too, in the *praeceptor*'s exhortation to his students: "Militiae species amor est" ("Love is a kind of warfare" [2.233]). By this he means to indicate not just conflict but the long campaign that conquering and colonizing a beloved involve: "Hoc quoque militia est, hoc quoque quaerit opes" ("this too [prolonging a love affair] is warfare, this too calls for your powers" [2.674]). Its rigors, he explains elsewhere, transform the body of a lover into that of a wan supplicant (1.723–38). The hardships of a soldier and humility of a slave, as Frank Olin Copley suggests, are two facets of the same thing for a lover.[28] For men and women alike, *amor* is mobile and dynamic, inflicting pain and breaking the bonds of friendship in the service of gratification. In the *Remedia amoris*, where Amor accedes to the Ovidian project of self-recovery (40), love remains deceptive (95), rebellious (246), fierce (530), alert (619), and rivalrous (768–80). Though the *praeceptor* advises an array of tactics, the only credible antidote for love is indifference (653–58).

This pattern of hyperbolic struggle stands against the second large claim made by the *praeceptor amoris* as a corollary to the controlling power of art. His art, the *praeceptor* asserts, can produce a safe and harmless love: "Nos venerem tutam concessaque furta canemus, / Inque meo nullum carmine crimen erit" ("Of safe love-making do I sing, and permitted secrecy, and in my verse shall be no wrong-doing" [1.33–34]). *Venus tuta* is love without consequences. It is a realm of erotic play, and when the master ends his instruction in book 3 of the *Ars amatoria*, he explicitly marks its boundary: "Lusus habet finem" ("Our sport is ended" [3.809]). What transpires in the space of play is licensed indulgence—"concessa furta," thefts, deceptions, and sexual intrigues that enjoy social tolerance and immunity. For that reason, the *praeceptor* consciously seeks to remove his poem from the domain of reproach and transgression. At the start of the *Remedia amoris*, he makes the same argument to Amor, contrasting the violence of war and unrequited passion to the harmless intrigues of lovers: "Tu cole maternas, tuto quibus utimur, artes, / Et quarum vitio nulla fit orba parens" ("do thou practise thy mother's art, which it is safe to use, and by whose fault no parent is bereaved" [29–30]).

In most commentary on this passage, the safety of Ovidian love depends on restricting its fictional audience and application. A. S. Hollis says that the women Ovid is writing about are *heteraerae* (high-class courtesans who were probably freedwomen).[29] Excluding those women whose dress and appearance carry the social badges of chastity ("vittae tenues, insigne pudoris" [1.31; cf. 2.600]), the *praeceptor* creates an imaginative community of women unable to control their passions adequately, who stand to lose nothing by indulgence. In his self-commentary as an elegiac poet in the *Remedia amoris*, Ovid confirms the point: "Thais in arte mea est; lascivia libera nostra est; / Nil mihi cum vitta; Thais in arte mea est" ("Thais is the subject of my art; unfettered is my love-making: naught have I to do with fillets; Thais is the subject of my art" [385–86]). Dalzell proposes that another section of the *Remedia* (611–616) implies that "all former slaves are fair game" and that "it was perfectly acceptable to betray the husband of a freedwoman"—explicit challenges to Augustan moral and social legislation.[30] Whatever their social and historical counterparts may be, these women are objects of male fantasy onto whom erotic wishes, anxieties, and aggression can be projected. Love with them is safe because they have no power or agency save that indirectly conceded by men who fail to regulate themselves. Conversely, the imagined disciples of the *praeceptor* are leisure-class Romans who have the time and means to devote to erotic intrigues and who become thereby a satirical target. Sharrock suggests that they are "educated Roman men of a detached and mildly subversive frame of mind, contemporary with Ovid."[31] Leisure, as the *praeceptor* reminds them in the *Remedia*, is the necessary condition of their erotic interlude: "Venus otia amat" (143).

In sounding his theme, Ovid at the same time relocates it within the elegiac tradition.[32] For earlier poets, the prospect of a safe love was wished for but not assumed. Catullus complains to Alfenus about the safety promised in love: "certe tute iubebas animam tradere, inique <me> / inducens in amorem, quasi tuta omnia mi forent" ("For truly you used to bid me trust my soul to you (ah, unjust!), leading me into love as if all were safe for me" [30.7–8]). Propertius contrasts his turbulent state with that of others favored by love who share their love in safety together: "in tuto semper amore pares" ("either to other make equal response of love unperilous" [1.1.32]). Tibullus asserts Venus's favor and beneficence for the lover: "Quisquis amore tenetur, eat tutusque sacerque / qualibet; insidias non timuisse decet" ("Whosoe'er hath love in his heart may pass safe and in heaven's keeping where he will; no ambush should he fear" [1.2.27–28]). These poets are among the ones that the *praeceptor* recommends for women to read (3.329–48) as part of the cultivation that constructs an inner self; in the *Remedia*, he will recommend their removal for the man seeking to escape love (759–66). If they were attentive readers, though, his students would see that Ovid has drastically shifted the meaning of safe love. His elegiac forebears see themselves profoundly at risk in love, and they hope for some measure of protection. Ovid promises not to make love safe but to confine erotic practice to a protected domain.

His means for doing so is to define love consciously as appetite and gratification. The logic of Ovid's hunting metaphor, which informs the project of finding and capturing a love object in book 1, depends on consumption. The cityscape containing the prey is marked by sites of appetite. The theater, circus, and banquet room stimulate by spectacle, drink, and social exchange, as Augustine recognized. Surface events in those domains both cover and signify the erotic subtext. Images of ripeness and harvesting provide a second and complementary metaphor of appetite. In his georgic guise, the Ovidian lover reckons the time to gather what he seeks: "Mens erit apta capi tum, cum laetissima rerum / Ut seges in pingui luxuriabit humo" ("Then will her mind be apt for winning when in the fulness of joy she grows wanton like the corn crop in a rich soil" [1.359–60]). The *praeceptor* emphasizes that erotic attachments are interchangeable—"nova grata voluptas" (" 'tis new delights that win welcome" [1.347]). Permanent liaisons allow novelty—"Nec mea vos uni damnat censura puellae" (2.387)—and the tyranny of one mistress can be escaped by replacement or alteration: "Successore novo vincitur omnis amor" ("all love is vanquished by a succeeding love" [*Remedia* 462]). As the example of Bacchus and Ariadne shows (1.565), even chance can offer up targets of opportunity. Moreover, as appetite, love draws on an inexhaustible source. Addressing his women disciples, the *praeceptor* admonishes them, "Ite, per exemplum, genus o mortale, dearum, / Gaudia nec cupidis vestra negate viris" ("Study, ye mortal folk, the examples of the goddesses, nor deny your joys to hungry lovers" [3.87–88]). As he formulates it here, the transactions of appetite move in one direction. *Gaudia vestra* are the joys that women provide; it is avaricious men who consume them.

In his remarks on pleasure, Ovid nuances this view of appetite, but love remains safe because it is confined to gratification. In his aetiological digression, Ovid credits pleasure with transforming mankind from an isolated brutishness: "Blanda truces animos fertur mollisse voluptas" ("Beguiling pleasure is said to have softened those fierce spirits" [2. 477]). Indiscriminate and mobile, pleasure is the end that gratifies men and women as both creatures and social beings. In book 2 it is what stands against the inexorability of time. Here Ovid speaks of mutual pleasure against the background of perishable youth and beauty: "Quod iuvet, ex aequo femina virque ferant. / Odi concubitus, qui non utrumque resolvunt" ("let both man and woman feel what delights them equally. I hate embraces which leave not each out-worn" [2.682–83]). He returns to the idea at the end of book 3—"ex aequo res iuvet illa duos" ("let that act delight both alike" [3.794])—and in the *Remedia amoris* (413–418). Both passages resist an uncritical glorification of pleasure. In the first, the alternative to mutual pleasure is the discrete simulation of contentment; in the second, when pleasure has reached its goal ("ad metas venit finita voluptas"), it furnishes an occasion to remark the defects in a lover's body. Nowhere, however, does Ovid address what might lie beyond pleasure and gratification. As Robert M. Durling has remarked, "The art of love is applicable only in an imaginary world, a world in which human beings have no profound needs or passions; as soon as the question of genuine passion arises, the problem of responsibility presents itself, and the cynical manipulation of others can no longer be treated lightly."[33]

Ovidian Desire

The confident claims that the *praeceptor* makes about the controlling power of art and the safety of love are at best compromised and at worse discredited as the *Ars amatoria* and *Remedia amoris* unfold their teaching. Within the fiction of erotodidaxis, control proves fragile and illustory, while love poses a threat to pupil and teacher alike. Taken on its own terms, the Ovidian program, as many commentators have remarked, is undercut by inconsis-tencies and contradictions that reflect Ovid's wit, his satiric aim, and his authorial presence. Volk says, "In control of his poem and in control of *amor*, the persona is central to the working of the *Ars amatoria* in a way that very few first-person speakers ever are, at least in ancient literature."[34] Downing proposes a second and more radical understanding: the program fails precisely to the extent that it succeeds. On this view, mastery and domination come at the price of an automatized, artificial self constructed by the violence required to make the lover an artwork.[35] Both the ironic failures and the unbearable success of the program point, I think, toward another dimension of Ovid's poems that remains only partially understood—desire, as distinct from appetite.

In the *Ars amatoria* and *Remedia amoris*, amatory technique and harmless love are confined to appetite and gratification. The metaphors of hunting and husbandry, the regimen of self-control, the tactics elaborated by precept and example—all these have to do with erotic demands that can be satisfied. Satisfaction, as the *praeceptor* says, may be mutual or, if circumstances require, individual and opportunistic (2.727–32); it can be heightened by deferral or difficulty. Yet it remains nevertheless tangible and immediate.

Ovidian pleasure (*voluptas*) is imagined as a specific, sensual goal. But by defining love as appetite and directing erotic practice toward pleasure as its terminal point, the *Ars* and *Remedia* obscure and evade the workings of desire.

Modern criticism has registered the presence of desire obliquely in its frequent assertion that Ovid's teaching about love is built over a void. For E. D. Blodgett, the void is the absence of any value besides an artistry dependent on irony, rhetoric, and fraud: "love, war and art are forms assumed from nothing at all. Their substance is their form."[36] Emphasizing the endless deferral of desire in Lacanian psychoanalysis, Philip Hardie contends that "Ovid revitalizes the conventional elegiac association of love and grief" to focus on the interplay of demand and absence; this dynamic informs both the love poetry and the repetitive narratives of the *Metamorphoses*, and it becomes a poetic emblem in the exile poetry, where presence necessarily signifies absence.[37] Alessandro Schiesaro, associating love poetry with issues of knowledge and understanding, proposes, "At the centre of Ovid's erotics, however, stands, more often than not, a void" because the object of desire can never be fully possessed.[38] For such readings, the impossibility of eros is a theme derived from Lucretius's discussion of perception, sensation, and sexuality. Turning briefly to Lucretius, we can trace the literary framework from which Ovidian desire emerges to destabilize external and internal control.

In book 4 of his *De rerum natura*, Lucretius explains that lovers (understood as men, though women, too, experience pleasure) are affected by images of other bodies (*simulacra*) and move toward those bodies driven by the cruel force of sexual passion ("dira lubido" [4.1046]). The material aim of this erotic turbulence is to transmit seminal fluid from one body to the other (4.1056). Lucretius's physiological account turns quickly, however, to a consideration of affect and to erotic prescriptions for managing passions. Images stimulate the internal mechanisms of sexuality and make the love object present: "nam si abest quod ames, praesto simulacra tamen sunt / illius" ("For if what you love is absent, yet its images are there" [4.1061–62]), insinuating it into consciousness. The remedy is to divert the mind to another object and redirect the fluid stimulated by perception to the receptacle of another but equally appropriate body (4.1064–65). This kind of displacement Lucretius calls a benefit without penalty ("sine poena commoda" [4.1074]), and it accrues especially to those healthy and disciplined men who can ration satisfaction for themselves and modulate the aggression that accompanies the love-making of appetitive bodies.

Though he offers a materialist account, Lucretius speaks largely in psychological terms, for he is concerned with somatic effects and the impact of love on the self as an agent. For him, love depends on a fantasy of repletion, the impossible hope that plenitude lies fully in another body and can be possessed there: "namque in eo spes est, unde est ardoris origo, / restingui quoque posse ab eodem corpore flammam" ("For here lies the hope that the fire may be extinguished from the same body that was the origin of the burning" [4.1086–87]). But unlike food and drink, the insubstantial images that fuel love cannot fill up the spaces of the body: "nil datur in corpus praeter simulacra fruendum / tenvia" ("nothing comes into the body to be enjoyed except thin images" [4.1095–96]). Eros thus offers a play of illusion: "in amore Venus simulacris ludit amantis" ("in love Venus mocks lovers with images" [4.1101]). Paradoxically, the impossibility of love resides precisely in the integrity of bodies, their ultimate inaccessibility to each other by capture, penetration, or carrying off. If bodies find some measure of solace in their embraces, it is a temporary respite. Described and experienced as "rabies" and "furor," love is repetitive, obsessive, and doomed to frustration. It is the "dira cupido" (4.1090) that continually restages the "dira libido" of attraction.

Lucretius is the authoritative didactic poet whose dismissive view of love counters the elegiac tradition from Catullus onwards and discredits the elegists' literary project of celebrating passion. Ovid's response to Lucretius's authority and doctrine is not challenge or assimilation so much as a troping of major themes. For example, his aetiological digression situates mankind within a Lucretian universe, but it is beguiling pleasure (*blanda voluptas* [2.477]), a phrase borrowed and dislocated from Lucretius, that replaces Lucretius's story of the gradual emergence of culture with a celebration of the civilizing power of sensuality.[39] In the passage on sexuality, Lucretius uses the rhetoric of hygiene to legitimate the workings of appetite, and his prescriptions for emotional distance are consistent with the doctrine of internalized control that the *praeceptor* expounds and with the strategies for removing a lover from a tyrannical mistress. Ovid, as J. Shullman insists, does not reject Lucretius's idea that love is madness or disease; but he does undercut the Lucretian assumption that love can be managed rationally, and he holds out the alternative that deception and self-deception are essential to love.[40]

Lucretius, then, gives us a source and an intertext but not an explanation for the void that inhabits Ovidian erotics. The Ovidian void is not, as some readers suggest, a dead zone bereft of affect that consequently makes possible the detached calculations of the *praeceptor* and his predatory, if sometimes incapable, disciples. Rather, it is the habitation of desire—a domain for eros whose presence is made known obliquely, through indirection and displacement. In the *Ars* and *Remedia*, Ovid provides vignettes of desire to counterpoint the *praeceptor*'s program of control. These are moments when lovers are taken unawares by passions that lie beyond their immediate objectives. Lawyers, as we have seen, are captured in the law courts by love (1.83–88); spectators in the grip of gladitorial games receive Cupid's wound—"vulnus habet" (1.166)—as they watch combatants wound one another. Moreover, as Ginsberg rightly observes, "Ovid suggests. . .that desire is always resisted from within, and that that resistance is already complicit with the desire that prompts it."[41] Ovid illustrates this complicity in the example of the rape of Deidamia by Achilles. Achilles's assault belies the female disguise intended to save him from fate and death. The *praeceptor*'s debatable point here is that a lover may use force on his mistress and that force is pleasing to women (1.673). What the example shows is not only that the regime of self-alienation is contradictory but that it falters before desire. The *vis* exercised by Achilles is desire, and it has multiple victims: Deidamia, Achilles's control and camouflage, and Deidamia's shame (*pudor*) as she habituates herself to the disgrace (*stuprum*) of his violations.

The vignette of Achilles, at once absurdly comic and brutally transgressive, is part of a larger pattern of disclosure and infiltration that marks the presence of desire in Ovid's erotodidactic poems. Lovers inadvertently lay bare their faculties at banquets (1.237–44), and maids can choose the right moment of vulnerability for Venus to penetrate their mistress, much like the stealthy capture of Troy (1.357–64). The set piece narrative of Vulcan's capture of Mars and Venus is ostensibly a warning to endure rather than act against a rival, but the scene Ovid describes is also about the anxiety of sexuality intruding into consciousness. Vulcan displays the adulterous lovers captured in his fine netting, as they desperately try to cover their nakedness. Yet his vengeful "spectacula" (2.581) for the other gods do not produce a corrective shame so much as a bitter acknowledgment of desire: "quod ante tegebant, / Liberius faciunt, ut pudor omnis abest" ("the affair they once kept dark they carry on openly, now that all shame is thrown to the winds" [2.589–90]). If desire subsequently equates to sacred rites performed in secrecy (2.607)—the "cura pudoris" (2.624) that reaches back even before culture—disclosing its presence remains the destabilizing threat. The *praeceptor* tries to present this threat as if it were merely careless boasting and unjust damage to reputations. The erotic *fama* (report) he censures is not baseless "fabula" but the acknowledgment, truthful or not, of desire in language.

In his excursus on the creation of the world and culture, Ovid locates desire before consciousness. Brutish mankind wanders the earth unaware of itself, and it is only eros that starts to curb an innate ferocity:

> Iamque diu nulli cognitus alter erat.
> Blanda truces animos fertur mollisse voluptas:
> Constiterant uno femina virque loco;

Quid facerent, ipsi nullo didicere magistro:

Arte Venus nulla dulce peregit opus.

(2.476–80)

[. . . and for long none knew his fellow. Beguiling pleasure is said to have softened those fierce spirits: a man and a woman had tarried together in one spot; what were they to do, they learnt themselves with none to teach them: artlessly did Venus accomplish the sweet act].

Here Ovid imagines a primal scene of untutored sexuality. The archaic parents find themselves arbitrarily in a place without the intervention of a teacher (*nullo magistro*) or the guidance of craft (*arte nulla*). What they perform is unambiguously an act of pleasure. Ovid brackets the scene with the phrases *blanda voluptas* ("beguiling pleasure") and *dulce opus* ("sweet act"). His stress is on affect rather than appetite, on eros as experience. Ovid's insistence on pleasure as the sign of desire can be seen, too, in the changes he brings to his source. In Lucretius, the story of civilization is the narrative of a progressive undermining of brutishness. Venus joins the bodies of primitive lovers, but their motives are intentionally ambiguous and disparate: "conciliabat enim vel mutua quamque cupido / vel violenta viri vis atque inpensa libido / vel pretium, glandes atque arbita vel pira lecta" ("for either the woman was attracted by mutual desire, or caught by the man's violent force and vehement lust, or by a bribe—acorns and arbute—berries or choice pears" [5.963–65]). Lucretius's alternatives are a graduated descent from pleasure to force, exchange, and appetite, and his multiplicity of motives suits the imperfect world of flawed compacts that he sees as the record of culture. Ovid sees instead an erotic force in circulation.

Circulation is one feature that distinguishes desire from love as appetite. Early in the *Ars amatoria*, as we have seen, the mobile desires of women are contrasted with the clearly punctuated, periodic consumption of male appetite. In his advice to women in book 3 of the *Ars amatoria*, the *praeceptor* claims that pleasure is inexhaustible: "omnia constant; / Mille licet sumant, deperit inde nihil" ("those joys abide; though they take a thousand pleasures, naught is lost therefrom" [3.89–90]). In the *Remedia amoris*, where he advises men to take two lovers at once, he addresses the economy of erotic circulation from the opposite position (441–88), as a force to be distributed within the limits of male powers. Later, he warns against accepting the modulations of desire at face value: "Flamma redardescet, quae modo nulla fuit" ("the flame that was lately naught will glow once more" [734]). Circe, the *praeceptor* notes, can change men into a thousand shapes, yet she is unable to transform love (269–70).

The most important acknowledgment of desire comes in a passage generally regarded as Ovid's most accomplished, if problematic, set piece in the *Ars amatoria*. At the beginning of book 2, as the *praeceptor* prepares to explain how love can be constrained and made to abide over time, the poem suddenly turns to an account of Daedalus and Icarus's flight from Minos. The master's expository frame and the narrative digression are linked by the images of wings and flying at the beginning and end of the passage. Most readers interpret the story itself as a self-reflexive parable of art. Fyler finds its "submerged implication" in the parallels between the *praeceptor* and Daedalus and in the overturning of each one's craft (*ratio*) by an impatient youth.[42] Molly Myerowitz argues that Ovid's theme is the limit of art, particularly in opposition to the laws of nature, which Daedalus seeks to transform through his craft and genius.[43] Charles Ahern sees Daedalus and Icarus as figures for Ovid and the Ovidian disciple respectively and thus for the contrast between controlled and immoderate love.[44] Sharrock, emphasizing Ovid's intertextuality, especially with Horatian and Vergilian versions of the story, contends that there are multiple and shifting analogies by which the episode functions as a commentary on art.[45] The reading I want to develop here sees it as a meditation on the power of desire.

Whatever correspondences they see, critics focus on Daedalus the *artifex* and treat Icarus as a tragic casualty. The decisive moment of the story occurs, however, specifically apart from Daedalus. What Icarus represents in Ovid's parable of artistry is the unforeseen arrival of desire. Daedalus takes Minos's confinement of him and Icarus as the *materia* on which he will exercises his *ingenium* (2.34): "Sunt mihi naturae iura novanda meae" ("I must devise new laws for my nature" [2.42]). He crafts the wings according to design ("in ordine") and then instructs Icarus to use them, following the middle way between the sun and the sea on their flight—in other words, to follow a trajectory of restraint and control (*modus*). Daedalus plans to make Icarus's path a journey without discovery: "ego praevius ibo: / Sit tua cura sequi" ("I will lead the way, let it be thine to follow" [2.57–58]). He prepares himself cautiously ("timide") for his *novum iter* (2.68)—the *labor* of his *novae artis* (2.48), the new and strange journey of flighted return to Greece from captivity in the Cretan labyrinth that he has constructed to contain the Minotaur whom he earlier helped to sire. Supervising Icarus, he follows the trajectory he has plotted: "cursus sustinet usque suos" ("[he] ever keeps on his own course" [2.74]). But if the *novum iter* is an ingenious and controlled means of escape to Daedalus, it is something radically different for Icarus. His journey is a flight of pleasure and sudden exhilaration unaccounted for by Daedalus's artifice and planning. In a single couplet, Ovid portrays the workings of an impulse beyond Daedalus's calculation or even Icarus's awareness: "Iamque novum delectat iter, positoque timore / Icarus audaci fortius arte volat" ("And now the wondrous voyage delights [him], and forgetting his fear Icarus flies more courageously with daring skill" [2.75–76]).

Viewed as part of a monitory exemplum, this moment captures, for Meyerowitz and Ahern, the difference between the self-possessed master and his undisciplined, intemperate pupil; viewed as poetic self-commentary, it signifies, for Fyler, the failure of *ratio* and, for Sharrock, Ovid's perpetually unsettled allegiance to lesser poetic forms and his rejection of higher genres. Yet the resonance and framing of the story suggest that *amor* rather than *ars* is the topic. Daedalus promises a safe journey—"me duce tutus eris" (2.58)—to echo the safe love (*venus tuta*) that the poet's persona makes his special topic. It is specifically under the artificer's supervision that the strange journey brings irresistible and terrifying delight. Icarus flies more powerfully (*fortius*) and higher (*altius*), impelled by a skill more daring (*audaci arte*) than Daedalus's. He is surprised by a sensual passion that Daedalus's art activates but cannot contain. Moreover, his sublimity is the reverse echo of the depravity of the Minotaur. Just as the labyrinth encloses the monstrous crime of Pasiphaë abetted by Daedalus ("clausit conceptum crimine matris" [2.23]) at the beginning of the tale, so water contains Icarus's cries at the end: "Clauserunt virides ora loquentis aquae" ("the green waters choked the words upon his lips" [2.92]). The *praeceptor* prefaces the story by remarking that it is difficult to set limits on Love's flight (2.20); he ends it by returning to the impossible task of holding Love in check: "Ipse deum volucrem detinuisse paro" (2.98). Between those two points, it is the *novum iter* of Icarus's desire that overtakes the trajectory of *ingenium* that Daedalus has plotted.

Ovid's erotodidactic poems thus embody a fundamental tension with the premises of their craft. The *praeceptor amoris* offers a technology of appetite that depends on a simultaneous control of love objects and oneself. His pedagogy assumes that erotic technique can be severed from erotic passion. It also assumes that passion can be rendered safe, by confining it to appetite and gratification. The superstructure of doctrine and illustration that the master builds in these poems aims to displace and contain desire, and this effort fails, sporadically and obliquely. There is no crisis in the *Ars* or *Remedia* where the master's program stands revealed as a hopeless and discredited enterprise. The master moves steadily ahead to his moments of willful closure. What Ovid does in these poems is much closer, rather, to his treatment of Vergil: desire undermines the *praeceptor*'s teaching as Ovid subverts Vergil. Desire intervenes in the middle of order, precisely within the exercise of craft and technique, most often with language that reveals more than it intends.

In the poetic apology he makes in the *Tristia*, Ovid blames his exile by Augustus on *crimen et error*, and he identifies the *Ars amatoria* as his *crimen*. His *error* remains unnamed, but we might recognize in the wandering, indirect path of *error* the insistent and unruly force of desire. The *Ars* and

Remedia seek to flee desire through art and displacement only to find it already waiting within the craft and mastery they espouse. This lesson awaited medieval writers in their own reading and rewriting of Ovid's works, themes, and strategies. In the succeeding chapters, I seek to map the interplay between Augustine's integration and Ovid's circulation of desire in texts that variously absorb and adapt these exemplary formulations.

CHAPTER 3

ABELARD AND HELOISE: CONVERSION
AND IRREDUCIBLE DESIRE

The literary correspondence between Peter Abelard and Heloise is at
once a narrative of desire and a sustained debate on whether desire can
be transformed. The eight letters traditionally ascribed to them tell differing
versions not just of their story but, equally important, of the meaning they
construct for it.[1] Abelard recounts an Augustinian narrative of conversion
in which he moves from Ovidian craft used in the service of lust and pride
to the integration of desire within spiritual and religious life. Claiming a
position beyond the demands of eros, he urges a similar conversion on
Heloise. She, however, asserts the irreducibility of desire. Though veiled
and suppressed, desire is, for her, a passionate attachment that can neither
be transformed fully into divine love nor reduced to appetite. Heloise
rejects both the Augustinian and Ovidian models in favor of a sustained
reflection on the place of desire within memory and selfhood.

A second epistolary collection, whose authenticity remains disputed,
may offer some perspective on the early phase of Abelard and Heloise's
love story. In the chronology of the story, these "lost love letters" would
have been written before the clandestine marriage and Abelard's mutilation.[2] These letters give a particular emphasis to reconciling friendship with
desire.[3] I shall refer to them chiefly as they bear on the generally accepted
correspondence. In addition, medieval testimony provides a frame of
reception for gauging, as Peter Dronke writes, "[w]hat was emotionally
and expressively possible for contemporaries of Abelard and Heloise, and
for the generations that followed them."[4] Contemporaries knew of the
love affair, if not the letters directly. Jean de Meun made the letters
available by translating them and referring to them in the *Roman de la Rose*.
Petrarch owned and annotated a manuscript of the letters.

The abiding interest of the correspondence remains the epistolary
dialogue of two intelligent, learned, passionate lovers who dispute what

their love meant and how eros must be negotiated after trauma and catastrophe. Though it is rich in historical, philosophical, and theological context, this is primarily a literary and rhetorical matter. The Abelard and Heloise who speak in these letters do so consciously within the conventions of medieval letter-writing and within textual self-representation—to themselves, to each other, and to their later readers. As Catherine Brown suggests for Heloise (the same applies to Abelard), their identities are not embodied in the letters but performed; and they engage in "a high-stakes struggle for erotic and intellectual power."[5] Among their readers, Jean and Petrarch present themselves as interlocutors for these textual selves. Like those of modern readers, their responses divide equally between the content of the story and its strategies of argument and representation.

The epistolary dialogue between Abelard and Heloise is an intricate transaction full of verbal and conceptual resonance and charged with its own erotic motives. We can track its negotiation of desire at several key moments. My discussion will focus on those moments and work out from them. Abelard's *Historia calamitatum* (Ep. 1) provides the initial narrative structure and imposes an interpretive frame of grace and salvation. Heloise's first letter (Ep. 2) is a brilliant reading of the *Historia* that resists its master narrative and devises an alternate structure for understanding desire. The letters that follow, including the *Problemata* in which Heloise seeks instruction on specific points of doctrine, represent an ongoing, though often submerged, struggle over the transformation of desire. Reading the letters in their literary and rhetorical contexts, in the framework of twelfth-century clerical culture and epistolary conventions, we can see that Abelard denies but continues to encounter the problem of desire, while Heloise situates desire as a form of interiority and selfhood.

Abelard's Narrative

In his *Historia calamitatum*, Abelard presents the story of his love affair with Heloise as part of a larger exemplary narrative. His professed aim is to offer consolation to an anonymous friend by furnishing a tale of his own tribulations that renders his reader's adversities meager or empty by comparison. Brian Stock remarks that Abelard, like Augustine, is "two persons, an actor and a narrator, each following different directives"—the actor largely unreflective and the narrator the source of inwardness.[6] The narrator's inwardness coexists, however, with an outward rhetorical purpose. Abelard's argumentative strategy in the *Historia* is to privilege a textualized life over spoken words ("amplius exempla quam verba") and to exploit the power of writerly absence over the immediacy of conversation and dialogue. Jean de Meun's translation nicely brings out the contrast: "aprés aucun confort de parole dite entre nous en ta presence, ai ge proposé a escripre a toy qui es ores lontains une confortable espitre des propres esperimens de mes meschances." ("after some comfort from words spoken between us in your presence, I have proposed to write you, since you are now at some distance, a consolatory letter about my own experiences of my misfortunes" [p. 3]). Abelard's broader aims may be, as Mary M. McLaughlin suggests, to anticipate institutional criticism and even offer himself consolation.[7] Within the fiction of his consolatory letter, he seeks to plot a conversion in the recipient that imitates his own process of recognition and acceptance. This entails a strategy of rivalry, mastery, subjugation, and containment. Abelard's friend, real or fictitious, biographical or readerly or both, can only belatedly imitate Abelard's conversion. He can follow the custom (usus) that Abelard everywhere points to with derision in comparison to his ingenium—his overmastering power of invention, innovation, and intellectual virtuosity.

The terms that govern the ostensible consolation of the Historia calamitatum overall are the ones that later shape Abelard's portrayal of Heloise. Étienne Gilson, arguably one of the most sympathetic modern readers of the correspondence, largely accepts Abelard's claim of exemplarity: "It is no love story, but the tale of the incontinence of Abélard, the victim of the noonday devil."[8] But more recent critics like Peggy Kamuf are certainly right to emphasize Abelard's concern with his mastery and control over an unruly female subject.[9] And if the reader needing consolation is a necessary fiction for Abelard's writing, a subject already constrained in the means and end of his reading, Heloise proves far more problematic in the textual economy of the Historia. In her own letters, as we shall see later, she is a figure of resistance, defiantly committed to desire. Some measure of her resistance emerges in Abelard's account, and the first challenge in the Historia is to situate Heloise within a defining framework. Only then can she serve as a foil to Abelard's ingenium and not merely as a condition for writing.

Heloise hovers uncertainly among several possible models of erotic attachment. Immediately before introducing her to his story, Abelard plots two endpoints in his isolation from women: "scortorum immunditiam semper abhorrebam et ab accessu et frequentatione nobilium feminarum studii scolaris assiduitate revocabar nec laicarum conversationem multum noveram" ("I had always held myself aloof from the unclean association with prostitutes, and constant application to my studies had prevented me from frequenting the society of gentlewomen: indeed I knew little of the secular way of life" [p. 10]). Prostitutes represent an unmediated and frightful sexuality; they are the uncleanness (immunditias) they carry as sexual creatures. Jean amplifies but does not distort Abelard's repulsion: "je tenoie a horreur et a hydeur les ordures des foles femmes" ("I held the filth of prostitutes in horror and disgust"). Folques de Deuil charges that Abelard indulged the sexual appetites that he rejects in this passage, and Roscelin de Compiègne, Abelard's rival and former master, names Heloise as Abelard's prostitute (*scortum*).[10] Their letters, the first a spiteful mock consolation and the second an undisguised attack, precede the composition of the *Historia*. Abelard may be responding belatedly to their accusations and to others that may have arisen, yet the most striking feature of his retrospective account is the intensity of his own denial, which gives some measure of the threat that desire poses and of the need to locate Heloise outside of merely carnal attachments.

Heloise is tacitly contrasted in this passage with the parallel model of aristocratic women. Abelard's devotion to study, an attachment already in place, makes such women inaccessible to him, and the eroticized world of stylized conversation and play supposedly remains an unknown domain. In this way, Abelard seeks to place Heloise outside courtly discourse and the vernacular chivalric world even before he introduces her.[11] As Heloise later reminds him, she does in fact enter courtly discourse, when the poems Abelard writes for her later circulate independently and take on a life of their own.[12] In a larger sense, the interior world that Abelard and Heloise create for themselves is the one that chivalric couples like Lancelot and Guenevere or Tristan and Iseut try to secure both within and against the courtly world.[13] Sustaining such a world, as we shall see in chapter 4, is a project explored by Marie de France in her *Lais*.

Two other models provides ways of locating Heloise as an object of desire, but each involves a significant and defining exception. Of the tragic heroes that Abelard evokes for comparison with himself (David, Ovid, Pompey, and Origen), the one he returns to in the later part of the *Historia* and in subsequent letters is St. Jerome. Abelard finds a typological resemblance between their exiles: "sicque me Francorum invidia ad Occidentem sicut Jheronimum Romanorum expulit ad Orientem" ("Thus the jealousy of the French drove me West as that of the Romans once drove St Jerome East" [p. 35]). He sees himself as Jerome's heir, particularly in suffering detraction. When he establishes Heloise and her nuns at the Paraclete, he reenacts Jerome's removal from Rome to Jerusalem with Paula, and he quotes Jerome's letter to Asella in defending himself from charges of concupiscence even after his mutilation.[14] In his instructional letter (Ep. 9) to the nuns of the Paraclete, he begins by citing Jerome's dedication to teaching "the virgins of Christ."[15] If Abelard fashions himself as Jerome, Heloise is to be like Paula, Asella, and Eustachium—women with a literary education and a degree of cultural authority who are deeply committed to Jerome's intellectual project. But unlike them, Heloise is not a benefactor from a powerful family, and she moves unwillingly from the world of letters and ideas to religious life. As Abelard presses this model on her in both the personal letters and the letters of direction, Heloise recuperates rather than sublimates the erotic attachment possible within Jerome's coterie.[16]

Another model of attachment succeeds in the *Historia* largely because of its defining exception. When Abelard plays Jerome to Heloise's imaginary Paula, he calls forth the sexual anxieties of a pedagogical relation between master and disciple. In Ovid's erotodidaxis, the master does not hesitate to assert himself as a claimant for the prey in his pupils' appetitive quests ("Naso erat magister"). In medieval pedagogy, the suppressed threat within teaching is homoeroticism. Monastic and cathedral schools produced a lyric subgenre whose central theme is the uncertain boundaries of homoerotic and homosocial desire. In the ninth-century poem "O admirabile Veneris ydolum," preserved in the *Cambridge Songs*, desire is openly expressed for a student who has gone off with a rival: "Quo fugis amabo, cum te dilexerim?" ("Where do you flee, I would like to know, since I loved you?").[17] Baudri of Bourgueil and Marbod of Rennes give desire a place in a poetic oeuvre composed for boys and girls as ostensible love objects. Gerald A. Bond observes, "Often marked by a frank eroticism, pedophilic verse was the most radical genre of contemporary poetry."[18] Baudri composes complaints for the canon Alexander of Tours, beloved by his companions ("Hunc plorat clerus Toronensis" ["The clerics of Tours lament for him"]), and in other poems he makes conversation (*colloquium*) a form of erotic exchange.[19] The famous equation of bad grammar and irregular sexuality that opens Alan of Lille's *De planctu naturae* implicates pedagogy as the scene where grammar is taught and syntactic permutations are carried out literally and figuratively.[20] Ernst Robert Curtius locates the discourse of homoerotic attraction directly in the age and cultural environment of Abelard: "for the end of the eleventh century and the beginning of the twelfth, an unprejudiced erotic candor even among the higher clergy, which, though it was not generally disseminated, was certainly to be found in humanistic circles."[21]

What Heloise represents, because of her education and literary achievement, is the prospect of translating desire from homoerotic attraction to clandestine heterosexual pleasure. Abelard's libidinal investment, diverted from prostitutes and aristocratic women and sublimated after his castration into ascetic religious life with women, finds its object in the student who comes to the pedagogical scene with the proper training and the right kind of body. His initial description of Heloise, counterposing understatement with hyperbole, works out the ratio of body and schooled intelligence: "Que cum per faciem non esset infima, per habundantiam litterarum erat

suprema" ("In looks she did not rank lowest, while in the extent of her
learning she stood supreme" [p. 10]). Heloise is a student physically
available as a woman, a woman available intellectually to him because she
is a student. She is a licit version of the homoerotic fantasy of beauty and
intelligence that Hilarius, Abelard's student, cultivates in his own rhetorical
portrait (*effictio*) of another student's alluring features: "Crinis flavus, os
decorum cervixque candidula, / Sermo blandus et suavis; sed quid laudem
singula" ("Long blond hair, a handsome face, a pretty white neck, charming and pleasant speech, but why should I praise separate parts").[22]
Heloise's gender is thus the supplement and difference that makes it
possible for Abelard to act on desire. He articulates these features through
an ambivalent mixture of misogyny and commendation. Heloise's gift for
letters is rare in women, and so makes her more attractive to him and
famous ("nominatissimam" [p. 10]) in France.

In Abelard's *Historia*, then, Heloise is a figure of desire who can be
defined only by approximation. No single model of attraction fully
captures or explains her. The reason lies, at least partly, in the letter's focus
on male desire. Indeed, in Abelard's story, Heloise is constructed from two
sets of male desire. Fulbert loves her not just within a family bond as her
uncle but with a libidinal investment that implicitly rivals Abelard's: "qui
eam quanto amplius diligebat tanto diligentius in omnem qua poterat
scientiam litterarum promoveri studuerat" ("he loved her so much
that he had done everything in his power to advance her education in
letters" [p. 10]). The rhetorical play between *diligebat* and *diligentius* marks
the vector of Fulbert's desire: his surplus of love ("amplius diligebat")
generates a further demand, which Abelard describes openly as a passion
("diligentius. . .studuerat"). As in classical and medieval discussions of
desire, Fulbert's love for Heloise is oriented toward the future and directed
to what he does not possesses. Abelard's phrasing characterizes it not simply
as a worldly or intellectual ambition but as an entilingly impossible
demand—an achievement in letters pushed to the vanishing point of its full
possibility ("in omnem qua poterat").

While Abelard portrays Fulbert's desire for Heloise as a form of erotic
stasis, he represents himself as a lover who succeeds and displaces Fulbert's
desires. It is a modern commonplace to remark the "cold calculation" of his
seduction of Heloise; she is the *adolescentula* and *joennette demoisele*—a
young woman in terms of social dependence rather than age—lodged in
Fulbert's household but apparently removed from other family ties. To do
so, however, is to overlook the consciously Ovidian structure that Abelard
applies to the love affair and the details he borrows from the *praeceptor
amoris*. His account reproduces the three-part program of the *Ars amatoria*
(to find, win, and extend love), and the ensuing correspondence will focus

on the fourth part (the retreat from an impossible mistress), as Heloise resists and subverts Abelard's demands that she convert fully to his version of religious life.

Abelard begins his account by situating Heloise in a landscape corresponding to the sensual geography that Ovid earlier mapped onto the civic and political space of Rome. He chooses his quarry as if she were the *apta puella* ("suitable girl") of the Ovidian hunter (*Ars amatoria* 1.44). Against a background of erotic circulation, Heloise is the appropriate and likely object: "Hanc igitur, omnibus circumspectis que amantes allicere solent, commodiorem censui in amorem michi copulare, et me id facillime credidi posse" ("I considered all the usual attractions for a lover and decided she was the one to bring to my bed, confident that I should have easy success" [p. 10]). His appraisal of her is paralleled by an assessment of himself as a suitor—he is young, good-looking, famous, and unlikely to be rejected. Abelard, in other words, seriously carries out the self-appraisal that is Ovid's witty, poetic troping of philosophy's *nosce te ipsum* (*Ars amatoria* 2.493–510).

Abelard captures his prey because, like the Ovidian lover, he recognizes the attachments that Heloise has already invested with desire: "Tanto autem facilius hanc michi puellam consensuram credidi, quanto amplius eam litterarum scientiam et habere et diligere noveram" ("Knowing the girl's knowledge and love of letters I thought she would be all the more ready to consent" [p. 10]). The exchange of letters they initiate when separated follows Ovid's advice and exploits the advantage he sees in writing to express the lover's intention (*Ars amatoria* 1.437–40).[23] If the *Epistulae duorum amantium* copied by Johannes de Vepria are authentic, Abelard shows himself aware of the power of letters as erotic substitutes and catalysts. In Letter *6*, for instance, he presents himself and his demand through the mechanism of a letter whose rhetorical purpose is the gesture of greeting.[24] In Letter *24*, before proceeding to a definition of love, he admits that the woman's letters satisfy and stimulate his desire ("desiderium meum et saturant et accendunt" [pp. 208–209]). In the *Historia*, Abelard sees the exchange as a means of amplifying and extending pleasure. The exchange allows the lovers to speak more frankly ("pleraque audacius") than in person and so maintain the pleasures of conversation (p. 10).[25]

When Abelard plays on Fulbert's greed and hopes for Heloise, he carries out Ovid's injunction to please the lover's husband in order to make him useful (*Ars amatoria* 1.579–80). Fulbert's participation is not limited to his *simplicitas*—the stunning credulity that leads him to commit his niece fully to Abelard's tuition and thereby to abet his project of seduction. Fulbert licenses the physical violence that attends teaching. Kamuf argues that this "was very close to rape."[26] Abelard certainly sees force as a means to compel Heloise to satisfy his wishes, if necessary. In a later letter (Ep. 5), he

contrasts Heloise's resistance ("te nolentem. . .reluctantem et dissuaden-
tem" [p. 80]) to the threats and blows that enforce his will. In the *Historia*,
physical blows disguise clandestine love making and offer further pleasure:
"verbera quandoque dabat amor, non furor, gratia, non ira, que omnium
ungentorum suavitatem transcenderent. Quid denique? Nullus a cupidis
intermissus est gradus amoris, et si quid insolitum amor excogitare potuit,
est additum" ("these blows were prompted by love and tender feeling rather
than anger and irritation, and were sweeter than any balm could be. In
short our desire left no stage of love-making untried, and if love could
devise something new, we welcomed it" [pp. 11–12]). The rhetorical play is
between words (*verba*) and blows (*verbera*). The advice is Ovidian, if ironic
and ambiguous: "Vim licet appelles: grata est vis ista puellis" ("You may
use force; women like you to use it" [*Ars amatoria* 1.673]).[27]

Lodged in Fulbert's house, Abelard has evaded the guardian (*custos*) and
passed beyond the door that repeatedly bars the lover's access in the *Ars amatoria* and symbolizes the obstacles and resistance to gratification.[28] Abelard
describes his entry to the household as a joining with Heloise first in domi-
cile and then in spirit ("Primum domo una coniungmur, postmodum
animo"). The third term in this equation—unstated but evident—is a
joining of flesh and bodies. Abelard's entry into Fulbert's house symbolizes
his capture and penetration of Heloise. The house, like the bedroom for
the Ovidian lover, is a place of sexual exploration and virtuosity ("Mille
modi veneris" [*Ars amatoria* 3.787]) and of mutual pleasure ("ex aequo res
iuvet illa duos" [*Ars amatoria* 3.794]). For Abelard, study is transformed
from the obstacle that keeps him from aristocratic women to the opportunity for erotic and verbal play: "Apertis itaque libris, plura de amore quam
de lectione verba se ingerebant, plura erant oscula quam sententie; sepius ad
sinus quam ad libros reducebantur manus, crebrius oculos amor in se
reflectebant quam lectio in scripturam dirigebat" ("then with our books
open before us, more words of love than of reading passed between us, and
more kissing than teaching. My hands strayed oftener to her bosom than to
the pages; love drew our eyes to look on each other more than reading
kept them on our texts" [p. 11]).[29] The scene of reading exemplifies the
lust of the eyes, but it is also the space of Ovidian play (*lusus*) where
inexperience underwrites the pleasure of erotic discovery.

Abelard describes his desire in the commonplace Ovidian imagery of consuming fire ("totus inflamatus" [p. 10]). The topos recurs in his subsequent
letters, especially when he tries to diminish the value of his love. This
obsessive love connects the narrative to two other features of Ovidian
erotodidaxis. Love's craft requires focus and concentration, a resignation
from public roles and citizenship. For Abelard, this takes the form of
redirecting the work of philosophy into pleasure, writing love poems

rather than expounding philosophical mysteries, and accepting the replacement of his *ingenium* by the *usus* of recycled lessons for his students. At the same time, his capture by desire restages the Ovidian irony of lawyers and other masters of disciplined technique, poets among them, caught unawares by love: "facile haremus" (*Ars amatoria* 3.543).

Abelard rounds out the Ovidian parallels at a moment of crisis— Heloise's pregnancy—by directly citing the episode in the *Ars amatoria* (2.559–600) where Mars and Venus are caught by Vulcan.[30] His citation reveals a subtle understanding of the Ovidian interext. At one level, Fulbert shares the shame and stupidity that the *praeceptor amoris* imputes to Vulcan: "Saepe tamen demens stulte fecisse fateris" ("yet often, madman, dost thou confess that thou didst act stupidly" [*Ars amatoria* 2.591]). At another, the disclosure serves only to bind the lovers closer. Ovid prefaces his story with the observation that disclosure abets passion (2.559–60). All Vulcan achieves is the lovers' release from obstacles and inhibitions: "quod ante tegebant, / Liberius faciunt, ut pudor omnis abest" ("the affair they once kept dark they carry on openly, now that all shame is thrown to the winds" [2.589–90]). The story of Mars and Venus, as Ovid tells it, is a "fabula" about the persistence of desire in the face of capture, exposure, and shame. Its inclusion in Abelard's narrative conveys the pleasure he shares with Heloise before his mutilation. It is this compound of pleasure and disclosure that Heloise will recall in her answering letters to the *Historia*.

Heloise finally enters Abelard's narrative as an active figure when he forces a clandestine marriage on her in hopes of propitiating Fulbert's anger. Her entrance is nonetheless a masterpiece of indirection and ventriloquism. Heloise's prescient argument against marriage is one of the longest sustained passages in Abelard's *Historia*, rivalling in emphasis the painful dispute over his tract on philosophy and theology and the forced burning of his book. Throughout Heloise's speech, Abelard moves between direct and indirect discourse: he reports, paraphrases, and in some measure performs her address to him. Jean's translation registers these textual dynamics in narrative voicing. It introduces the rubric "Or conclut son propoz la saige Heloys en eschivant le mariaige" ("Now the wise Heloise ends her remark on avoiding marriage") at the point where Heloise is most present, speaking directly to Abelard over distance and time yet within the framework of his own narrative. Jean marks the final section of Abelard's paraphrase with the rubric "Ci parle Pierre Abaielart" ("Here Peter Abelard speaks"), as if to indicate where the narrator's voice has reasserted its authorial control. The effect, perhaps unintended and certainly present nowhere else in his accounts of diputes and controversy, is to destabilize Abelard's grand narrative of conversion by allowing the repressed content to emerge through Heloise's voice and the indirections of his language.

The case Heloise makes for the philosophical life over marriage depends on absorbing the antifeminism of St. Paul, Jerome, and Theophrastus and setting the cares of ordinary life ("cura domestica") against the contemplative life and the constitution of what Alain de Libera calls a "philosophical aristocracy."[31] Constant J. Mews points out that the arguments Heloise uses appear in Abelard's *Theologia christiana*, which was written before the *Historia*.[32] Abelard reprises them here to lend force to Heloise's predictions of disaster and to prepare the catastrophe that leads to his conversion. Libera points out the incongruity of harnessing Pauline doctrine, which is designed to allow Christians to mediate the anxieties of spirit and flesh, to the service of philosophy.[33] At the same time, however, Abelard's narrative attributes to Heloise a daring formulation of philosophical desire, and it anticipates the fierce attachment that will inform Heloise's subsequent letters.

Heloise's argument goes beyond merely juxtaposing the world and the life of the mind. Philosophy, she says, is not just contempt for the world but a flight from it toward an erotic substitute: "Unde et insignes olim philosophi mundum maxime contempnentes, nec tam relinquentes seculum quam fugientes, omnes sibi voluptates interdixerunt ut in unius philosophie requiescerent amplexibus" ("Consequently the great philosophers of the past have despised the world, not renouncing it so much as escaping from it, and have denied themselves every pleasure so as to find peace in the arms of philosophy alone" [p. 15]). Earlier, Abelard had described his love affair as the replacement of philosophy by pleasure (*voluptas*). Here the prohibition of pleasures (*voluptates* / *toutes manieres de deliz*) is the specific difference separating philosophy from a life of study and teaching that customarily permitted concubinage. Finding analogues with the prophets of Jewish tradition and monks in the Christian tradition, Heloise argues that philosophers remove themselves from others in the social world and attain a special form of interiority based on their sexual continence and abstinence ("se a populo aliqua continentie vel abstinentie singularitate segregantes" [p. 15]).

This denial leads, however, to a still more powerful fantasy. Denial has as its object the plenitude of a full and continuing erotic embrace with philosophy alone ("ut in unius philosophie requiescerent amplexibus"). Philosophy thus replaces the world and worldly pleasures with an erotics isolated and sufficient to itself. It moves through a sequence of flight, segregation, and fulfillment. The repose it achieves is not the transcendence of contemplation or Abelard's interval of pastoral retreat with his students in Troyes or the *tranquilitas* he later seeks in ministering to the community at the Paraclete; its concrete form is closer to the embrace of satisfaction that Ovid describes as the end of mutual pleasure (*Ars amatoria* 2.727–28). It is in this context that Heloise boldly asserts to Abelard that she would rather be his lover than his wife and that she wishes to be bound to him by esteem alone rather than the chains of marriage: "quam sibi carius existeret, michique honestius amicam dici quam uxorem ut me ei sola gratia conservaret, non vis aliqua vinculi nuptialis constringeret" ("the name of mistress instead of wife would be dearer to her and more honourable to me—only love freely given should keep me for her, not the constriction of a marriage tie" [p. 17]).[34]

Criticism often treats this passage as an expression of Heloise's fidelity and devotion, though Abelard recounts it through indirect discourse. Neil Cartlidge sees "a relationship based absolutely on the continued expression of mutual free will."[35] Yet a more radical conception seems at work in Abelard's text. The eroticized project of philosophy offers Abelard and Heloise a common ground. Abelard's language, as he reports Heloise's declaration, reveals that it is of one piece with his own project of seduction. Where he earlier determines to join (*copulare*) with Heloise in love and takes advantage of Fulbertus's license to use force, Heloise now uses the imagery of binding (*vinculum*) and constraint (*constringere*) to define an alternative: her demand for radical freedom rather than marriage seeks to place desire within philosophy.

The imagery of binding and constraint appears again in the scene where Abelard describes Heloise's entry into religious life. This begins the fourth step of Ovid's erotic program, in which the lover ostensibly removes himself from passion and frees the heart from its own vices: "Utile propositum est saevas extinguere flammas, / Nec servum vitii pectus habere sui" (*Remedia amoris* 53–54). For Abelard, this recovery occurs under the pressure of deforming violence, shame, and grief; and it remains, as the *Historia* and other correspondence show, an effort mobilized against Heloise's resistance. Abelard describes his own monastic conversion as a confusion of shame rather than devotion, while Heloise is driven by a mixture of compulsion and consent that already characterizes their love affair. The incongruity of motives is apparent on the surface of Abelard's vexed description of Heloise's conversion: "Illa tamen, prius ad imperium nostrum sponte velata, et monasterium ingressa" ("Heloise had already agreed to take the veil in obedience to my wishes and entered a convent" [p. 19]). His command ("imperium nostrum") sorts oddly with her supposedly direct and unreflective wish ("sponte"). It may be, as Elizabeth Hamilton explains, that the contradiction is only apparent and that Heloise acts out of free will to submit to Abelard's intention.[36] But if she chooses freely, she elects the only option put before her. The obedience Abelard seems to demand is made to disappear, in his narrative, within her passionate abjection. It reappears in her subsequent letters in a way that signifies rather than denies Heloise's desire.

In the *Historia*, Heloise's obedience to Abelard's mastery takes the form of a textual citation of Lucan's *Pharsalia*. Hastening to accept the nun's veil,

Heloise repeats the lament uttered by Cornelia, Pompey's wife, after his defeat at Pharsalia. Cornelia is an icon of wifely fidelity, as she tries to assume guilt for Pompey's disastrous change of fortune. Just as Heloise willingly ("sponte") takes the veil, Cornelia willingly offers to bear her husband's punishment: "Nunc accipe poenas / Sed quas sponte luam" ("Now accept the penalty—a penalty which I will gladly pay" [*Pharsalia* 8.97–98]). In a commentary on Paul written about the same time as the *Historia*, Abelard refers to this scene in a narrow discussion of noble and true love—namely, the affection of a father for a son or a chaste wife for her husband.[37] Peter von Moos sees the reference to Cornelia as an illustration of a public and tragic catastrophe rather than merely personal loss.[38] David Luscombe says, "Pompey's Cornelia, as played by Heloise, posed a threat both to Abelard and to herself," which Abelard resolves by invoking Pompey's stoic rejoinder that her husband survives his loss of good fortune.[39] Mary Carruthers describes a complex performative and memorial dynamic in Heloise's identification: "she did not 'see herself as' Cornelia, in the sense of acting a role; rather, Cornelia's experience, given voice by Lucan, had been made hers as well—so much her own that she can use it, even, perhaps, with irony, in such an extreme personal situation."[40] If we read Heloise's citation in its full context, we can see that it, in fact, conveys a significant demurrer to Abelard's version of their story.

In Lucan's poem, Cornelia ends her speech by casting Pompey's defeat as the vengeance of Julia, Pompey's first wife. She offers herself as expiation to save Pompey from her rival, "Iulia crudelis" (*Pharsalia* 8.104). Her gesture of submission thus directs us to an earlier scene in Lucan's poem, in which the ghost of Julia appears to Pompey, claiming that the gods have allowed Caesar to fill his days and her to occupy his thoughts at night: "Sed teneat Caesarque dies et Iulia noctes" (3.27). Beneath the icon of Cornelia's tragic, wifely fidelity lies Julia's implacable, relentless presence. If Heloise fashions herself, on Abelard's report, after Cornelia's devotion, accepting the veil as the *poena* she shares with her husband, the text she invokes in doing so suggests that Cornelia is the veil covering a figure of irreducible desire.

Heloise as Reader

In Abelard's narrative, Heloise cites Lucan as the intertext for exemplary devotion built over fierce and implacable desire. Her citation reveals how deeply her self-representation and subjectivity are embedded in literary models. Martin Irvine argues that Heloise fuses the roles of a literate, masculine *amicus* and erotic *amica* to create a new form of subjectivity: "a dual-gendered *amicitia*" in which "she writes like an *amicus* but as a woman."[41] Barbara Newman suggests that Abelard's brief but intense tutelage allowed Heloise "to actualize—at least in writing—every one of the models that her splendid and thorough education had laid before her receptive spirit."[42] This identity stems not just from subject positions available within twelfth-century academic and literary discourse but also from Heloise's remarkable skill as a reader and interpreter of Abelard's letters. It is by now generally accepted that her reading and response are predominantly ethical.[43] The stress Heloise places on intention in her account of the love story is taken as a parallel, if not a source, for the voluntarist ethics that Abelard expounds in his *Ethica*. Her assertion of disinterested love seems to adapt Cicero's theory of virtuous friendship. The critical focus on ethics obscures, however, a complementary dimension of Heloise's achievement. The letters she writes responding to Abelard challenge him on his own grounds of argument, demonstration, and dialectic. Heloise develops a style of feminine reading that depends on metonymy and the logic of substitution to argue the claims of desire.[44]

Heloise's argumentative power in the correspondence depends significantly on revisiting Abelard's letters and resituating parts of their meaning. In the *narratio* of her first letter (Ep. 2)—that part, under the conventions of the medieval *ars dictaminis*, which typically recounts the occasion for writing to make a request of the recipient—Heloise accepts Abelard's equation of Fulbert's attack on his body with the doctrinal attack on his *Theologia*, and she acknowledges the controversy over naming the Paraclete as well as the continuing persecution of Abelard by the monks supposedly under his charge at St. Gildas. But as Katharina Wilson and Glenda McLeod show, Heloise devises her own structural parallels to Abelard's crises of lust and pride; cites the same Latin *auctores*, biblical sources, and Patristic writers; and challenges Abelard's portrayal of her and his framing of central themes like humility. In one passage, she chides him for not giving a full account of her arguments against marriage.[45] Equally important, she immediately grasps the disparity between the apparent and real aims of the *Historia*. Abelard's long letter offers consolation for his friend's troubles, but it attends, she notes, chiefly to his own. The displaced motives of Abelard's writing provide her a rhetorical occasion to mobilize her erotic demands against Abelard's official history of their love.

It is unclear whether Abelard's letter reached Heloise by chance, as she says (*forte*), or by design.[46] Jean strongly suggests the latter, for the unidentified messenger in Heloise's Latin text ("quidam") becomes "Voz homs" in his translation, while the friend who supposedly received the original letter is now "nostre ami."[47] In either case, Heloise distinguishes herself from the unknown addressee of the *Historia* by recognizing and subverting Abelard's strategy of mastering his reader. For modern interpreters of the letters, this resistance is generally thought to be short-lived, largely confined to her first two letters and the beginning of the third. On this view, their exchange of correspondence leads to Heloise's resignation or eventual conversion or her divided allegiance to love and duty or even, as she says, hypocrisy ("religioni deputares ypochrisim" [p. 67]).[48] I want to suggest instead that the resistance extends throughout the personal letters and the letters of instruction. Her strategies of reading and argument sustain a calculus of desire. Her first letter (Ep. 2) sets her interpretive structure in place and advances her demands for Abelard's presence by appealing to debt, devotion, and intention.

Heloise's rhetorical and argumentative methods are evident from the highly wrought salutation of her first letter: "Domino suo, immo patri; conjugi suo, immo fratri; ancilla sua, immo filia; ipsius uxor, immo soror; Abaelardo Heloysa" ("To her master, or rather her father, husband, or rather brother; his handmaid, or rather his daughter; wife, or rather sister; To Abelard, Heloise"). Cartlidge proposes that the salutation indicates "her uncertainty about the roles they should play towards each other" and particularly "her uncertainty about her status."[49] These stylized formulas of address reproduce Abelard's struggles to find a model for Heloise in the *Historia*, though she exploits his uncertainty and approximation to different effects. Her pattern of cancellations and corrections—lord to father, husband to brother, maid to daughter, wife to sister—presumably moves forward to mark the differences between worldly attachments in the past and spiritual bonds in the present and future. At the same time, these contrasts stipulate the emotional ties still in place: if Abelard and Heloise have become spiritual brother and sister, they nonetheless remain indissoluably man and wife. As Abelard concedes in a letter structured as a detailed refutation (Ep. 5), Heloise is his inseparable companion ("inseparabilis comes" [p. 81]), a phrase he uses elsewhere to define the relation of body and soul.[50] Moreover, the sequence of address in Heloise's letter is not temporal but metonymic and associative: the present roles of daughter and sister can be read backwards to signify the maid and wife ostensibly left behind in the secular world. In this way, Heloise establishes a resonant structure of reference and a dual time-scheme built on substitution, by which the fragile and mutable present and any claims for the future rest on the unchanging attachment of the past.

The arrival of Abelard's *Historia* affords the opportunity for Heloise to renew her erotic demands. Later (Ep. 5), Abelard will describe them as an old and incessant complaint against God ("veterem illam et assiduam querelam" [p. 70]). Later still, in his poem to their son Astrolabus, Heloise's "crebra querella" ("continual complaint") signifies her obstinate refusal to abandon the sweetness of old pleasures ("voluptatis dulcedo") for penance.[51] *Querella* associates Heloise with Monica in her laments at

Augustine's departure (*Confessions* 5.8.15) and with Augustine's source, the grieving Dido who threatens to inflame both Aeneas and herself with her complaints (*Aeneid* 4.360). In his textual evocation of Augustine and Vergil, Abelard forges a heroic role for himself based on a figurative and literal flight from desire. But Heloise has a far more complex goal than the renewal of carnal affection made impossible by Abelard's mutilation; she does not confuse sexuality with erotics. Like the retrospective narrator of the *Confessions*, she, too, demands presence. Such a demand differs categorically from the concupiscence that Abelard anticipates and hastens to reject in her writing. Concupiscence, as Augustine makes clear, is a movement toward what we lack but can possess; desire is for what we lack and what remains absent.[52]

Abelard's *Historia* inadvertently serves in Ep. 2 as a figure for the presence Heloise demands. Heloise seizes his letter ("ardentius eam cepi legere") because she recognizes its author as an object of passionate attachment ("scriptorem ipsum karius amplector"). Written words, like visual images, stand in for what she has lost. In Jean's translation, this lost thing ("cujus rem perdidi") is Abelard's self, the figurative sense of his literal, though absent, body: "celui dont j'é perdu le corps."[53] As Heloise indicates in quoting Seneca's letter to Lucilius, letters show one friend to another ("te michi ostendis"), and written characters from the author's hand are the true traces of an absent friend ("amici absentis veras notas"). Her forced conversion to religious life, she complains, has left her without conversation or compensatory letters. Defrauded of Abelard's actual presence, she asks for his semblance ("tue michi imaginis presenta dulcedinem" [p. 52]) and for the grace of words in place of things ("verba pro rebus" [p. 52]).

In doing so, Heloise creates a hermeneutic framework of reading in which the topics, images, similes, and other rhetorical figures in their exchange become intelligible as traces of her demands. Thus, for example, when Abelard replies to her first letter, his assertion that great miracles of resurrection have been performed for women (Ep. 3) not only confirms the efficacy of her prayers for him but symbolically acknowledges the return of desire in their exchanges. Similarly, his controversial choice in naming her convent the Paraclete signifies both the spiritual comfort he seeks for himself in the face of worldly tribulation and the comfort of exchange that Heloise demands of him. That her demand for presence was recognized is shown, in the immediate instance, by Abelard's repeated efforts to control what she evokes and, after his death, by Peter the Venerable's consolatory letter. Peter's letter ends with the image of Abelard, now cherished in God's bosom, eventually restored to Heloise at Judgment Day.[54] The image evokes Heloise's substitution of philosophy's erotic embrace for the marriage that Abelard forces on her in the *Historia*.

Heloise's demand for Abelard's presence is forcefully underwritten by the claims of debt. M. T. Clanchy says that she uses "the vocabulary of a money-lender rather than a lover," but her diction has a larger range of reference.[55] Heloise uses *debitum* in the context of both Pauline marriage doctrine (I Corinthians 7: 3) and the parable of the unforgiving servant (Matthew 18: 23–35). In the first, she employs Paul even more daringly than Abelard reports she does in the *Historia*, where she tries to redirect marriage to sustain philosophy rather than live under divine law, which is Paul's stated objective for marriage. In her first letter, Heloise carefully maneuvers Paul's notion that wives and husbands are mutual debtors, each with claims over the other's body, in order to recover Abelard's presence. The *Historia*, she says, discharges the debts of friendship and comradeship ("tam amicitie quam societatis debitum persolvisti"), but a larger claim binds Abelard to Heloise and her religious community ("sed majore te debito nobis astrinxisti"). Heloise sets out this larger claim in a series of graduated contrasts: "quas non tam amicas quam amicissimas, non tam socias quam filias convenit nominari" ("we should be called not friends but dearest friends, not comrades but daughters" [p. 47]). And she holds out a greater, if unspecified, possibility: "vel si quod dulcius et sanctius vocabulum potest excogitari" ("or if some sweeter or holier name could be devised"). Here the topos of inexpressibility conceals yet marks the existence of what Heloise does not directly name: as in her elaborate salutation, the next step in the chain of substitution must be from friend, companion, or daughter to sister and wife.

The debt that Heloise pursues in behalf of her community serves as a way of claiming the far more charged and problematic *debitum* that Abelard owes her. As the founder of the Paraclete, Abelard has the spiritual duty to care for his "novella plantatio," the new foundation raised from cuttings. For medieval interpreters, this figure taken from Psalms 143:12 signifies Israel and by extension the Church and its monastic institutions.[56] In Ep. 2, Abelard's duty takes the sexualized, metaphorical form of irrigating and cultivating the new plantings.[57] As Irvine remarks, the passage recuperates Abelard's paternity and masculinity.[58] Heloise invokes Jerome's tradition of pastoral care and instruction for women, which Abelard employes earlier in the *Historia* and commends throughout the correspondence. His general debt of attention to the community is payable to her in particular, however, for she exercises a greater and prior claim: "ut quod devotis communiter debes feminis, unice tue devotius solvas" ("repay the debt you owe a whole community of women dedicated to God by discharging it the more dutifully to her who is yours alone" [p. 48]).

Behind the pastoral and paternal duties Abelard has assumed since his conversion lie the greater bonds of husband and lover. Heloise argues, "cui quidem tanto te majore debito noveris obligatum quanto te amplius nuptialis federe sacramenti constat esse astrictum et eo te magis michi obnoxium quo te semper, ut omnibus patet, immoderato amore complexa sum" ("Yet you must know that you are bound to me by an obligation which is all the greater for the further close ties of the marriage sacrament uniting us, and are the deeper in my debt because of the love I have always borne you, as everyone knows, a love beyond all bounds" [p. 48]). The marriage that Abelard mistakenly forces on Heloise in the *Historia* returns, then, as a two-fold constraint. Abelard is bound by the mutual obligations of the marriage *debitum*, and he is answerable to her erotic demand. He is *obnoxius*—at once guilty and obligated—to the same extent that she is *complexa*—embraced and contained—by her excessive love for him.[59]

Heloise uses the other biblical context of *debitum* not to claim restitution but to turn Abelard's own assertion of divine grace to her advantage. In Matthew's parable, the servant is forgiven an enormous debt by his lord but then violently demands the repayment of a smaller debt owed him by another servant. Abelard has claimed that his worldly fall makes possible his salvation. Heloise reminds him that this disproportionate mercy obligates him to perform a similar act but on a smaller scale. As Augustine explains in his analysis of the parable in Matthew, there are two works of mercy— forgive, and you will be forgiven; give, and you will be given to.[60] Heloise invokes this appeal to mercy as the culminating petition of her first letter, asking Abelard to consider his obligation ("Perpende, obsecro, que debes"). She phrases her appeal so that her demand for his presence is the specific debt that Abelard owes in virtue of the larger mercy he has received: "te obsecro ut quo modo potes tuam michi presentiam reddas" ("I beg you to restore your presence to me in the way you can" [p. 53]).[61]

The *debitum* allows Heloise to position herself as a claimant and to give standing to her demand. Abelard's mutilation has robbed her as a wife; his withdrawal has grieved her as a lover. He is thus the source of her complaint and the remedy for it: "Solus quippe es, qui me contristare, qui me letificare seu consolari valeas" (p. 49). To this line of argument Heloise joins a second claim—the expression of pure devotion that has carried such extraordinary resonance for medieval and modern readers alike. As she reflects back on her desire, it is a singular and absolute demand: "Nichil unquam—Deus scit!—in te nisi te requisivi; te pure, non tua concupis- cens" ("God knows I never sought anything in you except yourself; I wanted simply you, nothing of yours" [p. 49]). In Jean's portion of the *Roman de la Rose* (8759–8832), it is this declaration of selflessness, devotion, and completely unmediated desire ("te pure. . .concupiscens") which the jealous husband in Ami's speech recalls. Petrarch admiringly comments on the passage in his manuscript of the correspondence, "Valde perdulciter ac blande per totum agis, Heloysa" ("You act very sweetly and charmingly in everything, Heloise.")

For modern readers after Gilson, the passage is a compelling example of Ciceronian *amicitia* transferred beyond the world of virtuous male friendship to disinterested yet passionate love.[62] The same conception of friendship seems at work in Letter 25, written by the woman in the *Epistulae duorum amantium*, which speaks of repaying and obeying her lover, and in Letter 49, in which she says she is compelled to love by preeminent virtue.[63] C. Stephen Jaeger observes, however, that "Heloise extends the ideal of perfect *amicitia* outside its conventional realm, appropriating it for a powerfully sexual and passionate relation to a man."[64] In claiming that she loves Abelard absolutely for himself and not for his possessions, Heloise adapts only part of Cicero's idea of friendship. The woman in Letter 49 of the *Epistulae* invokes the complete framework when she dismisses those who seem to love for riches or pleasures. It is precisely the erotic dimension that Heloise stresses in asserting her devotion: "te pure. . .concupiscens."

The subtlety of Heloise's rhetorical and argumentative strategy in this passage also lies in the way she connects debt and devotion. The crucial link is her obedience and abjection. Heloise pointedly recalls the scene of her forced conversion to religious life, where she changes habit and heart. The intended meaning of her conversion is symbolic, not literal; erotic, not religious. For her, conversion signifies Abelard's complete possession of her—"ut te tam corporis mei quam animi unicum possessorem ostenderem" ("in order to prove you the sole possessor of my body and my will alike" [p. 49]). Obedience, she argues, shifts the project of realizing her desires and wishes ("meas voluptates aut voluntates") to fulfilling his. From this subordination follows the denigration of status that Heloise famously tracks from wife to friend, concubine, and whore. It ends in her proclamation that she would rather be his whore than Augustus's wife confirmed in possession of the whole world: "karius michi et dignius videretur tua dici meretrix quam illius imperatrix" ("it would be dearer and more honourable to me to be called not his Empress but your whore" [p. 49]). The process of abjection, Heloise insists, is reciprocal: as she abases herself in Abelard's behalf, she gains grace with respect to him and lessens the damage to the glory of an incontinent philosopher. Heloise reminds Abelard that he has omitted some of the arguments she made against marriage. In most discussions, this is an assertion of her claim for freedom in prizing love over marriage and liberty over constraint: "amorem conugio, libertatem vinculo preferebam" (p. 49). The argumentative context of her letter makes it clear that obedience and abjection are inextricably tied to the claims of love and desire. Heloise reminds Abelard that her conversion stems not from spiritual commitments but his command. Her heart ("animus meus"/"mes couragies") is not with her but with him, so that she cannot exist without him—a sentiment that Petrarch pronounces "amicissime et eleganter" ("most lovingly and becomingly" [p. 52]). Unsure whether she is driven by love or lust, Heloise tropes her earlier version of philosophical erotics. She consciously forbids her own pleasures in the service of attending to his will ("Omnes michi denique voluptates interdixi ut tue parerem voluntati" [p. 52]). By making Abelard's wishes the replacement for her desire, Heloise thus forwards her demand ("quanta debeas attende"), while appropriating Abelard's will as the figurative stand-in for her desire.

The rationale Heloise provides for this substitution is the purity and disinterest of her intention. Perfect love, she tells Abelard, can preserve carnal relations like marriage not so much by bodily continence ("corporum continentia") as by purity of the soul ("animorum pudicitia" [p. 50]). Her assertion of the absolute value of intention finds eloquent expression in her rhetorical play on guilt and innocence (*nocens/innocens*): "Que plurimum nocens, plurimum—ut nosti—sum innocens: non enim rei effectus, sed efficientis affectus in crimine est, nec que fiunt, sed quo animo fiunt, equitas pensat" ("Wholly guilty though I am, I am also, as you know, wholly innocent. It is not the deed but the intention of the doer which makes the crime, and justice should weigh not what was done but the spirit in which it is done" [p. 51]). This passage is widely cited as a link between the correspondence and Abelard's *Ethica* and even as evidence of Heloise's influence on Abelard's dramatic reformulation of moral philosophy.

On this view, we can reach moral judgments based on the agent's intention rather than his actions. Gilson explains: "If her love is pure of all interest in that it only seeks its recompense in itself, it is justified, as by definition; and since it is the intention alone which determines the moral value of the act, every act, even one guilty in itself, if it is dictated by a sentiment of pure love, will be by the same token innocent." [65] Heloise holds to this position on doctrinal grounds in Ep. 4 and Ep. 6.[66] But as John Marenbon points out, there is a significant difference from the ethical approach Abelard espouses: "Abelard's morality is one of intended *actions*," while Heloise is concerned with the state of her mind.[67] In the context of her argument, Heloise's radical voluntarism serves an immediate purpose. The primacy of intention necessarily asserts the primacy of interiority. For Heloise, this means that the interior subject stands alone and complete as the ground of existence and moral being. The selflessness of her intention warrants her desire.

Writing Desire

Heloise's first letter sets the terms for the other personal and instructional letters that she and Abelard exchange in the decade of the 1130s.[68] Their exchange is a protracted debate over the terms that warrant Heloise's demand. The debate itself is a textualized erotic transaction in which language, figures, and images evoke Heloise's demand directly and obliquely in both personal and religious contexts. In Ep. 3, Abelard tries to restrict the scope of their letter-writing to spiritual matters. Heloise (Ep. 4) rejects these constraints, defining Abelard again as her remedy and contrasting her forbidden pleasures with his sporadic, compensatory presence. Even after she seemingly accepts his direction toward spiritual topics at the beginning of Ep. 6, he is a source of remedy ("Aliquod tamen dolori remedium" [p. 88]) and the question of desire remains stubbornly lodged within their imagination of religious life. In her critique of the Benedictine *Rule*, for instance, Heloise quotes Ovid, the poet of desire and teacher of lewdness ("poeta luxurie turpitudinisque doctor" [p. 89]) about the occasions for lust afforded by wine, as if the banquet scene in the *Ars amatoria* (1.233–44) could potentially find its way to the abbess's table. Her importation of the erotic into the religious becomes an issue that Abelard must address thereafter in his Rule (Ep. 8), where wine symbolizes the threat that desire might break into communal and devotional life and where prescriptions for attire are designed to forestall the sudden flaring of desire.[69]

Throughout the exchange, Abelard seeks to transform desire within a conversion narrative of past and present, while Heloise insists that desire is irreducible and constitutive, though its guises and signs may shift. In Ep. 5, Abelard offers a salacious recollection of furtive sex after their marriage and Heloise's entry into the convent: "Nosti post nostri federationem conjugii, cum Argenteoli cum sanctimonialibus in claustro conversareris, me die quadam privatim ad te visitandam venisse, et quid ibi tecum mee libidinis egerit intemperantia in quadam etiam parte ipsius refectorii, cum quo alias videlicet diverteremus, non haberemus." ("After our marriage, when you were living in the cloister with the nuns at Argenteuil and I came one day to visit you privately, you know what my uncontrollable desire did with you there, actually in a corner of the refectory" [p. 78]). His memory of the event is ostensibly subordinated to the themes of divine justice and spiritual salvation, and it recalls Augustine's admission that he took pleasure even in church (*Confessions* 3.3.5). Petrarch's marginal comment—"Vel iratus vel compunctus es, Petre" ("You are either angry or repentant, Peter")— captures part but not all of the ambivalence beneath Abelard's assertion of providential punishment. Angry or repentent, Abelard expresses the urgency of desire in memory where it remains a potential threat to salvation.

The transgression at Argenteuil is a striking example of the confessional pattern that Abelard imposes and of the double-voicing that carries its message. Though he addresses Heloise, the rhetorical model remains Augustine's confession of sin, faith, and praise to God. Abelard speaks simultaneously to

Heloise and through her to God: "Nosti quantis turpitudinibus immoderata mea libido corpora nostra addixerat, ut nulla honestatis vel Dei reverentia in ipsis etiam diebus dominice passionis vel quantarumcumque solempnitatum ab hujus luti volutabro me revocaret" ("You know the depths of shame to which my unbridled lust had consigned our bodies, until no reverence for decency or for God even during the days of Our Lord's Passion, or of the greater sacraments could keep me from wallowing in this mire" [p. 80]). The imagery of filth links him back to the prostitutes who disgust him in the *Historia*. His disgust leads him to recognize that he acts with unregulated desire ("immoderata mea libido"). Consequently, he insists to Heloise that his attachment to her was desire and not love: "Amor meus qui utrumque nostrum peccatis involvebat, concupiscentia, non amor, dicendus est. Miseras in te meas voluptates implebam, et hoc erat totum quod amabam" ("My love, which brought us both to sin, should be called lust, not love. I took my fill of my wretched pleasures with you, and this was the sum total of my love" [p. 84]).

Abelard thus resituates the Ovidian lover of the *Historia*, servicing his appetite through the body of his lover ("Miseras in te voluptates implebam"), to a different context. His admission of carnal desires is designed to support the Augustinian frame of his overall narrative. The third phase of Ovid's erotic project—holding a lover and dilating the interval of pleasure—is contained within the Christian equivalent to the fourth phase, a conversion now seen as already devised for both of them by God: "ipse jam tractaret ad se nos ambos hac occasione convertere" ("he was already planning to use this opportunity for our joint conversion to himself" [p. 82]). Though his opponents raise suspicions throughout his career, Abelard places himself beyond the goad of desire ("stimulus concupiscentie"/"aguillonnemens de charnel convoitise" [p. 86]).

Abelard's conversion narrative requires him to believe that desire can be transformed from then to now, from lust to love. It also requires him to to situate Heloise as a reader constrained by the movement of time. In his response to her first letter, he devises a formula that recurs throughout later instructional works: "soror in seculo quondam cara, nunc in Christo karissima" ("my sister once dear in the world and now dearest in Christ" [pp. 54–55]).[70] Irvine notes that Abelard tries to de-eroticize their letter-writing but succeeds instead in maintaining desire.[71] The play of *cara/karissima* evokes Heloise's earlier trope of *amicas/amicissimas* (Ep. 2), as she claims her debt. In Ep. 4, Heloise holds to the logic of substitution worked out in her first letter. Her opening quibble about the decorum of addressing those of lower rank before mentioning their superiors enumerates a hierarchy of paired male and female identities: "Miror, unice meus, quod preter consuetudinem epistolarum—immo contra ipsum ordinem naturalem rerum—, in ipsa

fronte salutationis epistolaris me tibi preponere presumpsisti, feminam
videlicet viro, uxorem marito, ancillam domino, monialem monacho et
sacerdoti diaconissam, abbati abbatissam" ("I am surprised, my only love,
that contrary to custom in letter-writing and, indeed, to the natural order,
you have thought fit to put my name before yours in the greeting which
heads your letter, so that we have a woman before man, wife before husband, handmaid before master, nun before monk, diaconess before priest
and abbess before abbot" [p. 61]). The rhetorical pretext is to chide Abelard
for violating natural law and epistolary convention. Meanwhile, the effect
of her list is to remind him, as in her first letter, that all the identities she
enumerates still apply uniquely to them. In its terms of substitution, the
hierarchy can be read forwards and backwards: the abbess is still a nun and
the servant still a wife.[72]

In Ep. 6, when Heloise makes what seems to be her definitive concession
to Abelard not to speak further of her feelings, her obedience is expressed
through a figure of erotic substitution and displacement whose literary
associations recapitulate the diverging views of desire. Adapting a simile
from Jerome and Cicero, she says, "Ut enim insertum clavum alius expellit,
sic cogitatio nova priorem excludit, cum alias intentus animus priorum
memoriam dimittere cogitur aut intermittere" ("As one nail drives out
another hammered in, a new thought expels an old, when the mind is
intent on other things and forced to dismiss or interrupt its recollection of
the past" [p. 88]).[73] For Jerome, the image of one nail driving another
originates in worldly philosophers; and it signifies the redirection, not the
conquest of desire. Jerome amplifies the simile by adding the biblical
example of King Ahasuerus, who is advised to gather young virgins to his
harem after Queen Vashti ignores his royal summons to display her beauty
(Esther 2: 1–4): "philosophi saeculi solent amorem ueterem amore novo
quasi clauum clauo expellere. quod et asuero septem principes facere
persarum, ut uasti reginae desiderium aliarum puellarum amore conpescerent.
illi uitium uito peccatumque peccato remediantur, nos amore uirtutum
uitia superemus" ("worldy philosophers usually drive out an old love with
a new one, like one nail pushing out another, which is what the seven
Persian leaders did for Ahasuerus, when they curbed his desire for Queen
Vashti by his love for other girls. They cured vice with vice, sin with sin;
we, however, overcome vice with the love of virtue").[74]

Jerome explicitly contrasts the pagan circulation of desire with the
Christian conquest of vice. What the example of Ahasuerus shows,
however, is that the immediate object of desire changes rather than desire
itself; the new nail can drive out the old one or drive it deeper: Ahasuerus's
desire, in fact, leads him to Esther. In Jerome's classical source, Cicero's
Tusculan Disputations, the replacement of old with new love changes

nothing; it may prove ineffective and, in any event, it misses the essential point for Cicero, which is the terrible, maddening power of love ("furor amoris").[75] For Cicero, the violence and disorder of the passions continually threaten to lead lovers to further depravity (ultimately, to incest—erotic fury turned on itself and its own). The only remedy he offers is the exercise of reason, will, and restraint against the extrinsic, pathological force of love.

Heloise rejects Cicero's diagnosis and his remedy as well as Jerome's contrast of pagan and Christian therapy. For her, love is internal, not extrinsic or somehow removed from human nature. She uses the image of the nail to signify the direction of the mind, as a new experience of perception and thought ("cogitatio nova") moves from one object of attention to another. Where Cicero sees an unstable and capricious mind, Heloise finds a logic of erotic substitutes. Her interest is primarily phenomenological, for she describes a dynamics of apprehension; and secondarily moral, for she stipulates that the new thought should be honorable and necessary. What she specifically does not do is repudiate or transform desire. Rather, as in her salutations and troping of Abelard's letters, she substitutes new topics that can stand for her erotic demands. The two topics she proposes to Abelard are simultaneously pastoral and affective. She first asks for a history and justification of the religious life that Abelard has imposed on her and then for a Rule for monastic life that takes account of women as intending agents. Both topics, as Glenda McLeod notes, concern religious life in the public sphere.[76] Both, as Heloise remarks at the end of Ep. 6, require Abelard's presence. As the earthly *fundator* and *institutor* of the community, he bears a continuing debt, an obligation to present himself directly to Heloise and her sisters: "Loquere tu nobis, et audiemus" ("Speak to us then, and we shall hear" [p. 106]).

Heloise reframes the conversion forced on her within a program of religious life that replaces yet still signifies the demand of desire. The apparent concession of Ep. 6 is a continuation of her demand by other means. By situating desire within writing and conversation, she establishes a hermeneutic exchange in which interpretation and contested meaning serve as forms of intimacy. This is largely but not exclusively an interior domain of readerly experience, of recognizing allusions, references, and their rhetorical contexts. In Ep. 8, for instance, Abelard answers Heloise's suggestion (Ep. 6) that continence added to the teachings of the Gospel would realize monastic perfection (p. 93). Her suggestion is itself a variation of the continence she proposes in his *Historia* as the specific difference defining the philosophical life (p. 15). In their last extant exchange, Abelard recognizes that the veiled referent of Heloise's question in *Problemata* 42—whether one can sin doing what God has allowed or ordered—is desire.[77]

Selfhood and Desire

The issue that connects and divides Abelard and Heloise as their correspondence unfolds, then, is the shape and emotional texture of an interior
world constituted by desire. Abelard stresses an ascetic flight from the
world. Evoking Augustine's powerful spiritual tempest ("procella ingens")
from the conversion scene in the *Confessions* (8.12.28), he retires from the
"tumultuosa seculi vita" ("the stormy life of the world" [p. 74]). Being
freed from life, he tells Heloise, would deliver him from suffering. Petrarch
remarks approvingly of the sentiment: "non ineleganter ais, Petre" ("not
without elegance do you speak, Peter"). But Abelard's flight is not simple
or uninflected contempt for the world. More precisely, it is a purposive,
egotistic withdrawal from what we might possibly desire through the
mediation of others. The self, as Abelard imagines it, is in danger because
others may activate the desire dwelling within it.[78] Along these lines
Abelard argues to Heloise that their marriage has had the unforeseen
benefit of converting them both, for otherwise she might have clung to the
world at her relatives' suggestion or in carnal pleasures.

Abelard's Rule for Heloise and her sisters (Ep. 8), like its monastic
predecessors, is premised on a flight from the world, which signifies the
external attractions that might activate desire. The self must be immured
within layers of defensive barriers as it awaits divine presence: "cum a
saeculo   corpore   quoque   recedentes,   claustris   nos   monasteriorum
recludimus, ne nos saeculares inquietent tumultus" ("when we withdraw
from the world in body too,. . .[we] shut ourselves in the cloisters of
monasteries lest we are disturbed by the tumult of the world").[79] The military architecture and social organization of the convent protect against the
outer world, and Abelard makes the metaphor explicit: "Sicut in castris saeculi, ita et in castris Domini."[80] For the individual, religious garments provide cloisters for the body ("corpore claustris recludamur"), which remains
nonetheless susceptible to worldly attractions because the mind desires and
pursues things outside ("foris").[81] Donna Alfonso Bussel points out that
monastic novices find indentity by adopting the dress of the community.[82]
Inclusion and identity work, however, through the same discipline that
aims at reducing the mind's attraction to external things, and Abelard warns
against rivalries even over coarse garments.

Of the three principles that Abelard expounds in his Rule—continence,
deprivation, and silence—the last sums up the temptations lurking in the first
two. Monastic life aims to free one from worldly attachments and thereby
achieve the tranquility and freedom of a solitary life which is conducted
simultaneously within and in isolation among a religious community.[83]
The means for doing so is to master the tongue by unrelenting silence

both in oneself and in places of communal devotion and human sociability. Inner silence quiets the worldly uproar ("saeculares. . .tumultus"), which is not just noise but disorder. Abelard's equation of monasticism with heremetic solitude not only rejects Heloise's idea of joining continence to the lesson of the Gospels as the basis of religious life; it seeks, finally, to efface the presence of others as a way of evading the possibility that they might bring the self to discover desire as a structural condition of its own being.[84]

For Heloise, desire is the interior condition that she knowingly cannot escape. In an extraordinary passage in her second letter, she describes how lascivious images of former pleasures ("obscena earum vuluptatum phantasmata" [p. 66]) intrude on her imagination during the Mass, causing her to grieve their loss rather than repent the acts. Unlike Abelard, she finds no antidote in isolation; for memory preserves pleasure, and the interior self surveys an erotic landscape in all its content: "Nec solum que egimus sed loca pariter et tempora in quibus hec egimus ita tecum nostro infixa sunt animo, ut in ipsis omnia tecum agam, nec dormiens etiam ab his quiescam. Nonumquam etiam ipso motu corporis animi mei cogitationes deprehenduntur, nec a verbis temperant improvisis." ("Everything we did and also the times and places are stamped on my heart along with your image so that I live through it all again with you. Even in sleep I know no respite. Sometimes my thoughts are betrayed in a movement of my body, or they break out in an unguarded word" [pp. 66–67]). If, in Abelard's conception of religious life, denial forestalls desire by depriving it of its stimulus in the tumult of the world, Heloise gives the lie to such denial by showing that desire is already located within subjectivity and that it is not wholly subordinate to conscious volition.[85]

Heloise's *exordium* at the opening of Ep. 6, where she accepts the bridle (*frenum*) of Abelard's injunction not to speak of her feelings, is a definitive staging of this formulation. Linda Georgianna observes, "Heloise explicitly and repeatedly distinguishes here between interior and exterior reality."[86] Writing, says Heloise, has the power to control and censor what speech cannot restrain. Speech conveys what overflows from the heart ("animus"). The heart, however, is beyond restraint: "Nichil enim minus in nostra est potestate quam animus, eique magis obedire cogimur quam imperare possimus" ("For nothing is less under our control than the heart—having no power to command it we are forced to obey" [p. 88]). As she reverses the sequence of heart, speech, writing, and hand, Heloise returns to the source of affect: "Revocabo itaque manum a scripto in quibus linguam a verbis temperare non valeo. Utinam sic animus dolentis parere promptus sit quemadmodum dextera scribentis" ("I will therefore hold my hand from writing words which I cannot restrain my tongue from speaking; would that a grieving heart would be as ready to obey a writer's hand!" [p. 88]). Writing will thus provide a means for negotiating desire, as new thoughts and topics serve as substitutes in the work of grief and memory. Yet Heloise is firm in her conviction that the line from the heart to the writer's hand is not direct but divided and oblique. Control diminishes as she recedes by stages from the written page to the speaking voice to the feeling heart (*animus/nostre couraige*). At the end of that regression, desire remains untransformed and irreducible.

CHAPTER 4

MARIE DE FRANCE AND *LE LIVRE OVIDE*

The *Lais* recounted by Marie de France are stories of desire working within the constraints of love in twelfth-century baronial culture. Marie insists that her stories originate in tales recounted by the Bretons to preserve adventures within cultural memory. Certainly the prominence of folk motifs, themes, and structural patterns argues for the origin of her courtly subject matter (*matiere*) in traditional narratives. Yet, as Marie makes clear in her Prologue, her own authorial grounding is in Latin—which is to say, written—literary culture. The *Lais* depend fundamentally on established traditions of writing, reading, and commentary. Marie says that she takes on the project of composing the *Lais* as a conscious alternative to translating "aukune bone estoire" ("Some good story" [prologue 29]) from Latin to French.[1] As she shifts her topic from history (*res gesta*) to romance (*aventure*), a signature topic for the vernacular, her approach to the stories nevertheless remains the same as it would be to a Latin text. She follows the model of the ancients who, according to Priscian, composed their works obscurely ("oscurement") so that later readers can gloss them and provide the supplement ("surplus") that completes their meaning within a community of schooled readers: "K'i peüssent gloser la lettre / E de lur sen le surplus mettre" (prologue 15–16). This "surplus," as R. Howard Bloch points out, directs the tales toward the future, not the originary past, toward an audience of readers moved by their own desires, at the same time that it presents reading—glossing the literal body of *aventure* and supplying something beyond what it possesses—as both hermeneutic and erotic.[2]

Marie makes a bold literary claim for her *matiere*, one as ambitious as Dante's assertion over a century later in the *De vulgari eloquentia* that the illustrious vernacular has a coherent and independent poetic tradition. Stephen G. Nichols contends, "she makes the first explicit canon revision in European literary history."[3] At a theoretical level, Marie argues that vernacular stories of love and desire function within the compositional and interpretive procedures of literary culture and that they carry the same exemplary and allegorical value as Latin texts. Like Latin texts, they can bear the attention and scrutiny of moral reflection, which is the possibility for meaning that they hold out for their readers to supply. Such readers, as Robert W. Hanning points out, are a constitutive element of Marie's authorship.[4]

For the *Lais*, scholars generally approach the influence of classical works as a source for specific borrowings, for material gathered discretely from other texts and then inserted into the narrative skein of her stories of *aventure*. They cite narrative parallels from Ovid's *Metamorphoses*, in particular, such as the influence of the tale of Piramus and Thisbe on "Les Deus Amanz" and "Laüstic" or of the Philomela story on "Laüstic," and, more generally, the impact of the Narcissus story as a model for narratives on the power of beauty or the *Metamorphoses* as the model for a thematically integrated collection.[5] In this chapter, I want to examine a different facet of Ovid's influence. I begin by focusing on the ekphrasis of Venus in "Guigemar" and the apparent repudiation of Ovid implied by that description. It is in Ovid's erotodidactic poems, I contend, that Marie finds a topic and conceptual frame for serious poetic invention rather than rhetorical adornment and learned allusion. Ovid's *Ars amatoria* and *Remedia amoris* furnish a way for Marie to imagine the workings of love and desire within a courtly sphere. She focuses on transforming a complex phase of Ovid's program—maintaining a love affair—into a social form of stable devotion and service. In "Eliduc," which ends the *Lais* in the only complete medieval arrangement of her stories, she ostensibly turns to an Augustinian transcendence of desire that nonetheless continues to serve some of its demands.

The Painted Room and Ovid's Book

In "Guigemar," Marie introduces Ovid's erotic teaching as part of an elaborate architectural description. The aging lord of the city to which the wounded Guigemar is carried by a mysterious ship protects the chastity of his young wife by placing her in an green marble enclosure situated beneath the donjon of his castle. The enclosure has a single, guarded entry and contains inside it a room where the wife is accompanied only by the lord's niece. The key to the gate of the enclosure is held by a castrated old priest who says mass in the chapel at the entrance to the room and serves meals to the wife. The sexual imagery of the phallic donjon looming over the enclosure translates immediately into the symbolism of male power seeking to contain and dominate female sexuality. It is an assertion of control that also reveals the anxiety at the heart of baronial power. For there is a mordant irony in an impotent old man acting as unlikely gate keeper, spiritual warden, and domestic staff in place of a vigilant and jealous old husband, driven now by envy rather than lust. The *senex amans* ("old lover") has accidentally and comically produced a sterile version of himself as the support staff in his wife's love story. The most striking detail of Marie's description, however, is her account of the paintings that adorn the inside of the room:

> La chaumbre ert peinte tut entur;
> Venus, la deuesse d'amur,
> Fu tres bien mise en la peinture;
> Les traiz mustrout e la nature
> Cument hom deit amur tenir
> E lealment e bien servir.
> Le livre Ovide, ou il enseine
> Comment chascuns s'amur estreine,
> En un fu ardant le gettout,
> E tuz iceus escumengout
> Ki jamais cel livre lirreient
> Ne sun enseignement fereint.
> La fu la dame enclose e mise.
>
>   (233–45)

[The walls of the chamber were covered in paintings in which Venus, the god-dess of love, was skilfully depicted together with the nature and obligations of love; how it should be observed with loyalty and good service. In the painting Venus was shown as casting into a blazing fire the book in which Ovid teaches the art of controlling love and as excommunicating all those who read this book or adopted its teachings. In this room the lady was imprisoned.]

Jean Rychner confidently glosses "Le livre Ovide" as the *Remedia amoris*.[6] For other commentators, the literal and figurative meaning of Marie's citation of Ovid remains a topic of critical debate and uncertainty. Herman Braet points out that a case can be made for identifying the Ovidian book as either the *Ars amatoria* or the *Remedia amoris*. Hanning sees a comprehensive reference: "Not just the *Remedia amoris* but the whole Ovidian system (*Ars* and *Remedia* alike), which seeks to control the force and course of love by artfulness and strategy, stands condemned by Venus and by Marie, for whom the goddess here stands surrogate."[7] He suggests elsewhere that Marie displaces Ovid and offers a "vernacular discourse of desire" in which writing gains its authority from pain and provides truthtelling from the margins.[8] SunHee Kim Gertz finds a "dissonant relation" between the description of the mural and the rest of the *lai*.[9] Marie's visual evocation of Ovid discloses its meaning, I believe, through the structure of his program, to which she gives a new configuration and revised content.

As we saw in chapter 2, Ovid sets out an erotic program with four distinct phases across the *Ars amatoria* and *Remedia amoris*: finding, capturing, keeping, and abandoning a lover when she becomes tedious or troublesome. The medieval *accessus ad auctores* describes the first three phases as the method of exposition in the *Ars amatoria*: "Modus istius operis talis est, ostendere quo modo puella possit inveniri, inventa exorari, exorata retineri" ("The mode of this work is such that it shows how a girl can be found, captured after she is found, and kept after she is captured").[10] The visual details in "Guigemar" show that Marie's concern is with the third phase—how a woman can be retained after she has been induced to take a lover ("exorata retineri"). The paintings reveal the nature of love and demonstrate how a man can extend and protract the duration of his love affair: "Cument hom deit amur tenir" (237). The burning of Ovid's book on controlling love ("Comment chascuns s'amur estreine" [240]) effectively cancels out the final stage of the Ovidian program contained in the *Remedia amoris*. It incidentally demolishes a book whose writing Cupid fully sanctions in a scene from Ovid's poem (*Remedia amoris* 40: "Et mihi 'propositum perfice' dixit 'opus' ").

The wife is immured, then, within a visual program whose topic is the maintenance of love after hunting and capture but before pleasure, satisfaction, and fulfilment erode. Marie transforms the erotic project from servicing Ovidian appetite against the decaying arc of gratification to sustaining courtly devotion ("lealment e bien servir" [238]). M. L. Stapleton argues that Marie, in effect, "domesticates" Ovid, divesting him of deceit and cynicism.[11] Donald Maddox contends that the scene portrays the need for "intersubjective *reciprocity*," which informs all of Marie's *Lais*.[12] R. Dubuis finds in Marie's *druërie* ("love") an innovative theory of reciprocal love.[13] Certainly, the emphasis on fidelity in love is expressed consummately later in "Guigemar," in the two knots that only Guigemar and his lady can untie and elsewhere in permutations of the phrase *amer lëalment* ("to love loyally").[14]

In the painted room in "Guigemar," Marie's transformation of eros is expressed in the contrast between the husband's obsessive desire to control his wife by layers of containment ("La fu la dame enclose e mise" [245]) and the devoted lover's task of drawing out and extending the duration of love within those walls and constraints. As Gertz notes, one point of critical debate is whether and how the paintings on the wall bear out the intentions of the husband who presumably authorized their execution in the chamber.[15] Do they represent what he hopes for himself or fears from his wife? Stapleton argues that we must separate the prescription about preserving love faithfully from its mode of representation.[16] To focus on the husband's intentions as a defining source for meaning is, however, to ignore the "surplus" that Marie makes an element of reading in her prologue to the *Lais* and the condition of desire in her writing.[17] It is the lover hovering in the future, the embodiment of husbandly anxiety and wifely desire, who will interpret and perform the scene painted on the walls of the wife's chamber.

"Mut fu delituse la vie"

The *ekphrasis* in "Guigemar" serves as a poetic emblem for one of the central concerns in the *Lais*—the fragile interim of pleasure which lovers cooperate on constructing for themselves. By canceling the *Remedia*, Marie truncates the four-step Ovidian project to direct the narrative focus to the problem of erotic dilation, to the interval of stolen pleasure unfolding in a joint venture of ingenuity and dedicated, clandestine betrayal. Distinguishing Marie's portrayal of love from both courtly love and romance chivalry, Philippe Ménard stresses its indulgence and *otium*: "In Marie knights hardly look for adventure and glory. By preference, they remain at home to savor untroubled loves at their leisure."[18] Marie's topic, put another way, is the enjoyment and maintenance of reciprocal pleasure operating against time and contingency. In "Guigemar" (537) and "Milun" (277), Marie uses the word *vie* ("life") to demarcate this erotic interval within the larger narrative. In "Eliduc," the *terme* ("fixed date" [550, 689]) of his military service overseas to the king of Exeter corresponds to his first erotic interval with Guilliadun.

Marie's poetic invention of Ovid builds on the point of greatest vulnerability for the teacher and students of love. As we have seen, the emergence of desire as a force beneath appetite and gratification threatens to disable Ovidian erotodidaxis. Desire is, however, already the starting point for Marie's lovers. Though pleasure and jouissance lead Equitan to chivalry ("Equitan" 15–16), he falls in love with the seneschal's wife without seeing her: "Sanz veüe la coveita" (41). So, too, does Milun's beloved, moved as she is by mention of his name. Marie thus poses the question implicit but largely suppressed in the *Ars amatoria*: how do lovers maintain and protract an erotic interim based on desire rather than appetite and simple gratification? The Ovidian lover draws out his liaison by subtrefuge and manipulation and finds a momentary resolution in the equity of sexual exhaustion. Marie explores an interval of erotic reciprocity that varies in time yet remains strikingly constant in structure and intensity. "Chievrefoil" recounts a brief meeting of Tristan and Iseut in the forest that encompasses satisfaction, intimacy, and pleasure: "Entre eus meinent joie mut grant. / A li parlat tut a leisir / E ele li dit sun pleisir" ("They shared great joy together. He spoke freely to her and she told him of her desire" [94–96]). The faery mistress of "Lanval" promises a succession of these encounters:

> "Quant vus vodrez od mei parler,
> Ja ne savrez cel liu penser
> U nuls puïst aveir s'amie
> Sanz repreoce e sanz vileinie,
> Que jeo ne vus seie en present
> A fere tut vostre talent. . ."
>
> (163–68)

["Whenever you wish to speak with me, you will not be able to think of a place where a man may enjoy his love without reproach or wickedness, that I shall not be there with you to do your bidding."]

Separated from external shame and internalized censorship ("Sanz repreoce e sanz vileinie"), this is the imaginary site of erotic plenitude, the fantasy of a libidinal object fully available and compliant to the lover's demands: "present / A fere tut vostre talent."[19] Sarah Kay points out that the tale turns paradoxically on what is not there—on the substitutions of fetishistic objects and the loss marked by language.[20] Structurally and thematically, Marie sets this illusory presence against the denials and omissions of favor at Arthur's court, which Lanval gladly abandons for Avalon at the end of his tale.

Some of Marie's stories portray the interval of pleasure as real but unreachable. The couple of "Deus Amanz," ostensibly bound in a committed love for each other ("s'entreamerent lëaument" [72]), perishes in their effort to meet the letter but circumvent the constraints imposed by the lady's father, who decrees that anyone seeking his daughter must be able to carry her up the high mountain outside the city of Pitres. What fails them in a practical sense is "mesure" (189), the self-possession and internalized discipline of the Ovidian lover (*modus*), for the lover resists drinking the potion that will assure success in his trial. The lady of "Chaitivel" proves a better Ovidian lover than her suitors, playing all four of them against each other but then losing three to the chance slaughter of a tournament designed to show their prowess. The survivor faces the prospect of endless service without pleasure. He is granted the company of his mistress but no comfort: "Si n'en puis nule joie aveir / Ne de baisier ne d'acoler / Ne d'autre bien fors de parler" ("I cannot experience the joy of a kiss or an embrace or of any pleasure other than conversation" [220–22]).

"Deus Amanz" and "Chaitivel" are stories of predicament, in which narrative action is contained by the governing fictional premise (an impossible task or choice), and their stasis reveals a key element of Marie's portrayal of desire. The conditions imposed by the father on his daughter's suitors in

"Deus Amanz" scarcely conceal his incestuous desire. His unwillingness to suffer the loss of her comfort and proximity ("Pres de li esteit nuit et jur" [30]) provokes widespread censure: "Plusur a mal li aturnerent, / Li suen meïsme le blamerent" ("Many people reproached him for this, and even his own people blamed him" [33–34]). In some measure, the daughter seems to accept and ratify his desire. When she rejects her lover's plea to flee with him, her sympathies lie with her father, and she imagines his response to her flight as that of a rejected lover:

> "Si jo m'en vois ensemble od vus,
> Mis pere avreit e doel e ire,
> Ne vivreit mie sanz martire.
> Certes tant l'eim e si l'ai chier,
> Jeo nel vodreie curucier."
>   (96–100)

> ["But if I went away with you, my father would be sad and distressed and his life would be an endless torment. Truly, I love him so much and hold him so dear that I would not wish to grieve him."]

The surviving lover of "Chaitivel," whose wound may be a sign of castration, faces the kind of predicament posed by a love question (*demande d'amour*): is it better for a lover to face rivals with the prospect of consummation, or to have no rivals yet no chance of pleasure?[21] Moreover, his lady's continued deferral after chance has produced a single result represents a flight from desire and from the interim of pleasure that other lovers seek in Marie's tales. These tales of predicament forestall the lovers' consummation precisely because the couple's erotic attachments are uncertain and contested from within. It is a critical commonplace that Marie's lovers must be committed to each other, even in a problematic case like "Equitan," where a lord wrongly desires his vassal's wife. But as "Deus Amanz" and "Chaitivel" demonstrate, reciprocity demands in turn a commitment to desire (hence "Equitan" as a monitory example, a critique not just of lordship blinded by lust but of desire as the condition of unforeseeable reversal).

In stories where Marie goes beyond predicaments to create a richly imagined and potentially unstable fictional world, the dilation of eros finds a complex and highly nuanced treatment. For Guigemar, this period begins with treatment for the wound ("la plaie" [113]) to his thigh caused by the ricocheted arrow during his hunt in the forests of Brittany. The external symbolic wound ("Sa plaie" [370]) healed by the lady in her chamber becomes the indwelling metaphorical wound of love ("Amur est plaie dedenz cors" [483]). When he discloses his love, Guigemar asks the lady not to act like a manipulative Ovidian lover or the conflicted lady of "Chaitivel." His request centers on the ethics of managing the erotic interim:

> Femme jolive de mestier
> Se deit lunc tens faire preier
> Pur sei cherir, que cil ne quit
> Que ele eit usé cel deduit. . . .
> (515–518)

[A woman who is always fickle likes to extend courtship in order to enhance her own esteem and so that the man will not realize that she has experienced the pleasure of love.]

Glyn Burgess finds in this passage a prescription for loyal service in love.[22] Hanning sees it as an example of Marie's using love casuistry against itself.[23] Jacques Ribard believes that it shows a natural and spontaneous love opposed to calculation and conferring liberty and selfhood.[24] The Ovidian background reminds us how closely Marie links temporality and desire. Ovid recommends that women use delay as a tactic for control, consolidation, and amusement: "Quod datur ex facili, longum male nutrit amorem: / Miscenda est laetis rara repulsa iocis" ("What is easily given ill fosters an enduring love; let an occasional repulse vary your merry sport" [Ars amatoria 3.579–80]). Delay (mora) hovers between two forms in Ovidian doctrine—tuta (safe) and brevis (short-lived). The praeceptor advises slow love-making to his male disciple (2.717–718). He counsels women to time their public entrances to their greatest advantage, adducing a proverb with larger applications to the management of eros: "maxima lena mora est" ("a great procuress is delay" [3.752]). Guigemar condemns the mystification of such tactics; they are, he says, a means for leveraging esteem while obscuring desire. He argues instead for the lady to act on her pleasure: "Ainz l'amerat, s'en avrat joie" ("she should rather love him and enjoy his love" [523]). Revealing desire produces the erotic "surplus" (533) of "Guigemar." What follows from that disclosure is a year-and-a-half interlude replete with sensual pleasure: "Mut fu delituse la vie" ("their life gave them great delight" [537]).

The acknowledgment of desire, such as Guigemar urges, is the precipating event of the parallel story "Yonec," where the aging husband isolates his wife within a paved chamber in his tower, attended by his sister. Here the patriarchal anxieties over lineage, inheritance, and cuckoldry in "Guigemar" and other tales are made explicit. The lady laments the isolation forced on her by her husband. The remedy she seeks lies in aventure as a social and discursive form, for she turns to stories like her own as they are memorialized within aristocratic culture:

> Chevalier trovoent puceles
> A lur talent, gentes e beles,

E dames truvoent amanz
Beaus e curteis, pruz e vaillanz,
Si que blasmees n'en esteient
Ne nul fors eles nes veeient.
(95–100)

[Knights discovered maidens to their liking, noble and fair, and ladies found handsome and courtly lovers, worthy and valiant men. There was no fear of reproach and they alone could see them.]

This story she acknowledges as the object of her wish and will ("ma volenté [104]). It is a textualized model of erotic subjectivity. Muldumarec, the princely lover who immediately arrives in the form of a hawk, reports that he has already desired her but could not come to her until her she has made her self-disclosure, until she has read and applied the story and so made possible the narrative and erotic surplus. Once the lady is reassured of her lover's belief in God, which adds no apparent scruple of conscience about adultery, the couple commits itself to the erotic plenitude of laughter, play, and intimacy ("unt asez ris e jué / E de lur priveté parlé" [193–94]). This period, Marie makes clear, is a dimension of time enclosed on itself: "E nuit e jur e tost e tart / Ele l'ad tut a sun pleisir" ("Night and day, early or late, he was hers whenever she wanted" [222–23]). The phrase *avoir tut a sun pleisir* echoes the promise of erotic repletion given by the faery mistress in "Lanval": "present / A fere tut vostre talent" (167–68). As in "Equitan," this period is punctuated and given an shape only by the comings and goings of the lady's husband, even though discovery and vengeance wait in the background.

In "Milun," Marie reformulates the periodicity of erotic fulfilment from "Lanval" into an incremental narrative structure. Milun and the lady who summons him as her lover enjoy their first interval of pleasure in her garden and bedchamber: "La justouent lur parlement / Milun e ele bien suvent" (51–52). This period ends with her pregnancy, the sending away of the child to Milun's sister, and the lady's subsequent arranged marriage to a local nobleman, as Milun leaves for paid service as a warrior. His return begins a second interval, in which the lady's husband replaces the father as the obstacle to pleasure, just as Meriaduc serves as a rival but unwanted suitor to replace the jealous husband in "Guigemar." The swan who serves as a messenger between Milun and the lady is the sole mechanism for sustaining a twenty-year love affair (277–88). Marie makes the swan a figure for the ingenuity of erotic craft: "Nuls ne poet estre si destreiz / Ne si tenuz estreitement / Que il ne truisse liu sovent" ("No one can be so imprisoned or so tightly guarded that he cannot find a way out from time to time" [286–88]). The starvation and feeding of the bird as it shuttles between the lovers carrying their messages symbolizes the epicycles of separation and plenitude.

The final interval in "Milun" begins as the lovers' son, who has unknowingly proved the chivalric equal of his father by unhorsing him at a tournament, prepares to kill the lady's husband, and a sealed message arrives announcing the husband's death. The son's betrothal of his mother to his father—done on his own authority ("Sanz cunseil de tute autre gent" [526])—fulfills his Oedipal desires and circumvents the anxieties of that desire by restoring the man he has mastered as his mother's partner. Reunited and freed from obstacles, Milun and the lady resume their roles as an erotic couple: "En grant bien e en grant duçur / Vesquirent puis e nuit e jur" ("Thereafter they lived night and day in happiness and tenderness" [529–30]). They live the life of pleasure in south Wales that Lanval finds by removing himself from Arthur's court to Avalon.

In portraying the interval of erotic plenitude for her lovers, Marie borrows and transforms structural devices from Ovid. The husbands and guardians—*vafer maritus* and *vigil custos* (3.611–612)—who stand as obstacles to the lover in the *Ars amatoria* have their counterparts in the *senex amans* of "Guigemar" and "Yonec," the seneschal of "Equitan," the violent husband of "Laüstic," the incestuous father of "Deus Amanz," the husband who replaces the father in "Milun," King Mark in the Tristan episode of "Chievrefoil," the retainers ("chevalier fiufé") of "Le Fresne," and even Guildeluëc, the wife of Eliduc. These figures simultaneously block the lover's satisfaction and bring the pressures of time and contingency that give definition to the lovers' shared erotic interlude. Lovers outwit these obstacles and communicate through intermediaries who function like the maids and go-betweens who must be cultivated in the *Ars amatoria*. In the *Lais*, they are not, however, as in Ovid, potential objects of seduction themselves. The old husband's niece in "Guigemar," assigned as a companion to the captive lady, becomes a collaborator in the love plot in a way that redounds to her credit and stature: "Mut ert curteise e deboneire" ("she was most courtly and noble" [464]). The abbess who raises Le Fresne abets her concubinage with Gurun. The chamberlain in "Eliduc" negotiates Guilliadun's cautious approach to her lover. The nightingale in "Laüstic" and the swan in "Milun" are devices for arranging the lovers' encounters.

In the *Ars amatoria*, the space for finding and capturing a lover is the Roman cityscape, but the site of desire and pleasure is the bedchamber (*thalamus*). The Ovidian teacher proclaims, "Conveniunt thalami furtis et ianua nostris" ("Chambers and a locked door beseem our secret doings" [2.617]). The obstacle of a barred door, he advises later, can be a stimulus to desire: "Adde forem, et duro dicat tibi ianitor ore / 'Non potes,' exclusum te quoque tanget amor" ("add but a door, and let a doorkeeper say to you with stubborn mouth, 'You cannot'; once shut out, you too, sir, will be touched by love" [3.587–88]). The bedchamber is a stronghold under siege by the recruits and veterans ("vetus miles") of the *militia Veneris* (3.559–74) whose tactics differ while their objective remains the same. Access to the chamber is thus a metaphor for access to the lover's body, and admission to the private space is a form of sexual penetration. Submerged under Ovid's pretext of harmless pleasure and displaced from the teacher's consciousness is the additional sense that entry to the chamber is also trespass on another man's household. It is here that Marie, imagining a baronial rather than cosmopolitan world, rejects Ovid's governing premise: "Nos venerem tutam concessaque furta canemus, / Inque meo nullum carmine crimen erit" ("Of safe love-making do I sing, and permitted secrecy, and in my verse shall be no wrong-doing" [*Ars amatoria* 1.33–34]). For her the erotic interim is framed not just by obstacles (all potentially comic in Ovid) but by violence within a militarized society, always potentially at war among and within its patriarchal households.

In the *Lais*, Marie exploits the Ovidian equation of bed, body, and property for its nuances as well as its basic structure. Guigemar is brought into the lady's chamber to be healed, and it is there that the wound in his thigh becomes the hidden wound of love. Equitan and his lover are discovered on the seneschal's bed, as he bursts into his chamber to discover his wife's betrayal and the means she has prepared to murder him. Le Fresne recovers her identity and her lover in Gurun's bedchamber, where she presides over the preparations for consummation that become, by chance disclosure and happy substitution, her own marriage. Lanval's lady has a portable chamber in the richly appointed pavillion where he first encounters her. The lady's bedroom window opens on her lover's house in "Laüstic," granting him a visual display of his otherwise unattainable beloved. The garden where Milun meets his lady is next to her bedchamber. Eliduc and Guilliadun disclose their love to each other in the bedroom that he enters with the king's encouragement, interrupting her chess lesson with another knight but securing access to her person in the most intimate space of the castle.

Marie's most striking use of the Ovidian *thalamus* occurs in "Yonec." Muldumarec, the shape-shifting lover who appears immediately after the lady's self-disclosure of desire, enters by a narrow window ("Par mi une estreite fenestre" [107]) that represents both her jealous husband's constraint and the sexual organs he seeks to protect and employ to assure himself of an heir, without success. The first interlude with the lover restores the lady's beauty, fuels her desire, and gives her a new appreciation of solitude: "Sun ami voelt suvent veeir / E de lui sun delit aveir" ("she wanted to see her beloved often and to take her pleasure with him" [219–20]). The old woman charged with guarding her, herself widowed and barren like the castrated priest of

"Guigemar," remarks that the lady now remains alone more willingly than before (239–40). In this way, the chamber is transformed from a site of privation, where the lady is removed from society and conversation by a sterile marriage.[25] The lover provides a "surplus" to its desolation, and this supplement is pleasure, sociability, intimacy, and progeny.

When the husband discovers the cause of his wife's restoration, he acts to prevent her body from penetration by rendering the space of her chamber lethal. The *engin* he prepares is both a deadly trap and a clever assertion of his right of seigneural possession:

> Broches de fer fist granz furgier
> E acerer le chief devant:
> Suz ciel n'ad rasur plus trenchant!
> Quant il les ot apparailliees
> E de tutes parz enfurchiees,
> Sur la fenestre les ad mises,
> Bien serreies e bien asises,
> Par unt li chevaliers passot,
> Quant a la dame repeirot.
>   (286–94)

[He had large iron spikes forged and the tips more sharply pointed than any razor. When he had prepared and cut barbs in them, he set them on the window, close together and well-positioned, in the place through which the knight passed whenever he came to see the lady.]

This fortified barrier does not simply defend the aperture that grants the lover entry to the lady and her body, nor does it make the passage inaccessible or forbidding. It is an aggressive, inverted phallic display designed to inflict a wound ("sa plaie" [334]) on the trespasser in vengeance for his transgression of household, property, and patriarchal ambitions. The symbolic aim of the sharply honed spikes is to castrate the lover, to reverse the sequence of wounds in "Guigemar" and to make Muldumarec as impotent as the lover in "Chaitivel." Muldumarec impales himself on the barrier, seemingly unaware of the trap, but enters the room and seats himself on the bed. His flow of blood on the sheets ("tuit li drap furent sanglent" [316]) represents his insemination of the wife, just as her tracking him by the trail of his blood back to his ornate chamber symbolizes the eventual succession of their son Yonec as lord of the city, after he beheads the lady's husband at the site of his father's tomb.

Impossible Desire

In her most richly plotted *Lais*, Marie transforms the interim of pleasure into some form of stable consolation, often marriage or restitution.

Guigemar destroys Meriaduc's castle, kills his rival, and goes off with his lover to a place beyond threat: "A grant joie s'amie en meine: / Ore ad trespassee sa peine" ("With great joy he took away his beloved. Now his tribulations were over" [881–82]). The love triangle of Gurun, Le Fresne, and La Codre is resolved by La Codre's marriage to another man when she returns with her parents to her country. Lanval and his faery mistress retire to Avalon. Milun and his lover are married by their son. Where erotic transformation fails, restitution prevails. Bisclavret, the werewolf betrayed by his wife out of fear, is restored to his land and possessions, while his wife goes off with the knight who had since married her. Yonec buries his mother at his father's tomb and becomes lord of Muldumarec's city before returning to the fief in Caerwent held by the stepfather he has murdered. The narrative mechanism that produces these transformations is disclosure. Disclosure forces the narrative crisis that brings *aventure* to closure, thence to public memory and literary form. The ending of "Le Fresne" plots the dual trajectories of closure and disclosure from fiction to writing and performance: "Quant l'aventure fu seüe, / Coment ele esteit avenue, / Le lai del *Freisne* en unt trové" ("When the truth of this adventure was known, they composed the lay of *Le Fresne*" [515–517]).

Marie writes other tales, however, that significantly resist the transformation of desire within narrative fiction and readerly understanding. "Deus Amanz" leaves its two dead lovers in a sepulchre on the mountain as a memorial to unconsummated desire. "Chaitivel" oscillates between two names (the other is "Les Quatre Deuls") to show the undecidability of its underlying love question. Both names signify thwarted desire, and the answer to the *demande* posed by the story is that neither tragic rivalry nor barren possession is preferable. "Chievrefoil" promises a future reconciliation between Tristan and King Mark, but its tradition tells us that the "acordement" ("peace" [98]) promised during their encounter is a device for deferred consummation. In "Eliaduc" and "Laüstic," to which we now turn attention, Marie goes beyond desire as stasis to examine the Ovidian interim in perhaps its most radical terms.

"Eliduc" in fact begins with the stable erotic interim that is the point of closure for Marie's stories of couples who overcome obstacles to achieve sustained fulfillment at the end of their *aventure*. In her opening summary of the tale, Marie locates Eliduc and Guildeluëc exactly at the point where nothing more can be told in "Guigemar," "Lanval," and "Milun": "Ensemble furent lungement, / Mut s'entreamerent lëaument" ("They lived together for a long time and loved each other with great loyalty" [11–12]). The intervening force in their happiness is external in the opening summary ("soudees," paid military service [14]) and internal in the narrative ("l'envie del bien de lui" [41]), yet in both cases it calls into question whether the erotic interim can be sustained within social structures based on a network of implicit allegiance and feudal loyalties: "amur de seignur n'est pas fiez" ("a lord's love is no fief" [63]). Eliduc's conflicted loyalty to his wife and mistress duplicates the competing claims that his Breton lord and English employer hold over his services. Terms like *fiance*, *fei*, and *leauté* apply equally to political allegiance and love.[26]

Though Eliduc's military service structures time and contingency, the poem's narrative concentrates on a series of erotic intervals. When Guilliadun falls in love with Eliduc, her chamberlain assures her that she can operate within the period of Eliduc's contracted service to her father: "Asez purrez aveir leisir / De mustrer lui vostre pleisir" ("Thus you will have enough opportunity to show him your desire" [453–54]). She accepts those limits in her ensuing interview with Eliduc (532–36), and there follows an interim of pleasure notable for its absence or suppression of sexual appetite:

> Mes n'ot entre eus nule folie,
> Joliveté ne vileinie;
> De douneier e de parler
> E de lur beaus aveirs doner
> Esteit tute la druërie
> Par amur en lur cumpainie.
>   (575–80)

[There was no foolishness between them, nor fickleness, nor wickedness, as their love consisted entirely of courting and talking, and exchanging fair gifts when they were together.]

Marie sets this restraint and sublimation against the desire that her characters so intensely experience. The circulation of words and gifts displaces but stands for sexuality. Sandra Pierson Prior observes that at the start of these exchanges Guilliadun becomes "the desiring Ovidian female," while Eliduc's feelings are those of "the desired object rather than of the desiring subject."[27] A second interval—Eliduc's temporary return to Brittany to aid his lord—repeats the first. Limited again by a promised term of service, Eliduc rejoins his wife and retainers but remains alienated from their joy and isolated within his concealed desire: "Mut se cuntient sutivement" ("He behaved most secretively" [717]). When Guildeluëc discovers Guilliadun after another return journey, she recognizes "la verité" (1017) of his withdrawal in a scene where she views Guilliadun's body, ironically adopting the lover's gaze and cataloguing the features it beholds (1010–1016). Motivated "[t]ant par pitié, tant par amur" (1027), Guildeluëc removes herself as an obstacle, taking the nun's veil and founding a religious community with thirty other women.

Guildeluëc's removal permits the kind of unforeseen closure we see at the end of "Milun," where the husband suddenly dies so that the son can marry his parents. This device returns the story to the erotic consolidation with which it began, though with a different couple. Eliduc and Guilladun marry and resume the life of apparent plenitude in a conscious echo of the restored couple in "Milun": "Ensemble vesquirent meint jur, / Mut ot entre eus parfite amur" ("They lived together for many a day and the love between them was perfect" [1149–50]; cf. "Milun" 530). Unlike "Milun," however, in "Eliduc" this new form of erotic interval, secured by trial, suffering, and generous resignation, is as untenable as the first. The life of plenitude that Eliduc and Guilliadun lead centers on charity and good works, which lead to religious conversion. In most modern readings of the poem, this final step demonstrates a movement from earthly to spiritual love.[28] Guildeluëc receives Guilladun as a sister in her community; the two pray for "lur ami" (1171), the shared husband turned patron who prays for them in return. The "bone fei" that Eliduc first pledges Guildeluëc when he leaves Brittany for England (84) presumably finds its proper object in their collaborative enterprise—a spiritual *amicitia* of rivalry in devotion and prayer: "Mut se pena chescuns pur sei / De Deu amer par bone fei / E mut par firent bele fin" ("Each one strove to love God in good faith and they came to a good end" [1177–79]). Placed in the final, emphatic position in the sequence of *Lais* in British Library MS Harley 978, the mid-thirteenth-century English manuscript that offers the only medieval disposition of the full collection, "Eliduc" seemingly gives Marie's last word on the Ovidian project of amplifying pleasure. In its portrayal of monastic flight from worldly attractions and the presence of an erotic other, it also effects the closure of spiritual conversion that Abelard seeks to impose on Heloise's irreducible desire.[29]

But if "Eliduc" follows a trajectory toward spiritual transcendence (*mut bele fin*), its narrative closure leaves open an interpretive "surplus" for Marie's readers. Marie says at the beginning that the poem used to be called *Elidus* but is now called *Guildeluëc ha Guilliadun* (21–28); at the end, she says that the Bretons made a lay "De l'aventure de ces treis" (1181). The undecidability of the title points toward the undecidability of the *matiere*. Is "Eliduc" about a knight who finds salvation after securing worldly pleasure? Is it about two women who eschew rivalry and become spiritual sisters? Is it about a love triangle transformed by something other than removing the obstacle or devising a double marriage?[30] The *aventure* all three share comes at the end to mean separation as well as reconciliation. Lodged in their monastic houses and communicating through messengers, the characters inhabit a sanctified version of the chambers holding unhappy wives elsewhere in the *Lais*. Their exchange of messages is a benevolent form of the "druërie" that sustains lovers.

The shift from worldly contentment in the Ovidian interval to spiritual transcendence marks the paradox of desire in "Eliduc"—its simultaneous impossibility and peristence. Throughout the poem, the erotic intervals cannot be sustained within the social structures where Marie locates human action, will, and gratification. Eliduc and Guildeluëc lose their happiness to envy and court rivalry. Eliduc and Guilladun cannot consummate their love during Eliduc's service to the king of Exeter. When they are legitimized as a couple, charity ("Granz aumoines e granz biens" [1151]) replaces eros in their "parfite amur" ("perfect love").[31] When they undergo conversion, they reenact their courtship, safely beyond the threat of pleasure and con-summation, its intimacy now fully contained in language.

"Eliduc" ends, then, with sublimation, not reconciliation, and its closure is perhaps more apparent than real. The husband and his two wives commit themselves to prayer as a form of exchange, a means of continuing transactions. The late conversion of Eliduc and Guilladun shows that Guildeluëc has failed or miscalculated in her gesture of resigning marriage for the nun's veil so that Eliduc can take his lover ("Elidus ad s'amie prise" [1145]). The problem of the poem is not to find the right couple but to find an arrangement for all three. This they discover in the exchange of messages, whose topic is the exposure of female emotion and affect ("Pur saveir cument lur estot, / Cum chescune se cunfortot" [1175–76]). Separated by agreement rather than jealous husbands, politics, or social constraints, Eliduc and his wives devise what we might call a spiritual Ovidianism. The messengers he sends to Guildeluëc and Guilladun contin-ually pose the lover's demand that his beloved reveal herself fully to him. Eliduc has appropriated Heloise's demand for erotic presence and her means of securing it through letters.

The demand for such disclosure is what constitutes the Ovidian interim of "Laüstic." Marie adapts the Piramus and Thisbe story for her fictional premise and evokes the story of Philomela at the point of narrative crisis. Yet the differences from Ovid's mythographic narratives are as important as the paral-lels. "Laüstic" is the story of adults, not children thwarted by their fathers; and it goes to the heart of baronial culture, not Semiramis's Babylon, by showing the contradiction of a social order centered simultaneously on rivalry and identity.[32] St. Malo, Marie's locale for the story, enjoys its reputation "Pur la bunté des deus baruns" ("Because of the fine qualities of the two men" [11]). Their two fortified houses opening onto each other, with no barrier except a wall, are the social core of the city. The wife whom one of the noblemen marries is the obstacle who disrupts their chivalric identification with one another and generates their rivalry. She accedes to her neighbor's importun-ing for all the qualities that he implicitly shares with her husband: "grant bien" ("so many qualities" [25]), reputation ("Tant pur le bien qu'ele en oï" [27]), and proximity. (The only difference that emerges between the men is the husband's later cruelty in strangling the nightingale.[33])

As this roster of qualities suggests, desire operates in "Laüstic" through language. The Ovidian interim made possible by the architecture of the houses is a traffic in signs and performance conducted through the lover's prudence and ingenuity. Conversation and gifts move across the wall and enter through the window of the lady's bedchamber, much as Muldumarec penetrates the window of his lover's room in "Yonec." Nothing impedes the lovers' display for each other in their facing windows: "Nuls nes poeit de ceo garder / Qu'a la fenestre n'i venissent / E iloec ne s'entreveïssent" ("no one could prevent their coming to the window and seeing each other there" [54–56]). Marie makes it clear that all these signs are linguistic substitutes for erotic consummation:

> N'unt gueres rien ki lur despleise,
> Mut esteient amdui a eise,
> Fors tant k'il ne poent venir
> Del tut ensemble a lur pleisir. . .
> (45–48)

> [There was scarcely anything to displease them and they were both very content except for the fact that they could not meet and take their pleasure with each other. . . .]

What she also demonstrates is that symbolic exchange not only replaces but comes to constitute desire. As Michelle Freeman points out, the lady finds an alternative to the role of the *mal mariée* under conditions not for lovemaking "*but for dialogue.*"[34] The interim for maintaining the love affair ("Lungement se sunt entreamé" [57]), as Paul Zumthor observes, is the sole marker of time in the poem.[35] It lasts until the lady exceeds the moderation (*modus*) of Ovidian craft and uses the nightingale as a pretext for their meetings. Asked by her husband why she rises in the night, she indirectly but fatefully speaks her dissatisfaction, the distance between him and the joy she finds in her nightly meetings: "Il nen ad joië en cest mund / Ke n'ot le laüstic chanter" ("anyone who does not hear the song of the nightingale knows none of the joys of this world" [84–85]).

The husband's capture and killing of the nightingale is the transgression (*vileinie*) that differentiates him morally and socially from his baronial double and reorders the economy of desire in "Laüstic." Thomas A. Shippey proposes that the nightingale stands for the "ideal love" sought by the lovers.[36] Emanuel J. Mickel, Jr. glosses the dead bird subsequently carried by the lover as the "agonizing memory of his lost love."[37] The wife describes the nightingale to her husband as desire that stands beyond him: "mut me semble grant deduit; / Tant m'i delit e tant le voil / Que jeo ne puis dormir de l'oil" ("it brings me great pleasure. I take such delight in it and desire it so much that I can get no sleep at all" [88–90]). When the husband breaks the nightingale's neck and splatters its blood on her tunic in an oblique echo of "Yonec," the crisis for the lady is hermeneutic. Deprived of her pretext for nightly display, she wonders how her lover will interpret her absence at the window. Her problem, in other words, is to control the interpretive "surplus" of possible meanings: "Il quidera ke jeo me feigne" ("He will think I am faint-hearted" [or dissumulating or that I have abandoned him, 131]). She solves her problem by generating her own surplus. The dead bird is transformed into a funerary artifact, wrapped in a rich silk cloth embroided with gold and writing. To assure the right reading of this overwrought sign, she sends with it a messenger as glossator to explain her intended meaning ("sun message" [143]) to her lover, who nonetheless adds his own surplus to what the messenger says and shows ("tut li ad dit e mustré" [145]).

The dead bird, as Bloch remarks, is sent to the lover as a poetic envoi that marks the impossibility of desire.[38] Without the pretext of the nightingale's song, the erotic exchanges between the wife and lover are no longer possible, and the Ovidian interim closes down under violence to the symbol of love lyric. The lavish reliquary that the lover orders made for the bird represents, however, a double, even contradictory meaning. At one level, the entombment equates death and desire, for the nightingale is not just placed inside the reliquary but the casket is sealed ("Puis fist la chasse enseeler" [155]), as the final act in the lovers' erotic exchanges. At another level, this fixing of desire is what allows desire to persist. The lover always carries the reliquary with him, as a memorial presence. Though sealed (*enseelee*), what the object represents cannot be concealed (*celee*): "Cele aventure fu cuntee, / Ne pot estre lunges celee" ("This adventure was related and could not long be concealed" [157–58]). In ordering the reliquary, the lover has shown that, unlike the husband (116), he is not "vileins" (148), and the object that contains impossible desire makes sure that desire persists and circulates in the lai preserving the *aventure*.

The reliquary of "Laüstic" inevitably recalls the marble tomb of "Deus Amanz." But the lovers of "Laüstic" do not have the unreachable desire of the young couple who possess the means but not the wisdom to overcome the obstacle placed in their way. The more revealing comparison is with "Eliduc." In "Eliduc," the Ovidian interval seemingly transforms into religious conversion. Similar interpretations have been made for "Laüstic," arguing that the reliquary retains its religious symbolism and that entombing the dead bird amounts to a transubstantiation of earthly love into "an ideal spiritual bond."[39] Whether spiritual, idealized, memorial, or morbid, love in "Laüstic" remains desire only partially transformed. The dead bird is not a metaphor but a metonymy for the lovers' Ovidian interval, the symbol of sustained pleasures arbitrarily brought into the economy of signs and performance when the wife improvises an excuse for her nightly displays. It is preserved in the vessel ordered by the lover, just as the three converts in "Eliduc" are situated in the houses and rules they create for themselves. Though the lady sends her message, the lover's continual possession of the reliquary ("Tuz jurs l'ad fete od lui porter" [156]) acts out Eliduc's demand that the women separated from him continue to reveal themselves by telling how they feel.

Marie engages "Le livre Ovide" imaginatively at the phase of the Ovidian project that demands the greatest craft and artfulness. In her rewriting of the *Ars amatoria*, keeping love is neither a domestic or harmless enterprise. Though the Ovidian interim in her stories remains somehow beyond moral condemnation, it still belies Ovid's claims to commit no trespass (*nullum crimen*) and to celebrate love without penalties (*venus tuta*). Resituated in a context of baronial power, the erotic interval is all about consequences. Only in the fantasy of "Lanval" does Marie approach something like the licensed intrigues (*concessa furta*) that Ovid claims to extoll. At the same time that she represents the Ovidian interim under time and contingency, Marie also discovers that the transformations of desire to marriage, restitution, and mourning offer provisional answers to its urgent demands. "Eliduc" and "Laüstic" suggest that in Marie's fictive realm the fixing of desire only masks its continuing circulation.

CHAPTER 5

REWRITING DESIRE IN THE
ROMAN DE LA ROSE

The *Roman de la Rose* is a poem in which love and desire are repeatedly contained within the desire of writing. At the beginning of the poem, Guillaume de Lorris gives a title and description of his work in one couplet: "c'est li *Romans de la Rose* / Ou l'art d'Amors est toute enclose" ("it is the Romance of the Rose, in which the whole art of love is contained" [37–38]).[1] By evoking the *Ars amatoria*, Guillaume signals his ambition to appropriate Ovid's erotodidaxis and summarize it inside the closed text of a courtly dream vision. The craft of love-making will reside in his dreamer's quest to possess the rose, while his text itself operates as a poetic analogue to the closed garden of Deduit, the locus of action in the poem. Guillaume's double ambition founders, of course, in his unfinished poem and likewise in the promised but unwritten glosses that will explain the dream's significance (1600–1602, 2067–72).[2] It returns later, however, significantly changed in Amors's pseudo-prophecy that Jean de Meun will succeed Guillaume and fashion a book renamed "Le *Miroër as amoreus*" (10651). Jean's mirror tropes "li mirëors perilleus" ("the perilous mirror" [1571]) in which the dreamer Amant first sees the rose in Guillaume's portion of the poem. Jean rewrites Guillaume's closed, aristocratic text to reveal its contents to audiences throughout France. He does so in an encyclopedic form that serves now as a satiric reflection of the erotic practice imagined by Guillaume.[3]

The account of poetic succession in the *Rose* is artfully, if profoundly, dislocated—belated in fact yet insistently prophetic in its authorial and authorizing fiction.[4] By the time Amors prophesies his arrival, Jean has long since taken over Guillaume's poem.[5] In doing so, he reconceives its poetic materials and its imaginative possibilities. He amplifies the earlier roles of Raison, Ami, and La Vielle, while adding other figures like Nature and

Genius and expanding the poem's literary and philosophical sources.[6] He replaces Amors with Venus as the deity who guarantees Amant's success, and he recasts the art of love as the craft of duplicity and guile. Jean also remedies the poetic losses ostensibly suffered by Amors, starting with the death of Tibullus, moving through those of Gallus, Catullus, and Ovid, and ending with Guillaume's—a collection of dead and rotting ("mors porris" [10525]) poets. Just as Ovid inherited and transformed the Latin elegiac tradition, so Jean reconceives Guillaume's vernacular invention of an aristocratic, courtly *ars* from Ovid while paying tribute to Guillaume's perfumed tomb (10562–63), the funerary memorial to the enclosed text that he has become. Amors cites the exact point of textual transition from Guillaume to Jean in Amant's discourse with Raison (4059) where, in the logic of already completed future succession, "quant Guillaume cessera, / Jehanz le continuera" ("when Guillaume shall cease, Jean will continue it" [10587–88]).

Medieval readers may well have seen Jean's succession as producing a single poem.[7] In the fifteenth-century quarrel over the *Rose*, Pierre Col, for example, refers to the speeches by Raison and Nature as "chapistres," and the implication is that they all belong to one book.[8] For modern readers of the poem, Jean's succession has largely structured interpretation. Guillaume's idealized vision of love is either cancelled out, according to a secular reading, or ironically realized, according to a religious reading, by Jean's scholastic, naturalistic continuation. In the first case, realism deconstructs the illusions of stylized courtly love; in the second, satire exposes the moral corruption and spiritual blindness at its core. The most persuasive alternative to reading along the lines of Jean's succession—a trajectory that Jean, of course, writes for himself—has its origin in the medieval debates over the *Rose* and finds a rationale in modern as well as medieval literary theory. David Hult sees the equivalent of Bakhtinian dialogism in the poem's debate structure.[9] Daniel Heller-Roazen identifies a radical poetics of contingency in the poem's exploration of "its own capacity to be otherwise than it is."[10] Nancy Freeman Regalado notes that Jean's intertextual citations and borrowings preserve the alterity of his sources.[11] Douglas Kelly argues that the *Rose* incorporates a poetic discourse whose formal properties render its meaning multiple and open-ended.[12] On this view, the poem invites hermeneutic repetition by readers and authors alike. In their interpretation of the composite text, readers restage the authorial reading of Guillaume conducted by Jean in order to invent and write his continuation of the poem.

Much turns in this critical debate on the play of temporality in the *Rose* and on the suture of the imperfect rhymes *cessera/continuera* in Amors's speech. How exactly does (or will) Guillaume stop and Jean carry on? Amors, we recall, marks the succession from one poet to another as a dead spot in time—a forty-year hiatus between Guillaume's death and Jean's birth, a void already passed over even if Amors pretends to await Jean's arrival and poetic inauguration, which is the necessary condition in this instance of his prophetic speech. As we read the poem, it becomes clear that while Jean continues Guillaume never ceases.[13] Amors's dislocation of time is not just a trope of authorship but a symptom. The symptom signifies the problem of situating desire within the poem's competing ideological systems, thus within claims of authorship.[14] In this chapter, I shall argue that it is Guillaume's portion of the *Rose* that presents the radical and desta-bilizing element of the poem, the repressed content that nonetheless finds continuing expression. Jean's satiric, material reduction of Guillaume— whether secular or religious in its aims—is a strategy that responds to the persistence of desire.[15] Jean, like Augustine in the *Confessions*, tries to effect the integration of desire.[16] I shall be concerned with three poetic strategies that he uses to rewrite desire from Guillaume. Jean balances the Narcissus story, Guillaume's founding moment of desire, with the Pygmalion myth; he tries to differentiate the varieties of love at the start of his continuation; at the end, he reverses the structure of Amant's approaches to the rose. Guillaume narrates Amant's erotic history prospectively, as a story that moves toward a culmination; Jean rewrites the story from the retrospect of an erotic career that follows from Amant's fulfillment.

Narcissus and Pygmalion: The Structure of Desire

Guillaume offers the poem's distinguishing formulation of desire in the scene where Amant reenacts the myth of Narcissus as he wanders in the garden of Deduit, stalked (unbeknownst to him) by Amors. Amant explores a landscape charged with multiple erotic possibilities, for Deduit has con-structed a network of shaded fountains with verdant borders suitable for lovemaking: "Aussi y peüst l'en sa drue / Couchier comme sor une coite" ("There one could couch his mistress as though on a feather bed" [1394–95]). Amant discovers the fountain of Narcissus as a memorial to erotic denial, vengeance, and death. Nature has placed the fountain in marble under a pine and inscribed the rock with small letters identifying it as the place where Narcissus died. The inscription generates the narrative gloss that Guillaume supplies by refashioning Ovid's story so that Narcissus's discourteous refusal of Echo's love leads to her prayer that he suffer a thwarted love ("eschaufés de tel amour / Dont il ne peüst joie atendre" [1462–63])—in other words, a condition of desire that can be neither escaped nor fulfilled.

In Guillaume's narrative gloss, Echo's vengeance is secured by the structural impossibility of desire.[17] Ovid's Narcissus goes through a process of seeing and pursuing an image that returns his gestures of affection before he recognizes himself as the erotic other contained in a true image of himself ("Iste ego sum: sensi, nec me mea fallit imago" [*Metamorphoses* 3.461]).[18] He portrays the full possession of self and other as death: "Nunc duo concordes anima moriemur in una" (3.471). In Guillaume, desire is misperception, not tragic recognition. Gazing into the fountain, Guillaume's Narcissus is deceived by the shadows: "Et cis maintenant s'esbahi, / Car ses ombres l'ot si trahi" ("Then he was struck with wonder, for these shadows so deceived him" [1485–86]). He loves "son umbre demaine" (1494), the darkened eroticized image of the self that parallels the secluded places of the garden and guarantees the continual failure of realizing pleasure: "Qu'il n'en pooit avoir confort / En nulle fin, ne en nul sens (1500–1501). The insistent negation of these last lines—no confort in any way or sense—cancels out even the ironic self-recovery that Ovid allows Narcissus before he perishes.

Amant repeats Narcissus's error in a way that Guillaume prepares at the beginning of the dream vision. Before Amant discovers and enters the garden, he washes his face in a river and notices the gravel covering the riverbed (102–21). At Narcissus's fountain, he sees gravel and two crystals at the bottom. The crystals have the power not just of reflection but of complete representation: "tel force ont que tous li leus, / Arbres et flors, et quanqu'aorne / Li vergiers, i pert tous a orne" ("[they] have such power that the entire place—trees, flowers, and whatever adorns the garden—appears there all in order" [1550–52]). Variously interpreted as the eyes of the beloved or of Amant or of the reader, they are a poetic emblem of the fused power of mimesis and eros, mirrors and a pair of testicles at the same time.[19] Gazing into "cil cristal merveilleus," the single surface created by the two crystals, one can see more than half the garden at any one time and the rest of it by turning; moreover, the smallest objects, however hidden and enclosed ("Tant soit repote ne enclose" [1568]), are reproduced as if they had been drawn in the crystal. Guillaume immediately names this "li mireors perilleus" (1571) both because of Narcissus's death and because of the transformative power that it exercises:

> Ci sort as gens noveles rages,
> Ici se changent li corage,
> Ci n'a mestier, sens ne mesure,
> Ci est d'amer volenté pure,
> Ci ne se set consillier nus;
> Car Cupido, li filz Venus,
> Sema ici d'Amors la grainne,
> Qui toute a tainte la fontainne,
> Et fist ses las environ tendre,
> Et ses engins i mist pour prendre

Damoiseles et damoisaus,
Qu'Amors ne veut autres oisiaus.
            (1583–94)

[Out of this mirror a new madness comes upon men: Here hearts are changed; intelligence and moderation have no business here, where there is only the simple will to love, where no one can be counseled. For it is here that Cupid, son of Venus, sowed the seed of love that has dyed the whole fountain, here that he stretched his nets and placed his snares to trap young men and women; for Love wants no other birds.]

Guillaume's explanation of these powers contains major elements that Jean will exploit in his rewriting of the poem. The "noveles rages" places lovers beyond clear judgment, self-regulation, and counsel, particularly the counsel of Raison. The fountain creates the condition of desire as uninflected will ("Ci est d'amer volenté pure"). Cupid's insemination of the fountain gives it the name "La Fontainne d'Amors" (1597) and anticipates Amant's insemination of the rose at the end of the poem. But if Guillaume offers the materials of his own revision, he also establishes themes that Jean and other successors cannot easily invent or exploit as poetic silences. In Guillaume's retelling, the Narcissus episode is Ovidian myth read through the optic of the *Ars amatoria* rather than the *Metamorphoses*.[20] Cupid's "las" and "engins" in the mirror belie the discipline of erotic self-mastery and reveal lovers as the quarry in Cupid's hunt, just as Amant is being tracked in the garden by Amors. Guillaume establishes a fundamental connection between desire and representation. Lovers transform and become vulnerable to their wishes and demands—and thereby to Cupid—through the aesthetic power of the mirror to present images. Erich Köhler astutely remarks that the figure in the mirror is both self and stranger, a more powerful version of the erotic subject contained in a reflected image.[21] It is for this reason that Jean will later write a repudiation of the power of representation in "la fontainne perilleuse" ("the perilous fountain" [20409]), claiming that lovers cannot know themselves (20437–38) and the crystals cannot show everything because of the darkness that envelops them ("Por l'occurté qui les onuble" [20453]).

Amant's quest for the rose begins precisely within representation. Among the thousand things shown in the mirror, he focuses on a rosebush laden with roses and surrounded by a hedge. Guillaume's language emphasizes that this attraction to the image within the mirror acts out the conditions of desire. Amant demonstrates his "volenté pure": "Choisi rosiers chargiés de roses" ("I saw rosebushes loaded with roses" [1616]). He experiences "cele rage" ("This madness" [1623]), which places him beyond reason and control. Drawn by the image and reinforced by the pleasure of

the smell, he approaches the mass of flowers and surveys the buds of varying sizes. When he selects a single bud, Amant puts in motion a mechanism
of erotic investment. He chooses one out of many buds ("Entre ces
boutons en eslui / Un si tres bel" [1655–56]) that becomes more valuable
than all the rest because of his gaze: "qu'envers celui / Nus des autres riens
ne prisé / Puisque je l'oi bien avisé" ("after I had examined it carefully,
I thought that none of the others was worth anything beside it" [1656–58]).
The aesthetic power of representation, then, creates desire, and the intending gaze selects its arbitrary object, whose pre-eminent value is confirmed
solipsistically by Amant's intent ("eslui") and attention ("avisé"). Guillaume
stages this moment, moreover, as the point of Amant's capture. While the
dreamer contemplates possession, Cupid recognizes that Amant's desire has
found its object, and so he shoots the five arrows that make Amant his vassal.
The quest to obtain the rose thus begins when Amors has completed his
hunt of Amant and claimed his quarry.

Jean's recognition of the link between desire and representation is
apparent in the Amant's retelling of the Pygmalion story immediately
before he penetrates the tower and inseminates the rose. Pygmalion is the
thematic counterpart and chiasmic balance of Narcissus. The parallel may
have been suggested by a comparison from the *Metamorphoses* that
Guillaume does not render in describing Narcissus's attraction to the image
in the fountain: the remarkable beauty of the image holds him like marble
statuary ("ut a Pario formatum marmore signum" [3.419]). Critics emphasize Jean's divergence from the Pygmalion story in the *Metamorphoses*. Peter
Allen observes that Jean amplifies his source by adding ornamental details
and giving Pygmalion "a good deal of depth and self-consciousness."[22]
Within the imaginative economy of the *Rose*, the story is equally striking
for its realization of the Narcissus story—that is, for the extent to which
Guillaume's paradigm of desire is both a source and limit in Jean's invention
of a poetic double.

The parallels begin with a significant troping of desire and representation.
If Guillaume's version of the Narcissus story reveals the origin of desire in
representation, Jean plots the origin of representation in Pygmalion's solipsistic desire to show his aesthetic power and secure reputation for himself:
"Por son grant engin esprouver, / [Car onc de li nus ne l'ot mieudre, /
Ausinc cum por grans los aquieudre]" ("[to] prove his skill (for no one was
better than he) and also gain him great renown" [20822–24]).[23] His demand
for fame is ironically realized in the predicament of his impossible love: "Il
n'est nus qui parler en oie / Qui trop merveillier ne s'en doie" ("There is
no one who heard of it who should not be thunderstruck" [20855–56]). Just
as the Narcissus story delays yet fulfills Cupid's taking of Amant, so the
Pygmalion story interposes itself in Jean's main narrative as Venus notches

her arrow and prepares to fire it toward the narrow aperture in the tower that symbolizes and contains the image of Amant's desire. When she launches the arrow after the story is finished, Amant begins his final movement toward consummation, much as Cupid's shooting the five golden arrows begins his career earlier as a lover. Pygmalion's creation of the ivory statue is an imitation of Nature's creation of the human body and the parallel construction of the pillars and opening in the tower. His love for the statue elicits a specific comparison between him and Narcissus (20876–88) that shows the structural mirroring of the episodes.[24]

Pygmalion mentions Narcissus by way of trying to exculpate himself. Narcissus is Pygmalion's textual proof that, however strange his own passion, others have loved more foolishly. The difference for Pygmalion resides in the practicalities of his desire. Narcissus, he says, loved the face seen in the fountain but could not embrace the shadow ("son ombre embracier" [20879]) that constituted its substance. He, by contrast, enjoys physical pleasure and possession: "quant je vuel, a ceste vois, / Et la prens et acole et baise / Si en souffre miex ma mesaise" ("when I wish, I go to this image and take it, embrace it, and kiss it; I can thus better endure my torment" [20884–86]). Surely, part of Jean's satiric purpose is furthered by Pygmalion's moral and spiritual blindness in this claim and by his subsequent remark that other women are loved just as futilely in many countries, with only the element of hope distinguishing courtly service from his literal idolatry. Yet Pygmalion reveals the persistence of desire even as he asserts some measure of satisfaction. Holding, embracing, and kissing are a stage in the definition of love that Raison parodies in her dismissal of Andreas Capellanus (4377–84); they have the Ovidian goal of mutual carnal pleasure ("por eus charnelment aisier" [4384]). Pygmalion and Amant are on the same path that Capellanus charts—a journey beginning with sight and thought, moving to embraces, and ending in sexual consummation. The "noveles rages" that seizes lovers in Narcissus's impossible love recurs in Pygmalion's obsession, his care in dressing the statue, and the songs and mock-liturgical love rituals he performs for it. Guillaume mentions the possibility of bedding one's mistress in the garden of Deduit, but Pygmalion acts on it fully: "Puis la rembrace et si la couche / Entre ses bras, dedens sa couche, / Et puis la baise et si l'acole" ("Then he took her in his arms again and laid her down on his bed and embraced her and kissed her again and again" [21059–61]).

Jean illustrates the impossibility of Pygmalion's desire in a conscious reenactment of Narcissus's misperception in Guillaume's story. Pygmalion holds the statue, unsure whether it is alive or dead:

Sovelment as mains la detaste,
Et croit, aussi cum se fust paste,

Que ce soit sa char qui li fuie,
Mes c'est sa main qu'il y apuie.
(20927–30)

[Softly he took her in his hands; he thought that she was like putty, that the flesh gave way under his touch, but it was only his hand which pressed her.]

Pygmalion enjoys a fantasy of possession that overcomes the imagined disdain and indifference of the statue, who symbolizes the courtly mistress toward whom lovers mobilize appetite and "esperance." Touch rather than sight is his medium of projection: the erotic gaze is made tactile. What Jean shows in the shaping pressure of the artist's hand against the unyielding ivory is the circularity of desire, which succeeds only in registering its own demands on itself. Pygmalion is the author and reader of his body's natural signs. Far from surpassing Narcissus, Pygmalion does not even reach his tragic recognition, and he continues to believe that the statue mistakenly thinks that she is made of ivory. His predicament is finally resolved not by will or futile service but through Venus's intervention in response to his prayer at a feast: "Et tu, qui dame es de ce temple, / Sainte Venus, de grace m'emple" ("And you, Saint Venus, who are the lady of this temple, fill me with grace" [21085–86]). The soul that Venus sends to the image (21117) merely corresponds in a parodic incarnation to Amant's demand; it is the erotic infusion of his wish into the lifeless image that otherwise sends back echoes of his desire.

Venus's intervention sets events in motion that suggest what Jean can and cannot invent from Guillaume's formulation of desire. Returning home to find the animated image, Pygmalion fears, first of all, that a ghost or demon has been placed inside the statue. His inspection of her nude body ("sa char nue" [21134]) tells him nothing decisive, nor does the throbbing pulse that now signals the circulation of her blood (21137–39) rather than the reflected pressure of his hand. He is convinced, rather, when she speaks back to him as "vostre amie" (21155), the erotic other who chooses to accept his demand and thereby requires not just his acceptance of her but his confirmation of the desire she now signifies: "Preste de vostre compaignie / Recevoir, e m'amor vous offer, / S'il vous plest recevoir tel offer" (21567–68). Kevin Brownlee observes that the animated statue reintroduces direct reference and signification into language after the characters in Jean's continuation had rendered language duplicitous.[25] Her lexicon, though, as Roger Dragonetti notes, is an echo of Pygmalion's speech.[26] Her acceptance of Pygmalion as a lover shows that Guillaume's earlier, cryptic moralization of the Narcissus episode, warning women not to neglect their suitors (1507–1510), has been absorbed by inert matter brought to life. Her reassurance leads to an erotic reciprocity that recalls Ovid's model of mutual satisfaction between lovers and finds rhetorical expression in the repetition of French compounds of –*entre*: "s'entrefacent" ("make for each other" [21167]), "s'entrebracent" ("embrace one another" [21168]), "s'entrebaisent" ("kiss each other" [21169]), "s'entr'aiment" ("love each other" [21170]). Such reciprocity has implications for the ending of the poem and for the idealization of friendship that many readers see as the moral frame of the poem.[27] At the same time, the concord of wills that the two lovers achieve proves the starting point for a mythological history of desire miscarried into death by Adonis and Mirra, who are the descendants of Pygmalion and the speaking but unnamed Galatea. Venus, as Marc Pelen observes, is ineffective in defending her votaries.[28]

Defining Love

The stories of Narcissus and Pygmalion bracket the *Roman de la Rose* and provide structural parallels, respectively, for the beginning and consummation of Amant's desire. The most extensive definition of love comes in Amant's dialogue with the allegorical figure of Raison. Raison is a vital link between the two parts of the poem, forecasting its development and turning back to Guillaume, as Alan Gunn points out.[29] She offers the lover a *remedia amoris* after he is driven away in his first attempt to possess the rose, and she returns, in a greatly amplified role, as the first figure in Jean's continuation. She is mentioned finally in the consummation scene where Amant pointedly excludes her from the list of "bienfaitors" ("benefactors" [21747]) who have helped him to possess the rose. The place of Raison in the thematic and conceptual structure of the *Rose* has been a major point of debate in interpretations of the poem. At issue for most critics is whether Raison offers an absolute moral standard for assessing the lover's conduct or whether her remedy for his anguish proves contradictory, impossible, or even irrelevant.[30]

Raison's account of love catalogues different possibilities of appetite and attachment. Its informing structure is the three-fold distinction among virtuous, utilitarian, and pleasurable friendship derived from Aristotle and Cicero and promulgated by medieval writers like Aelred of Rievaulx and Heloise, both of them sources for Jean. Raison's exposition also prepares for the Ovidian tactics later espoused by Ami and La Vielle as well as the metaphysical accounts given by Nature and Genius. Her long speech nonetheless makes a dramatic and highly problematic turn as Raison offers herself as the suitable "amie" for Amant. This gesture reflects not just an apparent clash of meaning between literal and allegorical levels but a profound questioning of the extent to which desire can be rationalized.

The first entry in Raison's catalogue of love's varieties is a rhetorical figure rather than a proper definition. In a long passage of amplification,

Raison describes love through repeated antithesis: "Amors, ce est paiz haïneuse, / Amors est haine amoreuse. . ." (4293–94). As Regalado notes, the technique anticipates the principle of definition by contraries at the end of the poem (21573–82).[31] However apt it may be as a description of love's ambivalence, Raison's rhetorical approach succeeds in the narrative merely in confusing Amant. Susan Stakel observes further, "The description of love and the lover's boggled response at the beginning of Raison's lecture lay the groundwork for continued misunderstanding."[32] Amant asks for a formal definition by means of clarification ("Prier vous veil au defenir" [4373]). Raison turns accordingly to the celebrated definition offered by Andreas Capellanus at the beginning of his *De amore*, and she gives a richly nuanced paraphrase:

> Amors, se bien sui apensee,
> C'est maladie de pensee
> Entre deus persones anexes,
> Franches entr' eus, de divers sexes,
> Venans as gens par ardor nee,
> Par avision desordonee,
> Por eus acoler et baisier
> Et por eus charnelment aisier.
>   (4377–84)

[Love, if I think right, is a sickness of thought that takes places between two persons of different sex when they are in close proximity and open to each other. It arises among people from the burning desire, born of disordinate glances, to embrace and kiss each other and to have the solace of one another's body.]

Raison's definition reads and interprets as well as translates Andreas. She follows Andreas in identifying the genus of love as an inborn suffering: "maladie de pensee" captures the interior experience expressed by the corresponding Latin phrase "passio quaedam innata."[33] Andreas stipulates, however, that the internal power of love over the subject is a response to the beauty perceived in the object of his desire. The malady, he says, proceeds from sight and excessive contemplation of the external, sensuous form of the beloved: "passio. . .procedens ex visione et immoderata cogitatione formae alterius sexus." The lover is the desiring subject acting on his own will, moved decisively by the image he sees and contemplates ("ob quam aliquis super omnia cupit"). He is effectively in the same position as Narcissus at the fountain in Guillaume's description. His material means is the embrace of the other, and the end he desires is sexual consummation proceeding from a shared volition with her ("cupit. . .et omnia de utriusque voluntate in ipsius amplexu amoris praecepta compleri"). The mystery of Andreas's definition, as we noted earlier, lies in the shift from the lover's interior obsession with the image of beauty to the common wish for physical pleasure.[34] Raison shifts Andreas's idea of reciprocity forward in the definition so that from the beginning desire is shared by men and women close and open to each other ("persones annexes / Franches entr' eus"). She treats vision in terms of its cognitive and moral effect on the couple ("avision desordonee"). In a formal sense, then, she transforms the specific difference of Andreas's definition, those features that characterize the indwelling suffering of love and complete the definition. The love born of desire and excessive thought joins two lovers and prepares, as we shall see, for the suggestion in the final scene of the poem that the rose responds in some measure to Amant's demands.

Raison makes a further change in Andreas's definition by glossing the final cause of love. Like Ovid, Andreas makes sexual consummation the goal of a lover's internal suffering and his obsessive reflection on the object of desire. He euphemistically phrases the goal as realizing all the commands of love in a mutual embrace ("in ipsius amplexu amoris praecepta compleri"). Raison, whose literalism will supposedly offend Amant when she calls body parts by their proper names, states the aim of love more concretely than does Andreas—"por eus charnelment aisier." She then goes on to assert that the purpose of such love is pleasure ("deliter" [4388]) rather than progeny. In this way, Raison aligns love with the friendship of pleasure that Aristotle and Cicero see as characteristic of youths rather than mature citizens.[35] She frames love as concupiscence and brings out semantic associations that may be already present in the language Andreas chooses.[36] At the same time, Raison anticipates the speeches by Nature and Genius near the end of the poem, which argue the need for procreation and fecundity as the rationale for sexual appetite and implicitly condemn Amant's sterile pursuit of pleasure.

In the second part of her discourse, Raison describes other species of love that differ from Amant's hedonism and covetousness. Each represents an impossible alternative. She fashions Ciceronian friendship ("Amitié") as a form of shared goodwill and charity: "C'est bonne volenté commune / De gens entr'eus sans demorance / Selon la lor bonne voillance" (4686–88). Though Cicero posits moral virtue as the end of true friendship, Raison emphasizes the stability of mutual trust and contrasts it with love governed by Fortune, which is a form of permanent alienation and anxiety (5315–5319).[37] When Amant protests that the classical exemplars are few and unmatchable, she offers a broader version of charity than heroic friendship: "Qu'il aint en generalité / Et laist especialité" ("He must love generally and leave particular loves" [5443–44]). Raison insists that she is merely restating love of friendship rather than describing another species altogether ("Autre? Non pas, mes cel meïmes" [5439]), though her subsequent injunction to act toward others as you would have them act toward you (5451–52) has little to do with elite friendship in antiquity. Regardless of how she combines Christian and classical ideals, her formulation remains the opposite from what Amant seeks. His quest is precisely for "especial-ité," the single bud chosen from the rosebush shown by the crystals in the mirror of Narcissus. The rose does not stand, as Raison would make it, for the class of roses or love objects in general; rather, it is the sign that makes desire visible and puts it in circulation.

The final species of love that Raison offers proves no more feasible than the others.[38] She describes "amor naturel" (5763), which has as its aim the preser-vation of a likeness of the self "par voie d'engendreüre / Ou par cure de nor-reture" (5773–74). Such love, Raison points out, is beyond judgments of virtue or vice ("N'a los ne blame ne merite" [5778]), and so implicitly its acts are beyond moral reflection. Augustine, as we have seen in chapter 1, makes the instinct to nourish a form of desire that signifies providence. Raison places the origin of natural love in the intermediary power of Nature, and she con-trasts its moral neutrality with Amant's "fole emprise" (5791) of pleasurable love alone. At the end of the poem, Jean will use natural love to frame his moral and satiric aim through the speeches of Nature and Genius. Nature will present the instinct to engender likenesses of the self as a desperate, frenzied effort to preserve the species against time and death. Genius will treat Amant's love based on pleasure as a form of nonproductive sodomy.[39]

At the end of her catalogue of loves, Raison takes the unlikely step of offering herself as Amant's lover, his courtly "amie." The apparent contra-diction between literal and allegorical levels generates a paradox that oper-ates both inside the poem and in the moral framework that readers use to interpret the *Rose*: what would it mean for Raison to be Amant's lover, and what kind of pleasure might she offer? Passion in most classical and medieval formulations is the diametrical opposite of reason, and only in mankind do the two operate simultaneously. Raison's phrasing of her offer refers obliquely to God's decision in Genesis 2:18 to create woman as a helpmate to man: "Ne por ice ne vuel je mie / Que tu demores sans amie" ("Nevertheless I don't want you to live without a friend" [5795–96]). Surely, the most startling implication is the disclosure of her affect. Raison identifies sympathetically with Amant's suffering, and she directs her will ("vuel") to providing a remedy—a literal solution to the metaphorical mal-ady of love sickness. She appraises herself as a fit object of attraction among the courtly personnel of Deduit's garden, asserting her beauty and her superior lineage as the daughter of God. She hints, too, at more menacing emotions by reminding Amant of Echo's vengeance when Narcissus rejected her love (5833–38). She thus reverses the warning to reluctant women that Guillaume earlier makes the lesson of the Narcissus story.

Raison promises Amant a repletion not offered by any of the other figures in the garden. Loving her brings the condition that later courtly poets, Chaucer among them, will describe as "suffisaunce." She says:

> Si vuel t'amie devenir;
> Se ja te vues a moi tenir,
> Ses tu que m'amor te vaudra?
> Tant que jamés ne te faudra
> Nulle cose qui te conviengne
> Por mescheance qui t'aviengne.
> (5801–5806)

[I want to become your friend, and if you wish to hold to me, do you know what my love will be worth to you? So much that you will never lack anything you need, no matter what misfortune comes to you.]

Raison promises, then, a love beyond mutability, a possession ("a moi tenir") not subject to Fortune. Loving Raison means loving the mean, and such love presumably entails pleasure experienced in the licit pursuit ("qui te conviengne") of progeny and virtue. The men Raison names as her lovers are philosophers—Socrates, Heraclitus, and Diogenes—who transcend changes in worldly fortune. As Gérard Paré suggests, Jean may have in mind Heloise's assertion in the *Historia calamitatum* that philosophy is a way of life and not just a speculative activity.[40] The love she offers likewise requires Amant to transform internally so that he becomes immune to Fortune's changes. The three demands that Raison makes of Amant—love her, despise Amors, have no trust in Fortune—are quickly reduced to the first alone, but for all practical purposes the first subsumes the other two. When Amant rejects her, he asserts his continuing fealty to Amors, and the scope of his rejection reveals the persistance of Guillaume's formulation of desire. Amant concedes that he may be "fol" (7207, 7211), but he affirms his willful commitment to the pleasure of his thoughts: "je ne vuel aillors penser / Qu'a la rose ou sont mi penser" (7221–22). Directed to the rose, his thoughts ("mi penser") signify his solipsistic desire. Amant recognizes that the sufficiency Raison offers him comes at the cost of transforming desire into practice, the constancy of moderated pleasure. Her love is an art of self-mastery that trades the mystery of desire for the domestication of passion. At the end of Raison's discourse, Amant accepts the role of Narcissus that she threatens at the beginning as the vengeful alternative to loving her.

Amant's rejection of Raison shows a dimension of Guillaume's story that resists Jean's rewriting. The episodes that follow it represent, however, Jean's thorough-going resituation of Guillaume's courtly eros. The figure of Ami who appears immediately after Raison withdraws brings the tactics of seduction as an alternate remedy to Amant's suffering. Ami's teaching and the parallel instruction that La Vielle gives Bel Acuel draw heavily on Ovid's *Ars amatoria*, but in each instance they shift the ground of erotic attachment. As Ami retails Ovid's advice about capturing a lover, Amant realizes that his doctrine goes beyond Ovid's theme of Protean improvisation to embrace an ethics of deceit. Urged to act with "traïson" ("treason") against Malebouche and other obstacles and to do whatever he thinks will please Bel Acuel and gain him entry to the rose, Amant initially resists: "Nulz honz, s'il n'est faus ypocrites, / Ne feroit ceste dÿablie; / Onc ne fu grignor establie" ("No man who was not a false hypocrite would commit such deviltry. No greater wickedness was ever started" [7796–98]). Told that he risks losing access to Bel Acuel, he quickly pledges himself to Ami's program of deception: "Compainz, a ce consel m'acort, / Je n'istrai mes de cest acort" ("Companion, I agree to this advice, and I shall never desert my agreement" [7877–78]).

Jean thus portrays Amant as abandoning the idealization of desire and the social forms that structure erotic values and conduct. By accepting deceit as a licit means, Amant betrays and impoverishes desire. He accepts expediency, compromises himself as a moral agent, and undermines eros as a project endowed with significance. In the narrative of the *Rose*, his acceptance prepares the way for Fausemblant and Abstinence Contrainte, two figures who embody deceit and add the element of malice to Ami's practical instructions for the lover's dissembling. These two join the ranks of Love's army as it assaults the castle of Jalousie, where Bel Acuel and the rose are immured. Amors's laconic acceptance of the pair—"Or soit" (10493)—repeats Amant's rapid concession to Ami's deceit, and when the barons seek confirmation of Fausemblant's acceptance, they use the same contractural language as Amant does earlier: "C'est nostre acort, c'est nostre otroi" ("That is our agreement, our compact" [10927]).

Inside the castle, La Vielle undertakes a comparable resituating of Guillaume's theme, when she learns that Malebouche has been killed and that she is not under threat of denunciation for aiding Fausemblant and Amant. She returns to Bel Acuel, the male symbol of the rose's own inclination to accept Amant's love, with a chaplet that Amant has given her for him. The chaplet represents Amant's invitation for the rose to participate in the play of courtly eros, and his sending it to Bel Acuel is a form of demand. The exchange between Bel Acuel and La Vielle is a sustained performance of the deceit that Ami and Fausemblant have introduced into the story. Bel Acuel, already anticipating La Vielle's lesson, pretends not to be particularly interested in Amant's gift. Meanwhile, La Vielle changes quickly from guardian to accomplice and discloses her experience as a form of vengeance on age and neglect: "Autrement ne m'en puis venchier / Que par aprendre ma doctrine" ("I have no other way to avenge myself than by teaching my doctrine" [12878–79]). If Raison surprisingly discloses an erotic attachment behind her exhortation to observe the mean, La Vieille reveals an anti-eros in her preparation of Bel Acuel for a career in manipulating love.

La Vieille begins by overturning the commandments that Amors gives Amant in Guillaume's portion of the *Rose*. Rejecting generosity and fidelity, she describes Amors's commandments as an untruthful and unreliable inscription. The commandments, she says, do not provide a lover a way of knowing love ("Mes gart qu'Amors a li nel sache" [13014]): "Cest faus texte, c'est fauce lettre" ("It is a false text, false in the letter" [13032]). The advice she gives reprises Ovid's advice to women in book 3 of the *Ars amatoria*, but she replaces Ovid's anticipation of pleasure with the mechanics of satisfying appetite. In the *Ars amatoria*, Ovid insists that love is play (*lusus*) and that it entails no crime. La Vieille offers Bel Acuel a starkly different appraisal of love's domain. Lovers, she says, are continually mobile and unstable (13141–42). Love is a succession of betrayals by men, who act indiscriminately on their pleasure: "Briement tuit les lobent et trichent, / Tant sont ribaut, par tout se fichent" ("Briefly, all men betray and deceive women; all are sensualists, taking their pleasure anywhere" [13265–66]). From male mutability and betrayal, she, like Ami, derives an ethics of deceit. La Vieille frames it as a moral compensation by which women can regulate their exchange value as objects circulating in the economy of male appetite.

La Vieille offers Bel Acuel a further rationale that claims a radical freedom but ends by describing the tyranny of love. Women, she proclaims, are born free ("franches nees" [13875]), and only positive law has subsequently placed constraints on them. In the imaginary moment before laws and history, Nature created men and women in an erotic circulation without constraints or singular objectives:

> Ains nous a fait, biau fix, n'en doutes,
> Toutes por touz et touz por toutes,
> Chascune por chascun commune
> Et commun chascun por chascune. . . .
> (13885–88)

[Instead, fair son, never doubt that she has made us all women for all men and all men for all women, each woman common to every man and every man common to each woman.]

All women, she reiterates, have a "naturel entencion" ("natural inclination" [13962]) willingly to seek whatever ways they can to possess "franchise" (13965). The "franchise"—freedom, liberty—that La Vielle extolls for women, however, merely trades compulsion for constraint. Jean indicates what this exchange entails by shifting the scale of the warrants for La Vielle's claims. She evokes Nature and plays with the grammatical differences of male and female endings in the passage above in order to make the point that the distinctions of language, like those of positive law, cover over the fundamental identity of human appetite. As she develops her case for freedom, La Vielle bases her claim in the world of domestic animals. Horses, cattle, and sheep—all seek and welcome all mates. The lesson she draws is phrased in a conscious verbal echo of the earlier appeal to Nature: "Aussi est il, biau fis, par m'ame, / De tout homme et du toute fame / Quant a naturel apetit" ("By my soul, fair son, it is thus with every man and every woman as far as natural appetite goes" [14087–89]). The turn to natural law, however, proves as constraining as laws and human conventions that impinge on erotic franchise. The imperative that works through the divisions of gender and species and that justifies the freedom of lovers to seek each other is pleasure. La Vielle describes its power in a language that reveals the indwelling problem of natural appetite: "Ainsi Nature nous justise, / Qui nos cuers a delit atise" ("Thus Nature regulates us by inciting our hearts to pleasure" [14157–58]). The freedom granted by natural appetite, in other words, is a form for exercising governance ("nature nous justise").

The freedom that La Vielle urges on Bel Acuel and the rose is part of her rhetorical seduction. It is premised on natural determinism, the condition of being an embodied, sensuous creature. She thus comes in her instruction to the same end that Raison reaches with Amant: *delit* is a structural feature of erotic attraction and of the ways of talking about attraction. But Raison places natural appetite in a neutral category beyond judgments of virtue and vice, while La Vielle makes it a feature that conditions a lover's social and moral action in securing pleasure. In later parts of the poem, Jean will render this description even more extreme. In the problematic episodes of Nature's confession and Genius's sermon, natural appetite operates against a background of profound bleakness. For Nature, it is the force that guarantees the preservation of the species (but not individuals) against death. Ovid's metaphor of the lover as hunter and Guillaume's troping of Ovid in Amors's pursuit of Amant reemerge grimly in Nature's speech as the "trop fiere chace" ("very cruel hunt" [15947]) where Death exterminates the living creatures who flee desperately before her across the domain of time. In Genius's sermon, those who neglect the productive duties that enable such flight and temporary escape are condemned to spiritual abandonment.

Approaching the Rose

As soon as he sees the rosebush in the mirror of Narcissus, Amant resolves to pluck at least one of the buds (1631–32)—a project that immediately narrows to a single rose invested with value by the lover (1655–58). *Cueillir la rose* is Guillaume de Lorris's locution for possession and sexual intercourse, and Jean de Meun uses it knowingly as a euphemism when he later describes his continuation of the poem: "enseignai la maniere du chastel prendre et de la rose cueillir" ("I taught the way to take the castle and pluck the rose").[41] Guillaume makes it clear that in his plan of composition Amant will take the castle where Jalousie has immured Bel Acuel and the rose. At the end of the poem, Jean describes the assault in lurid, phallic circumlocution as Venus's penetration of the castle-sanctuary and Amant's pilgrimage to its shrine. But if the outcome of the poem is already forecast by its authors and by other medieval writers who intervene in the text as well, the narrative that carries Amant toward consummation is nonetheless structured by repetition and delay. Amant makes three approaches to the rose before he finally possesses it. However much they may differ in their formulations of love, Guillaume and Jean jointly exploit the motif of Amant's approach as a vehicle to chart the disclosure and displacement of desire.

Amant's first approach to the rose follows immediately on Amors's commandments, whose promulgation and refinement is the ideological project that Guillaume's poem undertakes (2057–76). The commandments aim to fashion the lover socially as a courtly subject and individually as an attractive prospect in love. Amors describes the psychological experience of love as perpetual absence ("Amans n'avra ja ce qu'il quiert" [2419]), mitigated only by hope and the consolatory power of sweet thoughts, speech, and looks. Its characteristic state is anxiety and self-doubt. Amant's approach builds directly on this account in portraying the disclosure of desire. Facing the hedge surrounding the rosebush, Amant contemplates penetrating the barrier but hesitates lest he incur blame. He recognizes that moving toward the roses could be seen as wanting to steal them: "Mes assés tost peust l'en penser / Que les rosiers vousisse embler" (2785–86). His hesitation as a courtly subject is a denial of his desire as an erotic agent. When Bel Acuel guides him through the barrier to experience the pleasure of smelling the rose, his approach allows the desire he has supressed to resurface, if only hypothetically: "Si sachiés que mout m'agrea / Dont je me poi si pres remaindre / Que au bouton peüsse ataindre" ("I tell you that I was overjoyed at being able to remain so near that I might have attained the rose" [2820–22]).

Guillaume complicates the motif of approach when Bel Acuel presents Amant a leaf whose value lies in its nearness to the bud ("pres ot esté nee" [2878]). Here metonymy brings the full reference of the sign into view, as Amant poses the transgressive demand that Bel Acuel give him possession of the bud. He does so by addressing Bel Acuel literally as the feature of a courtly mistress that holds the power to remedy a lover's pain: "Ja les dolors n'en seront traites / Se le bouton ne me bailliés" ("their pain will never cease if you do not give me the rosebud" [2902–2903]). Bel Acuel's rejection is phrased as a courtly rebuff: "Vilains estes du demander" ("you are base to ask it" [2915]). Amant is guilty, then, of transgressing Amors's first commandment to avoid villainy (2077–80). The surprise appearance of Dangier, who has overheard the exchange, decisively transfers the hesitations in Amant's erotic demand to the rose. Lover and beloved thus move in parallel but opposite directions. Amant's approach, though punctuated with hesitation, ends with the demand of possession and the disclosure of desire. The rose's reception of Amant and her metonymic concession of the leaf end with her resistance in the churlish form of Dangier, who drives off Amant and Bel Acuel.

Amant makes his second approach to the rose through a combination of Ami's Ovidian advice to flatter Dangier and the intervention of Franchise and Pitié, who persuade Dangier to act courteously. Reunited with Bel Acuel, Amant encounters a rose grown somewhat larger to symbolize both physical maturity and a greater willingness to accept the lover—an embodied and intending agent responding to the erotic demand.[42] Amant's demand on this occasion is to kiss the rose. Bel Acuel's initial refusal is motivated externally by the allegorical figure Chastaé. Chastity's constraint follows, however, from Bel Acuel's recognition of what the kiss signifies in a chain of metonymic substitution. He tells Amant, "Et sachiés bien, cui l'en otroie / Le baisier, qu'il a de la proie / Le plus bel et le plus avenant" ("Know well that he to whom one grants a kiss has the best, most pleasing part of his prize" [3405–3407]). The kiss is a deposit, he says, for claiming what remains ("erres du remanant" [3408]) in the amatory sequence of wish, seduction, and fulfillment. Amant secures the kiss not by persuading Bel Acuel himself but through Venus's intervention. Venus represents Amant to Bel Acuel as the courtly subject that Amors has formed and warms Bel Acuel with her torch. Guillaume's turn to Venus as the intermediary between Amant and Bel Acuel presents his own form of textual disclosure, for it tacitly acknowledges the impossibility of his own imaginary order. Beneath courtesy lies desire; beneath a literature of courtesy lies a narrator's demand, the reward that a woman reader ("la bele")— Guillaume's or Amant's?—can bestow better than any other when she wishes (3505–3510).[43] At the point where Amant makes his symbolic conquest by kissing the rose, courtly persuasion reaches an impasse, and the sensuous demands of the body prevail: "Bel Acuel si senti l'aer / Du brandon" ("Fair Welcoming. . .felt the breath of Venus's torch" [3473–74).

Jean stages the same form of approach but frames a different view of desire in his continuation of the poem. Amant makes his third approach after La Vielle has finished her instruction of Bel Acuel, which overturns Amors's commandments. Amant is aided by Amors and his barons in assaulting the castle where Jalousie has confined Bel Acuel and the rose, but La Vielle's betrayal in leaving the back gate unsecured allows Amant to rejoin Bel Acuel. Bel Acuel seemingly grants full access: "se j'ai chose qui vous plese, / Bien vuel que vous en aiés ese" ("if I have anything that may please you, I certainly want you to have its comfort" [14797–98]). His offer is an eroticized form of the *consensio* ("agreement") that Cicero places at the foundation of friendship and that Capellanus treats as the shared volition of lovers. Bel Acuel assumes further that Amant acts out of the same motives as he ("Par bien et par honor, cum gié" [14800]).

Amant describes the moment, however, as erotic repletion and the approach to fulfillment: "Lors m'avançai por les mains tendre / A la rose que tant desir, / Por acomplir tout mon desir" ("Then I advanced to stretch out my hands toward the rose that I long for so greatly, in order to fill my whole desire" [14809–14810]). Stretching out his hands ("les mains tendre"), Amant reaches toward the possession that eludes him in the first approach but returns now as a verbal echo ("au bouton peüsse ataindre" [2822]). The rime riche of "desir" / "desir" rhetorically connects the intending subject and the condition of desire. The rose he approaches becomes, by substitution, the figure for his erotic demand—"tout mon desir." After Dangier, Honte, and Poor restrain his outstretched hand, they will protest that Amant has misconstrued Bel Acuel's offer ("Malement entendre savés" [14848]) and understood it in a simple sense. They give Amant their own literal gloss on Bel Acuel's speech: "Il ne vous offri pas la rose" ("He never offered you the rose" [14867]). Amant's description invites us to read it for the solipsism that Guillaume has already anticipated and that Jean now names literally by his repetition: "I desire my desire."

In Amant's final, successful approach, Jean exploits his insight that the rose is a complex sign for Amant's desire, a symptom rather than a symbol of the internal condition which operates independently from its ostensible object. Readers of the poem have long remarked Jean's graphic description of the consummation scene. Venus shoots her burning arrow toward the tower and into the reliquary where an image is situated between two pillars, which represent a young girl's body and genitalia. Amant's approach to the rose is figured as a pilgrimage; his sack and pilgrim's staff symbolize his testicles and phallus. Jean's poetic invention here is to rewrite Amant's approach and insemination not as the narrative culmination that Guillaume originally envisioned but as a retrospect that only he can supply as the poetic successor. Just as he delays the release of Venus's arrow to tell the Pygmalion story, so he retards Amant's struggling entry into the sanctuary and the beloved's body. In the process, he reveals that plucking the rose, the last action of the dream, has been the starting point of an erotic career. Just as Jean has already succeeded Guillaume when Amors makes his prophecy, so the taking of the rose has already been surpassed by other exploits by the time Amant recounts his conquest.

Celebrating his phallic staff, Amant describes its usefulness on his journeys to remote places: "je le boute / Es fosses ou je ne voi goute / Aussi cum por les gués tenter" ("I put it into the ditches where I can see nothing, to see if they can be forded" [21401–21403]). He exults in his capacities to test the fords and explore the concave spaces that represent the hidden, inner surfaces of the female body: "Tant sai bien les gués essoier, / Et fier par rives et par fons" ("so well do I know how to test the fords and probe the banks and brooks" [21406–21407]). He claims nonetheless to leave wide roads to other travelers and follow smaller paths ("les jolives senteletes" [21432]) in his metaphorical journeys. Amant's digression ends with an Ovidian consideration of older women—old roads ("Viex chemins" [21436])—as lovers whose seduction requires particular craft and young women whose variety requires extensive sampling. In substance, Jean recounts Amant's career as wandering in the Augustinian "land of unlikeness," but to do so he turns the narrative frame of Augustinian retrospect to the service of an erotic picaresque.

In the composite story of the *Rose*, Amant's wandering is the reverse image of his erotic approaches, just as digression is the generic counter to narrative resolution. By inserting the errant narrator into the final, dilatory movement of the poem, Jean frames the consummation of Amant's desire by its posthistory. As in Amors's prophecy of succession, he draws attention to the dislocated narrative phase that lies between Amant's past actions as a character and his present account as a narrator. This retrospective framing is an authorial strategy for dealing with the erotic topic that Guillaume establishes through the Narcissus myth and begins to analyze in Raison's first encounter with Amant. Rather than dismiss Guillaume, Jean takes him seriously as a theorist of erotics who has posed a specific challenge to self-understanding and moral life by asking what it is we seek in an object of desire. This is, as Jean recognizes, a question that does not cease, though it may be reframed, anatomized, and debated. Jean's rewriting amplifies the scope and probes the complexities of Guillaume's question. Prefacing the consummation that Guillaume promised by disclosing the consequences that follow from it, Jean imagines for himself an authorial position that allows him to show the persistent circulation of desire in the overlapping spheres of love and writing.

CHAPTER 6

"SIMULACRA NOSTRA": THE PROBLEM OF
DESIRE IN DANTE'S *VITA NUOVA*

Dante's *Vita nuova* is a work of sustained erotic and poetic revision.
Using the retrospect of Augustine's conversion narrative, Dante
transcribes the meaning ("sentenzia"), if not the actual words, of an imagined
text located under the rubric "Incipit vita nuova"in his metaphoric book of
memory.[1] As compiler, commentator, and narrator, he omits fictional text
above the rubric, which is scant or illegible or both ("poco si potrebbe leg-
gere"), as well as writing found below it, which supposedly has no bearing
on his master narrative of reform and renovation. The narrative trajectory
that Dante follows as the protagonist of his *libello* moves through selected
encounters with Beatrice and her avatars and onwards to Beatrice's sudden
yet foretold death and thereafter to Dante's efforts not just to mourn but to
understand his loss. As in Augustine, key events proleptically anticipate a
future that is already fixed.[2] Advancing through these stages, Dante ostensibly leaves behind an earthly attachment based on his demands as a lover
and comes to embrace a disinterested and objectified spiritual love that
exists beyond yet informs and makes intelligible his individual experience.

Inscribed within this narrative of erotic conversion is a poetic movement through internal programs of writing and a history of Italian love
lyric. Praise of Beatrice's greeting leads to self-transcending praise of
Beatrice, thence to memory and understanding. At the same time, Dante
adapts the poetry of Guittone d'Arezzo, Guido Guinizelli, and Guido
Cavalcanti and of the earlier Sicilian and Tuscan schools broadly. Nor is
this development strictly linear or chronological. Enrico Gragnani shows
that Guittone influences Dante at several points in his effort to theorize love.
Domenico De Robertis observes that Dante's borrowings from Cavalcanti
concentrate on a specific portion of Cavalcanti's lyric production—the
tragic equation of love and death.[3] Guinizelli's lyric ideology is implicit in

the first poem of the *Vita nuova* yet decisively present in Dante's turn from Cavalcanti to the poetry of praise. As María Rosa Menocal suggests, we might usefully debate whether the erotic or poetic narrative comes first, or whether indeed they may be the same thing after all.[4] Both narratives find provisional closure after Beatrice's death in Dante's promise to write something of her unexampled in the discourse applied to women. This promise originates in another narrative omission—an undescribed wonderful vision (42.1) that balances his first prophetic sight of Beatrice (2.1). The vision moves him to silence and marks the point where the retrospect of the *Vita nuova* ends and the poet presumably speaks in an authorial present tense oriented toward a future of poetic repletion and erotic resolution in Beatrice.

Dante's self-commentary in the *Vita nuova* complements the twin narratives of erotic and poetic conversion. Few great poets have devoted as much effort to controlling the reception and interpretation of their works. Dante's commentary and divisions foreground the performance of interpretation. The poet's material is the "sentenzia" of his memory, a term that designates, as Robert Pogue Harrison notes, both "meaning" and "the principle of narrative coherence that orders the temporal mass of the past and places its events on a linear and teleological trajectory."[5] Dante's first sonnet is a love vision and a hermeneutic puzzle whose true meaning ("verace giudicio") was not understood at the time but is now apparent (3.15). The formal divisions that Dante outlines in his commentary on the poems ostensibly open up their meaning ("aprire la sentenzia" [14.13]) or the author's intention ("aprire lo intendimento" [19.22]), or they disclose the poet's rationale for figurative language ("aprire per prosa" [25.8]). Robert Durling and Richard Martinez see the divisions as counterparts to formal and philosophical order.[6] Steven Botterill notes that they focus on structured content (the rhetorical *forma tractatus*) rather than external form (*forma tractandi*).[7] But as Sherry Roush has persuasively argued, Dante's self-commentary opens up the meaning of his poems not by restricting their significance but by relocating the poems to other textual settings.[8]

These other textual settings hold out the prospect for seeing both what the *Vita nuova* achieves as a revisionary text and what it flees through its revisions. These two aspects, as Antonio D'Andrea remarks, need not imply contradiction but succession—a clarification that emerges from putting the poems into time and discovering what they come to mean in new explanatory contexts.[9] Still, the poetry and interpretive prose differ at several points.[10] Dante's contemporary Cecco Angiolieri famously points out the contradiction in the final sonnet (ch. 41) of the *Vita nuova*.[11] Moreover, poems excluded from the collection, as Teodolinda Barolini notes, "testify to the possibility of an anti-*Vita nuova*, a Cavalcantian *Vita nuova*, whose Beatrice brings not life but death."[12] In this chapter, I want to extend Barolini's observation by arguing that this alternate history goes beyond Cavalcanti, for whom love remained securely, if tragically, in the realm of sensation. In both the *Vita nuova* and the poetry excluded from it, the unresolved and persistent challenge to Dante's master narrative of reform is desire. Giuseppe Mazzotta rightly points out the abiding tension in the *Vita nuova* between the Christological language that underwrites its expectant ending and the workings of poetic imagination, "which in this text comes forth in the shifting forms of memory and desire."[13] The challenge of desire, I shall argue, is made concrete in the *libello* by those figures whom Love names as "simulacra nostra," the women who variously stand-in for Beatrice. These surrogates signify Beatrice as the object of Dante's love, but they also occasion moments of profound crisis early and late in the conversion narrative. Dante's unforeseen attachments to them raise the possibility that, while he waits to write more worthily of her ("più degnamente"), Beatrice may not contain or exhaust the resources of desire.

"Fierissima e importabile passione d'amore"

In his *Trattatello in laude di Dante*, Boccaccio describes eros as a constant in Dante's life: "quasi dallo inizio della sua vita infino all'ultimo della morte, Dante ebbe fierissima e importabile passione d'amore" ("almost from the beginning of his life to the day of his death, Dante was the prey of the fierce and unendurable passion of love").[14] Later, in his appraisal of Dante's strengths and defects of character, Boccaccio transforms this passion from moral incontinence into the vice of lust: "trovò ampissimo luogo la lussuria, e non solamente ne' giovani anni, ma ancora ne' maturi" ("lust found a large place, and not only in his youth but also in his mature years" [172/114]). The sources for these descriptions lie squarely in Dante's poetry and in his exchanges with other poets, which define his themes. However limited they may be in their biographical value, Boccaccio's comments nonetheless offer a historical reading of the poems.[15] In the "Tenzone del duol d'amore," an exchange with Dante da Maiano roughly contemporary with the first sonnet of the *Vita nuova* and therefore part of 'the "fabuloso parlare" (2.10) of youth excluded from the *Vita nuova*, Dante portrays himself as one often in the grip of the pain of love-longing: "e 'l proprio sì disio saver dol, como / di ció sovente, dico, essendo a serra" ("But I desire to understand this suffering precisely, being, as I say, one who is often gripped by it").[16] Cecco Angiolieri says in his response to the last sonnet of the *Vita nuova* that Dante has long been a servant to the God of Love: "lo quali è stato un tu signor antico" ("your lord from of old" [line 4]).

As Boccaccio suggests, desire follows Dante well beyond the anticipated conversion from praise of Beatrice to a new and more worthy project of writing after her death. In the Lisetta poem, to be sure, a young woman is turned away from the figurative tower of will and consent where another lady reigns under the sceptre given by Love.[17] But four different sequences record Dante's attachments after Beatrice's death—to the compassionate lady who sees Dante's sorrow (discussed below), to the "pargoletta," the "giovane," and the "donna pietra."[18] Perhaps a decade after the *Vita nuova*, Dante writes from exile to Cino da Pistoia, who serves as his model for the erotic poet in the illustrious Italian vernacular (*De vulgari eloquentia* 2.2.9). Dante's topic is their continuing subjugation to love: "Perch'io non trovo chi meco ragioni / del signor a cui siete voi ed io" ("Since I find no one here with whom to speak of the Lord to whom you and I are subject").[19] In another exchange, he rebukes Cino for shifting affections from one woman to another but concedes that human will is inadequate to resist love's dictates and so one is constrained to follow the objects of desire as they wax and wane: "e qual che sia 'l piacer ch'ora d'addestra, / seguitar si vien, se l'altro è stanco" ("and whatever the attraction may be that is now leading us, follow we must, if the other is outworn").[20] Opening his poem with the biographical detail that he has been with the God of Love since his ninth year, Dante speaks as the narrator of the *Vita nuova* who, much like the narrator of the *Roman de la Rose*, has strayed far beyond its supposed ending. The letter accompanying his sonnet (Epistola 3) makes the same point. It situates love in the sensitive rather than rational soul and maintains that the soul can move from one passionate attachment to another, remaining the same ("eandem potentiam") while the objects of passion differ not in kind ("specie") but in identity ("numero"): "de passione in passionem, dico, secundum eandem potentiam et obiecta diversa numero sed non specie."[21]

In a final exchange of sonnets, Dante renews his reproof of Cino's wandering affections, which move uncertainly from place to place ("or qua, or là"). Here Cino presents a rationale that resonates significantly against the *Vita nuova*. He rejects both the strategy of the screen ladies who preserve the identity of Beatrice and the program of praise that advances from Beatrice's greeting to Beatrice herself and then to something greater in a new but deferred poetic project. In effect, he challenges the achievements in style and metaphysical conceit that the stilnovisti claim and that the *Vita nuova* consolidates. Exile, the figure for losing Beatrice that Dante evokes in his *libello* from the Book of Lamentations (28.1), is for Cino the very condition of writing and desire. Separated from homeland and his lady, Cino finds in other women the instantiation of a singular beauty located in his beloved: "e s'ho trovato a lui simil vicino, / dett'ho che

questi m'ha lo cor ferito" (but when I've found near me any beauty like to
that one, I've said it was *this* one that wounded my heart."[22] His mutability,
says Cino, is the paradoxical evidence of constancy. For the pleasures he
finds in the erotic particulars of exile all lead back to their source in the
original lady: "ch'un piacer sempre me lega ed involve, / il qual conven
che a simil de beltate / in molte donne sparte mi diletti" ("for it is always
one and the same beauty that binds and trammels me; and this perforce
delights me in whatever is like it in beauty in many different women" (lines
12–14). As Warren Ginsberg points out, Cino enlists medieval ideas about
beauty and the power of analogy here but turns them to different aims:
"This is an argument that does not strive to persuade us it is true, only that
it is witty."[23]

Cino's argument about the one and the many is clearly a theme that
Dante does not embrace. Beatrice may be the source for stimulating virtues
in others, but she remains a singular miracle and so not a source for erotic
and moral emanations. Other women may stand in for her in the narrative
frame of the *Vita nuova*, but none approximates her in kind. At the same
time, desire persists as a moral and poetic issue for Dante, largely in the terms
of Cino's challenge to stilnovism. Dante's last lyric poem is the "mountain
song" dispatched to Florence to announce an erotic entanglement that
incidentally cancels any political threat of his return to the city. The poem
is addressed directly to Love, the figure who appears in the first vision of
the *Vita nuova* to assert his sovereignty over the poet. Here Dante asks
Love, "chi mi scuserà, s'io non so dire / ciò che mi fai sentire? / chi cred-
erà ch'io sia omai sì colto" ("Who will excuse me if I cannot put into
words what you make me feel? Who will believe that I am now so in the
power of another").[24] This sense of capture and constraint ("colto") stems
from the image of a woman, at once beautiful and evil ("com'ella è bella e
ria") which stimulates a desire in the poet that turns against itself and overcomes reason. The "nemica figura" ("hostile image") of the woman holds
sway over the will, and Dante captures its allure in a metaphor of tragic
inevitability: "Ben conosco che va la neve al sole" ("Well I know that it is
snow going to the sun" [line 37]).[25] The language of Dante's canzone
recalls other poems directed to impossible mistresses, such as the *donna
pietra* of an earlier sequence. His isolation in this poem from other women
and "genti accorte"—accomplished readers of the love complaint, an audience that he has broadened from the "trovatori" and redefined imaginatively through the *Vita nuova*—may refer obliquely to Beatrice.[26] Whatever
the identity of the lady, the power and threat of desire arguably remain
undiminished long after the completion of the *Vita nuova*, even as Dante's
reflections on desire deepen into a moral consciousness of his own agency
and the dialectic of will and desire.[27]

"Soave sonno. . .maravigliosa visione"

The first vision that Dante recounts in the *Vita nuova* forecasts the larger trajectory of his book. It restages Dante's first sight of Beatrice at age nine, which impedes the working of his mental faculties and leaves Love as the ruler of his soul ("D'allora innanzi dico che Amore segnoreggiò la mia anima, la quale fu sì tosto a lui disponsata" [2.7]). Precisely nine years after this event, Dante sees Beatrice dressed in white, flanked by two gentle ladies, passing on the street; and she offers him her greeting, which seems to possess all the "terms"—the furthest limits as well as the constitutive language—of his beautitude ("tutti li termini de la beatitudine"). Returning to his room, he experiences a *visione*, a term that Dante the narrator applies to only three events, two of them dreams with the God of Love (chs 3 and 12) and the other Beatrice's undescribed appearance which prompts the suspension of his writing about her (ch. 42).[28]

In the first vision, Love appears joyously in a cloud of fire and speaks to Dante, who understands only the portion where Love claims his lordship: "Ego dominus tuus." He shows a naked figure sleeping in his arms, clad lightly in a crimson cloth, whom Dante recognizes as Beatrice: "Ne le sue braccia mi parea vedere una persona dormire nuda, salvo che involta mi parea in uno drappo sanguigno leggeramente" (3.4). Love holds what seems to be a burning object in one hand, which is the poet's heart. He appears to waken the sleeping figure and through the power of his art and persuasion ("ingegno") forces her to eat the heart, which she consumes hesitantly. Thereafter his happiness changes into weeping, and he gathers the lady into his arms and seems to rise toward heaven. The anguish of this scene is so great that it wakens Dante from his sleep. The sonnet he composes to commemorate the event is the work that presumably introduces him to contemporary writers ("famosi trovatori in quello tempo") and launches his friendship with Cavalcanti.[29] The retrospective narrator of the *libello* remarks that the sonnet attracted many responses and that its meaning, opaque at the time, is now transparent to the most naïve readers. This last assertion, as Gregory B. Stone argues, may undermine more than confirm the idea of a single meaning ("lo verace giudicio" [13.5]) for the vision.[30]

Though Dante surrounds the vision with the theological overtones of the number nine, it is undoubtedly the most erotically charged scene in the *Vita nuova*. Marianne Shapiro describes the chapters following it as "a convalescence from erotic shock" occasioned by the dream.[31] As Robert Pogue Harrison contends, the focus of the scene falls as much on the veil covering Beatrice's nude body as on her body itself. Dante recognizes the sleeping nude as the lady who had given him her greeting. The color symbolism changes from the pure white garment of the street to the crimson veil of the dream vision. Dante retains the materiality of perception even as the function of covering changes. Beatrice's white garment, like her subsequent allegorical veiling in virtue ("vestita d'umilitade" [26.2]) blocks the sight of her body and directs attention elsewhere, to other dimensions of affect and perception.[32] The crimson veil of the dream vision organizes perception and directs it toward the body: "The veil sends the eye through the veil and allows the body to appear as the image figured by the veil itself."[33] By evoking the crimson dress that Beatrice wore when he first saw her at age nine (2.3), Dante locates the origin of desire in the interplay between object and covering. The veil becomes the fetish that provides a mechanism for erotic attachment as well as concealment and semiosis. It obscures the body at the same time that it allows the penetration of sight and the sustained focus of a lover's gaze: "io riguardando molto intentivamente" (3.4).

In poetic terms, Dante draws on the medieval distinction between external covering (*involucrum* or *integumentum*) and internal hidden meaning only to suggest their practical equivalence. He uses the distinction in an early poem to Lippo Pasci dei Bardi that asks the poet to clothe "esta pulcella nuda" (line 13), the accompanying canzone, presumably with music, so that she might become known ("che sia conosciuda" [line 19]).[34] The canzone he refers to by this image begins with a poetic request that essentially duplicates the eroticized scene of the *Vita nuova*, though in seemingly conventional language: "Lo meo servente core / vi raccomandi Amor, [che] vi l'ha dato" ("May Love commend to you my loyal heart— Love who gave it to you").[35] The power of the veil to figure Beatrice's body and call forth Dante's erotic attachment is also suggested in a contrasting scene from the *Vita nuova*. When a young woman associated with Beatrice suddenly dies, Dante can see her body directly as it is framed by attendant women: "lo cui corpo io vidi giacere sanza l'anima in mezzo di molte donne" (8.1). In the first of two sonnets written to honor her, Dante says that his final words are direct and unveiled: "appare manifestamente a chi lo intende" (8.3).

The sonnet Dante writes to memorialize his vision of Beatrice, the first poem recorded in the *Vita nuova*, serves the same function as the veil covering her body. The two *voltae* ending the sonnet depict the same scene as the prose account, though the figure is not nude and Love does not rise toward heaven but goes off weeping. Dante remarks that the poets to whom he sends the sonnet misconstrue it but that now the true meaning is fully clear ("manifestissimo") to the most simple (3.15). Mazzotta points out that their particular misreadings represent broader poetic approaches that Dante rejects.[36] Though mistaken, the poets' responses nonetheless identify the erotic content of the poem. Dante da Maiano offers a medical diagnosis of lovesickness. Cino da Pistoia interprets the crimson veil as protective covering from suffering and construes the lady's eating of the heart as a recognition of love's pain, which the God of Love registers in his weeping. Cavalcanti grasps the power and idealization of Dante's portrayal: "Vedeste, al mio parere, onne valore / e tutto gioco e quanto bene om sente" ("What you saw, I think, was all nobility and all joy and all the good that man can know").[37] He sees the feeding of the heart as a way of restoring the lady as she sinks toward death, but he stops short of interpreting Love's withdrawal. As Harrison points out, Cavalcanti seems to ignore the tragic fatalism attached to death and eros in Dante's sonnet, which so closely echoes the themes of his own love lyrics.[38] The scene he interprets, however, is one that focuses on the poet's heart rather than the veiled body. The heart, Ginsberg rightly observes, is at the center of a system of analogies that links Dante, Beatrice, and Love in a dual perspective of memory and understanding.[39] As we shall see later, its demands structure the narrative stasis of the *Vita nuova*.

Dante's inspiration for the fetishized veil of his first vision may lie in a contemporary dream poem sent out to poets, for which the young Dante offered an interpretation. In "Provedi, saggio, ad esta visïone," Dante da Maiano depicts a love vision in which a lady gives him a garland and he then finds himself dressed in her shift. He embraces her and, as she smiles, begins to kiss her. Bound by his promise to the lady, the speaker coyly refuses to disclose the rest of what occured. His final line introduces a macabre motif of death and maternity: "E morta, ch'è mia madre, era con ella" ("And a dead woman—my mother—was with her").[40] Dante interprets the garland as true desire which seldom comes to an end ("u' rado fin si pone"), the woman's shift as love, and the dead figure as the constancy she will have in her heart.[41] As in his idealization of Beatrice, he associates desire with merit or beauty ("mosse di valore o di bieltate"). The word he uses for the lady's shift ("camicia") now worn by the poet is not Dante da Maiano's "vestigione" (line 7) but "Lo vestimento." The only rhyme that Dante carries over in answering the earlier poem is *-one*, but the word he substitutes for "vestigione" is a term that emphasizes the sense of covering that is made explicitly to signify love.

For all the differences in tone, style, and approach, Dante da Maiano's "visïone" (line 1) offers the poetic materials for Dante to invent his dramatic scene in chapter 3 of the *Vita nuova*. Dante's adaptation fuses the recognition of desire with the covering that simultaneously obscures and represents the body of Beatrice. The covering, which moves from the beloved to the poet in Dante da Maiano's poem, is glossed by Dante as love, but the gift that initiates the exchange is desire ("Disio verace").[42] In the *Vita nuova*,

Dante reverses the direction of eros from poet to the beloved by having her eat the burning heart, the poet's gift to her. Equally important, Dante da Maiano's poem establishes the thematic connection of desire and death. In the first poem, the dead figure of the poet's mother accompanies the beloved whose pleasures with the poet are remanded to silence. Dante tropes this macabre link of death, sexuality, and maternity in his image of Love's forcing Beatrice to eat his burning heart, and he interprets the dead figure in Dante da Maiano's poem as constancy ("fermezza"). Beatrice's death, already prefigured in Love's weeping as he withdraws, is the loss that serves as the necessary and sustained condition of his writing.[43]

Screen Ladies and Stand-Ins

The veil that blocks yet signifies Beatrice's naked body recurs as a structural feature in other scenes in Dante's narrative, and it represents an effort to mobilize Ovidian craft in the service of an elevated love. The first of these scenes is the seeming accident of the screen lady who happens to intersect the gaze Dante directs toward Beatrice when he sees her in church: "nel mezzo di lei e di me per la retta linea sedea una gentile donna di molto piacevole aspetto, la quale mi mirava spesse volte, maravigliandosi del mio sguardare, che parea che sopra lei terminasse" ("halfway between her and me in the direct line sat a gentle lady of quite pleasing aspect, who stared at me repeatedly, wondering at my gazing, which seemed to rest upon her" [5.1]). P. J. Klemp rightly observes that there are four points in the straight line ("retta linea") of Dante's sight—Dante the observer, the intervening screen lady, Beatrice, and the Madonna—and that Beatrice is "an earthly obstacle" placed between Dante and the divine queen of glory, just as the screen lady is an obstacle between Dante and Beatrice.[44] The occasion for the scene is ritual devotion to the Virgin Mary ("parole de la regina de la gloria"), and Dante will remark Beatrice's reverence for the Virgin in his disclosure of her death (28.1) and mention her dwelling with Mary in his first opening to the anniversary poem for her death (34.7). In an allegorical reading, the Virgin is the final referent of the poet's gaze, the real terminus of observation and intent. But even within an allegorical framework, Dante foreshortens and reverses the direction of sight and observation.

Perhaps the most striking and undervalued feature of the scene is that the objects of the gaze look back in a gesture that recalls both the lover's projection of desire and the workings of language itself. The lady seated in the line between Dante and Beatrice returns his unintended look repeatedly ("spesse volte"), thinking herself its destination and intended object ("parea che sopra lei terminasse"). It is her staring rather than Dante's gaze that generates the other "parole" which circulate outside the devotions to

the Virgin in the church, when she is named by others and said to be the
cause of the poet's disability. Moreover, Dante perceives her as the middle
point of the line, again foreshortened, that reverses his initial gaze and now
runs from Beatrice back to him: "io intesi che dicea di colei che mezzo era
stata ne la linea retta che movea da la gentilissima Beatrice e terminava ne
li occhi miei" ("it spoke, I understood, of the lady who had been intermediate in the direct line that proceeded from the most gentle Beatrice and
ended in my eyes" [5.2]). In this circuit of eroticized sight, the Virgin
disappears as an endpoint and Beatrice replaces her, as the line progressively
shortens from Dante to Beatrice and from the screen lady back to Dante.
As in the earlier "maravigliosa visione," Dante has transposed the hidden
meaning ("lo mio secreto" [5.3]) and the covering that supposedly veils it.
Similarly, he has succeeded in animating the objects onto whom he
projects desire. Not only does the screen lady look back, astonished by his
gaze ("maravigliandosi del mio sguardare"); Beatrice, too, is the starting
point of the line that leads back to the poet's eyes. The erotic substitution
of the scene can be plotted in the two uses of the verb *terminare*, a rhetorical and thematic echo of the earlier "termini de la beatitudine" (3.1)
applied to Beatrice. The screen lady mistakenly thinks Dante's gaze ends
with her, while he believes the interrupted sight is answered by a look from
Beatrice that passes through the screen lady and returns to his eyes.

The overt value of the screen lady is that she permits Dante to conceal
himself over a long period of time by serving as the covering to disguise the
real object of desire. Omitting the verses composed for her, Dante posits
Beatrice as the referent and final destination of this suppressed double
writing (5.4). The lady's departure demonstrates, however, the unstable
difference between veil and hidden object within the logic of erotic substitution. When the lady leaves the city and removes herself to a distant place,
Dante finds himself not only deprived of his defense but surprised by his
sense of loss. The removal to a "paese molto lontano" ("faraway place
[7.1]) adumbrates Beatrice's death, figured by her removal from Florence
and her enrollment among "li cittadini de vita eterna" (the "citizens of
eternal life" [34.1]). But at the same time, the poet-narrator discovers his
unacknowledged attachment to her proxy. He recognizes the screen lady as
a figure of erotic surplus, a "schermo di tanto amore" ("screen to so much
love" [6.1]), and finds himself responding more than he would have
expected: "quasi sbigottito de la bella difesa che m'era venuto meno, assai
me ne disconfortai, più che io medesimo non avrei creduto dinanzi"
("rather fearful that my fair defense was being lost, [I] became greatly
disheartened, more than I myself would have previously believed" [7.1]).
In the poem addressing her withdrawal ("O voi che per la via d'Amor
passate"), he makes concealment a double sign. Beatrice is the cause of

certain words whose meaning, he says, can now be seen in retrospect (7.2). Meanwhile the effect of the lady's withdrawal is a division of the self that refers uncertainly to either her removal or Beatrice's inaccessibility or both: "di fuor mostro allegranza, / e dentro da lo core struggo e ploro" ("outwardly I show joy, / and inwardly at the heart I waste away and weep" [7.6]).

Though accidental, the "simulacra" for Beatrice are inevitably an Ovidian tactic, which Dante stumbles upon and turns to his own purposes. A later scene offers a narrative commentary on the conflicting attachments that emerge in the Ovidian pretense of maintaining a screen lady. Dante has occasion to travel toward the screen lady, though not so far as the place where she now dwells; and he suffers because, in doing so, he distances himself from Beatrice ("mi dilungava de la mia beatitudine" [9.2]). The "linea retta" now has two endpoints with Dante as the middle term. On his journey, Love appears to him in his imagination as a frightened, shabby pilgrim to announce the screen lady's indefinite removal. He carries the poet's heart and names the next women who will serve as a defense for Beatrice's identity. His instruction to Dante is to maintain the fiction of love ("lo simulato amore" [9.6]) so that the veil of deception remains in place and merely transfers to the new woman. The sonnet that records this scene preserves the secrecy enjoined by Love in his instructions, but Love himself is a changed and diminished figure.[45] The claim of dominion that he makes over Dante in chapter 3 of the *Vita nuova* seems attenuated by his appearance: "meschino, / come avesse perduto segnoria" ("poor, / as if he had lost his lordship" [9.10]). Though he bears the heart that he possesses through his will ("per mio volere"), he effectively puts it into circulation. As De Robertis observes, Dante returns here to the insistent problem within a traditional ideology of courtly love, in which one love succeeds another.[46] Yet the scene offers a different formulation from the courtly translation of love from one object to another. The destination for Dante's heart—the locus of affect and appetite—is not just the other woman ("altri"), as in the prose narrative, but a new pleasure ("novo piacere"), mentioned in the sonnet, in which desire operates alongside the directives of Love.[47] Dante will echo his phrasing later in the *Vita nuova* when the heart speaks against the soul, the seat of reason, in the episode with the compassionate lady (38.10). In the scene of Dante's journey, the power of eros is registered in two ways to show the interplay of dominion and consent. In the prose, Love leaves Dante stunned by the magnitude of seemingly giving himself to the poet: "per la grandissima parte che me parve che Amore mi desse di sé" (9.7). In the sonnet, it is the poet who exercises his will to absorb Love: "Allora presi di lui sì gran parte, / ch'elli disparve" ("Then I took of him so great a part / that he disappeared" [9.12]).

The new pleasure of the second screen lady prompts a defining trauma within Dante's narrative. Just as the first screen lady revealed an unsuspected surplus of attachment in Dante, the second lady generates an erotic and linguistic excess. In his prose account, Dante fuses the two: "in poco tempo la feci mia difesa tanto, che troppa gente ne ragionava oltre li termini de la cortesia" ("in a brief time I made her my defense to such an extent that too many spoke about it beyond the bounds of courtesy" [10.1]). Making the lady so much his defense is Dante's euphemism for erotic attachment, and it applies specifically to the Ovidian craft of simulation that discovers more and deeper affect than it intends. This excess produces in turn the super-abundance of speakers ("troppa gente") who discuss Dante's attentions to the screen lady beyond the bounds of decorum ("oltre li termini de la cortesia"). This double transgression of language and courtesy—"questa soverchievole voce che parea che m'infamasse viziosamente" ("these excessive voices that appeared to defame me viciously" [10.2])—leads Beatrice to withdraw her greeting, which has been his beatitude.

The repetition of *termini* links this scene to both the first marvelous vision and the first screen lady. In the vision, Beatrice is the condition and language of Dante's beatitude ("tutti li termini de la beatitudine"); in the episode in church, the screen lady is the mistaken destination of the poet's gaze ("parea che sopra lei terminasse"). Love will tell Dante in the next chapter that Beatrice already has some intuition of his secret love (12.7), and it might be argued that the transgression of courtesy that causes her to withdraw her greeting is the threat of disclosing Dante's secret, of making the real referent of speech and the real destination of the gaze publicly known. Such a reading would be consistent with *cortesia* as a sign for courtliness in general.[48] But Dante's prose cites a different cause. It is the accelerated circulation of eros and language together that makes Beatrice withdraw the *salute* that is both her greeting and Dante's salvation: too many people, speaking beyond courtesy; too many voices, viciously defaming.

Through his Ovidian tactics, Dante surely had a hand in forming this impression. The ballad included in the *Vita nuova* to make his excuses claims that Love made him look at another woman but his heart has not changed (12.12). But in the ballad "Per una ghirlandetta," Dante sees Fioretta, who may be a screen lady or merely an imagined courtly lover, wearing a garland of flowers rather than the garments of virtue that cover Beatrice in public. The flowers transform into the poet's sighs, and then "per crescer disire / mïa donna verrà / coronata da Amore" ("my lady will come crowned by Love, to increase desire").[49] Like the "pulcella nuda" in his poem to Lippo, the ballad needs music to clothe the words.[50] Dante's use of the motif suggests, however, not just the joining of words and music but the uncertain, wandering reference of the poem itself. The music— "una vesta ch'altrui fu data" ("a garment given to another" [line 21])—is the melody from another ballad and the borrowed *involucrum* that hides and replaces meaning. Dante has put a song into circulation that pretends to address a screen lady in terms that can only fail to represent Beatrice even as they reveal the poet's absorption in their surface and his complicity in the subterfuge. He repeats the tactic in a poem addressed to Violetta, who appears to him in an otherworldly form ("in forma più che umana"), perhaps as a figure for Love but certainly not as an angel. Beauty, Dante says, kindles a fire in the mind that spurs hope. What sustains his hope, at least in part, is the lover's smile ("in parte mi sana / là dove tu mi ridi" [lines 9–10]), the analogue here to Beatrice's greeting but the failed equivalent later, in the poetry of praise, to the smile that memory cannot retain.[51] Yet as Dante reveals at the end of the sonnet, desire rather than hope is his topic: "ma drizza li occhi al gran disio che m'arde" ("but consider rather the great desire that burns me" [line 12]). His rhetorical aim is to position Violetta in the conventional posture of lyric complaint, in which she ministers to his pain in order to avoid her own.

As the narrative of the *Vita nuova* shows, the logic of the screen ladies is constituted against itself. Beatrice in some measure already knows the secret these women are supposed to disguise. She is the referent of the affect and poetry ostensibly directed toward them. To the extent that Dante addresses them in courtly discourse in the poems excluded from the book of memory, he inevitably misdirects his address to Beatrice. At the same time, pursuing the screen ladies runs the risk of uncovering desire, which always threatens the illusions of erotic self-mastery in Ovidian craft. When Love appears to Dante after Beatrice withdraws her greeting, he concedes the impossibility of the screen ladies as an erotic and poetic strategy: "Fili mi, tempus est ut pretermictantur simulacra nostra" ("My son, it is time to end our fabrications" [12.4]). The women are likenesses of Beatrice (the general sense of *simulacrum*), but, more precisely, they are idols.[52] For the prophets Isaiah and Ezekiel, from whom Dante takes the concept and terminology, worshipping such idols brings divine vengeance and the catastrophe of exile.[53] As Love remarks in equating himself with the center of a circle, he can survey the entire geometry of lines and circumferences, while Dante cannot: "Ego tanquam centrum circuli, cui simili modo se habent circumferentie partes; tu autem non sic" ("I am like the center of a circle, to which all the points of the circumference bear the same relation; you, however, are not").

The withdrawal of Beatrice's greeting inspires two poetic programs, and the movement from one program to the other reproduces the shift from *simulacra* toward Beatrice herself. Beset by internal conflict, Dante turns first (chs 13–16) to Cavalcanti's tragic style in sonnets that record his turmoil and confusion, Beatrice's mockery, and the near-fatal power of love. These poems, he realizes, concern his own condition ("lo mio stato"); and he resolves, accordingly, to take up a new topic ("matera nuova e più nobile" [17.1]), whose signature canzone "Donne ch'avete intelletto d'amore" (ch. 18) marks a decisive shift to a poetry of praise, self-transcending love, contemplation, and understanding.[54] At a poetic level, then, Dante advances through mediating images toward his true topic of writing. But this narrative obscures another story, sustained by poems attached to the same occasions, in which erotic demands are not sublimated or transcended and the lover remains the focus.

In "Lo doloroso amor che mi conduce," Dante amplifies the Cavalcantian themes of the sonnets included in the *Vita nuova*, while concentrating on Beatrice's withdrawal of herself rather than the greeting whose signifance he glosses in some detail (*Vita nuova* 10.3–11.4). Beatrice's direct withdrawal is expressed through the image of light. Dante names Beatrice in this canzone and, more important, makes her the cause of death rather than the source of love or beatitude: " 'Per quella moro c'ha nome Beatrice' " (" 'Through her I die, whose name is Beatrice' ").[55] Her name creates the bitter heart ("il cor agro" [line 15]) that renews his sorrow and ravages his body. This new sorrow (*nuovo dolor*, line 17) tropes the "novo piacere" ("new delight") that Love promises on the road of sighs when he introduces the second screen lady ("Cavalcando l'altr'ier per un cammino," line 12). Separated from the body, the soul, like the pilgrim spirit of "Oltre la spera che più larga gira," mounts to the heavens, where divine pardon awaits or at least the redemptive contemplation of Beatrice's image. In his congedo, Dante sends Death rather than Love to ask Beatrice why she has withdrawn from him; and he raises the possibility, unimaginable within the decorum of the *Vita nuova*, that someone else may be receiving the light she has denied him: "se per altrui ella [*sc.* luce] fosse recolta, falmi sentire, a trarra'mi d'errore" ("If another is receiving it, let me know; deliver me from illusion" [lines 48–49]).

An even more drastic alternative to Dante's account emerges in the canzone "E' m'increscie di me sì duramente," where the same motifs combine to challenge the narrative of erotic and poetic conversion. De Robertis shows that the canzone returns to the somatic language of trembling and torment in Dante's first vision of Beatrice (*Vita nuova* ch.2) and to the central metaphor of the book of memory, yet the poem resituates these elements within Cavalcanti's poetics.[56] Barolini notes that "the birth of a lady who possesses 'occhi micidali' ('death-dealing eyes') is described in language resonant of the *Vita nuova*" but that Dante tries to create "an impossible hybrid" in this poem of elements otherwise kept separate in the story of Beatrice.[57] Foster and Boyde likewise comment on Beatrice's "aggressive cruelty" and human attributes, which make the poem unacceptable for inclusion in the *Vita nuova*.[58] Beatrice's rejection, as Dante makes clear, stems from his desire: " 'Venne, misera, fuor, vattene omai!' / Questo grida il desire / che me combatte così come sole" (" 'Away with you, wretch, away now! Such is the cry of the one I desire, assailing me as she always did").[59]

If this separation is less painful than the lover might have expected, it is precisely because of the relation of affect to understanding, heart to soul, which is the itinerary of conversion. The soul has been all but divided from the heart in its quest for love: "e ora quasi morto / vede [l'anima] lo core a cui era sposata, / e partir la convene innamorata" ("now she sees the heart to which she was joined in marriage almost dead, while she must go on her separate way full of love" [lines 26–28]). The radical alternative of the poem, in other words, is that it accepts the spiritual trajectory of the *Vita nuova* in order to frame a worldly complaint against Beatrice's failure to show pity. Moreover, the source for Dante's desire lies within reason, which supposedly transcends the demands of earthly affection. Reason—"quella virtù che ha più nobilitate" (line 74)—looks into beauty ("piacere") and sees the origin of its own sorrow in its reflected erotic gaze: "conobbe 'l disio ch'era creato / per lo mirare intento ch'ella fece" ("[it] recognized the desire that was caused by its own intense gazing" [lines 77–78]). Desire is thus inseparable from reason and the conditions of knowing. The disinterested love that motivates Dante's poetry after Beatrice's withdrawal of her greeting stands not as a point of transition in a conversion narrative but as a formulation that must suppress its own contradictions by silence and omission. Furthermore, the recognition of desire that the canzone registers discloses the force of the qualification that Dante makes when he says that from the outset Love has governed him with "lo fedele consiglio de la ragione in quelle cose là ove cotale consiglio fosse utile a dire" ("the faithful counsel of reason, in those things where such counsel was useful to heed" [2.9]). Reason may offer guidance in love, but it is counsel inescapably working in some measure against itself.

Primavera

Dante presents an anti-type to the abandoned *simulacra* in an episode in which he feels a tremor in the heart, as if Beatrice were present. He then experiences an *imaginazione* in which Love approaches him from Beatrice's direction and tells him to bless the day that he fell under Love's power. Shortly afterwards, Giovanna, the lady loved by Cavalcanti and called Primavera on account of her beauty, approaches, and Beatrice follows behind her. As the women pass, Love explains that he has inspired Primavera's name specifically for this particular moment of pageant and display: "cioè prima verrà lo die che Beatrice si mosterrà dopo la imagi-nazione del suo fedele" ("because she will come first on the day that Beatrice will show herself following the imagining of her faithful one" [24.4]). He links the etymological play on Primavera's name ("prima verrà") to John the Baptist's proceeding Christ and reveals that Beatrice could be called Love "per molta simiglianza che ha meco" (for the great likeness she bears to me" [24.5]). The sonnet Dante subsequently sends to Cavalcanti about this episode omits Love's etymologizing and exegesis, but it preserves the processional order of the experience and the identification of the women.

The episode clearly echoes the event that gives rise to the first screen lady, and it rectifies the erotic uncertainty and circulation that have emerged in the *simulacra* for Beatrice and thereby robbed Dante of her *salute*. As with the first screen lady, Dante's vision moves in a straight line of sight (Love–Primavera–Beatrice) and in a straight progression of mean-ing (Primavera–Beatrice–Love). Love's gloss in the prose narrative specifies and regulates the meaning of sign and referent: Primavera's beauty points toward Beatrice as the embodiment of Love. Dante thus precludes the risk of an Ovidian discovery of desire or the chance that a "simulato amore" might generate unexpected attachment. Insisting on the semiotic character of the episode, he cancels out the possibility that *simulacra* might assume the signifying and erotic power of idols or that he might potentially return to the bondage that Augustine describes as the outcome of mistaking signs for their referents.[60] Charles Singleton takes Love's gloss as a declaration that reveals the principle of unity and secret of form in the *Vita nuova*, which is Beatrice's identification with Christ.[61] Besides the resemblance by analogy, the procession also signifies the poetic movement from Cavalcanti's poet-ics to Dante's new matter: the lyrics of complaint and tragic lament written after the withdrawal of Beatrice's greeting lead toward the poetry of praise. As if to signal the change, Dante describes Primavera's beauty in the con-tinuing action of the imperfect tense ("era di famosa bieltade") and her attachment to Cavalcanti in the past absolute ("e fue già molto donna di questo primo mio amico"). Praise of Beatrice, though inflected by the idiom of Guinizelli's lyrics, becomes the thematic goal of Cavalcanti's poetry.

Dante's assertion of his new program and of his shift beyond Cavalcanti becomes even clearer if we contrast this episode with a poem that frames Primavera in a very different context. In the sonnet "Guido, i' vorrei che tu e Lapo ed io," Dante devises a fantasy in which a magician sets him, Cavalcanti, and Lapo Gianni in a boat whose direction follows their wishes ("al voler vostro e mio"), as they grow in desire to be together: "vivendo sempre in un talento, / di stare insieme crescesse 'l disio" ("our desire to be together in fact always increasing, living as we would in unceasing harmony").[62] The affective bond between poets ("voler," "talento," and "disio") is matched by each one's attachment to his lady, who is also placed in the boat by the magician: Cavalcanti with Monna Vana, Lapo with Monna Lagia, and Dante with the thirtieth woman mentioned in his *sirventese* recording the names of the sixty most beautiful women in Florence. In the *Vita nuova* (6.2), Dante makes a point of mentioning that Beatrice's name appears as the ninth entry on that list, and so the woman referred to in the sonnet is likely the first screen lady. Though De Robertis sees the poem as outdated in its conventions, J. F. Took describes it as "a confession of faith in the new poetic" of the *dolce stilnuovo*.[63]

More important, what connects the affective bonds between the poets with their attachments to the ladies is the project that Dante seeks to transcend in his praise of Beatrice. The poets and the women are joined in erotic discourse, in a conversation between poets that is simultaneously a conversation between sexes, the stated goal of poetry in the vernacular (*Vita nuova* 25.6). The core of the sonnet's fantasy—its demand and desired form of repletion—is speech: "e quivi regionar sempre d'amore, / e ciascuna di lor fosse contenta, / sì come i' credo che saremmo noi" ("there to talk always of love; and that each of them should be happy, as I'm sure we would be" [lines 12–14]). It is worth noting that Cavalcanti's reponse to the poem ("S'io fosse quelli che d'amor fu degno") intimates his alienation from Monna Vanna and registers his ambivalent attraction toward destructive love. The Primavera who unambiguously announces Beatrice in the *Vita nuova* is in effect a beloved and a poetics already abandoned. In the lateral context of writing outside Dante's book of memory, Primavera is potentially the erotic idol for whom one forms an attachment of sterility and death.

La donna pietosa

Except for the eroticized vision of Beatrice in Love's hand covered only by a veil, the most unsettling episode for Dante's narrative is his involvement with a compassionate lady who happens to observe his grief after Beatrice's death. Dante places this episode after his struggle to write an anniversary poem on Beatrice's death, in which two different openings—first spiritual, then courtly—reflect the kinds of love that he seeks to reverse in the final chiasmic pattern at the end of the *libello*.[64] The "donna pietosa" is a recursion to the erotic-poetic courtly world that Dante had seemingly transcended before the loss of Beatrice. As James T. S. Wheelock notes, Dante sees the woman on the vertical axis of an elevated courtly lady rather than the horizontal plane of civic life where he encounters Beatrice. In De Robertis's formulation, she is the dimming of memory, the forgetfulness (and implicit self-alienation) of error.[65] Enrico Fenzi associates her with *vanitas*, the emptiness and deception of erotic *simulacra* and the interruption of Dante's ascent to understanding Beatrice.[66] I propose to read her as the insistent erotic demand whose presence threatens to unwrite the poetic program of the *Vita nuova*.

Interpretation of this episode is complicated by the two accounts that Dante offers. In the *Vita nuova*, he describes his ambivalence, contrasting the pleasure of seeing the lady with a repudiation of the "vanitade de li occhi miei" (37.2). His internal battle is a contest of appetite and reason, symbolized respectively by the heart and soul (38.5). In the *Convivio*, he offers a literal (2.2–11) and allegorical (2.12–15) reading of the episode as he glosses the canzone "Voi che 'ntendendo il terzo ciel movete," a poem contemporary with the *Vita nuova*.[67] In this account, the compassionate lady becomes a figure for philosophy, and Dante follows a path of attraction and consent so that love for her expels and destroys every other thought ("che lo suo amore cacciava e distruggeva ogni altro pensiero" [2.12.7]), including the memory of Beatrice. This new love, Dante recounts, was an unexpected discovery made when he was seeking only consolation (2.12.5); and his exposition, as D'Andrea notes, faithfully represents the content of the episode in the *Vita nuova* while giving it a new meaning.[68] Likewise, the four sonnets inspired by the "donna pietosa" (*Vita nuova* 35–38) stand uncertainly between lyric complaint and philosophical allegory. As Took remarks, "The difficulty about this is that while there is nothing in the poems to preclude [an allegorical] reading, there is, equally, nothing in them to prompt it, nothing crying out for such drastic reinterpretation."[69] Finally, the status of the lady herself is uncertain as Dante moves from describing her in the *Vita Nuova* to the *Convivio*. Is she a purely imaginary figure, a real woman, an allegorical personage, or a concrete figure who becomes a larger symbol? Should the "donna pietosa" of the *Vita nuova* be distinguished from the "donna gentile" of the *Convivio*? Peter Dronke seeks to reconcile the literal and allegorical identifications while tacticly admitting their limits: "Sensuality. . .guides reason towards the fuller recognition of that lady who in the *Convivio* will be revealed as reason's supreme embodiment."[70]

This synthesis of appetite and reason lies, of course, outside Dante's narrative in the *Vita nuova*, and the compassionate lady commands our attention precisely because of the erotic demands that she evokes. Dante begins the episode in a memorial space that is poignant but already Ovidian. The woman first sees him "in parte ne la quale mi ricordava del passato tempo" ("in a place in which I remembered times past"[35.1]). Like Troilus in Boccaccio and Chaucer, Dante ignores the Ovidian warning "Et loca saepe nocent" ("Places too are often harmful" [*Remedia amoris*

725]).[71] Ovid, like Boccaccio and Chaucer, refers to places where sensual pleasure was shared, but his stress falls on remembered places as reminders of loss that render the self vulnerable to its own desire: "Admonitu refricatur amor, vulnusque novatum / Scinditur" ("Love brought to mind is stung to life, and the wound is rent anew" [729–30]). Conscious of himself and his outward appearance, Dante looks to see if he has been discovered in this place fraught with memory, much as he does in the earlier chapters where he tries to keep his love and Beatrice's identity secret.

The woman who sees him in this moment of anxiety immediately fills the roles that Beatrice has vacated by her social withdrawal from Dante and by her death. Like the first screen lady, she returns a gaze that Dante is directing elsewhere and for entirely different purposes. She furnishes the affective quality that Beatrice has denied in life: "Allora vidi une gentile donna giovane e bella molto, la quale da una finestra mi riguardava sì pietosamente, quanto a la vista, che tutta la pietà parea in lei accolta" ("I then saw a gentle lady, young and very beautiful, who from a window watched me so compassionately, to judge by her look, that all pity seemed to be gathered in her" [35.2]). In the prose narrative, Dante describes her pity as something perceived, but he makes it directly present in the accompanying sonnet: "Videro li occhi miei quanta pietate / era apparita in la vostra figura" ("My eyes saw how much pity / had appeared on your face" [lines 1–2]). Earlier in the *Vita nuova*, pity signifies sorrow in the loss of Beatrice's greeting, her response to her father's death, and Dante's anticipation of her eventual death; it is a demand for compassion and remedy after Beatrice's mocking and in the Cavalcantian lyrics. In the poetry of complaint, Love is associated with pity. Thus, if his thoughts produce wildly differing views of love, "sol s'accordano in cherer pietate" ("they accord only in craving pity" ["Tutti li miei penser parlan d'Amore," line 7]). In his encounter with the compassionate lady, pity unambiguously signifies love. Retreating from his encounter and reflecting on it later, Dante realizes, "E' non puote essere che con quella pietosa donna non sia nobilissimo amore" ("It cannot be but in that compassionate lady there is a most noble love" [35.3]). The sonnet he writes on this occasion, addressing her, makes the same link: "Ben è con quella donna quello Amore / lo qual mi face andar così piangendo" ("Surely, with that lady is that Love / who makes me go thus weeping" [lines 13–14]). Dante's phrasing in the last line of the sonnet tropes the first vision of the *Vita nuova*, where Love ascends weeping to the heavens in the prose ("così piangendo. . .si ne gisse verso lo cielo" [3.7]) but merely goes off in the accompanying sonnet ("gir lo ne vedea piangendo" [line 14]). Love, burdened with foreknowledge of Beatrice's death, is replaced in this episode by the erotic subject already in a posture of complaint as he goes off weeping.

By supplying pity, the compassionate lady makes available an exchange that remains only potential while Beatrice lives and becomes seemingly inaccessible with her death. In their first encounter, her compassion nearly provokes the tears that Dante struggles to contain within himself. In subsequent encounters, she takes on the pitiful appearance ("vista pietosa" [36.1]) and color of love, which reminds Dante of Beatrice. Serving as a catalyst for grief, she draws out his tears "per la sua vista" ("by her sight" [36.2]). But as with the first screen lady, desire overtakes her signifying function and obscures Beatrice as the real referent of Dante's acts and feelings. Dante discovers again an erotic surplus in the proxy for Beatrice: "li miei occhi si cominciaro a dilettare troppo di vederla" ("my eyes began to delight excessively in seeing her" [37.1]). He retrospectively names the emotion that develops in these encounters as a form of lust ("la vanitate de li occhi miei" [37.2]) and stages another battle of sighs to mark his ambivalence, yet his attachment is compelling. He experiences a "nuova condizione" characterized by excessive pleasure ("troppo mi piacesse") that carries the prospect—in fact, the disavowed wish—that Love has perhaps sent it in order to bring repose into his life: "apparita forse per volontade d'Amore, acciò che la mia vita si riposi" (38.1). The contrast with a "vita nuova" or even "la mia vita oscura" of the sonnet ("Videro li occhi miei quanta pietate," line 6) is clear. So, too, is the contrast between repose and peace (*pace*). Repose, as Dante suggests earlier (13.1) refers to the lover's internal state, not the objective *pace* associated only with Beatrice in her earthly and heavenly aspects. Dante's new condition is overtly erotic in content; the will assents to it in substance and in its seductive rationalizations: "E molte volte pensava più amorosamente, tanto che lo cuore consentiva in lui, cioè nel suo ragionare" ("And I often thought more amorously, so much so that my heart consented to it, that is, to that reasoning" [38.1]).

Though she inspires an unexpected attachment, the compassionate lady is not a "simulato amore" like the screen ladies. In one sense, she may be, as Jerome Mazzaro suggests, a memory token for Beatrice working by contiguity; but Dante contemplates her in sensuous terms ("amorosamente"), as if he were the courtly lover suffering in the way that Andreas Capellanus describes the inner experience of solipsistic desire in his definition of love.[72] The lady may offer repose but not the *salute* of Beatrice's beatitude. She threatens the primacy of Beatrice's memory not merely by her sensuous presence but, more important, by the desire that she activates—or recuperates—in Dante. Like Heloise, she interrupts the flight from desire by making the lover confront the erotic demands that continue to circulate in him.

Dante's response to this threat is to fragment both the lady and himself. Shame contends with a realization that the lady holds out an escape from "tanta tribulazione" ("so much tribulation") and "tanta amaritudine"

("such bitterness"), that her appearance is inspired by Love ("uno spira-
mento d'Amore"), that it makes internal desire evident ("ne reca li disiri
d'amore dinanzi"), and that its source is indisputabily noble ("è mosso da
così gentil parte" [38.3]). In the sonnet "Gentil pensero che parla di vui,"
which ends the episode, Dante prepares his disavowal by division. He
restricts the adjective "gentil" to the lady and treats the rest of his thought
as "vilissimo" (38.5).[73] In the first part of the sonnet, thought of the lady
resides with Dante as a form of habit ("a dimorar meco sovente"), the second self that augments the defining qualities of character in classical and
medieval ethics. As in the fantasy sonnet to Cavalcanti and Lapo Gianni,
this thought speaks of love ("ragiona d'amor sì dolcemente") so that the
heart consents. Echoing the phrasing of the Song of Songs and Cavalcanti's
"Chi è questa che vèn," the soul remarks the power of the thought to
displace any other—implicitly to drive out the memory of Beatrice with
new love for the lady.[74] The heart responds to the soul by naming the
woman as "uno spiritel novo d'amore / che reca innanzi me li suoi desiri"
("a new little spirit of love, / who brings before me its desires" [lines
10–11]). The source of her power lies in her capacity to identify with
Dante and his sufferings ("si turbava de' nostri martiri" [line 14]). The sorrow that Dante struggles to contain and master at the start of the episode
(ch. 35), when her compassionate look nearly moves him to tears, stands
revealed in the debate of heart and soul as Dante's desire itself. Grief and
mourning are the markers of an impossible erotic demand.

Dante's gloss on this sonnet identifies the heart as appetite and the soul
as reason (38.5). His viewpoint here, he argues, is consistent with the
previous sonnet "L'amaro lagrimar che voi faceste," where the desire to
remember Beatrice is said to be greater than the desire to see the compassionate lady (38.6). His quibble over greater and lesser desires obscures,
however, the more important argumentative step that Dante takes in
separating heart from soul and dividing the faculties of the self. This
division prepares for Beatrice's decisive entrance in the next chapter in an
"imaginazione" that cancels out the noble thought of the lady as the "avver-
sario de la ragione" (39.1). His attachment to the woman is transformed into
"cotale malvagio desiderio" ("this malicious desire" [39.2]), and suffering
returns to displace "cotale desiderio malvagio e vana tentazione" (39.6) and
to disable the mutual gaze that makes desire recognizable: "li occhi son
vinti, e non hanno valore / di riguardar persona che li miri" ("the eyes are
vanquished and have not the strength / to look on anyone who gazes upon
them" ["Lasso! per forze di molti sospiri," lines 3–4]).

Dante's alienation of affect from understanding produces a conceptual
and thematic stasis, and he inserts this stasis into time in the deferred ending
of the *Vita nuova*. Though Dronke contends that sensuality guides reason in

the *Convivio*, it is not until the middle of the *Purgatorio* that Dante resolves the issue he leaves in suspension in the *Vita nuova*. Readers have long noted that Dante returns to his lyric poetry in the *Purgatorio*, first in Casella's song of canto 2 and most forcefully in the encounters with Bonagiunta of Lucca (canto 24) and Guinizelli (canto 26), the poetic father he consigns to the circle of the lustful. In *Purgatorio* 17–18, Dante offers a formulation that synthesizes desire within understanding. Love, Vergil tells the pilgrim, is a condition of being, and it is "o naturale o d'animo" ("either natural or of the mind" [17.93]). Natural love, instilled by the Creator, is beyond the possibility of error, hence "malvagio desiderio." Elective love can err by selecting a wrong object or by being excessive or defective because it concerns secondary goods and means rather than ends. Explaining the relation of love and cognition, Vergil sets out a three-fold process that recapitulates Dante's erotic history on a different plane. As we saw in the introduction, the mind "creato ad amar presto" ("created quick to love" [18.19]) inclines toward objects that promise pleasure, enters into a state of desire ("ch'è moto spiritale" [18.32]), and does not rest until it enjoys the thing loved. Vergil offers in these cantos an explanation explicitly limited by human reason, and he asserts that Beatrice will supply a fuller explanation based on revelation. The point, however, is not just that revelation supersedes reason; it is also that desire operates with reason in things we would know and judge.

In the *Vita nuova*, the problem of desire is deferred and unresolved. Beatrice's intervention cancels Dante's attachment to the "donna pietosa" by imposing reason on appetite in a formulation that Dante will later reverse. As the master narrative of conversion moves forward, then, the counter narrative of desire remains in place. While we anticipate the work that will finally treat Beatrice in her full and proper dimensions, Dante the protagonist comes to occupy the middle ground between the then and now of conversion narrative. At the end of the book of memory, the question is whether Dante has read his story well enough to accommodate eros within understanding and to reorganize himself as a subject who can integrate desire and reason.

CHAPTER 7

THE DESOLATE PALACE AND THE SOLITARY
CITY: CHAUCER, BOCCACCIO, AND DANTE

The texts we have studied so far represent desire as a force operating broadly through love and writing. In this final chapter, I focus on a particular moment in which absence and loss pose the demand for plenitude and then disclose the impossibility of desire. The disclosure reveals in this case the limits of desire within history and the endpoint of erotic attachment. My text is Chaucer's *Troilus and Criseyde*, a poem whose celebration of passionate, sexual love unfolds simultaneously with a critique of desire. Chaucer's poem is a detailed and conscious rewriting of Boccaccio's *Filostrato*. Boccaccio's poem in turn revises parts of Dante's *Vita nuova*, reading it along the lines we suggested in the previous chapter. In all three texts, Augustinian and Ovidian models of desire are clearly at issue, and they are connected in the poetic figure of an empty city despoiled of love. For medieval readers, such a figure acquired an additional and defining resonance, for it evokes Jerusalem as the solitary city mourned in the Book of Lamentations. The exegetical tradition applied to Lamentations in the Middle Ages reads the figure as a sign of both erotic loss and the promise of repletion. For medieval poets, the figure marks a point where worldly attachments come face to face with transcendence.

The particular moment I want to examine through these multiple contexts occurs late in Chaucer's poem, after Criseyde has left Troy and been delivered to the Greek camp, having assured Troilus privately that she will soon find a way to return. In book 5, Troilus journeys around Troy after his return from enforced leisure at Sarpedon, as he futilely awaits Criseyde's promised return. He goes first to Criseyde's palace, then by the "places of the town / In which he whilom hadde al his plesaunce"

(5.563–64), and finally to the gates from which Criseyde left the city.[1]
The crucial stanzas are those in which Troilus addresses Criseyde's palace:

> "O paleys desolat,
> O hous of houses whilom best ihight,
> O paleys empty and disconsolat,
> O thow lanterne of which queynt is the light,
> O paleys, whilom day, that now art nyght,
> Wel oughtestow to falle, and I to dye,
> Syn she is went that wont was us to gye!
>
> "O paleis, whilom crowne of houses alle,
> Enlumyned with sonne of alle blisse!
> O ryng, fro which the ruby is out falle,
> O cause of wo, that cause hast ben of lisse!
> Yet, syn I may no bet, fayn wolde I kisse
> Thy colde dores, dorste I for this route;
> And farwel shryne, of which the seynt is oute!"
>   (5.540–53)

These stanzas are one of the most commented-on passages in modern
criticism of *Troilus and Criseyde*. Lawrence Besserman and John V. Fleming
contend that Chaucer through Boccaccio is deeply indebted here to Ovid.
Besserman notes that Troiolo and Troilus ignore Ovid's warning about
revisiting sites on an erotic landscape, something Boccaccio claims in the
"Proemio" of the *Filostrato* that he has avoided.[2] Fleming sees a large
pattern of influence: "It seems to me quite certain that in the episodes of
the fifth book of the *Filostrato* (the festivities at Sarpedon's and the secret
visitation to Criseida's empty house) Boccaccio was schematically playing
off against the themes of Ovid's *Remedia*." The abortive trip to Sarpendon
follows Ovid's advice that a distraught lover should seek company, but
when Troiolo reads Criseida's letters and returns to the sites of former
sexual pleasures, he violates Ovid's specific injunctions.[3] Michael Calabrese
argues that Chaucer's borrowings from Ovid augment and intensify those
in Boccaccio, but he proposes that as the poem draws to a close even
the *Remedia* would offer no remedy for Troilus.[4]

Fleming suggests that the *Roman de la Rose* serves as a mediator between
Ovid and Chaucer, both in its appropriation of lines from Ovid and its parallel, though distinctly Christian, aims of parody and satire.[5] The conclusion he reaches is, I think, generally the right one—namely, that Chaucer
exploits the theme of sexual idolatry. But the Ovidian influence operates in
a larger literary and interpretive context. In this passage, Chaucer inserts his
poem within the rich and superbly nuanced intertextuality that joins
Boccaccio and Dante, and he sets the portrayal of Troilus's love in relation to

an exegetical tradition that signals what is finally at stake in his poem. Chaucer depends not only on the *Filostrato* but also, indirectly, on the *Vita nuova*, which is Boccaccio's subtext. These two sources consciously use the figure of the solitary city from the opening of the Book of Lamentations to express the workings of absence and desire. To appreciate fully what Chaucer achieves in *Troilus and Criseyde*, we must begin with the originary text in Lamentations and with the hermeneutic tradition within which Christian writers like Augustine and subsequent medieval commentators understood the solitary city. From there we can trace the sequence of poetic response that links Dante, Boccaccio, and Chaucer in their formulations of desire.

Lamentations and Its Readers

The Book of Lamentations, traditionally (though mistakenly) ascribed to the prophet Jeremiah, consists of five closely related poems mourning the fall of Jerusalem and the destruction of the Temple by the Babylonians in 587 B.C. (2 Kings 25: 8–12). These poems draw on earlier Middle Eastern traditions of poetic laments for ruined cities and on funeral songs, but they are unique in recording a moment of terrible historical consciousness, in which God evidently withdraws his favor from the Jewish people as his chosen servants becuse of Israel's sin. Throughout Jewish history, God's destruction had been a means of correction and chastisement, and restoration had followed reliably from atonement. But in Lamentations the nature of the sin is never revealed and remains unnamed and unknown. Consequently, the poems record, as Norman K. Gottwald observes, a "historical crisis" in which faith in the simple correspondence between virtue and reward is tested by bitter adversity without the prospect of restoration.[6] The opening strophe of Lamentations serves as a synecdoche to evoke the entire sequence of five poems, and it was understood as such by medieval writers. In Jerome's Vulgate it reads:

> Quomodo sedit sola civitas plena populo
> facta est quasi vidua domina gentium
> princeps provinciarum facta est sub tributo.

> [How deserted lies the city that once was full of people!
> Once greatest among nations, she is now like a widow;
> Once the noblest of states, she is set to forced labor.]

The city here is a polysemous term; it means Zion, the Jewish kingdom, and the people of the covenant present, past, and future. Personified as an abandoned women, doubly defiled by her own promiscuity and her rape by the Babylonian conquerors, the widowed city is isolated from all social and spiritual community. She is, as Alan Mintz describes her predicament, "a living witness to a pain that knows no release," who suffers "continuing exposure to victimization" because she has no legal standing and "may thus be abused with impunity."[7] Her abasement is intensified by the shame of her enemies' exultation, for they are not just the blind instruments of God's vengeance but her apparent successors in a history that has suddenly taken on new contours in the rise and fall of nations rather than the enduring covenant between God and Israel.

It is the shock of abandonment more than sheer destruction that lends thematic and emotional unity to the poems of Lamentations and makes them such a powerful, evocative source for later writers. At various points, abandonment is expressed as exile, mourning, captivity, hunger, and slaughter. The writer of the opening poem complements these metaphors with images of the city's desolate gates (1:4) and fire descending (1:13), of disavowing lovers (1:19), groans (1:22), and the repellant sight of the enemies' exultation (1:5, 7, 21). What organizes all these rhetorical figures is the lost presence of God, the full embodiment of numinous power now removed and for the first time seemingly irrecoverable. Lamentations offers no consolation through prophecy, and so it registers the psychological, historical, and spiritual impact of an end to the covenant, to the means of atonement, to the possibility of any reconciliation and restoration.

Christian writers appropriate this rich collection of themes in rhetorical and hermeneutic forms that bear significantly on subsequent vernacular poetry. The rhetorical power of the metaphors and images from Lamentations is nowhere more evident than in Augustine's *Confessions*. In book 4 Augustine recalls his friendship with a young man who shared his enthusiasm for literary studies and followed him into heresy. When the friend falls ill, he receives baptism. During a brief recovery, Augustine jokes with him about the baptism, but the friend reproves Augustine for mocking the sacrament. The friend dies a few days thereafter, before Augustine can reconcile with him. Augustine's expression of grief (*Confessions* 4.4.9) takes its language of alienation and spiritual exile from Lamentations:

Quo dolore contenebratum est cor meum, et quidquid aspiciebam mors erat. Et erat mihi patria supplicium et paterna domus mira infelicitas, et quidquid cum illo communicaueram, sine illo in cruciatum immanem uerterat. Expectabant eum undique oculi mei, et non dabatur; et oderam omnia, quod non haberent eum, nec mihi iam dicere poterant: "Ecce ueniet," sicut cum uiueret, quando absens erat.

[My heart was darkened over with sorrow, and whatever I looked at was death. My own country was a torment to me, my own home was a strange unhappiness. All those things which we had done and said together became, now that he was gone, sheer torture to me. My eyes looked for him every-where and could not find him. And as to the places where we used to meet I hated all of them for not containing him; nor were they able to say to me now, "Look, he will come soon," as they used to say when he was alive and away from me.][8]

In the *Convivio* (1.2.14), Dante explains how the *Confessions* served him as literary model, and certainly the topical elements of the solitary city, as they will appear later, are already directed toward rhetorical ends in Augustine's lament.[9] Grief, alienation, the *loci* of memory, the poignancy of expectation set against the impossibility of restoration—all these wait to be reshuffled into later poetic configurations. For Augustine, the informing idea—what emerges as the hermeneutic clarification of his rhetorical use—comes slightly later in his narrative, and we see it only from the retrospect that controls the forward unfolding of time in his story of conversion. Augustine advances to two stages of understanding about his friend's death. He first realizes that his grief for his friend is grief for himself. If the friend is, as Horace (*Odes*, 1.3.8) and Ovid (*Tristia* 4.4–72) would have it, "the soul's other self" (*dimidium animae suae*), to suffer his death is to suffer the loss of oneself.[10] Eventually however, Augustine realizes that the classical model of friendship—Cicero's "rivalry of virtue" (*honesta certatio*) and the otiose life of cultured conversation among intimates—is "one huge fable, one long lie" (*ingens fabula et longum mendacium*): "fuderam in harenam animam meam diligendo moriturum ac si non moriturum" ("I had poured out my soul like water onto sand by loving a man who was bound to die just as if he were an immortal" [4.8.13]).[11] The false unities of self with other and of the self in a circle of intimates prove to be, in the dual frame-work of the *Confessions*, mere adumbrations of what Augustine calls "friendship with God." Augustine's narrative of desolation, then, offers the promise of abundance and plenitude that he reaches by working through false embodiments of presence as it is simultaneously eroticized and sublimated. In the end, the affective bond of friendship signifies God's incommensurable love. Seen from the retrospect of conversion, all desire has its final object in God.

The reading I am offering of this passage operates, of course, within the hermeneutic established by Augustine's narrative framework. The loss rep-resented rhetorically by evoking Lamentations discloses its significance to Augustine only belatedly, in the distance of time and from the perspective of faith. Taken by itself, Augustine's rhetorical strategy is limited and localized. He relies chiefly on analogy, and his aim is to express the measure of grief: his experience is like that of the poet and the widowed city in Lamentations because the feelings of grief, loss, abandonment, and exile are the same. By contrast, medieval commentaries on Lamentations imposed a structure closer to the hermeneutic retrospect that finally controls the *Confessions*. In their textual commentaries, Christian exegetes recognized the importance of the historical level that gave Lamentations its immediate expressive power, yet they emphasized figurative aspects that yielded applications to the individual soul and to the Church as a social paradigm. The medieval commentary on Lamentations is vast (Friedrich Stegmüller's *Repertorium Biblicum* lists nearly seventy works),[12] but the key text in this medieval reading is the *Expositio in Lamentationes Hieremiae* by the Carolingian writer Paschasius Radbertus.[13] Radbertus's commentary was incorporated in the *Glossa ordinaria* and so became the dominant reading in the exegetical tradition; it served, for example, as a direct source for Guibert of Nogent and Hugh of St. Victor and for late-medieval commentators like the Oxford Franciscan John Lathbury (fl. 1350).

Radbertus treats divine presence as the symbolic constant among the text's multiple meanings. Drawing on Jerome and Rabanus Maurus, Radbertus offers a literal interpretation of the historical fall of the city, which for him includes the prophecy, since realized, of its second fall under the Romans; he then reads the text as an allegory of the Church and explains its tropological application to the individual soul.[14] The major hermeneutic step in Radbertus's interpretation is to suggest that Lamentations should be read not alone but in the context of the Song of Songs and the Psalms.[15] Just as the Canticle is the preeminent text about lovers' embracing, he contends, so Lamentations stands above other scriptural laments in bemoaning the withdrawal of the husband from his wife: "Quia sicut omnino praecellunt illa in quibus sponsus ac sponsa dulcibus fruuntur amplexibus ita et Lamentationes istae uincunt omnia Scripturarum lamenta in quibus abscessus sponsi ab sponsa magnis cum fletibus uehementius deploratur" ("Just as the Song of Songs entirely surpasses those in which a husband and wife delight in sweet embraces, so these Lamentations excel every lament of the Scriptures in which the withdrawal of the husband from his wife is violently mourned with great weeping").[16] E. Ann Matter proposes that this comparison is crucial to the plan of exposition: "For Radbertus, the Song of Songs and Lamentations describe contradictory spiritual states; the former tells of the joy of God's mystical embrace, the latter describes the desolation of God's absence."[17] Radbertus cites the Psalms, with their repeated theme of God's absence, as parallels because Lamentations shows the feelings and reproduces the complaints for which the Psalms serve as exemplary texts: "Quae nimirum lacrimarum genera

Scriptura diuina latius explanat cum in diuersis Scripturarum locis singulorum uarios demonstrat affectus et lamenta replicat." ("The Bible of course explains these kinds of tears in a broader sense when it shows different feelings of individuals and recreates their complaints in various places in scripture").[18] Like the Canticle, then, Lamentations connects eros and absence, while it bewails, through the Psalms, God's abandonment of his chosen.[19]

In Radbertus's explication of multiple meanings, God's withdrawal is expressed concretely through the figure of the husband abandoning his wife. Radbertus takes the Vulgate phrase *sola civitas* in a spiritual sense to mean that Christ the bridegroom of the Canticle has been driven off by sin.[20] The lament is not merely for the city but for mankind. Furthermore, the prophet grieves not because the city is sitting in the dust but because it sits alone; therefore, the adjective *sola* is correlated with the phrase *quasi vidua*: "Porro *sola* quia *quasi uidua*" ("Moreover, *alone* because *like a widow*).[21] The city is like a widow, he reiterates, because her foulness has induced her husband to leave her. Nonetheless, Radbertus insists that the figure is only a simile: the city is like a widow; it is not a widow strictly speaking, for the marital bonds (*sponsalitatis iura*) remain in place, as does the possibility of returning to an earlier promise of love. Thus, read tropologically, the deserted city as it sits like a widow signifies a soul stripped of virtues and subjugated by vice as its captor.

Rabanus earlier made the same point in his interpretation of the passage. He offers a reading that juxtaposes fullness and loss, control and abjection. In a figurative sense, Rabanus says, the passage laments the loss of virtue and self-regulation and the soul's consequent isolation and vulnerability: "Mystice autem plangitur anima fidelis hominis, quae plena quondam fuit numerositate virtutum, et imperabat diversis affectibus, dominans concupiscentiis carnis: postea autem a malignis spiritibus flamma libidinis succensa, destituta angelorum solatio, et carens divino consortio, tot servit sceptris dedita quot vitiis" ("Tropologically, the faithful soul of man is lamented, which was once full with the abundance of virtues, holding sway over the lusts of the flesh; but afterwards burned by the flame of desire from evil spirits, left without the comfort of the angels, lacking divine fellowship, it is given as a slave to as many kingdoms as vices").[22]

The elements of Radbertus's commentary reappear in later exegetical writers. Guibert of Nogent interprets the widowed city along tropological lines, explaining its isolation as the consequence of the flight of reason and God its spouse: "*Domina gentium quasi vidua* fit, cum ratio, quae vitiorum gentibus discretionis sceptro praesidere debuerat, expers divini seminis, et Deo conjuge vacat" ("It is said *The Queen of nations like a widow*, when reason, free from divine essence, which should have watched over the people of vices with the staff of judgment, is without God as her husband").[23] Hugh of St. Victor reads the passage on historical, allegorical, and tropological levels. Like Guibert, he stresses the soul's regulation of vices and senses. Though Hugh does not explicitly connect Lamentations with the Canticle, he nonetheless draws on the marital imagery Radbertus had elaborated: "Propterea vero Deus vir dicitur plebis illius; quia eam ad cultum suum casto sibi amore copulaverat, ne per varias idolorum culturas fornicaretur" ("Therefore, truly God is said to be the husband of that people because he joined it to his faith with a chaste love, lest it commit adultery through various idolatrous rites").[24] Moreover, Hugh stresses divine presence as God's habitation of the soul: "Secundum intellectum moralem civitas significat animam quae sola sedet, quando a Deo derelinquitur; plena autem populo virtutum, quando a Deo inhabitatur" ("According to the moral sense, the city means the soul which sits alone when it is abandoned by God but which is full of people of grace when it is inhabited by God"). He poses a set of questions that builds successively to an understanding that the soul's virtues proceed from God's presence: "Quomodo sedet sola civitas plena populo? Quomodo anima mea desolata est? Quomodo bonum illum habitatorem perdidit, quo praesente olim plena populo virtutum fuit?" ("How does the city sit solitary that was full of people? How has my soul been forsaken? How did it lose that good inhabitant, by whose presence the people were once full of virtues?" [PL 175: 258]).

Radbertus's commentary exercised a wide influence not only through its inclusion in the *Glossa ordinaria* but also through direct citation by later exegetes. Lathbury places Radbertus at the head of a tradition of commentators that includes Isidore, Gregory, Nicholas Lyra, and Gilbert of Poitiers. Lathbury's *Liber moralium super trenis iheremie* employs an extrinsic prologue to explain the author, subject matter, form, and intention of Lamentations.[25] The subject matter is three-fold: historically, the ruin of the city first by the Babylonians and then the Romans; allegorically, the overthrow of the Roman Church by numerous heretics; and tropologically, the overthrow of the Christian soul through sin and invisible enemies. Lathbury continues, "Et hac de causa legam lamentationem lamentationum sicut predecessor legit cantica canticorum. Quia sicut canticum canticorum conuenit patrie benedicte sic lamentacio lamentationum conuenit uie huius uite maledicte" ("And for this reason I should read Lamentations just as my predecessor read the Song of Songs, because just as the Song of Songs is appropriate to the blessed homeland, so the lament of Lamentations is appropriate to the ways of this cursed life" [sig. C2vb–C3ra]).[26] He restates Radbertus's contrast between the Canticle as a poem about the embrace of husband and wife and Lamentations as a work "in quibus absencia sponsi a sponsa multimodis fletibus deploratur" ("in which the absence of the husband from his wife is lamented in various tears" [sig. C3ra]). The Canticle leads unlike people—"diuerse persone," literally, people turned away from each other—to nuptial joy ("nuptialia gaudia"), while Lamentations bemoans the separation of dissimilar persons ("diuerse persone abducte"). Lamentations further contains within it two distinct parts—"lamentationes et orationes" (sig. C4vb). Its lament deals with sin, while its prayer joins divine power and human need: "In oracione uero copulat et connectit dei omnipotenciam et huius rei indigenciam ut ipse deus in clemencia consolatoria et ipse in confidencia meritoria firmius perseuerat" ("In this prayer, it joins and connects the omnipotence of God and the lack of this thing, for God persists in his comforting mercy and more strongly in his just confidence" [sig. C4vb]). Thus whoever reads Lamentations can see himself portrayed in its prophetic mirror as blessed or miserable.

Within and across its exegetical levels, then, the Christian tradition read the image of the solitary city in Lamentations in a way that complicated the themes of abandonment and alienation by discovering further possibilities of textual meaning. If Lamentations represents within Jewish history a crisis of belief in God's justice, medieval Christian writers understood that the text chiefly embodies a metaphysics of presence—in this case, God's favor now withdrawn but still immanent, hence capable of restoration. For them, the absence and abandonment grieved in Lamentations imply the restoration promised by the Song of Songs.[27] Seen alone or paired with others, the biblical text becomes a meditation on desire. Like Augustine, who offers friendship with God as a prospect, structuring his life story as a forward movement seen from the retrospect of conversion, the exegetes envision a temporal continuum from past to future along which desire moves from absence to repletion and plenitude.

This hermeneutic structure of abandonment and return, absence and plenitude is critical in the intertextual sequence that connects Dante's *Vita nuova*, Boccaccio's *Filostrato*, and Chaucer's *Troilus and Criseyde*. All three texts employ the figure of the desolate, widowed city in a way that signifies not just the loss of love but, more important, the problematics of restoration. For love restored is not merely love returned, a kind of compensatory justice. What is restored turns out to be radically different, and the lover as desiring subject discovers himself profoundly transformed. He gains not just a perspective on desire, as in Augustine; he also serves the writers as a means for authorial understanding of the final objects of desire, hence of the literary themes that underwrite the authors' own projects of composition.

Dante and Boccaccio

In the *Vita nuova*, Dante quotes the opening of Lamentations at the most crucial point in his work. It is his only direct citation of the Bible in a text otherwise resonant with biblical echoes. As Charles Singleton proposed long ago, the solitary, widowed city is Dante's typological figure for Beatrice's death.[28] In his prose narrative (ch. 27), Dante relates that he began composing a *canzone* to express Beatrice's miraculous powers over him and so to remedy the incomplete account of her given in two previous sonnets, which register her social virtues in the manner of Guido Guinizelli and the poets of the Dolce stilnuovo. Having completed the first stanza of the new poem (itself a complete sonnet), Dante learns of Beatrice's death. The passage from Lamentations opens the subsequent chapter (ch. 28) with striking and dramatic force, and it takes the place of any discursive announcement of Beatrice's death:

> *Quomodo sedet sola civitas plena populo! facta est quasi vidua domina gentium.* Io era nel proponimento ancora di questa canzone, e compiuta n'avea questa soprascritta stanzia, quando lo segnore de la giustizia chiamoe questa gentilissima a gloriare sotto la insegna di quella regina benedetta virgo Maria, lo cui nome fue in grandissima reverenzia ne le parole di questa Beatrice beata.

> ["How doth the city sit solitary that was full of people! How is she become a widow, she that was great among the nations!" I was yet involved in composing this *canzone*, and I had completed the above stanza when the God of Justice called this most gracious one to glory under the banner of the Blessed Virgin Mary, whose name was always spoken with the greatest reverence by the blessed Beatrice.][29]

The passage marks the loss of Beatrice by her absence and by the remarkable strangeness of the typological figure. Not only is Beatrice's death veiled, but Beatrice herself is removed as a referent. Dante speaks of her simply as "questa gentilissima" ("this most gracious one"), and her name (troped as an etymological figure, "Beatrice beata") reenters only by displacement, in mention of her devotion to the Virgin, the first mention of such devotion in the text. Beatrice's death is further removed to a species of textual commentary. Dante explains on a historical level that he was composing a *canzone* that survives as a finished sonnet, and this account provides a context for interpreting the symbolism of the genres: the finished sonnet signifies a secular love theme carried to its fulfillment, while the *canzone* represents the larger poetic project of moral and exemplary discourse.[30]

In the next chapter (ch. 30), Dante portrays Beatrice's departure by a textual citation of Lamentations that is already an allegorical reading of the city's bereavement: "rimase tutta la sopradetta cittade quasi vedova dispogliata da ogni dignitade; onde io, ancora lagrimando in questa desolata cittade, scrissi a li principi de la terra alquanto de la sua condizione, pigliando quello cominciamento di Geremia profeta che dice: *Quomodo sedet sola civitas*" ("all of the previously mentioned city was left a widow, stripped of all dignity; wherefore, still weeping in this barren city, I wrote to the princes of the earth concerning its condition, taking my beginning from the prophet Jeremiah where he says: 'How doth the city sit solitary.' "). The passage is cited, he remarks, "quasi come entrata de la nuova materia che appresso vene" ("as if to serve as a preface for the new material that follows"). The solitary city appears again in the next chapter (ch. 31), where Dante begins a new *canzone*. There he diverges from his usual practice and divides the poem into three parts beforehand rather than afterwards in order to make it appear "widow-like" ("più vedova").[31] Later, he sees pilgrims passing through the middle of the city and knows them to be foreigners because "if they were from a neighboring town they would in some way appear distressed while passing through the center of the mournful city": "Io so che s'elli fossero di propinquo paese, in alcuna vista parrebbero turbati passando per lo mezzo de la dolorosa cittade" (ch. 40). The sonnet he addresses to them is calculated to cause them to depart in tears after he explains how the city has lost its source of blessings, which is identical in name and substance to Beatrice: "Ell'ha perduta la sua beatrice."

Singleton explains the absence of historical details and the typological use of Lamentations for Beatrice's death on the grounds that Beatrice resembles Christ. What he calls the "underground presence. . .of that resemblance" makes the figure "not too lofty and sacred a proclamation of the death of a mortal creature," and the "same hidden metaphor" explains the address to the princes of the earth and to the pilgrims on their way to Rome to see Veronica's veil, itself "the image of the departed Christ."[32] Other readers have looked for a narrative logic beyond Singleton's pattern of typological resemblance. Margherita de Bonfils Templer finds a justification for citing Lamentations in Dante's insistence from the very start that his Book of Memory records significance rather than circumstances, essence rather than accident.[33] Vittore Branca sees Beatrice in the tradition of the *speculum Christi*, by which human contemplation of Christ operates through intermediate material substances.[34] Of late, revisionist critics have begun to resist Singleton's doctrinal explanations and find instead contradictory and problematic motives behind the employment of Lamentations. Robert Pogue Harrison insists that Dante's efforts to veil Beatrice and especially Beatrice's physical body succeed paradoxically in drawing attention to them.[35] John Kleiner argues, "while Dante's vision of Beatrice's death is cast as a revelation, her actual death is closer to a rhetorical 'reveiling'; at the climax of Dante's story, Beatrice vanishes into a fold of the narrative that Dante refuses to open."[36]

The veiling of Beatrice is less problematic—and surely less aesthetically suspect—if we see Dante's use of Lamentations in the context of the dominant medieval reading of the text. Dante's representation proceeds from the dual structure articulated in the commentaries. He insists that Beatrice is a historical and social being; the city left empty by her departure is preeminently a social structure, a web of relations among men and women stratified by status and common values. Though Beatrice is now lost to Dante, her full significance lies in the deferred restoration promised in prophecy. For while the present city is by turns *dolente* ("grieving"), *desolata* ("desolate"), and *dolorosa* ("painful"), Beatrice has been made one of "li cittadini di vita eterna" (34.1). Dante builds a promise of repletion and plenitude into his text in the final chapter of the *Vita nuova*, where he records his hope "di dicer di lei quello che mai non fue detto d'alcuna" ("to write of her that which has never been written of any other lady") and to ascend "a vedere la gloria" ("to behold the glory") of Beatrice as she gazes on God (ch. 42). The first of these hopes is sometimes taken as an anticipation of the *Commedia*, but Harrison is probably right in insisting that Dante's real innovation is to connect two orders of time, human chronology and "God's eternal now."[37] Dante's second hope is the promise of numinous presence that Beatrice only signifies but does not embody and of a restoration that is not the remedy of her loss but the end of his own spiritual estrangement.

Dante's use of the solitary city from Lamentations marks a point where textual discourse hovers between Scripture and literature, and it is arguably Dante's poetic objective to cultivate precisely such ambiguity. His text registers both the loss signified by Lamentations and the restoration promised by the Song of Songs. Much as Beatrice is called to glory under the banner of the Virgin, she is seen in the end in the double vision of her beholding God directly. It would be wrong, however, to suggest that such careful thematic and structural balance closes the narrative. Dante as poet and protagonist remains in time, though Beatrice does not. The complex time scheme of Dante's book, like the dual framework of Augustine's *Confessions*, continually plays off the temporal difference between then and now; the poet is sometimes the protagonist moving forward in time, sometimes the author looking back. Only in the retrospect of Beatrice's death does a circular, repetitive pattern become clear. Absent, she is seen definitively as a miracle, and we realize, too, that a sequence of visions has already announced her death. Time thus becomes for Dante the condition of desire, while desire is for Beatrice the condition of full and authentic being.

In the *Filostrato*, Boccaccio sets out to deconstruct the promise of restoration that Dante extracts from the shock of loss. In effect, he reverses the trajectory of the *Vita nuova*, moving from repletion to absence and turning the text from spiritual aims back to the secular tradition Dante had sought to transcend, if not transform.[38] The clearest evidence of

Boccaccio's strategy is the double inscription of Lamentations. In the Proem to the *Filostrato*, the poet-narrator reports that his lover, real or fictitious, has abandoned Naples for Sennio, taking from his eyes what he should value most. Naples is the "dilettevole città" (18), not Dante's "dolorosa cittade." The lady's angelic face ("vostro angelico viso") is a stilnovist conceit rather than, as in Dante, a miracle whose utter difference and strangeness is a sign of God's mystery. The poet prays for a return that is an ambiguous peace restored: "se [sc. così] Iddio tosto coll'aspetto del vostro bel viso gli occhi miei riponga nella perduta pace. . . ." (that God "soon restore to my eyes, by the sight of your fair face, the peace which they have lost"). His eyes turn away from the civic landscape that desire has eroticized and filled with private significance:

> Oh me, quante volte per minor doglia sentire si sono essi spontanamente
> ritorti da riguardare li templi e le logge e le piazze e gli altri luoghi ne' quali
> già vaghi e disiderosi cercavano di vedere, e talvolta lieti videro, la vostra
> sembianza, e dolorosi hanno il cuor costretto a dir con seco quel misero
> verso di Geremia: 'O come siede sola la città la quale in qua addietro era
> piena di popolo e donna delle genti!

> [Alas, how often, to save themselves suffering have [my eyes] of their own
> accord avoided looking at the temple, the balconies, the public squares, and
> the other places, where once, full of longing and desire, they sought to see
> and sometimes did see your countenance; and in their grief they have forced
> my heart to utter that verse of Jeremiah: "How doth the city sit solitary that
> was full of people, she that was great among the nations."]

The solitary city is Jerusalem and Naples superimposed on each other, and this image underwrites the metafction of Boccaccio's narrative, which is directed not to a future project of writing but to a lover on spring holiday.

The second inscription of Lamentations replicates the first, connecting the metafiction of the *Filostrato* with the narrative of the love affair between Troiolo and Criseida. After Priam exchanges Criseida for Antenor, Troiolo consoles himself during her absence by visiting her "closed house" ("la magione / chiusa," 5.51.7–8) and the other *loci* of their pleasure.[39] By means of the visit, Boccaccio formulates a chain of amatory reasoning, a logic of desire. The house contained joy and light, just as Criseida contained Troiolo's peace of mind. Lacking her now, the house is left in darkness. Troiolo does not know if it will contain her again and so, by substitution, whether he will possess peace of mind again. His lament before her house and his journey through the solitary city are a topical and partial allegory for the poet's imagined situation: Criseida is lost to Troiolo as Fiammetta is lost to the poet. In his Proem, Boccaccio explains that Troiolo's weeping and his lamenting the departure of Criseida are a figure for his own "words, tears, sighs, and agonies," while Criseida's beauty, manners, and excellent qualities stand for the corresponding virtues in his lover:

> Nelle quali se avviene che leggiate, quante volte Troiolo piangere e dolersi della partita di Criseida troverete, tante apertamente potrete conoscere le mie medesime voci, le lagrime e' sospiri e l'angosce; e quante volte la bellezza e' costumi, e qualunque altra cosa laudevole in donna, di Criseida scritta troverete, tante di voi esser parlato potrete intendere.
>
> [And if by chance you read them, as often as you find Troilus weeping and lamenting the departure of Criseida, you will be able to understand and know my very words, tears, sighs, and agonies; and whenever you find portrayed the beauty of Criseida, her manners, and any other excellent quality in a woman, you can understand that it is spoken of you.]

As Robert Hanning notes, the decoding of the allegory in the frametale is "notoriously incomplete" and may include "beneath its refined discourse of yearning a current of resentment and accusation directed at the recalcitrant object of desire."[40] What Boccaccio leaves temptingly undefined are the vices proper to Criseida but ostensibly inapplicable to the departed lover.

At first glance, Boccaccio's reinscription of Lamentations must seem ironic and satirical. Hanning proposes that Boccaccio's parallels between the narrator's situation and Troiolo and Criseida "constitute an obvious parody of Beatrice's death and Dante's decision to write his *Commedia*."[41] Chauncey Wood contends, "Boccaccio's use of Jeremiah is more boldly inapposite in all respects than Dante's," which he takes as a device "to show the self-indulgent young lover [of the *Vita nuova*] at his worst."[42] For even if Beatrice is Christ by analogy, how can Criseida resemble Beatrice except as a grotesque distortion? And what of the absent lover who is only partially (which is to say, potentially) Criseida? One might argue that the very distance between the *Vita nuova* and the *Filostrato* is intended to provide a moral perspective on Boccaccio's love story. On this view, Boccaccio, rewriting the *Vita nuova* in secular and sensual terms and so returning to its origins, ironizes both his story and the conditions of his own writing. But it is more likely, I think, that Boccaccio grasped Dante's analogical strategy perfectly well and called it forth to make a point whose seriousness is not mitigated by irony any more than Boccaccio's powerful ambivalence is resolved by revising Dante. Boccaccio shows what happens when Dante's bold strategy of creating a textual discourse between Scripture and literature is relocated in literary conventions, for Troiolo's love seeks to enact the promise of restoration and plenitude that medieval exegetes had made a feature of Lamentations and that Dante seized as the prospect of future writing that lay beyond his Book of Memory. Boccaccio's final address to young lovers certainly invites a restrictive moral reading. He urges them, "nell'amor di Troiol vi specchiate" ("see yourselves imaged in the love of Troiolo" [8.29.5]), and so not to choose an inconstant woman over one of true nobility. But more is meant in Boccaccio's poem. His narrator sends the poem in the garb of exile to seek the promise of the lady's return (canto 9), much like the pilgrim spirit in the final poem of the *Vita nuova* (ch. 41). Though the narrative ends in loss and death, the metafiction remains open to the lover's return and the restoration of an undefined peace that is the token of plenitude.

Troy, Lamentations, and Loss

In *Troilus and Criseyde*, Chaucer, like Dante, portrays the empty city at a moment of defining crisis in his poem, as civic and personal destiny, largely deferred heretofore, impinges on the narrative and gives it a historical shape. After the Trojans agree to exchange Criseyde for Antenor, Troilus spends a fitful night dreaming of the "dredefulleste thynges / That myghte ben" (5.248–49). Pandarus, detained by attendance on the king, comes belatedly to comfort him. After he dismisses Troilus's dreams (in a way that incidentally dismisses the dream lore of Chaucer's early poetry), Pandarus sounds the theme of Troy's plenitude, the civic corollary to Criseyde's presence.[43] He exhorts Troilus to action, speech, and remembrance: "Ris, lat us speke of lusty lif in Troie / That we han led, and forth the tyme dryve; / And ek of tyme comyng us rejoie" (5.393–95). His rhyming of Troy and joy is, of course, only one of many instances of a narrative irony that begins in the very first stanza of the poem. Echoing his earlier and cynical, if apt, claim that the "town is ful of ladys al aboute" (4.401), he says, "This town is ful of lordes al aboute" (5.400) and urges Troilus to rejoin their numbers and the shared spectacle of their lusty life.[44] The sojourn with Sarpedon that Pandarus proposes fails, however, to improve Troilus's disposition, and as they come back to Troy, Pandarus rightly predicts that Criseyde's return will be delayed. She remains in the Greek camp, not the city, and her absence is the point dramatized in the journey that Troilus begins at her desolate palace.

Troilus's journey around the city recapitulates the love narrative in processional form. His circuit resembles civic spectacle, with attendant retainers and retinue; but its aim is private, and the mock spectacle has been made to celebrate a secret that cannot be divulged. The journey begins at the place where, in book 2, Criseyde first sees him as he triumphantly enters the city and she begins to incline toward him..It passes by the temple where Troilus first saw her and the house where "My lady first me took unto hire grace" (5.581). It ends at the place where Troilus handed her over to Diomede, a separation he now marks by gesturing over "yonder hille" (5.610). At the level of poetic technique, Troilus's journey enacts the precepts traditionally set down for the exercise of artificial memory.[45] Like the orator coached by pseudo-Cicero, Troilus moves through familiar *loci*, each containing the subject matter to be recalled in his discourse—in this case, the material is his lament and his tale of "newe sorwe, and ek his joies olde" (5.558). At a thematic level, the journey transposes absence and repletion. Criseyde's removal has emptied the city of its joy. As Troilus stands at the city gate, gesturing beyond to where Criseyde now abides, he locates the vanishing point of his emotional landscape and gives voice to a desolation that is identical to the city's: "And here I dwelle out cast from alle joie, / And shal, til I may sen hire eft in Troie" (5.615–616).

Memory works here as the consequence and ostensible remedy of absence. If Criseyde is gone, Troilus can effect some measure of repletion by summoning images of her presence: he can fill the city with tokens of his lover.[46] As the text makes clear, Troilus's memory is not only of events but sensation. He rides by locales associated with sight, sound, and touch:

"Lo, yonder saugh ich last my lady daunce. . . ." (5.565)

"And yonder have I herd ful lustyly / My dere herte laugh. . . ." (5.568–69)

". . .in that yonder place / My lady first me took unto hire grace." (5.580–81)

Troilus's memory, in other words, is sensitive memory.[47] The affective images are impressed from lived experience on the soul. Yet by evoking them so powerfully through "the places of the town," Troilus paradoxically demonstrates the emptiness of Troy. Chaucer thus signals the profound complications of love and desire in a city where, as Pandarus says earlier, "love of frendes regneth" (2.379) and friends are joined in their common project of being lovers.[48] As Eugene Vance observes, "Troy is now a mirror that will not reflect what Troilus desires. It is a city without love, which, in a universe of courtiers, is to say that it is without life."[49]

Though Troilus apostrophizes Criseyde's "paleys desolat," it is the entire city that has been made barren for him. His bereavement recalls Augustine's account of finding familiar places rendered intensely alien. But Criseyde's house is only the initial destination in a tour of his matrix of pleasures recalled, and his journey at length produces a prayer to Cupid: "I n'axe in guerdoun but o bone— / That thow Criseyde ayein me sende sone" (5.594–95). Troilus asks Cupid for a congruence of desires that will leave the city replete and his visual appetite satisfied: "Destreyne hire herte as faste to retorne / As thow doost myn to longen hire to see" (5.596–97). For her part, Criseyde looks on Troy as a place where pleasure and joy have turned to gall (5.732). She resolves to return; but in an authorial interjection that equates empty Troy and forlorn Troilus, the narrator signals the ebbing away of her resolve: "For bothe Troilus and Troie town / Shal knotteles thorughout hire herte slide; / For she wol take a purpos for t'abide" (5.768–70).

Chaucer's reworking of Boccaccio in the scene before Criseyde's house is a measure of the conceptual differences that separate the two poets, just as Boccaccio's citations of Dante and Lamentations mark the difference of the *Filostrato* from the *Vita nuova*. The stanzas addressing the "paleys desolat" that I quoted at the start of this chapter represent Chaucer's specific addition to Boccaccio's text. They are a conscious reinscription of Lamentations into a scene that Boccaccio had already associated with the biblical text. Chaucer retains the imagery of light and darkness from Boccaccio, but he replaces Boccaccio's amatory reasoning about absence and desire with a cluster of visual images, beginning with the desolate palace. Criseyde's palace is not only "empty and disconsolat" (5.542), a lantern with an extinguished light, a ring without its stone; it is also a shrine that has lost its relic. In these additions, Chaucer evokes other figures that he has earlier added to Boccaccio, particularly in the consummation scene of book 3. The ring without its stone recalls the brooch Criseyde gives Troilus "[i]n which a ruby set was lik an herte" (3.1371). The ring image is repeated soon thereafter in Troilus's wish that he "[w]ere in youre herte iset so fermely / As ye in myn" (3.1488–89), a passage in which Barry Windeatt notes that Chaucer's "imagery of fixity, inwardness, replaces B[occaccio]'s stress on duration (*star continuamente*, 'remain continually')."[50] Both images are anticipated by Pandarus's speech in book 2, which discloses Troilus's love to Criseyde and argues the lovers' fitness to each other: "And be ye wis as ye be fair to see, / Wel in the ryng than is the ruby set. / Ther were nevere two so wel ymet" (2.584–86). The last image in Chaucer's sequence, in which the distraught Troilus imagines himself kissing the "colde dores" (5.552) of the house, evokes the final image of the *Roman de la Rose*. The empty shrine "of which the seynt is oute" is iconically the architectural structure that Jean de Meun uses to represent the rose's genitalia as the dreamer symbolically penetrates the aperture of the castle. In some measure, Troilus's sterile worship reenacts the dreamer's joyless consummation in the *Rose*.

If the scene is a parody and satire of sexual idolatry at a moral level, it also opens up a more complex spiritual domain that Chaucer's biblical, exegetical, and literary sources help to identify. As Troilus stands "bitwixen hope and drede" (5.630), he mourns not only the false icon of earthly desire but, more important, the promise of superabundant and incommensurable love. As in the commentaries on Lamentations, the desolate palace and the solitary city of *Troilus and Criseyde* represent this promise in a double movement of withdrawal and restoration. The images are primarily symbols of loss. Independently from Dante and Boccaccio, Chaucer adds stylistic echoes of Lamentations to enforce the desolation of the scene. Criseyde's "hous of houses" (541) echoes the Vulgate "princeps provinciarum." Similarly, the phrase "crowne of houses alle" (547) is a reminiscence of "domina gentium." Yet the added images also carry the promise of return, as the commentaries suggest that a full reading of Lamentations must. Empty or replete, the desolate palace and the solitary city promise divine presence. Through them, Chaucer offers a critique not only of idolatry and Boethian "false felicity" but of the metaphysics of desire with its demand for the absolute presence of the other. While Criseyde repeatedly seeks and attains "suffisaunce" (3.1309, 4.1640, 5.763), Troilus asks for the wrong thing *and* for too much. He goes beyond Palamon's desire in the Knight's Tale to "have fully possessioun / Of Emelye" which means to die in Venus's service (I.2242–43). He seeks instead to satisfy an impossible absence, and so he demands numinous presence, a divine plenitude rendered doubly impossible because he stands outside both the Old Law and the New Covenant, situated as he is in the fallen world of pagan tragic history. What is at stake for Troilus, then, is not merely a false object of desire but an impossible desire directed toward an immeasurable order of magnitude.

AFTERWORD

When Jean de Meun takes over the *Roman de la Rose* from Guillaume de Lorris, his first authorial gesture is to return the allegorical figure Raison to the poem with a description of love. Raison's description is a catalogue of possible definitions drawn from classical and medieval sources. The range of her definitions—from natural appetite to friendship to charity—reminds us that love is more often a literary and cultural discourse than a cohesive theory in medieval texts. Her subsequent proposal that she become the narrator-lover's "amie" ("beloved") shows us that desire is located somewhere unexpectedly, even paradoxically in the discourse of love. My contention in this book has been that desire functions dialectically within this multiform discourse in ways that remain resistant and unaccommodated to the definitions that might be proposed for love. By elevating love as a topic for serious literary treatment, medieval writers provided the necessary condition—a structure of established conventions, generic codes, and readerly expectations—for expressing desire, even if such expression is oblique or only partially acknowledged or even disavowed. The demands that desire thus registers address fundamental issues in medieval literature such as selfhood, subjectivity, knowledge, virtue, social identity, and spiritual values. Desire is also, as we have seen, a condition of writing and especially of inventing and rewriting earlier texts.

The texts we have examined in this book represent exemplary desire— that is, they explore the problems and complexities of erotic attachment in works from a variety of historical and imaginative contexts. Augustine's formulation of desire and Ovid's discovery of eros beneath appetite and mastery shape many of the problems embodied in those works. As a practical matter, interpreting exemplary desire means reading texts in their particularity, the "especialité" that the lover in the *Rose* tells Raison he will choose against loving universally, "en generalité." By way of a provisional conclusion, though, I want to read across these particular texts of exemplary desire and set the problems they pose in some relation to each other. Seen in this framework, the texts can give us a somewhat larger view of what may be at stake in their complex and sometimes problematic depictions of passionate attraction and attachment.

Augustine's *Confessions* offered medieval writers a theory of desire and a form for describing its workings. The theory radically integrates the particulars of erotic experience, and it holds out the prospect of erotic plenitude in the divine love that lies at the source of particular desires as their true and final referent. Integration and plenitude, we have seen, are the reverse and obverse of the same thing, and they alternately impoverish and make impossible the specific objects of desire. Most of Augustine's loves disappear, unnamed and presumably effaced by what they signify. Against that background, Heloise has been a prominent figure in my discussion precisely because she does not disappear and because she insists on naming the roles she plays for Abelard. Most important, she resists the impoverishment of desire and demands Abelard's presence as a source of erotic plenitude. Marie de France gives us different examples of untransformed desire in her stories of love's frustration. The couple of "Deus Amanz" never consummates their love in the face of the father's incestuous demands. The four rivals of "Chaitivel" inadvertently destroy each other, leaving one alive but unable to find pleasure with the lady who sought to orchestrate her surplus of suitors.

As these stories suggest, untransformed desire falls victim to chance and miscalulation. But other examples formulate the problem as structural and internal. Desire in "Laüstic" reveals itself in the erotic display that the two lovers stage for each other across the space separating their houses, but it ends in the fetishized coffin that contains the dead symbol of these exchanges. Troilus's desire is celebrated in the consummation scene with Criseyde, but its full meaning is not clear until we recognize that his demand is for erotic plenitude, which remains impossible both in his story and in his unredeemed pagan history. If death is the far goal of desire according to modern theories, medieval texts certainly hold open that possibility, but they see other possibilities, too, in Heloise's heroic resistence to transcendence and in the tragic stasis of "Laüstic" and the Troilus story.

Augustine adapts the literary form of conversion narrative to represent the integration and plenitude of desire. In the *Confessions*, he writes from the rhetorical vantagepoint of a narrator turning back toward the past as the future of grace and plenitude approaches him. Commentators rightly point out that, despite this fictive positioning, his narrative remains subject to time and the ongoing struggle for salvation. The sense of completion that Augustine conveys within his narrative reemerges, however, with different effects in medieval writers. In Abelard's letters, conversion serves as a means to cancel rather than integrate desire, to silence Heloise as much as celebrate Abelard's unsought but providential release from carnality. Abelard makes Augustine's narrative posture a literal fact in order to place himself beyond desire and to urge a complementary, obedient conversion in Heloise. Dante moves in much the same direction in the erotic-poetic revisions of the *Vita nuova*. As the *libello*'s narrator, he stands at the juncture of retrospect and anticipation. What he has silenced, though, is not the voice of another but of himself, and what he cancels by exclusion is his own writing. Desire reenters his book in powerful and unexpected ways because its source lies within him as a lover and poet. The final position Dante occupies is thus not the convert's vantagepoint of understanding but the refuge of delay, a deferral of writing in the hope that desire can be transformed to another project of writing and to spiritual plenitude.

Other medieval texts add perspective to what conversion narrative might offer as a discursive form for desire. The story of "Eliduc" is frequently read as the thematic culmination of Marie de France's *Lais* because it shows both the endpoint and the transcendence of mutual desire. Guildeluëc plays the structural role of the obstacle to the lovers' erotic fulfilment, and her removal of herself to monastic life allows Eliduc and Guilliadun successively to realize a perfect worldly love and then to discover greater perfection in charity and their own monastic withdrawal. Within this sequence of conversion, desire stays ambiguously in place, however, in the messages that circulate among all three characters as signs of their continuing attachment. At the end of the *Rose*, circulation poses a still larger challenge to the thematic trajectory of conversion narrative. In taking over Guillaume's poem, Jean continues the story's forward movement toward the lover's possession of the rose, but he locates his narrator in a position of retrospect and disenchantment. Though he plucks the rose as the climax of his dream, the lover is already past this conquest, wandering without escape or refuge among the successors and substitutes of desire. If Augustine's conversion narrative traces desire to its source, Jean's adaptation of it finally reverses direction to move from the source of erotic attachment in the rose to repetition and mutability in the paths and byways that represent aimless sexuality.

Ovid's *Ars amatoria* and *Remedia amoris* furnished medieval writers with works that were canonically interpreted as illustrations of behavior yet still remained available in all their poetic subtlety and nuance. Ovid's erotic doctrine, as we have seen, was frequently adapted to an Augustinian framework. Jean's medieval readers and many modern ones see the lover in the *Rose* as a "fol amoureux" who reenacts Ovid's erotic teaching and ends, like the *praeceptor amoris*, caught by what he sought to master. Other texts show us how Ovid's erotic program can be reimagined and grounded in different contexts. This recontextualization inevitably challenges several governing premises in Ovid's didactic fiction, particularly his claim that love can be safe and harmless and that it occurs within a self-sustaining realm of ingenuity. Marie takes the Ovidian project of maintaining a love affair as the framework for her stories of desire within baronial culture. Critics have remarked that the informing value in Marie's stories is loyalty to one's lover. Perhaps a more precise description would be the stabilization of mutable desire. If "Lanval" represents a fantasy of plenitude, other stories like "Milun," "Le Fresne," and "Guigemar" describe a protracted trial of desire rewarded at length by resolution. But unlike Ovid, Marie situates her lovers in a social world where appetite and desire risk the consequence of violence, for which "Yonec" and "Laüstic" remain memorable examples. Maintaining passionate attachment, nonetheless, is a form of freedom and a way of defining selfhood within the external constraints of unhappy marriages and patriarchal culture. Guigemar and Milun become who they are (or should be) not just by finding lovers but also by collaborating with them to exercise ingenuity in the service of mutual pleasure.

Certainly, one of the most interesting problems posed by the texts is the Ovidian challenge to Augustinian transcendence. The *Rose*, as I read it, ends with the lover in the grip of Ovidian circulation and mutability. Dante not only discovers unexpected attachments to the "simulacra" who stand-in for Beatrice; even as he fictively defers writing until he can say something more noble about Beatrice, he continues writing, notably in the *Convivio* where Philosophy emerges as a rival mistress but also in the late love lyrics he writes. Chaucer amplifies the Ovidian elements of the *Troilus* beyond what he found already present in Boccaccio's *Filostrato*. Pandarus's counsel in the seduction of Criseyde draws on the *Ars amatoria*, but his guidance as Troilus suffers the loss of Criseyde turns to the *Remedia amoris*. His description as Troy as a town full of lovers is an anachronistic restatement of Ovid's description of Rome as a hunting preserve in which women are the quarry. The remark proves irrelevant, of course, to Troilus's singular investment of desire in Criseyde, but it remains a credible account for medieval readers who saw Troy as the doomed city of fecond Priam and of Helen, Paris, and Deiphoebus. Ovid's teaching, in other words, threatens to deconstruct the promise of plenitude that Augustine holds out for desire. As in his own poems, it is an alternative but not a resolution to desire.

Writing desire within the medieval discourse of love, as we have observed throughout this study, entails the desire to write. This chiasmic reversal is, of course, a trope of modern criticism; but it has, I think, a specific formulation in the medieval texts we have examined. The desire to write or, more accurately, rewrite follows from reading. Heloise negotiates desire within epistolary conventions and by recasting what Abelard writes in the *Historia calamitatum* and subsequent letters. For her letter-writing becomes the means of securing the presence she demands. Marie shapes her project of memorializing Breton *aventure* around a particular reading of Ovid's erotic program. Within her stories characters like the lady of "Yonec" realize their demands by reading them as chivalric romance; for the *Lais* as a whole, readers will supply the "surplus" that completes their meaning. Jean can rewrite Guillaume's *Rose* to the extent that he has attentively read the episodes of Narcissus and the dreamer's approach to the rose and then found counterparts to them in Pygmalion and Venus's assault on the castle. Dante rereads his lyric corpus in the *Vita nuova* and recontextualizes it in order to flee desire. Chaucer's *Troilus and Criseyde* depends on a detailed reading of the *Filostrato* not just for its narrative but also for its context of allusions and interpretive resonance.

At one level, the connection between writing and reading mirrors medieval theories of invention. To compose their own works, writers read antecedent texts to discover what might have been left unexpressed in them. At another, this compositional practice produces an authorial counterpart to narratives of desire. The texts of exemplary desire operate through the discourse of love in order to discover and assert demands that can be spoken only obliquely. Medieval writers reinscribe texts to reimagine and claim possession of their unsaid possibilities and so to secure a place for themselves within the sphere of authorship. Their invention—"discovery" in its original sense—can prove as uncanny as the lover's fraught recognition of what he or she wants. As we read the texts of exemplary desire, then, we see how passion and its urgent attachments are given expression in the Middle Ages by the process that allows writers to uncover them within their own desires and demands. Inevitably, we glimpse, too, our own investments in their texts and practices of writing. Those moments of recognition remind us as modern readers of the crucial play of difference and similarity in our aesthetic and historical understanding of medieval works.

NOTES

Introduction

1. Botterill, *De vulgari eloquentia*, pp. 52–53. On Dante's use of *venus* to designate love, see Welliver, p. 198. Singleton, "Dante," argues that love ("amoris accensio") comes to be contained by another of Dante's great topics—rectitude ("directio voluntatis"). Haller, *Literary Criticism of Dante Alighieri*, gives a different flavor to his translation of the passage: "[we say] that thing is most delightful which gives delight as the most precious object of the appetite: and this is the enjoyment of love" (p. 35). The difference between "pleasure" in Botterill and "delight" in Haller points to a larger debate about the role of pleasure within moral judgments. Aristotle, for instance, admits the consideration of pleasure, while Kant does not. I am grateful to Emily Grosholz for providing the philosophical context of this larger debate. The issues involved in translating *appetitus* as "desire" (Botterill) or "appetite" (Haller) are discussed later in this introduction. *Magnalia*, Dante's term for the major poetic topics, is used in both the Vulgate and Christian commentaries to denote God's miracles.
2. The implicit contrast is with the classical *cursus* of epic, georgic, and pastoral.
3. *The Poetry of Arnaut Daniel*, pp. 36–37.
4. Ambrose's treatise combines a graduated approach of ascetic discipline with the urgency of flight: "Fugiamus hinc" ("Let us flee from here" [*De fuga* 8.45 and 8.46]).
5. *La vie et les epistres*, p. 15.
6. Discussing the passions of the soul, Aquinas (*Summa theologiae* 1a2ae. 30.2 ad 3) contrasts concupiscence with a passion that cannot be named directly but might be called elsewhere *fuga* or *abominatio*. Albert Plé, *Somme théologique I-II*, p. 211, notes that in monastic writings this emotion corresponds to despair (*accidia, taedium vitae*).
7. My discussion here draws on Zizek's analysis of ideological fantasy in the social and political spheres (pp. 30–33), which treats ideology not as mere illusion but as a working rationale for practices that also entail their own demands and potential contradictions of ideology.
8. *Vita nuova*, ed. and trans. Cervigni and Vasta, pp. 108–109. Dante retracts his claim that love is the topic of vernacular poetry in the canzone "Le dolci rime d'amor," written between 1295 and 1300; text in *Dante's Lyric Poetry*, 1: 128–39 and commentary in 2:210–213.

9. The aim of writing in this account is identical to the account of language in general in *De vulgari eloquentia* 1.2.3: "nostre mentis enucleare aliis conceptum" ("to expound to others the concepts formed in our minds"). Dante's formulation in turn paraphrases Augustine's theory of signs in *De doctrina christiana* 2.3: "Nec ulla causa est nobis significandi, id est signi dandi, nisi ad depromendum et traiciendum in alterius animum id quod animo gerit qui signum dat" ("we have no other reason for signifying—that is, giving signs—except extracting and conveying to someone else's mind what is in the mind of the person who gives the sign").

10. In this connection, Cogan's insistence that Dante adapts rather than reproduces Aristotle and Aquinas (pp. 3–19) is a useful reminder of the interplay between poetry and the history of ideas.

11. *Rhetoric* 1.11.10–12; cf. Aquinas, *Summa theologiae* 1a2ae 30.1 resp.

12. *Summa theologiae* 1a2ae 30.2 resp. ad 1; cf. Aristotle, *De anima* 3.9–11.

13. Cicero, *Tusculan Disputations* 4.6.

14. Augustine, *De civitate Dei* 14.7.

15. Augustine, *Enarrationes in Psalmos* 118, sermo 8.4; cf. Augustine, *Sermones* 177.

16. Moi, p. 21.

17. Cicero defines friendship in *De amicitia* 6.20:"Est enim amicitia nihil aliud nisi omnium divinarum humanarumque rerum cum benevolentia et caritate consensio" ("For friendship is nothing else than an accord in all things, human and divine, conjoined with mutual goodwill and affection"). His definition recurs in its basic elements in Jerome (*Epistulae* 130) and Sedulius Scottus (*Collectaneum miscellaneum* 52) and with alternate wording in Aelred of Rievaulx, *De spiritali amicitia* 1.11: "amicitia est rerum humanarum et diuinarum cum beneuolentia et caritate consensio." *Consensio*, understood as a concordance and mutuality of will ("eadem uelle et eadem nolle"), reflects not just a commitment to virtue but also the presence of another as an equal. In classical times, the other is male and patrician. For medieval secular adaptations of Cicero, see Jaeger. See chapter 2, below, for Ovid and erotic reciprocity.

18. The shortened version of Andreas's definition is quoted from a fifteenth-century miscellany printed in *Drouart la Vache*, p. 254, under the rubric "Quid sit amor."

19. Walsh's translation is typical of other renderings in that it breaks Andreas's sentence into two sentences exactly at the point where Andreas states the final cause of love.

20. Boyde, pp. 276–77; cf. Cogan, pp. 19–22.

21. Vlastos, p. 26.

22. Halperin, p. 169.

23. Augustine, *In Iohannis epistulam ad Parthos tractatus* 4.

24. Aristotle, *De anima* 3.10.

25. Aquinas, *Summa theologiae* 1a2ae 30.3.

26. Halperin, p. 175.

27. Ragland-Sullivan, p. 81. Kay offers the best recent application to medieval literature of Lacan's theorizing of desire.

28. Bloch, *Medieval Misogyny and the Invention of Western Romantic Love*, pp. 173–78.

29. Singer, 1: 39–44.

30. Dollimore, pp. xvi–xvii.

31. Foster, p. 53.

32. Zeitlin, p. 63.

1 Desire in Saint Augustine's *Confessions*

1. Chadwick, p. 66; and Hagstrum, p. 191. In the "Epilogue" added to his new edition of *Augustine of Hippo*, pp. 500–502, Peter Brown notes that interest in Augustine's views on sexuality and marriage represents a recent critical shift; but he also stresses the relative moderation of Augustine's views compared to those of Jerome, Ambrose, and the Greek Fathers.

2. Le Goff, p. 96.

3. Hagstrum, p. 193.

4. Thonnard, p. 60. My general discussion depends greatly on Thonnard's study. For discussion of the influence of Stoic thought on Augustine, see Colish, 2: 142–238.

5. *De civitate Dei* 14.2.1 and 14.5.

6. Thonnard, p. 74. After his discussion of various appetites, Augustine says that desire used in an absolute sense, uninflected by any specific object of desire, normally refers to sexual arousal (*De civitate Dei* 14.16).

7. Thonnard, p. 61, n. 8, derives the distinction from Augustine's commentary on Psalm 118: "An aliud est concupiscere, aliud desiderare? Non quod non sit desiderium concupiscentia, sed quia non omnis concupiscentia desiderium est. Concupiscuntur enim et quae habentur et quae non habentur: nam concupiscendo fruitur homo rebus quas habet; desiderando autem, absentia concupiscit. Desiderium ergo quid est, nisi rerum absentium concupiscentia?" ("Is it one thing to want and another to desire? Not because desire is not a form of wanting but because not every want is a desire. We want both what we have and what we do not have, for in wanting something a man enjoys things that he has, but in desiring he wants things that are absent. Therefore, what is desire except wanting things that are absent?"). Rist, pp. 135–36, by contrast, describes *concupiscentia* not as an active drive of appetite but a weakness or inclination inherited from man's fall that becomes sinful when we consent to it.

8. See *De civitate Dei* 14.6, and Thonnard, p. 74; Stump points out that desire involves first- and second-order volition—a movement of the will toward action if nothing impedes it and a will to will. My discussion of Augustine focuses on the workings of first-order volition because of the sensual nature of erotic demands.

9. See the discussion in *Confessions* 8.5.

10. Discussion in Colish, 2: 207–210. In *De civitate Dei* 14.16, Augustine describes the power of desire (*libido*) to organize corporal appetite, overwhelm reason, and move the whole soul with carnal appetite.

11. Aimé Solignac, "Notes complémentaires" to *Confessions* 8, *Oeuvres de Saint Augustin*, 14: 537.

12. Courcelle, *Les Confessions de Saint Augustin dans la tradition littéraire*, p. 101; translation mine.

13. Le Goff, p. 96.

14. Chadwick, pp. 70–74, situates Augustine's discussion of time against the background of Platonic and Aristotelian paradoxes.

15. O'Donnell, *Confessions*, 3: 289–90, discusses the literature on the psychological qualities of *distentio* and its possible connections with Neoplatonism.

16. I cite Skutella and Verheijen's text of the *Confessions* and Warner's translation. O'Donnell, *Augustine*, pp. 116–117, remarks on this passage:

> Time is inherent in the created intellect, a category for describing the apparent transience and impermanence of reality. Time is not even a created thing, for it is a creation of created things. Intelligent created beings see the world around themselves in a framework of their own invention, which they call time. This characteristic distinguishes their experience from that of their creator. God as creator sees all things simultaneously in a single vision, perceiving process and change but, freed of experiencing those things in temporal succession, he does not experience time.

O'Donnell, *Confessions*, 3: 294, suggests parallels with *Confessions* 10.14.21, 10.17.26, and 10.25.36.

17. O'Donnell, *Confessions*, 3: 184, notes that Augustine here and elsewhere does not equate mind with memory, though the formulation invites such a confusion of the two.

18. Freccero, p. 4.

19. Since Augustine's abstract view of time is consistent with his narrative strategies, Freccero may overstate the case in saying, "As in all spiritual autobiographies, so in the *Confessions* and in the *Divine Comedy* there is a radical division between the protagonist and the author who tells his story" (p. 25). The divided self, Augustine makes clear, is an inauthentic self.

20. Peter Brown, *Augustine of Hippo*, p. 169.

21. O'Donnell, *Augustine*, p. 82.

22. The unity of Augustine's *Confessions* is a matter of debate, some holding that the autobiography of books 1–9 is separate from the speculations in books 10–13. The literature is too vast to be surveyed here; see for background K. Grotz, "Die Einheit des 'Confessiones,'" Diss. Tübingen, 1970. For my purposes, the remarks on desire in the last four books provide extensions and commentary on the materials of the autobiography.

23. Pellegrino, p. 62, thinks Augustine's first social experience is going to school, but the convergence of motives described in this passage is fundamentally social.

24. O'Donnell, *Confessions*, 2: 35–36, observes that *ordo* represents the will in action and so corresponds to the second person of the Trinity: "*Ordinatus*

affectus, then, is carefully phrased to identify the place of the impulse to offer nourishment both in human affairs (whence it arises) and in divine affairs (whence it is governed)—the love of a mother that offers this nurture is human love in harmony with divine love."

25. O'Donnell, *Confessions*, 2: 59, comments here, "Speech begins in the fallen man as the assertion of *voluntas*"; he notes the iteration of verbs of willing in the paragraph.

26. Vance, p. 13. Vance goes on to explain that mastering the laws of grammar is also an initiation into lust (p. 15) and that Augustine's figurative fornication in desiring signs is coincident with the beginnings of his physical fornication (p. 19). These parallels are contained in turn within a larger analogy between grammar and the Mosaic Law, which must be replaced by the New Law of charity.

27. Miles, p. 57.

28. In *Confessions* 10.6.8, the imagery of nourishment is correlated with the five senses in Augustine's love for God. At 10.31.44, Augustine situates the "laqueus concupiscentiae" ("snare of concupiscence") at the point of transition between bodily hunger and satiety, and argues the need for regulating physical desires.

29. O'Donnell, *Confessions*, 2: 126–29, 133–34, on Augustine's use of the classical convention that Cataline is a model of evil.

30. Montecelli, *Confessioni*, p. 605, notes that the wordplay demonstrates the equivalence of being and goodness.

31. O'Meara, *The Young Augustine*, p. 55, reports the common opinion that the passage refers to Augustine's first meeting with his future mistress.

32. See Peter Brown, *The Body and Society*, for discussion of the ideal of self-regulation in Mediterranean cultures in late antiquity.

33. The schema set out in 10.30.41 is anticipated at 3.8.16, where Augustine distinguishes the lusts of power, sight, and feeling. The source for both passages is 1 John 2:16 (Skutella and Verheijen, *Confessiones*, pp. 176, 35).

34. O'Meara, "Augustine the Artist and the *Aeneid*," pp. 260, 255.

35. The phrase first appears after Dido has completed her funeral preparations: "magnoque irarum fluctuat aestu" (4.532). It reappears in Mercury's second speech: "certa mori, variosque irarum concitat aestus" (4.564).

36. Fulgentius, *Virgiliana Continentia* in *Opera*, p. 94; *Fulgentius the Mythographer*, p. 127.

37. Bernardus Silvestris, p. 23: "In hoc quarto volumine natura iuventutis exponitur mistice"; and p. 24: "Manifeste ac mistica narratione iuvenilis natura describitur." See Baswell, pp. 101–120, for discussion of parallel materials.

38. Bernardus Silvestris, p. 12.

39. Augustine, *De musica* 6.11.32; see discussion in Edwards, *Ratio and Invention*, pp. xviii–xx, 5–11.

40. McNamara, p. 4.

41. Peter Brown, *The Body and Society*, p. 389.

42. Horace, *Odes* 1.3.8; and Ovid, *Tristia* 4.4–72. In the *Retractationes* (2.6.2), this is one of only two parts of the *Confessions* that Augustine repudiates; he

rejects it lest the idea of the "soul's other half" lead to an affirmation of the World Soul. I owe this observation to Carl Vaught.

43. For Dante's later use of friendship with God, see Mazzaro, "From *Fin Amour* to Friendship."

44. See Courcelle's summary remarks in *Les Confessions de Saint Augustin dans la tradition littéraire*, pp. 191–97.

2 "Nullum crimen erit": Ovidian Craft and the Illusion of Mastery

1. Connolly, p. 75. Ovid names the elegiac poets as his predecessors in *Tristia* 4.10.51–55. Mariscal, p. 163, notes that, while Ovid exhausts the erotic elegy as a form, he influences later Roman writers linguistically, rhetorically, and conceptually.

2. The key sources for Ovid as an ethical poet are Hexter, *Ovid and Medieval Schooling*; Olsen; and Huygens, *Accessus ad auctores*.

3. Ginsberg, "*Ovidus ethicus?*," p. 63.

4. The opening claim of art's ability to regulate love echoes the language of Ovid's description of himself as the elegiac poet-lover at the beginning of his *Amores*: "uror, et in uacuo pectore regnat Amor" ("I am on fire, and in my but now vacant heart Love sits his throne" [1.26]).

5. Gavilán, pp. 95, 109, reviews arguments for the fundamental unity of the *Ars amatoria* and the *Remedia amoris*.

6. Ahern, "Ovid as Vates in the Proem to the *Ars amatoria*," p. 48.

7. Sharrock, *Seduction and Repetition in Ovid's "Ars Amatoria" 2*, p. 21.

8. Dalzell, pp. 136–37, notes Ovid's combination of didactic form with elegiac material as well as the existence of slight didactic themes before Ovid.

9. Fyler, p. 200.

10. Allen, p. 23.

11. Stephen Harrison, p. 84, argues that the opening address to Cupid in the *Remedia amoris* (7–8) describes Ovid as devoted not to love but continuing as an elegiac poet.

12. Tarrant, p. 22.

13. Dalzell, p. 146. Dalzell, pp. 144–46, notes that *ars* as technical skill shades into "cunning" and "deception"; *fides* (1.740) becomes a "meaningless word"; *pudor* means rustic; chastity is turned from the needed attribute of a mistress in elegy to something lost in the *Ars amatoria*: "One by one the pieties of elegy are subjected to a process of reinterpretation and debasement" (p. 146).

14. Green, pp. 222, 226.

15. Green, p. 232.

16. For Ovid's redirection of the meaning, figured in buildings, of Augustus's ideological program from *pietas* to *amor*, see O'Gorman, p. 109.

17. For *commoda* as "fringe-benefits," see Hollis, p. 86.

18. The jurisconsult Gaius (*Institutiones* 3.106) rules the *furiosus* out of business transactions and legal testimony because he does not understand what he is

doing: "Furiosus nullum negotium gerere potest, quia non intellegit, quid agat"; cf. Ulpian, *Liber singularis regularum* 20.7 and 20.13.

19. Tarrant, p. 15, points out that the list of mythological heroines who could have avoided their fates (*Remedia amoris* 55–68) is an inversion of this catalogue.

20. Leach, pp. 146–49.

21. Downing, "Anti-Pygmalion," p. 235.

22. Hexter, "Ovid's Body," p. 331.

23. Sharrock, "Gender and Sexuality," pp. 96–97.

24. Cf. *Ars amatoria* 3.433 and 3.447, where the point is made inversely: women should beware men who are overly concerned with their appearance.

25. Downing, "Anti-Pygmalion," p. 243.

26. Cicero, *Partitiones oratoriae* 88; cited in Lewis and Short, s.v. *amor*.

27. Volk, pp. 168–73.

28. Copley, p. 293.

29. Hollis, p. 85. Wilkinson, p. 51, points out that at least in book 2 of the *Ars amatoria* Ovid seems to be thinking of fairly permanent liaisons.

30. Dalzell, p. 159.

31. Sharrock, *Seduction and Repetition in Ovid's "Ars Amatoria" 2*, p. 10.

32. Ovid's tragic variation on this theme emerges in the *Heroides*, where Oenone contrasts her love for Paris to the dire consequences of his bringing Helen to replace her: "Denique tutus amor meus est: tibi nulla parantur / Bella, nec ultrices advehit unda rates" ("Remember, too, my love can bring no harm; it will beget you no wars, nor bring avenging ships across the wave" [*Heroides* 5.89–90]).

33. Durling, p. 30.

34. Volk, p. 188; cf. pp. 193, 194.

35. Downing, *Artificial I's*, p. 15.

36. Blodgett, p. 331.

37. Hardie, pp. 8–9.

38. Schiesaro, p. 69.

39. Miller, pp. 388–93; Sommariva, pp. 142–46.

40. Shullman, pp. 242–47.

41. Ginsberg, "*Ovidus ethicus?*," p. 65.

42. Fyler, p. 203.

43. Myerowitz, pp. 151–67.

44. Ahern, "Daedalus and Icarus in the *Ars Amatoria*," pp. 275, 277–80.

45. Sharrock, *Seduction and Repetition in Ovid's "Ars Amatoria" 2*, pp. 87–195.

3 Abelard and Heloise: Conversion and Irreducible Desire

1. Abelard is the author of Ep. 1 (his *Historia calamitatum*), Ep. 3 and 5 (responses to Heloise's letters), and Ep. 7 and 8 (the so-called letters of instruction which give a history of monastic life and a Rule for the Paraclete, respectively). Heloise writes Ep. 2 (in response to reading Abelard's *Historia*), Ep. 4, and Ep. 6 (the latter usually included among the

letters of instruction). Muckle, p. 47, establishes the division between the personal letters early in the exchange and the instructional letters that begin with Heloise's Ep. 6. I quote the Latin text and Jean de Meun's French translation of the letters from *La vie et les epistres*, except for the Latin text of Abelard's Ep. 7, for which I cite the edition in PL 178: 225–56; the English translation quoted is Radice with minor changes. Newman, pp. 46–75; and Marenbon, "Authenticity Revisited," pp. 19–33, offer the most influential recent reviews of the debate over the authenticity of the correspondence. I accept the letters as genuine.

2. Scholars like Jaeger, pp. 157–73, accept Mews's argument for the authenticity of these twelfth-century extracts collected by Johannes de Vepria in the fifteenth century. Mews, "Philosophical Themes in the *Epistolae duorum amantium*" and Ward and Chiavaroli report the parallels between the two collections. Meckler's review of Mews's book finds the evidence inconclusive and suggests instead that the texts were an exercise in applying *dictamen* to love letters.

3. The definition of love in letter *24* in Mews, *The Lost Love Letters of Heloise and Abelard*, pp. 208–209, tries to balance an awareness of the beloved with the lover's appetite and desire: "Est igitur amor, vis quedam anime non per se existens nec seipsa contenta, sed semper cum quodam appetitu et desiderio, se in alterum transfundens, et cum altero idem effici volens ut de duabus diversis voluntatibus unum quid indifferenter efficiatur" ("Love is therefore a particular force of the soul, existing not for itself nor content by itself, but always pouring itself into another with a certain hunger and desire, wanting to become one with the other, so that from two diverse wills one is produced without difference").

4. Dronke, *Abelard and Heloise in Medieval Testimonies*, p. 14.

5. Catherine Brown, p. 28.

6. Stock, p. 843.

7. McLaughlin, pp. 468–69. McLaughlin contends that Abelard has little of Augustine's introspection and insight in his *Confessions* (p. 471).

8. Gilson, p. 6.

9. Kamuf, pp. 8–10.

10. See discussion in Dronke, *Abelard and Heloise in Medieval Testimonies*, pp. 26–27.

11. Zumthor, *Abélard and Héloïse: Correspondance*, pp. 14–25, argues for the importance of courtly discourse in the letters. Jolivet, p. 22, disputes the courtly connection because it emanates from a different cultural sphere that does not influence Paris until later in the twelfth century.

12. Heloise, Ep. 2, complains that Abelard's love song made her widely known, roused the envy of other women, and echoed her name in every plaza and household: "me platee omnes, me domus singule resonabant" (p. 53). As Mews points out (*Peter Abelard*, p. 28), reference to the love affair works its way as illustration into several of Abelard's works on logic. In the fifteenth century, Heloise is portrayed as the master of erotic teachings in an "Art d'Amour" that is a partial translation of book 1 of Capellanus's *De amore*; see *Two Late Medieval Love Treatises*.

13. I am grateful to Winthrop Wetherbee for pointing out the structural parallel between the contained, secretive world described in the *Historia* and the example of courtly romance.

14. Jerome, letter 45 (to Asella) in *Epistulae* 1: 324.

15. "De studio litterarum" (Ep. 9) in PL 178: 325–36. Heloise directly echoes Abelard's citation of Jerome in the preface to her *Problemata* (PL 178: 677).

16. Georgianna, p. 199, notes that halfway through Ep. 6 Heloise turns from the details of monastic life to a larger concern: she "mounts an argument that love, not the law, is the object of the spiritual life." The emphasis on particularity and interiority links the personal and religious letters. Blamires, p. 295, suggests, "it seems apt to argue that *all* the consolatory options that Heloise urges her husband to exercise are 'outlets for incontinence' "; he goes on to show how Abelard's letters of instruction absorb Jerome's letters by combining mutual obligations with marital imagery.

17. Text in Stehling, pp. 22–23.

18. Bond, p. 51.

19. For Alexander, see Stehling, nos. 51–55; and for *colloquium*, Stehling, nos. 56, 58, and 63. Bond points out, "the culminating act of *amor* for Baudri is the meeting and discourse of friends (*colloquium*)" (p. 53).

20. Alan of Lille, *De planctu naturae* I.15–20.

21. Curtius, p. 116. As Johnson and Percy point out (p. 181 n. 34), Curtius's brief remarks on sodomy (pp. 113–117) are the starting point for modern discussion of the poetry. Ailes, pp. 228–37, follows Curtius's lead in distinguishing vernacular from Latin texts in their representation of affective bonds between men. Bullough, pp. 55–71, surveys the range of practices that fell under the designation of sodomy.

22. Quoted in Curtius, p. 116.

23. Ovid discusses letter-writing as a tactic for female lovers in *Ars amatoria* 3.469–98 and 3.627–30.

24. Mews, *The Lost Love Letters of Abelard and Heloise*, p. 192–93; cf. letter *54* (pp. 236–37) and letter *110* (pp. 284–85).

25. Though Jean's translation omits the last point ("et sic semper jocundis interesse colloquiis"), Abelard makes it clear that the letters are also a form of erotic exchange. Beebee, p. 116, contends that in the later correspondence Heloise finds an expressive outlet "only in the interstices of the epistolary system."

26. Kamuf, p. 3.

27. The play on *verba* and *verbera* is attested in Terence, Ovid, and Seneca; but the use in ecclesiastical writers such as Augustine, Ambrose, Gregory, and Bernard of Clairvaux seems more extensive.

28. For the door and guardian, see *Ars amatoria* 2.525, 2.635, 3.228, 3.560, 3.592, 3.611.

29. The erotics of reading is a topos that Boccaccio, for instance, utilizes in his *Filocolo*, as reading Ovid instills desire in his protagonists, Florio and Biancifiore.

30. Abelard further signals the Ovidian source by echoing the term *fabula* and the verb *narrare* from the *Ars amatoria:* "Actum itaque in nobis est quod in Marte et Venere deprehensis poetica narrat fabula" (p. 13). Ovid begins his story proper, "Fabula narratur toto notissima caelo" (2.561).

31. Libera, p. 23.

32. Mews, *The Lost Love Letters of Heloise and Abelard*, p. 33.

33. Libera, p. 188.

34. Jean's text omits this passage in his translation, but he refers to it in the *Roman de la Rose* (8777–88); cited by Hicks, ed. cit., p. 17n.

35. Cartlidge, p. 64.

36. Hamilton, pp. 54–55.

37. *Commentaria in epistolam Pauli ad Romanos* (3.7), p. 204: "Quod bene in consolatione uxoris Corneliae Pompeius uictus et profugus commemorans ait: 'Quod defles id amasti.'" The passage that Abelard cites ends Pompey's speech and leads immediately to Cornelia's lament. Abelard also cites *Pharsalia* 3.108 in his *Theologia 'Summi boni'* 2.10.vi, written around 1120.

38. Moos, "Lucan und Abelard."

39. Luscombe, pp. 167–68.

40. Carruthers, p. 179.

41. Irvine, p. 92.

42. Newman, p. 70.

43. See, for example, Clanchy, p. 279; and Marenbon, *The Philosophy of Peter Abelard*, pp. 314–315. This position has a particular attraction to those critics who attribute the *Epistulae duorum amantium* to Abelard and Heloise. The woman in the correspondence strives to link Ciceronian friendship with passionate attachments to her lover. See Mews, "Philosophical Themes in the *Epistolae duorum amantium*," pp. 36–47; and Ward and Chiavaroli, p. 58.

44. I borrow the term feminine reading from Dinshaw, pp. 28–64, who offers it as an alternative to imposing a single, restrictive meaning on a potentially unruly text.

45. *La vie et les epistres*, p. 49: "sed plerisque tacitis quibus amorem conjugio, libertatem vinculo preferebam." Jolivet notes that Heloise makes three related arguments: the marriage will not placate Fulbert and disclosure would ruin Abelard; she would rather be joined by intent than constrained by marriage vows; and if they were temporarily separated, the reunion would be sweeter. If the arguments are taken together, Jolivet contends, it looks as if Heloise wants a free union without cohabitation; if they are separated, she seems resigned to it (p. 21).

46. Dronke, *Women Writers of the Middle Ages*, p. 113, believes that the letter was designed to reach Heloise.

47. Hicks notes that "voz homs" might be read as "uns homs" and "nostre ami" as "vostre ami" (*La vie et les epistres*, p. 45).

48. Heloise is resigned for Kamuf, p. 22, and Wilson and McLeod, p. 123. She is converted to religious life for McGuire, p. 312, and earlier critics like D. W. Robertson, Jr. She remains divided in her allegiances for Gilson, p. 102,

and Georgianna, p. 191. Bourgain, and Moos, "Le silence d'Héloïse" survey the historical and critical reception of Heloise.

49. Cartlidge, p. 69, following Dronke's interpretation in *Women Writers of the Middle Ages*, p. 112.

50. *Theologia christiana* 1.75 and *Theologia 'scholarum'* 1.131.

51. Relevant text in Dronke, *Abelard and Heloise in Medieval Testimonies*, pp. 43–44.

52. See above, ch. 1, n. 7.

53. Godefroy, s.v. *cors*, "personnage, personne."

54. Peter the Venerable, Letter 115, in *La vie et les epistres*, p. 161: "[Deus] hunc, inquam, loco tui, vel ut te alteram, in gremio suo confovet, et in adventu Domini, in voce archangeli, et in tuba Dei descendentis de celo, tibi per ipsius gratiam restituendum reservat."

55. Clanchy, p. 165.

56. For Jerome, the "novella plantatio" represents Israel in the prophetic books of the Bible; see his *Commentarii in Isaiam*, 1: 13, 67–68. Caesarius of Arles (Sermo 205) addresses his auditors as a "novella plantatio" in an Easter sermon; *Sancti Caesarii Arelatensis Sermones*, p. 824. In their monastic histories, Hugues le Poitevin, p. 418, applies it to Vézélay, and Sigebert of Gembloux, p. 512, to Gembloux.

57. Dronke, *Women Writers of the Middle Ages*, p. 116; and McLeod, p. 66, argue in favor of the sexual reading; Blamires, p. 289, argues against.

58. Irvine, p. 97.

59. Clanchy, p. 166, contends that *obnoxius*, in the sense of "liable" is stronger than *obligatus:* "An *obnoxius* debtor is rendered 'submissive' or even 'crippled' by his debt." Heloise's term *complexa* has the further sense, in philosophical usage, of drawing a conclusion, making an inference, and taking possession of something; Lewis and Short, s.v., *complector*. In Jean's translation, her excessive love contains him: "je t'aye tousjours embracié par desatrampee amur."

60. Augustine, "Sermo 83," in PL 38: 514–519.

61. For the application of *debitum* to another narrative context, see Baldwin.

62. Gilson, p. 57; Newman, p. 69.

63. Mews, *Epistulae duorum amantium*, pp. 210–211, 228–29.

64. Jeager, p. 169.

65. Gilson, p. 59.

66. As in her first letter, Heloise continues, for instance, to assert the power of intention as a moral criterion. She asks in Ep. 4 how penance can work when the mind retains the will to sin ("ipsam peccandi. . .voluntatem") and burns with its old desires ("pristinis. . .desideriis" [p. 66]). In Ep. 6, she invokes Christ's teaching that the soul is corrupted by evil intent before the body acts: "Nisi enim prius prava voluntate animus corrumpatur, peccatum esse non poterit, quicquid exterius agatur in copore [sic]" [p. 102]).

67. Marenbon, *The Philosophy of Peter Abelard*, p. 92; cf. Georgianna, p. 203: "Unlike Abelard, who distinguishes between desire and consent, the constitutive element

of sin, Heloise seems to equate the two and thus to damn herself as unworthy of God's forgiveness."

68. The dating is approximate, but it falls within the decade: 1132/33–35 for the personal and instructional letters, and 1136–39 for the *Problemata*; see Mews, *Peter Abelard*; pp. 50, 91 for dating; and Barrow, Burnett, and Luscombe, pp. 242, 244–45, and 251 for manuscript sources.

69. Abelard, Ep. 8, in PL 178: 300–301.

70. The formula reappears in Abelard's prefaces to his "Confession" to Heloise (PL 178: 378), *Expositio in Hexaemeron* (PL 178: 731), and *Hymni* (PL 178: 1771–72).

71. Irvine, p. 102, cf. Newman, p. 73.

72. Heloise's rhetorical strategy in this passage is connected as well to the salutation of Ep. 6: "Suo specialiter, sua singulariter" ("To him who is hers specially, from her who is his singularly"). Gilson, p. 102, reading "Domino" for "Suo," rightly observes that Heloise is part of the species as a bride of Christ but a singular individual as Abelard's bride. Mews, "Philosophical Themes in the *Epistolae duorum amantium*," p. 43, and Georgianna, p. 197, point out that the question of intimacy lies with the philosophical distinctions.

73. Georgianna, p. 209 n. 32, and Blamires, p. 294, following Gilson, p. 188 n. 21 and Dronke, *Women Writers of the Middle Ages*, p. 305 n. 39, favor Jerome as the immediate source of the image.

74. Jerome, Epistula 125.14 in *Epistulae*, 3:132. The example of Ahasuerus also connects Heloise's quotation of Jerome to the *Historia*, where Abelard refutes suspicions that he still has carnal interests (p. 37).

75. Cicero, *Tusculan Disputations* 4.35.75.

76. McLeod, pp. 79–82.

77. Heloise, *Problemata Heloissae* in PL 178: 726: "Ille autem, qui ultra istam necessitatem [generandi] progreditur, jam non rationi, sed libidini obsequitur" ("Whoever goes beyond the mere necessity of reproduction yields not to reason but to lust").

78. Wetherbee notes that Abelard abandons self-analysis as the narrative goes forward and presents his spiritual state as "constant and beyond question": "All that matters is Abelard's endurance of suffering" (p. 56).

79. Text in PL 178: 294.

80. Text in PL 178: 266.

81. Text in PL 178: 302.

82. Bussell, p. 235.

83. PL 178: 262. The text gives variant readings for the attachments that monastic life allows one to escape: "saecularium rerum [*var.*: virorum, vitiorum] vinculis absolutus."

84. PL 178: 265: "monachi, hoc est solitarii nomen."

85. Catherine Brown, p. 37, connects the division of body and soul in this passage to Heloise's strategy of using her supposed "hypocrisy" as a tool of resistance and aggressive submission.

86. Georgianna, p. 191.

4 Marie de France and *Le livre Ovide*

1. I quote from *Les Lais de Marie de France*; the translation is by Burgess and Busby.
2. Bloch, *The Anonymous Marie de France*, pp. 42–48. Fitz, "Desire and Interpretation" traces the dialectic of exegesis and eros in Marie's Tristan episode. For desire as the supplement operating through the social sphere, see Stein, p. 289. Pickens observes that Marie as a feminine poet effectively inseminates her audience and patrons.
3. Nichols, "Marie de France's Commonplaces," p. 135.
4. Hanning, "The Talking Wounded," p. 144.
5. Discussion in Segre, Cargo, Gertz, and Brightenback.
6. *Les Lais de Marie de France*, p. 244.
7. Hanning, "Courtly Contexts for Urban *cultus*," p. 45.
8. Hanning, "Talking Wounded," pp. 141–42.
9. Gertz, p. 382.
10. *Accessus ad auctores*, p. 33.
11. Stapleton, p. 294.
12. Maddox, p. 36.
13. Dubuis, p. 397.
14. Burgess, pp. 147–58.
15. Gertz, p. 382; Whalen.
16. Stapleton, p. 293.
17. Fitz, "The Prologue to the *Lais* of Marie de France and the *Parable of The Talents*," p. 563.
18. Ménard, *Les Lais de Marie de France*, p. 237; translation mine.
19. For Marie's contemporary Walter Map, author of the antimatrimonial tract "Dissuasio Valerii ad Ruffinum," the women who bestow this plenitude are sources of fear and demonic power; see *De nugis curialium* 2.12–14, 4.8–9, 11.
20. Kay, pp. 202–203.
21. For the reading of castration, see Bloch, *The Anonymous Marie de France*, p. 93.
22. Burgess, pp. 135–36.
23. Hanning, "Courtly Contexts," p. 51.
24. Ribard, pp. 143–45.
25. Paupert, pp. 177–81, notes the equivalence of love and speaking for the heroines of the *Lais*.
26. Burgess, pp. 152–57.
27. Prior, p. 129.
28. Nelson, and Howard S. Robertson.
29. Brook, pp. 15–16, conveniently sets the textual against the historical evidence.
30. Kelly, " 'Diversement comencier' in the *Lais* of Marie de France," p. 109, notes that the triangle is not just a fundamental or inherited structure in the *Lais* but also the point from which Marie begins the process of rhetorical invention that connects her to Latin literary culture.
31. Mickel, "A Reconsideration of the *Lais* of Marie de France," p. 64.

32. In this respect, the story addresses its audience directly, the "Cunte, barun e chivaler" and the aristocratic ladies whose pleasure with the *Lais* is mentioned by the twelfth-century Anglo-Norman writer Denis Piramus; quoted in Ménard, "Marie de France et nous," p. 7.

33. Cottille-Foley, pp. 157–61, suggests that the husband's killing the nightingale removes him from the love triangle and substitutes the entombed bird; in a further substitution, the bird comes to represent Marie's story itself.

34. Freeman, p. 868.

35. Zumthor, p. 389.

36. Shippey, p. 51.

37. Mickel, "A Reconsideration of the *Lais* of Marie de France," p. 56.

38. Bloch, *The Anonymous Marie de France*, p. 73.

39. Tudor, and Cottrell, p. 504.

5 Rewriting Desire in the *Roman de la Rose*

1. I quote from *Le Roman de la Rose*, ed. Poirion; the translation is by Dahlberg, with minor changes.

2. Kelly, " 'Li chastiaus. . .Qu'Amors prist puis par ses esforz,' " p. 65, argues that the seizure by Amors was to terminate Guillaume's poem. Regalado, "The Medieval Construction of the Modern Reader," pp. 96–97, points out that Jean will make Amant a reader who refuses to gloss.

3. Eberle, pp. 244–45, connects the encyclopedic quality of the mirror to developments in thirteenth-century optics, which produced an instrument with multiple perspectives. The mirror underwrites "a poem *for* lovers and at the same time a poem *about* lovers" (p. 259). Brownlee, "Reflections in the *Miroër aus Amoreus*," shows how Jean's addresses to different kinds of readers add up to "a potentially universal audience" (p. 70). Fleming, "Jean de Meun and the Ancient Poets," pp. 83–84, asserts that the encyclopedism is selective and that Jean is oriented toward the classical and away from the vernacular romance tradition.

4. Hult, *Self-Fulfilling Prophecies*, pp. 10–14, gives a useful account of the permutations and literary effects of the passage.

5. Regalado, "The Medieval Construction of the Modern Reader," p. 101, remarks that Jean's prophesied birth is also the birth of a reader for the *Rose*.

6. Kelly, "Du Narcisse des poètes à la rose des amants," observes, "La matière de Jean de Meun, c'est Guillaume de Lorris" (p. 794).

7. Luria, pp. 3, 12, 16, 30. My discussion of additions and continuations in the *Rose* is necessarily limited to Guillaume and Jean; it does not take into account other writers and scribes who reconceive the poem, nor does it consider the condensing effects of lacunae in Poirion's base manuscript, which are restored from other editions. For recent discussion of textual problems bearing on interpretation, see Huot, "Authors, Scribes, Remanieurs"; Huot, *The "Romance of the Rose" and Its Medieval Readers*; and Hult, *Self-Fulfilling Prophecies*, pp. 10–104.

8. Pierre Col, "Response aux traitiés precedens" [by Christine de Pisan and Jean Gerson], in *Le Débat sur le Roman de la Rose*, pp. 91, 96, 98, 102, 103.

9. Hult, "Language and Dismemberment: Abelard, Origen, and the *Romance of the Rose*," pp. 106–108.

10. Heller-Roazen, p. 10.

11. Regalado, " 'Des contraires choses,' " pp. 63–65; see Minnis, *Magister amoris*, pp. 17–21 and 82–118, on the multiplicity of poetic *integument*. Cherniss, pp. 233–38, gives an account of the contrast between literal and figurative levels that works toward a final meaning for love in moral systems outside the poem.

12. Kelly, *Internal Difference and Meanings in the "Roman de la Rose"* proposes that the *Rose* has more than one literal level (pp. 28, 32) and offers more than one context for interpreting action (pp. 128–30).

13. Strubel, pp. 107–111, rightly points out that the succession involves connections far more complex than Amors suggests. Brownlee, "Jean de Meun and the Limits of Romance," p. 116, notes that the situation of rhetorical address changes from Amant as the protagonist-narrator to other figures in the poem (e.g., Bel Acuel, Amors's barons) just at the point that Amors remarks that Guillaume has ceased and Jean will continue.

14. Baumgartner observes that Guillaume creates a five-year gap in time between Amant's dream and his narrative (p. 24) and suggests that the search to recover the rose as an object of desire is an effort to regain the panoptic vision conferred by the crystals (p. 34).

15. Poirion, "De la signification selon Jean de Meun," p. 180, argues that, at the level of linguistic reference, Jean tries to put his continuation of Guillaume beyond desire.

16. I follow the suggestion of Fleming, *Reason and the Lover*, p. 83, that Jean's "supertext" is the *Confessions*, though I read it as a source used to a different effect.

17. Poirion, "Narcisse et Pygmalion dans *Le Roman de la Rose*," pp. 158–59, suggests that the episode critiques the rhetorical situation and circularity of courtly lyric. Köhler, pp. 163–64, sees it as the idealization of a culture that has already been overtaken and surpassed by historical forces. Hult, *Self-Fulfilling Prophecies*, pp. 268–73, stresses the parallel isolation of Echo and Narcissus.

18. Steinle, p. 253, contends, "The essence of Narcissus is *forma*, outer beauty" with no capacity for self knowledge.

19. Thut, p. 111, finds allusions to rhetoric, hence poetic craft, in the description of the crystals.

20. Knoespel, pp. 66–93, discusses the details of Guillaume's invention from the *Metamorphoses* and sees the turn to Ovid's erotic poems only in the continuation of the *Rose* (p. 93).

21. Köhler, pp. 159–60.

22. Allen, p. 101.

23. Thut, pp. 121–22, sees Pygmalion as the representative of art and of the narrator as artist.

24. Huot, *From Song to Book*, interprets Pygmalion as "Jean's corrected image of the lyric poet as writer" (p. 98) and notes that manuscript miniatures of Pygmalion asleep clearly recall those of Guillaume's dreamer asleep at the start of the poem (p. 99).
25. Brownlee, "Pygmalion, Mimesis, and the Multiple Endings of the *Roman de la Rose*," p. 197.
26. Dragonetti, pp. 108–109.
27. Kelly, *Internal Difference and Meanings in the "Roman de la Rose,"* pp. 76–78.
28. Pelen, pp. 46, 167. Thut, pp. 128–29, points out that Adonis is not only the lover with whom Venus betrays Mars but also the incestuous partner whose birth she has made possible by aiding Pygmalion.
29. Gunn, pp. 147–50.
30. Fleming, *Reason and the Lover*, p. 30: "For Jean de Meun, Reason is exactly what Guillaume de Lorris said she was and something more besides. She is human reason, the image of the sapiential Christ in man, and the mirror of *sapientia* in the created world." The alternate interpretation follows Cherniss's claim (p. 230) that Raison's authority is impossible in the fallen world of the *Rose* and Wetherbee's sense that she can think "only in terms of an allegorically coherent universe," not one in which cosmic harmony has been lost (*Poetry and Platonism in the Twelfth Century*, p. 259).
31. Regalado, " 'Des contraires choses,' " p. 72.
32. Stakel, p. 77.
33. *Andreas Capellanus On Love*, p. 32.
34. See introduction, pp. 5–6.
35. Kelly, *Internal Difference and Meanings in the "Roman de la Rose,"* p. 61, argues that Andreas's shared sexual aim is contained somewhat in Reason's definition of friendship as shared goodwill.
36. See discussion in Karnein, pp. 216–218.
37. Heller-Roazen, pp. 6, 97–98, proposes that Fortune defines the necessary conditions for love.
38. Dahlberg, p. 573, contends that natural love is the base for other kinds of love and implies them.
39. Kelly, *Internal Difference and Meanings in the "Roman de la Rose,"* pp. 113–115.
40. Paré, pp. 95–98.
41. "Boethius' *De consolatione* by Jean de Meun," p. 168.
42. Uitti, pp. 56–58, describes a process of growth from erotic demand toward a sense of service and reciprocity.
43. This passage and mention of a courtly beloved at the start of the poem who should be called Rose (40–44) lay the groundwork for Amors's assertion that Amant represents Guillaume (10526–36).

6 "Simulacra nostra": The Problem of Desire in Dante's *Vita nuova*

1. Quotations and translations taken from *Vita nuova*, ed. and trans. Cervigni and Vasta, based on Barbi's text; for reference, I cite Barbi's divisions of the text.

2. See Barolini, " 'Cominciandomi dal principio infino a la fine' (*V.N.*, XXIII, 15)" for a lucid discussion of prolepsis and recursion and for the *contaminatio* of narrative and lyric.

3. De Robertis, p. 80.

4. Menocal, p. 13, would reverse the priority of the narrative over the poetic history, or, rather, treat the narrative as only a consequence of Dante's focus on writing.

5. Robert Pogue Harrison, p. 140.

6. Durling and Martinez, p. 62, referring to the divisions of "Donne ch'avete intelletto d'amore." For a critique of these divisions as a general model and a reading that emphasizes the eroticization of division, see Stillinger, pp. 97–100.

7. Botterill, p. 67. Because they are focused on content, Dante's divisions, says Botterill, can be replaced by narrative (p. 76).

8. Roush, p. 29.

9. D'Andrea, pp. 505–506, sets out principles for gauging the revisions between the *Vita nuova* and the *Convivio*.

10. Mazzaro, *The Figure of Dante*, pp. 89–94, traces the discrepancies between prose and poetic accounts as scholastic predicaments and predicables.

11. Cecco Angiolieri, "Dante Allaghier, Cecco, 'l tu' servo e amico"; text and translation in *Dante's Lyric Poetry*, 1: 98–99. This edition will be cited for Dante's lyrics outside the *Vita nuova* and for poems associated with them.

12. Barolini, "Dante and the lyric past," p. 27.

13. Mazzotta, "The Light of Venus and the Poetry of Dante," p. 195.

14. Boccaccio, *Trattatello in laude di Dante* [29], p. 444. I quote from the first redaction; the second redaction reads, "quasi dello inizio della sua puerizia infino allo stremo della sua vita" (3:501). The translation is from Nichols.

15. The influence of Dante's poetry on Boccaccio's rendering of his life can also be seen in Boccaccio's account of the prophetic dream of Dante's mother. Boccaccio specifically echoes the language of Dante's comment at the end of the prose account of his first *visione* in the *Vita nuova*: "come che ciò non fosse allora da lei conosciuto né da altrui; e oggi, per lo effetto seguìto, sia manifestissimo a tutti" ("Although this dream was not then understood by her or by anyone else, it is now clear to all from what followed" [*Trattatello* 16]); the second redaction of the *Trattatello* 14 preserves the echo but phrases it differently.

16. "Lasso, lo dol che più mi dole," lines 7–8 in *Dante's Lyric Poetry*, 1:98–99. I accept Foster and Boyde's division of the poems between Dante and Dante da Maiano.

17. "Per quella via che la bellezza corre," in *Dante's Lyric Poetry*, 1: 98–101.

18. The texts are printed in *Dante's Lyric Poetry* as nos. 59–61, 64–66, 67–68, and 77–80.

19. "Perch'io non trovo," lines 1–2, in *Dante's Lyric Poetry*, 1: 194–97.

20. "Io sono stato con Amore insieme," lines 13–14, in *Dante's Lyric Poetry*, 1: 198–201.

21. *Dantis Alagherii Epistolae*, p. 22. See Took, p. 79, on Dante's recursion to Cavalcanti. Foster, pp. 50–51, reads *Purgatorio* 16 and 18 as a direct refutation of the erotic determinism expressed in Dante's reply to Cino.

22. "Poi ch'i' fu', Dante, dal mio natal sito," lines 7–8, in *Dante's Lyric Poetry*, 1: 204–205.

23. Ginsberg, *Dante's Aesthetics of Being*, p. 5.

24. "Amor, da che convien pur ch'io mi doglia," lines 8–10, in *Dante's Lyric Poetry*, 1: 204–211.

25. Contini, *Dante Alighieri: Rime*, p. 208n, cites sources for the image in vernacular writers, but see Giannarelli, pp. 101–102, for Ovidian influence. To Giannarelli's remarks on the Christian tradition of the image, one might add the description of Christ's Transfiguration in Matthew 17:2 and commentary on the passage by Augustine, Jerome, Cassiodorus, Bede, and Bernard of Clairvaux.

26. Boccaccio, *Trattatello* 175, notes that the *Vita nuova* appeals "massimamente a' volgari." Ricci, 3:890 takes the phrase to mean those who love to read writings in the vernacular, a group comprised of a small circle of poetic correspondents and a larger, though less distinct, group of women addressees. Ricci also remarks that Boccaccio is in error when he claims that Dante was later embarrassed by the *Vita nuova*; cf. *Convivio* 1.1.16.

27. I follow Took's discussion here of the "the notion that the lover, far from being a *victim* of love, connives at his own subjection" (p. 80). Cavalcanti offers one source for this awareness, and in the narrative of the *Vita nuova* it is apparent from the time that Beatrice withdraws her greeting. In "De gli occhi de la mia donna si move" (*Dante's Lyric Poetry*, 1:52), for example, as the light from Beatrice's eyes instills fear, the poet recognizes, "ma poscia perdo tutte le mie prove, / e tornomi colà dov'io son vinto" ("But then, losing all power to resist, I return to the place where I am overcome").

28. Hollander differentiates the dream visions of Love from the Pauline *raptus* of the last vision, which may not be oneiric. Singleton, pp. 13–20, takes Dante's delirious recognition that Beatrice must die (ch. 23) as the third vision; the terms applied to it are *imaginazione* and *fantasia*.

29. Sturm-Maddox, p. 131, remarks the inadequacy of the traditional audience that Dante first envisions and the progressive expansion of his audience as Dante redefines the scope of love poetry.

30. Stone, p. 144.

31. Shapiro, p. 112.

32. De Robertis, p. 30n, points out that the manuscript tradition records alternate phrasing for Beatrice's investiture in virtues—e.g., "umilemente d'onestà vestuta."

33. Robert Pogue Harrison, p. 24.

34. "Se Lippo amico se' tu che mi leggi," in *Dante's Lyric Poetry*, 1: 18–21. If the association of lyric and music is traditional, Dante nonetheless suggests by evoking the tradition that the inner linguistic meaning of the canzone becomes intelligible precisely because of its outer musical covering.

35. "Lo meo servente core," in *Dante's Lyric Poetry*, 1: 20–21. Contini, *Dante Alighieri: Rime*, p. 25, notes the echo of the phrase "secondo il mio parvente" (line 10) from this poem in the first sonnet of the *Vita nuova* ("suo parvente" [line 3]).

36. Mazzotta, "The Language of Poetry in the *Vita nuova*," p. 6: "Against the materiality of the one [Dante da Maiano] and the abstraction of the other [Cavalcanti] Dante is involved in probing ever-equivocal signs, disguises, and masks through which love and poetry come into being."

37. Guido Cavalcanti, "Vedeste, al mio parere, onne valore," in *Dante's Lyric Poetry*, 1: 14–15.

38. The motif of the heart held in the hand refers to Cavalcanti's "Perchè non fuoro"; see *Dante's Lyric Poetry*, 2: 27 (where Death, not Love, holds the heart) and Robert Pogue Harrison, p. 21. De Robertis, pp. 42–43, notes that the biblical echoes of the scene also resonate with Cavalcanti's poetry.

39. Ginsberg, *Dante's Aesthetics of Being*, pp. 42–43.

40. Dante da Maiano, "Provedi, saggio, ad esta visïone," in *Dante's Lyric Poetry*, 1: 2–3. Although Took, p. 14, doubts the seriousness of the poem, it offers Dante a vocabulary ("visione" and "sentenza") and a model for the uncanny dreamwork of his vision. Contini, ed. *Dante Alighieri: Rime*, p. 3, notes the diverse interpretations of the last line made by Dante da Maiano's correspondents. Foster and Boyde, *Dante's Lyric Poetry*, 2:4 observe that the line can be punctuated several ways with corresponding shifts in meaning.

41. Dante, "Savete giudicar vostra ragione," in *Dante's Lyric Poetry*, 1: 2–4.

42. I am grateful to Warren Ginsberg for suggesting that Dante da Maiano's poem successively translates the image of covering from the woven garland to the texture of the shift to the poet's flesh covering the beloved but taking original form from the mother's flesh to the poet's textual veiling of the lovers' physical consummation. As an intertext for Dante's vision and accompanying sonnet in the *Vita nuova*, Dante da Maiano's poem comes strikingly closer to registering the desire that Dante subsequently obscures.

43. Martinez notes, "we can understand the unfolding of the plot of the *Vita nuova* as a series of separations and losses" (pp. 15–16).

44. Klemp, p. 187.

45. For an interpretation that emphasizes the prophetic dimensions of this episode, see Nolan, pp. 44–47.

46. De Robertis, p. 58, bases the problem of erotic succession in Andreas Capellanus's *De amore*. The dynamic I am tracing has to do, however, with repetition rather than succession.

47. My reading of Dante's shift from the first to the second screen lady extends the argument made in Piccone, pp. 60–61, which revises Spitzer's analysis of the sonnet as a pastorella.

48. Barolini, *Dante's Poets: Textuality and Truth in the "Comedy,"* pp. 9–13, suggests that *cortese* remains a stable term with shifting applications in the *Vita nuova*, *Convivio*, and *Commedia*.

49. "Per una ghirlandetta," in *Dante's Lyric Poetry*, 1: 38–39.

50. Contini, ed., *Dante Alighieri: Rime*, p. 39n.

51. "Deh, Vïoletta, che in ombra d'Amore," in *Dante's Lyric Poetry*, 1: 38–39. Beatrice smiles as she comes to resemble Love (ch. 24), and in his division of the sonnet "Ne li occhi porta la mia donna Amore," Dante says that he omits discussion of the workings of her smile "però che la memoria non

puote ritenere lui né sua operazione" ("because memory cannot retrain her smile or its operation" [21.8]).

52. Singleton, p. 16, simply equates *simulacra* with the screen ladies. De Robertis, p. 20, says that the screen ladies remain perfectly coherent within the circuit of courtly love, while Beatrice, the sole object of love, is sublimated by being identified with love itself and becoming an exemplum of a divine idea. He suggests elsewhere (pp. 68, 70) that the source for the screen ladies is the muses that Lady Philosophy drives away from Boethius's bed at the beginning of the *Consolation of Philosophy*. Shaw, p. 84, argues that the phrase "simulacra nostra" refers not just to the screen ladies but also to "the forms in which he, Love, has hitherto appeared to him, the modes in which Dante has hitherto imagined Love—the peremptory master and the heart-peddling patron."

53. Citing Isaiah 40:18 ("cui ergo similem fecistis Deum aut quam imaginem ponetis ei") and stressing the anagogical dimension of spiritual seeing, Nolan extends the meaning of *simulacra* from screen to the technical sense of "idols and vain appearances which are mistakenly worshipped in place of the true God" (p. 48). Perhaps closer to the sense of trauma in the *Vita nuova* is the vengeance in Ezechiel 7: 21–22, noted by Jerome, *Commentarii in Ezechielem* 2.7.

54. De Robertis, pp. 145–46, remarks that the lyrics recorded in the "extravagant" tradition—that is, the poems with manuscript sources outside and presumably earlier than the *Vita nuova*—are subsequently revised to reflect the shift in emphasis away from Dante as lover and toward Beatrice as an object of contemplation.

55. "Lo doloroso amor che mi conduce," line 14, in *Dante's Lyric Poetry*, 1: 44–47. In the fantasy and delirium that accompany his realization that Beatrice must die (*Vita nuova* 23), Dante stops short of naming Beatrice publicly. She is named in *Vita nuova* 31.

56. De Robertis, pp. 31–36.

57. Barolini, "Dante and the lyric past," p. 27.

58. *Dante's Lyric Poetry*, 2: 92.

59. "E' m'incresce di me sì duramente," lines 51–53, in *Dante's Lyric Poetry*, 1: 54–59.

60. Augustine, *De doctrina christiana* 3.5: "ea demum est miserabilis animi seruitus, signa pro rebus accipere; et supra creaturam corpoream, oculum mentis ad hauriendum aeternum lumen leuare non posse" ("It is surely a wretched slavery of the soul to take signs for things, and not be able to raise the eye of the mind above the physical body to draw in the everlasting light").

61. Singleton, p. 22.

62. "Guido, i' vorrei che tu e Lapo ed io," in *Dante's Lyric Poetry*, 1:31–32.

63. De Robertis, p. 81; Took, p. 20.

64. Moleta, pp. 3–5, argues that the first beginning of the poem was written after the second and inserted after it in the *Vita nuova* because of the episode with the "donna pietosa." The contrived sequence shows that the "donna pietosa" is a detour on the way toward the beatific vision of the final sonnet.

65. De Robertis, p. 24.

66. Fenzi, p. 198.

67. See "The Biographical Problems in 'Voi che 'ntendendo' (no. 59)," in *Dante's Lyric Poetry*, 2: 341–62.

68. D'Andrea, pp. 503–505.

69. Took, p. 27.

70. Dronke, *Dante's Second Love*, p. 9.

71. In *Vita nuova* 25.9, Dante quotes the opening of the *Remedia amoris* in his defense of prosopopoeia.

72. Mazzaro, *The Figure of Dante*, p. 22; Andreas Capellanus, pp. 32–33 (cf. discussion in introduction, pp. 5–6). For Dante and Capellanus, see De Robertis, pp. 44–52.

73. As D'Andrea notes, p. 504, the "vilissimo" of this passage will be transformed into the "virtuosissimo" of the *Convivio* (an ethical but not a spiritual term).

74. Dronke, *Dante's Second Love*, pp. 8–9, suggests that Dante borrows the phrasing from the Song of Songs and Cavalcanti, though in forms sapiential as well as erotic; cf. De Robertis, p. 45 n. 1. De Robertis, p. 50, also cites Capellanus as the source for the motif of erotic displacement (see above, chapter 3, for Jerome and Cicero as the sources for Heloise).

7   The Desolate Palace and the Solitary City: Chaucer, Boccaccio, and Dante

1. Quotations of Chaucer's poetry are taken from *The Riverside Chaucer*. For comparisons between *Troilus and Criseyde* and Boccaccio's *Filostrato*, I rely on the text of the *Filostrato* edited by V. Pernicone, as printed in Windeatt, *Troilus and Criseyde*; English translation by Gordon, *The Story of Troilus*.

2. Besserman, p. 307.

3. Fleming, *Classical Imitation and Interpretation in Chaucer's "Troilus,"* pp. 26–27.

4. Calabrese, pp. 67–69.

5. Henry Ansgar Kelly, pp. 119–20, suggests a possible source for the lines in a poem cited in Hermanus Alemannus's translation of Averroes's commentary on Aristotle's *Poetics*. Robert Holcot cites the poem in his commentary on the Book of Wisdom, which Chaucer knew, but there are no close echoes.

6. Gottwald, pp. 48–53. Gottwald, p. 34, contends that the primary literary type is the national lament and that its expression of common misery contains the funeral song and the individual lament.

7. Mintz, p. 24.

8. Augustine, *Confessionum libri XIII*, ed. Skutella and Verheijen, p. 44; translation by Warner.

9. Dante Alighieri, *Il convivio*, ed. Simonelli, pp. 5–6; for discussion, see Freccero.

10. Augustine turns this realization into an explanation of the fear that accompanies his grief; see discussion above, ch. 1, pp. 32–34.

11. See Peter Brown, *The Body and Society*, pp. 388–95, for discussion of friendship and *otium*.

12. Stegmüller, 3: 342 for general information and 9: 210–211 for supplement.

13. Contreni, p. 87, observes, "Paschasius Radbertus, in the absence of an earlier commentary on Lamentations, wrote his own."

14. Lubac, 1: 199–209, argues against the claim that Radbertus is a literalist along the lines of Jerome. A short tract "In Lamentationes Jeremiae" (PL 25: 827–32), falsely ascribed to Jerome and possibly by Bede, likewise maintains the dual emphasis on historical and figural levels, though much of its stress falls on reading Lamentations as an allegory of the Church and the failings of its prelates.

15. In pairing Lamentations with the Song of Songs, medieval Christian exegetes take the same step as postexilic Jewish commentators who repair the absence of any prophecy and consolation in Lamentations by reading the text against other parts of the Hebrew Bible; see Mintz, pp. 49–83.

16. Paschasius Radbertus, p. 4.

17. Matter, p. 151. Matter adds later that the Bible is a source in every passage: "Radbertus set about explicating Lamentations by a system of resonances to other biblical passages" (p. 155).

18. Paschasius Radbertus, p. 5.

19. Martinez, pp. 3–7, emphasizes the sense of separation and loss that the exegetical tradition makes available to interpreters.

20. Paschasius Radbertus, p. 9.

21. Paschasius Radbertus, p. 10.

22. Rabanus Maurus, *Expositio super Jeremiam libri viginti*, in PL 111:1185.

23. Guibert of Nogent, *Ad tropologias in prophetas Osee et Amos ac Lamentationes Jeremiae* 5.1.1 in PL 156: 451.

24. Hugh of St. Victor, *Adnotatiunculae elucidatoriae in threnos Jeremiae*, in PL 175: 257.

25. Lathbury, sig. C1ra; on the prologue, see Minnis, *Medieval Theory of Authorship*, pp. 180, 275 n. 51. On Lathbury, see Smalley, pp. 221–39.

26. Bloomfield, p. 18, quoting Smalley, notes that Robert Holcot deals with the deserted palace as a figure of the transitoriness of human life in his commentary on the Book of Wisdom.

27. The element of hope that Gottwald (pp. 91–111) finds in the text of Lamentations derives from the restrictive basis of God's righteousness and self-determination and man's subsequent submission.

28. Singleton, *An Essay on the "Vita Nuova,"* p. 6.

29. Quotations and translations from Cervigni and Vasta, *Vita nuova*; for reference, I cite Barbi's divisions of the text.

30. For Dante's conception of the *canzone* as a poetic form that encompasses the full range of themes possible in the lyric, see *De vulgari eloquentia* 2.3.1–10; in the *Convivio*, the claims Dante makes for the value of the vernacular are, as a practical matter, inseparable from the ability of the *canzone* to express elevated themes.

31. The repetition of image is supplemented by a formal repetition that likewise recalls the citation of Lamentations. As in the incomplete *canzone* of ch. 27,

each stanza of this *canzone*, except the six-line *envoi* of part three, is a complete sonnet, though written in a different rhyme scheme from earlier sonnets.

32. Singleton, *An Essay on the "Vita Nuova,"* p. 23.
33. De Bonfils Templer, pp. 115–21.
34. Branca, pp. 128–30.
35. Robert Pogue Harrison, p. 24.
36. Kleiner, p. 91.
37. Robert Pogue Harrison, p. 134.
38. McGregor, p. 149, argues that in his *Trattatello in laude di Dante*, Boccaccio offers a "patient deflation and explaining away of precisely those spiritual elements that in the *Vita Nuova* vibrate in the charged presence of Beatrice."
39. Boccaccio, *Filostrato*, p. 170.
40. Hanning, "Come in Out of the Code," p. 129.
41. Hanning, "Come in Out of the Code," p. 127n.
42. Wood, p. 13.
43. For discussion of Pandarus's speech in relation to Chaucer's earlier dream lore, see Edwards, *The Dream of Chaucer*, pp. 155–56.
44. For discussion of Pandarus's remark, see Edwards, "Pandarus's 'Unthrift' and the Problem of Desire in *Troilus and Criseyde*."
45. On memory systems, see Carruthers; Mazzaro, *The Figure of Dante*; and Schibanoff.
46. In this respect, Troilus's alignment of Criseyde with the work of memory ironically tropes the scene in book 1 in which his imagination is drawn to the empty space defined by Criseyde (1.169–77, 295–98).
47. It is what Philosophy calls "the derknesse of desceyvynge desyrynges" (*Boece* 1, pr.6, 103–104). Later she says of "delyces of body," "Of whiche delices I not what joie mai ben had of here moevynge, but this woot I wel, that whosoevere wol remembren hym of hise luxures, he schal wel undirstonden that the issues of delices ben sorweful and sorye" (3 pr.7, 7–12).
48. Lambert observes, "This poet's Troy is the city of kindness and friendship, of an unheroic and, because not free of foibles, unintimidating loving-kindness" (p. 61).
49. Vance, p. 300.
50. Windeatt, *Troilus and Criseyde*, p. 325.

WORKS CITED

Note on Texts

Primary texts are cited in the original languages, accompanied by translations where available; otherwise translations are mine. For classical authors, I use the texts and translations in the Loeb editions. For patristic and exegetical works, I use the standard series and electronic texts in CETEDOC. I do not cite texts and editions for incidental and parenthetical references. Medieval writers are generally listed below under their first names. Greek terms are transliterated. The following abbreviations are used:

CCCM   Corpus Christianorum Continuatio Mediaeualis
CCSL   Corpus Christianorum Series Latina
CSEL   Corpus Scriptorum Ecclesiasticorum Latinorum
PL   Patrologia Latina
TAPA   Transactions and Proceedings of the American Philological Association

Primary Texts

Abelard, Peter. *Petri Abaelardi Opera Theologica* 1–2, ed. Eligius M. Buytaert. 2 vols. CCCM 11–12. Turnhout: Brepols, 1969.

———. *Epistolae.* In PL 178: 113–380.

——— and Heloise. *Abélard and Héloïse: Correspondance*, trans. Paul Zumthor. Paris: Christian Bourgeois, 1979.

———. *The Letters of Abelard and Heloise*, trans. Betty Radice. Harmondsworth: Penguin, 1974.

———. *La vie et les epistres: Pierres Abaelart et Heloys sa fame*, ed. Eric Hicks. Paris: Champion, 1991.

Aelred of Rievaulx. *De spiritali amicitia*, ed. A. Hoste. In *Aelredi Rievallensis opera omnia* 1: *Opera ascetica*, ed. A. Hoste and C. H. Talbot. CCCM 1. Turnhout: Brepols, 1971. Pp. 279–350.

Alan of Lille. *De planctu naturae*, ed. Nikolaus M. Häring. *Studi Medievali.* 3rd ser. 19 (1978): 787–879.

Ambrose. *De fuga saeculi*. In *I patriarchi, La fuga dal mondo, Le rimostranze di Giobbe e di Davide*, ed. Karl Schenkl and trans. Gabriele Banterle. Milan: Biblioteca Ambrosiana, 1980. Pp. 71–133.

The Anchor Bible: Lamentations, ed. Delbert R. Hillers. Garden City, NY: Doubleday, 1972.

Andreas Capellanus. *Andreas Capellanus on Love*, ed. and trans. P. G. Walsh. London: Duckworth, 1982.

Anon. "In Lamentationes Jeremiae." In PL 25: 827–32.

Aquinas, Thomas. *Summa theologiae*, ed. and trans. Blackfriars of the Dominican Province. 60 vols. New York: McGraw-Hill, 1964–66.

———. *Somme théologique I–II*. Paris: Éditions du Cerf, 1993.

Aristotle. *The "Art" of Rhetoric*, trans. John Henry Freese. Cambridge, MA: Harvard University Press, 1991.

———. *De anima*. In *On the Soul, Parva naturalia, On Breath*, trans. W. S. Hett. Rev. ed. Cambridge, MA: Harvard University Press, 1986. Pp.1–203.

Arnaut Daniel. *The Poetry of Arnaut Daniel*, ed. and trans. James J. Wilhelm. New York: Garland, 1981.

Augustine. *De civitate Dei*, ed. B. Dombart and A. Kalb. 2 vols. CCSL 47–48. Turnhout: Brepols, 1955.

———. *Confessioni*, ed. Roberta de Montecelli. Milan: Garzanti, 1990.

———. *Confessions*, ed. James J. O'Donnell. 3 vols. Oxford: Clarendon Press, 1992.

———. *The Confessions of Saint Augustine*, trans. Rex Warner. New York: Penguin, 1963.

———. *Confessionum libri XIII*, ed. M. Skutella, rev. L. Verheijen. CCSL 27. Turnhout: Brepols, 1981.

———. *De doctrina christiana*, ed. S. J. Martin. CCSL 32. Turnhout: Brepols, 1962.

———. *Enarrationes in Psalmos*. In PL 36: 67–1968.

———. *De musica*. In PL 32: 1081–1194.

———. *In Iohannis epistulam ad Parthos tractatus*. In PL 35: 1977–2062.

———. *Oeuvres de Saint Augustin*. Bibliothèque Augustinienne. 85 vols. 5th Series. Paris: Desclée de Brouwer, 1947–77.

———. *Retractiones*. In PL 32: 583–656.

———. *Sermones*. In PL 38: 23–1637.

Bernardus Silvestris. *The Commentary on the First Six Books of the "Aenied" of Vergil Commonly Attributed to Bernardus Silvestris*, ed. Julian Ward Jones and Elizabeth Frances Jones. Lincoln: University of Nebraska Press, 1977.

Biblia sacra juxta vulgatam versionem, ed. Robert Weber et al. 2 Vols. Stuttgart: Württembergische Bibelanstalt, 1975.

Boccaccio, Giovanni. *Filostrato*, ed. V. Pernicone. In Windeatt, *Troilus and Criseyde*.

———. *Filostrato*, ed. Alberto Limentani. Vol. 2 of *Tutte le opere di Giovanni Boccaccio*.

———. *Life of Dante*, trans. J. G. Nichols. London: Hesperus, 2002.

———. *Trattatello in laude di Dante*, ed. Pier Georgio Ricci. In *Tutte le opere di Giovanni Boccaccio*. 3: 423–538.

———. *Tutte le opere di Giovanni Boccaccio*, gen. ed. Vittore Branca. 12 vols. Milan: Mondadori, 1964–83.

Caesarius of Arles. *Sancti Caesarii Arelatensis Sermones*, ed. Germain Morin. 2 vols. CCSL 103–104. Turnhout: Brepols, 1953.

Catullus. *Catullus, Tibullus and Pervigilium Veneris.* 2nd ed., rev. G. P. Goold. Cambridge, MA: Harvard University Press, 1988.

Chaucer, Geoffrey. *The Riverside Chaucer*, gen. ed. Larry D. Benson. 3rd ed. Boston: Houghton Mifflin, 1987.

———. *The Story of Troilus*, ed. and trans. R. K. Gordon. 1934; rpt. Toronto: University of Toronto Press, 1978.

———. *Troilus and Crisyede: A New Edition of "The Book of Troilus,"* ed. Barry A. Windeatt. New York: Longman, 1984.

Cicero. *Tusculan Disputations*, trans. J. E. King. Cambridge, MA: Harvard University Press, 1966.

———. *Partitiones oratoriae.* In *De oratore III, De fato, Paradoxa Stoicorum, De partitione oratoria*, trans. H. Rackham. Cambridge, MA: Harvard University Press, 1982.

———. *De amicitia.* In *De senectute, De amicitia, De divinatione*, trans. William Armistead Falconer. Cambridge, MA: Harvard University Press, 1992. Pp. 101–211.

Dante Alighieri. *Il convivio*, ed. Maria Simonelli. Bologna: Pàtron, 1966.

———. *Convivio*, ed. Franca Brambilla Ageno. Vol. 3 of Edizione nazionale delle opere di Dante Alighieri. Florence: Le Lettere, 1995.

———. *Dante Alighieri: Rime*, ed. Gianfranco Contini. Turin: Einaudi, 1939, 1995.

———. *Dante's Lyric Poetry*, ed. Kenelm Foster and Patrick Boyde. 2 vols. Oxford: Oxford University Press, 1967.

———. *Dantis Alagherii Epistolae: The Letters of Dante*, ed. Paget Toynbee. Emended ed. Oxford: Clarendon Press, 1920.

———. *De vulgari eloquentia*, ed. and trans. Steven Botterill. Cambridge: Cambridge University Press, 1996.

———. *The Divine Comedy*, ed. and trans. Charles S. Singleton. 6 vols. Princeton: Princeton University Press, 1973.

———. *Literary Criticism of Dante Alighieri*, ed. and trans. Robert S. Haller. Lincoln, NB: University of Nebraska Press, 1973.

———. *La vita nuova*, ed. Michele Barbi. Edizione nazionale delle opere di Dante Alighieri 1. Florence: Bamporad, 1932.

———. *Vita nuova*, ed. and trans. Dino S. Cervigni and Edward Vasta. Notre Dame, IN: University of Notre Dame Press, 1995.

Le Débat sur le Roman de la Rose, ed. Eric Hicks. Geneva: Slatkine, 1996.

Drouart la Vache. *Drouart la Vache: Traducteur d'André le Chapelain* (1290), ed. Robert Bossuat. Paris: Champion, 1926.

Epistulae duorum amantium. See Mews, Constant J. *The lost Love Letters of Heloise and Abelard.*

Fulgentius. *Opera*, ed. R. Helm, rev. Jean Préaux. 1898; Stuttgart: Teubner, 1970.

———. *Fulgentius the Mythographer*, trans. Leslie George Whitbread. Columbus: Ohio State University Press, 1971.

Gaius. *Institutiones*, ed. Emil Seckel and Bernhard Kuebler. Leipzig: Teubner, 1935.

Guibert of Nogent. *Tropologiae in prophetas Osee et Amos ac Lamentationes Jeremiae.* In PL 156: 341–488.

Guillaume de Lorris and Jean de Meun. *Le Roman de la Rose*, ed. Daniel Poirion. Paris: Garnier-Flammarion, 1974.

———. *The Romance of the Rose*, trans. Charles Dahlberg. Princeton: Princeton University Press, 1971.

Heloise. *Problemata Heloissae*. In PL 178: 677–730.

——— [pseudo-Heloise]. *Two Late Medieval Love Treatises: Heloise's "Art d'Amour" and a Collection of "Demandes d'Amour,"* ed. Leslie C. Brook. Oxford: Society for the Study of Mediæval Languages and Literature, 1993.

Horace. *Odes and Epodes*, ed. and trans. Niall Rudd. Cambridge, MA: Harvard University Press, 2004.

Hugh of St. Victor. *Adnotatiunculae elucidatoriae in threnos Jeremiae*. In PL 175: 255–322.

Hugues le Poitevin. *Chronique de l'abbaye de Vézélay*. In *Monumenta Vizeliacensis: Textes relatifs à l'histoire de l'abbaye de Vézélay*, ed. R. B. C. Huygens. CCCM 42. Turnhout: Brepols, 1976. Pp. 395–607.

Huygens, R. B. C., ed. *Accessus ad auctores, Bernard d'Utrecht, Conrad d'Hirsau, "Dialogus super Auctores."* Rev. ed. Leiden: Brill, 1970.

Jean de Meun. "Boethius' *De consolatione* by Jean de Meun," ed. V. L. Dedeck-Héry. *Mediaeval Studies* 14 (1952): 165–275.

Jerome. *Commentarii in Ezechielem*, ed. F. Glorie. CCSL 75. Turnhout: Brepols, 1964.

———. *Commentarii in Isaiam*, ed. M. Adriaen. 2 vols. CCSL 73–73a. Turnhout: Brepols, 1963.

———. *Epistulae*, ed. Isidorus Hilberg. 3 vols. CSEL 54–56. Vienna: Tempsky, 1910–1918.

Lathbury, John. *Liber moralium super trenis iheremie*, Oxford: T. Root, 1482.

Lucan. *The Civil War (Pharsalia)*, trans. J. D. Duff. Cambridge, MA: Harvard University Press, 1988.

Lucretius. *On the Nature of Things*, trans. W. H. D. Rouse. Rev. ed. Martin Ferguson Smith. Cambridge, MA: Cambridge University Press, 1992.

Map, Walter. *De nugis curialium; Courtiers' Trifles*, ed. and trans. M. R. James, rev. C. L. N. Brooke and R. A. B. Mynors. Oxford: Clarendon Press, 1983.

Marie de France. *Les Lais de Marie de France*, ed. Jean Rychner. Paris: Champion, 1971.

———. *The Lais of Marie de France*, trans. Glyn S. Burgess and Keith Busby. 2nd ed. London: Penguin, 1999.

Ovid. *The Art of Love and Other Poems*, trans. J. H. Mozley. Cambridge, MA: Harvard University Press, 1969.

———. *Heroides and Amores*, trans. Grant Showerman. Cambridge, MA: Harvard University Press, 1971.

———. *Metamorphoses*, trans. Frank Justus Miller. 2 vols. Cambridge, MA: Harvard University Press, 1971–76.

———. *Tristia, Ex Ponto*, trans. Arthur Leslie Wheeler. Cambridge, MA: Harvard University Press, 1975. 2nd ed., rev. G. P. Goold. Cambridge, MA: Harvard University Press, 1988.

Paschasius Radbertus. *Expositio in Lamentationes Hieremiae libri quinque*, ed. Beda Paulus. CCCM 85. Turnhout: Brepols, 1988.

Propertius. *Propertius: Elegies*, ed. and trans. G. P. Goold. Cambridge, MA: Harvard University Press, 1990.

Rabanus Maurus. *Expositio super Jeremiam*. In PL 111: 793–1272.

Sedulius Scottus. *Collectaneum Miscellaneum*, ed. Dean Simpson. CCCM 67. Turnhout: Brepols, 1988.

Sigebert of Gembloux. *Vita Wicberti Gemblacensis*. In *Monumenta Germaniae Historica: Scriptores*, 8, ed. Georg Heinrich Pertz. Hannover: Hahn, 1848. Pp. 507–516.

Stehling, Thomas, ed. and trans. *Medieval Latin Poems of Male Love and Friendship*. New York: Garland, 1984.

Tibullus. See Catullus.

Ulpian. *Liber singularis regularum*. In *Iurisprudentiae anteiustinianae reliquas*, ed. Emil Seckel and Bernhard Kuebler. 2 vols. Leipzig: Teubner, 1908. 1: 442–91.

Vergil. *Virgil: Eclogues, Georgics, Aenied*, ed. and trans. H. Rushton Fairclough. 2 vols. Cambridge, MA: Harvard University Press, 1935, 1974.

Criticism and Scholarship

Ahern, Charles F., Jr. "Daedalus and Icarus in the *Ars Amatoria*." *Harvard Studies in Classical Philology* 92 (1989): 273–96.

———. "Ovid as Vates in the Proem to the *Ars amatoria*." *Classical Philology* 85 (1990): 44–48.

Ailes, M. J. "The Medieval Male Couple and the Language of Homosociality." In *Masculinity in Medieval Europe*, ed. D. M. Hadley. New York: Longman, 1999. Pp. 214–237.

Allen, Peter. *The Art of Love: Amatory Fiction from Ovid to the Romance of the Rose*. Philadelphia: University of Pennsylvania Press, 1992.

Arcaz, J. L., G. Laguna Mariscal, and Antonio Ramírez de Verger, eds. *La obra amatoria de Ovidio: aspectos textuales, interpretación literaria y pervivencia*. Madrid: Ediciones Clásicas, 1996.

Baldwin, Anna. "The Debt Narrative in *Piers Plowman*." In *Art and Context in Late Medieval English Narrative: Essays in Honor of Robert Worth Frank, Jr.*, ed. Robert R. Edwards. Cambridge: D. S. Brewer, 1994. Pp. 37–50.

Barolini, Teodolinda. " 'Cominciandomi dal principio infino a la fine' (*V.N.*, XXIII, 15): Forging Anti-narrative in the 'Vita Nuova.' " In Moleta, *La gloriosa donna de la mente*. Pp. 119–40.

———. "Dante and the lyric past." In *The Cambridge Companion to Dante*, ed. Rachel Jacoff. Cambridge: Cambridge University Press, 1993. Pp. 14–33.

———. *Dante's Poets: Textuality and Truth in the "Comedy."* Princeton: Princeton University Press, 1984.

Barrow, Julia, Charles Burnett, and David Luscombe. "A Checklist of the Manuscripts containing the Writings of Peter Abelard and Heloise and Other Works Closely Associated with Abelard and his School." *Revue d'histoire des textes* 14–15 (1984–85): 183–302.

Baswell, Christopher. *Virgil in Medieval England: Figuring the "Aeneid" from the Twelfth Century to Chaucer*. Cambridge: Cambridge University Press, 1995.

Baumgartner, Emmanuèle. "The Play of Temporalities; or, The Reported Dream of Guillaume de Lorris." In Brownlee and Huot, *Rethinking the "Romance of the Rose."* Pp. 21–38.

Beebee, Thomas O. *Epistolary Fiction in Europe 1500–1850.* Cambridge: Cambridge University Press, 1999.

Besserman, Lawrence. "A Note on the Sources of Chaucer's *Troilus* V, 540–613." *Chaucer Review* 24 (1989–90): 306–308.

Blamires, Alcuin. "No Outlet for Incontinence: Heloise and the Question of Consolation." In Wheeler, *Listening to Heloise.* Pp. 287–301.

Bloch, R. Howard. *The Anonymous Marie de France.* Chicago: University of Chicago Press, 2003.

———. *Medieval Misogyny and the Invention of Western Romantic Love.* Chicago: University of Chicago Press, 1991.

Blodgett, E. D. "The Well Wrought Void: Reflections on the *Ars Amatoria.*" *Classical Journal* 68 (1973): 322–33.

Bloomfield, Morton W. "Troilus' Paraclausithyron and its Setting: *Troilus and Criseyde,* V, 519–602." *Neuphilologische Mitteilungen* 73 (1972): 15–24.

Bond, Gerald A. *The Loving Subject: Desire, Eloquence, and Power in Romanesque France.* Philadelphia: University of Pennsylvania Press, 1995.

Botterill, Steven. " 'Però che la divisione non si fa se non per aprire la sentenzia de la cosa divisa' (*V.N.*, XIV, 13): The '*Vita Nuova*' as Commentary." In Moleta, *La gloriosa donna de la mente.* Pp. 61–76.

Bourgain, Pascale. "Héloïse." In *Abélard en son temps,* ed. Jean Jolivet. Paris: Les Belles Lettres, 1981. Pp. 211–237.

Boyde, Patrick. *Perception and Passion in Dante's "Comedy."* Cambridge: Cambridge University Press, 1993.

Braet, Herman. "Note sur Marie de France et Ovide (Lai de *Guigemar,* vv. 233–244)." In *Marche romane: Mélanges de philologie et de littérature romanes offerts à Jeanne Wathelet-Willem.* Liège: Association des romanistes, 1978. Pp. 21–25.

Branca, Vittore. "Poetics of Renewal and Hagiographic Tradition in the *Vita nuova,*" trans. Rosemary Foy. *Lectura Dantis Newberryana* 1, ed. Paolo Cherchi and Antonio C. Mastrobuono. Evanston: Northwestern University Press, 1988. Pp. 123–52.

Brightenback, Kristine. "The *Metamorphoses* and Narrative *Conjointure* in 'Deuz Amanz,' 'Yonec,' and 'Le Laüstic.' " *Romanic Review* 72 (1981): 1–12.

Brook, Leslie C. "A Note on the Ending of *Eliduc.*" *French Studies Bulletin* 32 (1989): 14–16.

Brown, Catherine. "*Muliebriter:* Doing Gender in the Letters of Heloise." In *Gender and Text in the Later Middle Ages,* ed. Jane Chance. Gainesville: University Press of Florida, 1996. Pp. 25–51.

Brown, Peter. *Augustine of Hippo: A Biography.* Berkeley and Los Angeles: University of California Press, 1967; new ed. 2000.

———. *The Body and Society: Men, Women and Sexual Renunciation in Early Christianity.* New York: Columbia University Press, 1988.

Brownlee, Kevin. "Pygmalion, Mimesis, and the Multiple Endings of the *Roman de la Rose.*" *Yale French Studies* 95 (1999): 193–211.

————. "Reflections in the *Miroër aus Amoreus*: The Inscribed Reader in Jean de Meun's *Roman de la Rose*." In *Mimesis: From Mirror to Method, Augustine to Descartes*, ed. John D. Lyons and Stephen G. Nichols, Jr. Hanover, NH: University Press of New England, 1983. Pp. 60–70.

Brownlee, Kevin and Sylvia Huot, eds. *Rethinking the "Romance of the Rose": Text, Images, Reception*. Philadelphia: University of Pennsylvania Press, 1992.

Bullough, Vern L. "The Sin against Nature and Homosexuality." In *Sexual Practices and the Medieval Church*, ed. Vern L. Bullough and James A. Brundage. Buffalo: Prometheus Books, 1982. Pp. 55–71.

Burgess, Glyn S. *The Lais of Marie de France: Text and Context*. Athens, GA: University of Georgia Press, 1987.

Bussell, Donna Alfonso. "Heloise Redressed: Rhetorical Engagement and the Benedictine Rite of Initiation in Heloise's Third Letter." In Wheeler, *Listening to Heloise*. Pp. 233–54.

Calabrese, Michael A. *Chaucer's Ovidian Arts of Love*. Gainesville: University Press of Florida, 1994.

Cargo, Robert T. "Marie de France's *Le Laustic* and Ovid's *Metamorphoses*." *Comparative Literature* 18 (1966): 162–66.

Carruthers, Mary J. *The Book of Memory: A Study of Memory in Medieval Culture*. Cambridge: Cambridge University Press, 1990.

Cartlidge, Neil. *Medieval Marriage: Literary Approaches, 1100–1300*. Cambridge: D. S. Brewer, 1997.

Chadwick, Henry. *Augustine*. New York: Oxford University Press, 1986.

Cherniss, Michael D. "Irony and Authority: The Ending of the *Roman de la Rose*." *Modern Language Quarterly* 36 (1975): 227–38.

Clanchy, M. T. *Abelard: A Medieval Life*. Oxford: Blackwell, 1997.

Cogan, Marc. *The Design in the Wax: The Structure of the "Divine Comedy" and Its Meaning*. Notre Dame, IN: University of Notre Dame Press, 1999.

Colish, Marsha L. *The Stoic Tradition from Antiquity to the Early Middle Ages*. Corr. ed. 2 vols. Leiden: Brill, 1990.

Connolly, Joy. "Asymptotes of Pleasure: Thoughts on the Nature of Roman Erotic Elegy." *Arethusa* 33 (2000): 71–98.

Contreni, John M. "Carolingian Biblical Studies." In *Carolingian Essays*, ed. Uta-Renate Blumenthal. Washington, D.C.: Catholic University of America Press, 1983. Pp. 71–98.

Copley, Frank Olin. "*Servitium amoris* in the Roman Elegists." TAPA 78 (1947): 285–300.

Cormier, Raymond J. and Urban Tigner Holmes, eds. *Essays in Honor of Louis Francis Solano*. Chapel Hill: University of North Carolina Press, 1970.

Cottille-Foley, Nora. "The Structuring of Feminine Empowerment: Gender and Triangular Relationships in Marie de France." In *Gender Transgressions: Crossing Normative Barrier in Old French Literature*, ed. Karen J. Taylor. New York: Garland, 1998. Pp. 153–80.

Cottrell, Robert D. "*Le Lai du Laustic*: From Physicality to Spirituality." *Philological Quarterly* 47 (1968): 499–505.

Courcelle, Pierre. *Les Confessions de Saint Augustin dans la tradition littéraire: Antécédents et Posterité*. Paris: Études Augustiniennes, 1963.

———. *Recherches sur les Confessions de Saint Augustin*. Paris: E. de Boccard, 1950.

Crane, Susan. "Anglo-Norman Cultures in England, 1066–1460." In *The Cambridge History of Medieval English Literature*, ed. David Wallace. Cambridge: Cambridge University Press, 1999. Pp. 35–60.

Curtius, Ernst Robert. *European Literature and the Latin Middle Ages*, trans. Willard R. Trask. New York: Harper Row, 1963.

Dahlberg, Charles. "Love and the *Roman de la Rose*." *Speculum* 44 (1969): 568–84.

Dalzell, Alexander. *The Criticism of Didactic Poetry: Essays on Lucretius, Virgil, and Ovid*. Toronto: University of Toronto Press, 1996.

D'Andrea, Antonio. "Dante interprete di se stesso: le varianti ermeneutiche della *Vita Nuova* e la 'Donna Gentile.' " In *Miscellanea di studi in onore di Aurelio Roncaglia*. Modena: Mucchi, 1989. Pp. 493–506.

De Bonfils Templer, Margherita. *Itinerario di amore: Dialettica di amore e morte nella "Vita Nuova."* Chapel Hill: Publications of the Department of Romance Languages, University of North Carolina, 1973.

De Robertis, Domencio. *Il libro della "Vita Nuova."* Florence: Sansoni, 1961.

Dinshaw, Carolyn. *Chaucer's Sexual Poetics*. Madison: University of Wisconsin Press, 1989.

Dollimore, Jonathan. *Death, Desire and Loss in Western Culture*. New York: Routledge, 1998.

Downing, Eric. "Anti-Pygmalion: The *Praeceptor* in *Ars Amatoria*, Book 3." In Porter, *Constructions of the Classical Body*. Pp. 235–51.

———. *Artificial I's: The Self as Artwork in Ovid, Kierkegaard, and Thomas Mann*. Tübingen: Max Niemeyer, 1993.

Dragonetti, Roger. "Pygmalion ou les pièges de la fiction dans le *Roman de la Rose*." In *Orbis Mediaevalis: Mélanges de langue et de littérature médiévales offerts à Reto Raduolf Bezzola à l'occasion de son quatre-vingtième anniversaire*, ed. Georges Güntert, Marc-René Jung, and Kurt Ringger. Berne: Francke, 1978. Pp. 89–111.

Dronke, Peter. *Abelard and Heloise in Medieval Testimonies*. Glasgow: Glasgow University Press, 1976.

———. *Dante's Second Love: The Originality and the Contexts of the Convivio*. Exeter: The Society for Italian Studies, 1997.

———. *Women Writers of the Middle Ages*. Cambridge: Cambridge University Press, 1984.

Dubuis, R. "La notion de *druërie* dans les *Lais* de Marie de France." *Le Moyen Age* 98 (1992): 391–413.

Dufournet, Jean, ed. *Amour et Merveille: Les "Lais" de Marie de France*. Paris: Champion, 1995.

Durling, Robert M. *The Figure of the Poet in Renaissance Epic*. Cambridge, MA: Harvard University Press, 1965.

———, and Ronald L. Martinez. *Time and the Crystal: Studies in Dante's "Rime Petrose."* Berkeley and Los Angeles: University of California Press, 1990.

Eberle, Patricia J. "The Lovers' Glass: Nature's Discourse on Optics and the Optical Design of the *Romance of the Rose*." *University of Toronto Quarterly* 46 (1976–77): 241–62.

Edwards, Robert R. *Ratio and Invention: A Study of Medieval Lyric and Narrative.* Nashville, TN: Vanderbilt University Press, 1989.

———. *The Dream of Chaucer: Representation and Reflection in the Early Narratives.* Durham, NC: Duke University Press, 1989.

———. "Pandarus's 'Unthrift' and the Problem of Desire in *Troilus and Criseyde*." In Shoaf, *Chaucer's "Troilus and Criseyde*." Pp. 74–87.

Fenzi, Enrico. " 'Costanzia de la ragione' e 'malvagio desiderio' (*V.N.* XXXIX, 2): Dante e la donna pietosa." In Moleta, *La gloriosa donna de la mente*. Pp. 195–224.

Fitz, Brewster E. "Desire and Interpretation: Marie de France's *Chievrefoil*." *Yale French Studies* 58 (1979): 182–89.

———. "The Prologue to the *Lais* of Marie de France and the *Parable of The Talents*: Gloss and Monetary Metaphor." *MLN* 90 (1975): 558–64.

Fleming, John V. *Classical Imitation and Interpretation in Chaucer's "Troilus."* Lincoln: University of Nebraska Press, 1990.

———. "Jean de Meun and the Ancient Poets." In *Rethinking the "Romance of the Rose."* Pp. 81–100.

———. *Reason and the Lover*. Princeton: Princeton University Press, 1984.

Foster, Kenelm. *The Two Dantes and Other Studies.* Berkeley and Los Angeles: University of California Press, 1977.

Freccero, John. *Dante: The Poetics of Conversion*, ed. Rachel Jacoff. Cambridge, MA: Harvard University Press, 1986.

Freeman, Michelle A. "Marie de France's Poetics of Silence: Implications for a Feminine *Translatio*." *PMLA* 99 (1984): 860–83.

Fyler, John M. "*Omnia vincit amor*: Incongruity and the Limitations of Structure in Ovid's Elegiac Poetry." *Classical Journal* 66 (1970–71): 196–203.

Gavilán, Francisco Socas. "Entre la moral e la estética: intenciones del maestro de amor." In Arcaz et al., *La obra amatoria de Ovidio*. Pp. 95–120.

Georgianna, Linda. " 'In Any Corner of Heaven': Heloise's Critique of Monastic Life." In Wheeler, *Listening to Heloise*. Pp. 187–216.

Gertz, SunHee Kim. "Echoes and Reflections of Enigmatic Beauty in Ovid and Marie de France." *Speculum* 73 (1998): 372–96.

Giannarelli, Elena. "L'immagine della neve al sole dalla poesia classica al Petrarca: contributo per la storia di un 'topos.' " *Quaderni petrarcheschi* 1 (1983): 91–129.

Gilson, Étienne. *Héloïse and Abélard*, trans. L. K. Shook. Chicago: Henry Regenry, 1951.

Ginsberg, Warren. *Dante's Aesthetics of Being.* Ann Arbor: University of Michigan Press, 1999.

———. "*Ovidius ethicus*?: Ovid and the Medieval Commentary Tradition." In Paxson and Gravlee, *Desiring Discourse*. Pp. 62–71.

Godefroy, Frédéric. *Dictionnaire de l'ancienne langue française*. Paris: Librarie des sciences et des arts, 1938.

Gottwald, Norman K. *Studies in the Book of Lamentations*. Rev. ed. London: SCM Press, 1962.

Gragnani, Enrico. "La revisione della produzione guittoniana nelle rime danteschi." *Esperienze letterarie* 24 (1999): 39–57.

Green, C. M. C. "Terms of Venery: *Ars Amatoria* I." TAPA 126 (1996): 221–63.

Grotz, K. "Die Einheit des 'Confessiones.' " Diss., Tübingen, 1970.

Gunn, Alan M. F. *The Mirror of Love: A Reinterpretation of "The Romance of the Rose."* Lubbock: Texas Tech Press, 1952.

Hagstrum, Jean. *Esteem Enlivened by Desire: The Couple from Homer to Shakespeare*. Chicago: University of Chicago Press, 1992.

Halperin, David. "Platonic *Erôs* and What Men Call Love." *Ancient Philosophy* 5 (1985): 161–204.

Hamilton, Elizabeth. *Héloïse*. Garden City: Doubleday, 1967.

Hanning, Robert W. "Come in Out of the Code: Interpreting the Discourse of Desire in Boccaccio's *Filostrato* and Chaucer's *Troilus and Criseyde*." In Shoaf, *Chaucer's "Troilus and Criseyde."* Pp. 120–37.

———. "Courtly Contexts for Urban *cultus*: Responses to Ovid in Chrétien's *Cligès* and Marie's *Guigemar*." *Symposium* 35 (1981–82): 34–56.

———. "The Talking Wounded: Desire, Truth Telling, and Pain in the *Lais* of Marie de France." In Paxson and Gravlee, *Desiring Discourse*. Pp. 140–61.

Hardie, Philip, ed. *The Cambridge Companion to Ovid*. Cambridge: Cambridge University Press, 2002.

Harrison, Robert Pogue. *The Body of Beatrice*. Baltimore: The Johns Hopkins University Press, 1988.

Harrison, Stephen. "Ovid and Genre: Evolutions of an Elegist." In Hardie, *The Cambridge Companion to Ovid*. Pp. 79–94.

Heller–Roazen, Daniel. *Fortune's Faces: The "Roman de la Rose" and the Poetics of Contingency*. Baltimore: Johns Hopkins University Press, 2003.

Hexter, Ralph J. *Ovid and Medieval Schooling*. Munich: Arbeo Geselleschaft, 1986.

———. "Ovid's Body." In Porter, *Constructions of the Classical Body*. Pp. 327–54.

Hœpffner, Ernest. "Marie de France et l'*Eneas*." *Studi medievali* n.s. 5 (1932): 272–308.

Hollander, Robert. "*Vita Nuova*: Dante's Perceptions of Beatrice." *Dante Studies* 92 (1974): 1–18.

Hollis, A. S. "The *Ars Amatoria* and *Remedia Amoris*." In *Ovid*, ed. J. W. Binns. London: Routledge and Kegan Paul, 1973. Pp. 84–115.

Hult, David. "Language and Dismemberment: Abelard, Origen, and the *Romance of the Rose*." In *Rethinking the "Romance of the Rose."* Pp. 101–130.

———. *Self-Fulfilling Prophecies: Readership and Authority in the First "Roman de la Rose."* Cambridge: Cambridge University Press, 1986.

Huot, Sylvia. "Authors, Scribes, Remanieurs: A Note on the Textual History of the *Romance of the Rose*." In *Rethinking the "Romance of the Rose."* Pp. 203–233.

———. *From Song to Book: The Poetics of Writing in Old French Lyric and Lyrical Narrative Poetry*. Ithaca: Cornell University Press, 1987.

———. *The "Romance of the Rose" and Its Medieval Readers: Interpretation, Reception, Manuscript Transmission*. Cambridge: Cambridge University Press, 1993.

Irvine, Martin. "Heloise and the Gendering of the Literate Subject." In *Criticism and Dissent in the Middle Ages*, ed. Rita Copeland. Cambridge: Cambridge University Press, 1996. Pp. 87–114.

Jaeger, C. Stephen. *Ennobling Love: In Search of a Lost Sensibility*. Philadelphia: University of Pennsylvania Press, 1999.

Johnson, Warren and William A. Percy. "Homosexuality." In *Handbook of Medieval Sexuality*, ed. Vern L. Bullough and James A. Brundage. New York: Garland, 1996. Pp. 155–89.

Jolivet, Jean. *Abélard ou la philosophie dans le langage*. Paris: Éditions du Cerf, 1994.

Kamuf, Peggy. *Fictions of Feminine Desire: Disclosures of Heloise*. Lincoln: University of Nebraska Press, 1982.

Karnein, Alfred. "Amor est Passio: A Definition of Courtly Love?" In *Court and Poet*, ed. Glyn S. Burgess, A. D. Deyermond, W. H. Jackson, A. D. Mills, and P. T. Ricketts. Liverpool: Cairns, 1981. Pp. 215–221.

Kay, Sarah. *Courtly Contradictions: The Emergence of the Literary Object in the Twelfth Century*. Stanford, CA: Stanford University Press, 2001.

Kelly, Douglas. " 'Diversement comencier' in the *Lais* of Marie de France." In Maréchal, *In Quest of Marie de France*. Pp. 107–122.

———. "Du Narcisse des poètes à la rose des amants: Le jeu de la vérité chez Guillaume de Lorris." In *Et c'est la fin pour quoy sommes ensemble: Hommage à Jean Dufournet*. 3 vols. Paris: Champion, 1993. Pp. 793–800.

———. *Internal Difference and Meanings in the "Roman de la Rose."* Madison: University of Wisconsin Press, 1995.

———. " 'Li chastiaus. . .Qu'Amors prist puis par ses esforz': The Conclusion of Guillaume de Lorris' *Rose*." In *A Medieval French Miscellany*, ed. Norris J. Lacy. Lawrence: University of Kansas Publications, 1972. Pp. 61–78.

Kelly, Henry Ansgar. *Chaucerian Tragedy*. Cambridge: D. S. Brewer, 1997.

Kennedy, Duncan F. "Bluff Your Way in Didactic: Ovid's *Ars Amatoria* and *Remedia Amoris*." *Arethusa* 33 (2000): 159–76.

Kleiner, John. "Finding the Center: Revelation and Reticence in the *Vita Nuova*." *Texas Studies in Literature and Language* 32 (1990): 85–100.

Klemp, P. J. "The Women in the Middle: Layers of Love in Dante's *Vita Nuova*." *Italica* 61 (1984): 185–94.

Knoespel, Kenneth J. *Narcissus and the Invention of Personal History*. New York: Garland, 1985.

Köhler, Erich. "Narcisse, la fontaine d'amour et Guillaume de Lorris." In *L'Humanisme médiéval dans les littératures romanes du XIIe au XIVe siècle*, ed. Anthime Fourrier. Paris: Klincksieck, 1964. Pp. 147–66.

Lambert, Mark. "Telling the Story in *Troilus and Criseyde*." In *The Cambridge Chaucer Companion*, ed. Piero Boitani and Jill Mann. Cambridge: Cambridge University Press, 1986. Pp. 59–73.

Le Goff, Jacques. *The Medieval Imagination*, trans. Arthur Goldhammer. Chicago: University of Chicago Press, 1988.

Leach, Eleanor Winsor. "Georgic Imagery in the *Ars amatoria*." TAPA 95 (1964): 146–49.

Lewis, Charlton T. and Charles Short. *A Latin Dictionary*. Oxford: Clarendon, 1969.

Libera, Alain de. *Penser au moyen âge*. Paris: Seuil, 1991.

Lubac, Henri de. *Exégèse médiévale: Les quatre sens de l'Écriture*. 4 vols. Paris: Aubier, 1961.

Luria, Maxwell. *A Reader's Guide to the "Roman de la Rose."* Hamden, CN: Archon Books, 1982.

Luscombe, David. "Peter Abelard and the Poets." In *Poetry and Philosophy in the Middle Ages: A Festschrift for Peter Dronke*, ed. John Marenbon. Leiden: Brill, 2001. Pp. 155–71.

Maddox, Donald. *Fictions of Identity in Medieval France*. Cambridge: Cambridge University Press, 2000.

Maréchal, Chantal A., ed. In *Quest of Marie de France, A Twelfth-Century Poet*. Lewistown, NY: Mellen, 1992.

Marenbon, John. "Authenticity Revisited." In Wheeler, *Listening to Heloise*. Pp. 19–33.

———. *The Philosophy of Peter Abelard*. Cambridge: Cambridge University Press, 1997.

Mariscal, Gabriel Laguna. "Recepción de Ovidio amatorio en la antigüedad tardía." In Arcaz et al. *La obra amatoria de Ovidio*. Pp. 163–83.

Martinez, Ronald L. "Mourning Beatrice: The Rhetoric of Threnody in the *Vita nuova*." *MLN* 113 (1998): 1–29.

Matter, E. Ann. "The Lamentations Commentaries of Hrabanus Maurus and Paschasius Radbertus." *Traditio* 38 (1982): 137–63.

Mazzaro, Jerome. "From *Fin Amour* to Friendship: Dante's Transformation." In *The Olde Daunce: Love, Friendship, Sex, and Marriage in the Medieval World*, ed. Robert R. Edwards and Stephen Spector. Albany: State University of New York Press, 1991. Pp. 121–37.

———. *The Figure of Dante: An Essay on the "Vita Nuova."* Princeton: Princeton University Press, 1981.

Mazzotta, Giuseppe. "The Language of Poetry in the *Vita nuova*." *Rivista di Studi Italiani* 1 (1983): 3–14.

———. "The Light of Venus and the Poetry of Dante: 'Vita Nuova' and Inferno XXVII." In *Dante*, ed. Harold Bloom. New York: Chelsea, 1986. Pp. 189–204.

McGregor, James H. "Is Beatrice Boccaccio's Most Successful Fiction?" *Texas Studies in Literature and Language* 32 (1990): 137–51.

McGuire, Brian Patrick. "Heloise and the Consolation of Friendship." In Wheeler, *Listening to Heloise*. Pp. 303–321.

McLaughlin, Mary M. "Abelard as Autobiographer: The Motives and Meaning of His 'Story of Calamities.'" *Speculum* 42 (1967): 463–88.

McLeod, Glenda. "'Wholly Guilty, Wholly Innocent': Self-Definition in Héloïse's Letters to Abélard." In *Dear Sister: Medieval Women and the Epistolary Genre*, ed. Karen Cherewatuk and Ulrike Wiethaus. Philadelphia: University of Pennsylvania Press, 1993. Pp. 64–86.

McNamara, Marie Aquinas. *Friendship in Saint Augustine*. Studia Friburgensia n.s. 20. Fribourg: The University Press, 1958.

Meckler, Michael. Review of *The Lost Love Letters of Heloise and Abelard: Perceptions of Dialogue in Twelfth-Century France*, by Constant J. Mews. *Speculum* 78 (2003): 572–74.

Ménard, Philippe. *Les Lais de Marie de France: Contes d'amour et d'aventure du Moyen Age*. Paris: Presses universitaires de France, 1979.

———. "Marie de France et nous." In Dufournet, *Amour et merveille*. Pp. 7–24.

Menocal, María Rosa. *Writing in Dante's Cult of Truth From Borges to Boccaccio*. Durham, NC: Duke University Press, 1991.

Mews, Constant J. *The Lost Love Letters of Heloise and Abelard: Perceptions of Dialogue in Twelfth–Century France*. New York: St. Martin's Press, 1999.

———. *Peter Abelard*. Vol. 2. No. 5. of Authors of the Middle Ages, Historical and Religious Writers of the Latin West. Aldershot, Hants: Ashgate, 1995.

———. "Philosophical Themes in the *Epistolae duorum amantium*: The First Letters of Heloise and Abelard." In Wheeler, *Listening to Heloise*. Pp. 35–52.

Mickel, Emanuel J., Jr. "Antiquities in Marie's *Lais*." In Maréchal, *In Quest of Marie de France*. Pp. 123–37.

———. "A Reconsideration of the *Lais* of Marie de France." *Speculum* 46 (1971): 39–65.

Miles, Margaret R. "The Body and Human Values in Augustine of Hippo." In *Grace, Politics and Desire: Essays on Augustine*, ed. H. A. Meynell. Calgary: University of Calgary Press, 1990. Pp. 55–67.

Miller, John F. "Lucretian Moments in Ovidian Elegy." *Classical Journal* 92 (1997): 384–98.

Minnis, A. J. *Magister amoris: The "Roman de la Rose" and Vernacular Hermeneutics*. Oxford: Oxford University Press, 2001.

———. *Medieval Theory of Authorship: Scholastic literary attitudes in the Later Middle Ages*. 2nd ed. Philadelphia: University of Pennsylvania Press, 1988.

Mintz, Alan. *Hurban: Responses to Catastrophe in Hebrew Literature*. New York: Columbia University Press, 1984.

Moi, Toril. "Desire in Language: Andreas Capellanus and the Controversy of Courtly Love." In *Medieval Literature: Criticism, Ideology, and History*, ed. David Aers. New York: St. Martin's Press, 1986. Pp. 11–33.

Moleta, Vincent, ed. *La gloriosa donna de la mente: A commentary on the "Vita Nuova."* Florence: Olschki, 1994.

Moos, Peter von. "Lucan und Abelard." In *Hommages à André Boutemy*, ed. Guy Cambier. Brussels: Latomus, Revue d'études latines, 1976. Pp. 438–40.

———. "Le silence d'Héloïse." In *Pierre Abélard, Pierre le Vénérable: Les courrants philosophiques, littéraires et artistiques en Occident au milieu du XIIe siècle*, ed. R. Louis, J. Jolivet, and J. Châtillon. Paris: Éditions du CNRS, 1975. Pp. 425–68.

Muckle, J. T., C. S. B. "The Personal Letters Between Abelard and Heloise." *Mediaeval Studies* 15 (1953): 47–94.

Myerowitz, Molly. *Ovid's Games of Love*. Detroit: Wayne State University Press, 1985.

Nelson, Deborah. "Eliduc's Salvation." *The French Review* 55 (1981): 37–42.

Newman, Barbara. *From Virile Woman to WomanChrist: Studies in Medieval Religion and Literature.* Philadelphia: University of Pennsylvania Press, 1995.

Nichols, Stephen G. "Marie de France's Commonplaces." *Yale French Studies*, Contexts: Style and Values in Medieval Art and Literature (1991): 134–48.

Nolan, Barbara. "The *Vita Nuova* and Richard of St. Victor's Phenomenology of Vision." *Dante Studies* 92 (1974): 35–53.

O'Donnell, James J. *Augustine.* Boston: Twayne, 1985.

O'Gorman, Ellen. "Love and the Family: Augustus and the Ovidian Legacy." *Arethusa* 30 (1997): 103–123.

Olsen, Birger Monk. *L'étude des auteurs classiques latins aux XIe et XIIe siècles.* 3 vols. Paris: Éditions du CNRS, 1982–89.

O'Meara, John J. "Augustine the Artist and the *Aenied.*" In *Mélanges offerts à Mademoiselle Christine Mohrmann.* Utretcht: Spectrum, 1963. Pp. 252–61.

———. *The Young Augustine: The Growth of St. Augustine's Mind up to his Conversion.* New York: Longman, Green and Co., 1954.

Paré, Gérard. *Les idées et les lettres au XIIIe siècle: La Roman de la Rose.* Montréal: Bibliothèque de philosophie, 1947.

Paupert, Anne. "Les femmes et la parole dans les *Lais* de Marie de France." In Dufournet, *Amour et Merveille.* Pp. 169–87.

Paxson, James J. and Cynthia A Gravlee, eds. *Desiring Discourse: The Literature of Love, Ovid through Chaucer.* Selinsgrove, PA: Susquehanna University Press, 1998.

Pelan, Margaret. *L'influence de "Brut" de Wace sur les romanciers français de son temps.* Paris: Droz, 1931.

Pelen, Marc M. *Latin Poetic Irony in the "Roman de la Rose."* Liverpool: Cairns, 1987.

Pellegrino, Michel. *Les Confessions de Saint Augustin: Guide de lecteur.* Paris: Alsatia, 1960.

Piccone, Michelangelo. "Modelli e struttura nella *Vita nuova.*" *Studi e problemi di critica testuale* 15 (1977): 50–61.

Pickens, Rupert T. "Poétique et sexualité chez Marie de France: L'exemple de *Fresne.*" In *Et c'est la fin pour quoy sommes ensembles: Hommage à Jean Dufournet.* 3 vols. Paris: Champion, 1993. Pp. 1119–31.

Poirion, Daniel. "De la signification selon Jean de Meun." In *Archéologie du signe,* ed. Lucie Brind'Amour and Eugene Vance. Toronto: Pontifical Institute of Mediaeval Studies, 1983. Pp. 165–85.

———. "Narcisse et Pygmalion dans *Le Roman de la Rose.*" In Cormier and Holmes, *Essays in Honor of Louis Francis Solano.* Pp. 153–65.

Porter, James I., ed. *Constructions of the Classical Body.* Ann Arbor: University of Michigan Press, 1999.

Prior, Sandra Pierson. " 'Kar des dames est avenu / L'aventure': Displacing the Chivalric Hero in Marie de France's *Eliduc.*" In Paxon and Gravlee, *Desiring Discourse.* Pp. 123–39.

Ragland-Sullivan, Ellie. *Jacques Lacan and the Philosophy of Psychoanalysis.* Urbana: University of Illinois Press, 1986.

Regalado, Nancy Freeman. " 'Des contraires choses': la fonction poétique de la citation et des *exempla* dans le 'Roman de la Rose' de Jean de Meun." *Littérature* 41 (February 1981): 62–81.

————. "The Medieval Construction of the Modern Reader: Solomon's Ship and the Birth of Jean de Meun." *Yale French Studies* 95 (1999): 81–108.

Ribard, Jacques. "Le *Lai de Guigemar: Conjointure* et *Senefiance*." In Dufournet, *Amour et Merveille*. Pp. 133–45.

Richards, Earl J. "Les Rapports entre le *Lai de Guigemar* et le *Roman d'Eneas*: considérations génériques." In *Le Récit bref au moyen âge*, ed. D. Buschinger. Paris: Champion, 1980. Pp. 45–55.

Rist, John M. *Augustine: Ancient Thought Baptized*. Cambridge: Cambridge University Press, 1994.

Robertson, D. W., Jr. *Abelard and Heloise*. New York: Dial Press, 1972.

Robertson, Howard S. "Love and the Other World in Marie de France's *Eliduc*." In Cormier and Holmes, *Essays in Honor of Louis Francis Solano*. Pp. 167–76.

Rocher, Daniel. "Marie de France et l'amour tristanesque." In *Tristan et Iseult: mythe européen et mondial*. Göppinger: Kümmerle, 1987. Pp. 341–51.

Ronchi, Gabriella. "Sulla questione dei rapporti tra il *Tristan* di Thomas e i *Lais* di Maria di Francia." *Medioevo romanzo* 16 (1991): 261–70.

Rougemont, Denis de. *Love in the Western World*, trans. Montgomery Belgion, rev. ed. New York: Pantheon, 1956.

Roush, Sherry. *Hermes' Lyre: Italian Poetic Self-Commentary from Dante to Tommaso Campanella*. Toronto: University of Toronto Press, 2002.

Schibanoff, Susan. "Prudence and Artificial Memory in Chaucer's *Troilus*." *ELH* 42 (1975): 507–517.

Schiesaro, Alessandro. "Ovid and the Professional Discourses of Scholarship, religion, rhetoric." In Hardie, *The Cambridge Companion to Ovid*. Pp. 62–75.

Segre, Cesare. "Piramo e Tisbe nei *Lai* di Maria di Francia." In *Studi in onore di Vittorio Lugli e Diego Valeri*. 2 vols. Venice: Pozza, 1961. 2: 845–53.

Shapiro, Marianne. *Dante and the Knot of Body and Soul*. New York: St. Martin's Press, 1998.

Sharrock, Alison. "Gender and Sexuality." In Hardie, *The Cambridge Companion to Ovid*. Pp. 95–107.

————. *Seduction and Repetition in Ovid's "Ars Amatoria" 2*. Oxford: Clarendon Press, 1994.

Shaw, J. E. *Essays on The Vita Nuova*. Princeton: Princeton University Press, 1929.

Shippey, Thomas A. "Listening to the Nightingale." *Comparative Literature* 22 (1970): 46–60.

Shoaf, R. A., ed. *Chaucer's "Troilus and Criseyde": "Subgit to alle Poesye"— Essays in Criticism*. Binghamton: Medieval & Renaissance Texts & Studies, 1992.

Shullman, J. "*Te quoque falle tamen*: Ovid's Anti-Lucretian Didactics." *Classical Journal* 76 (1981): 242–53.

Singer, Irving. *The Nature of Love*. 2nd ed., 3 vols. Chicago: University of Chicago Press, 1984.

Singleton, Charles S. "Dante: Within Courtly Love and Beyond." In *The Meaning of Courtly Love*, ed. F. X. Newman. Albany: State University of New York Press, 1968. Pp. 43–54.

———. *An Essay on the "Vita Nuova."* Cambridge, MA: Harvard University Press, 1949.

Smalley, Beryl. *English Friars and Antiquity in the Early Fourteenth Century.* Oxford: Basil Blackwell, 1960.

Sommariva, Grazia. "La parodia di Lucrezio nell'*Ars* e nei *Remedia* ovidiani." *Atene e Roma* n.s. 25 (1980): 123–48.

Spitzer, Leo. *Bemerkungen zu Dantes "Vita Nuova."* Istanbul: Devlet Basimevi, 1937.

Stakel, Susan. *False Roses: Structures of Duality and Deceit in Jean de Meun's "Roman de la rose."* Saratoga, CA: ANMA Libri, 1991.

Stapleton, M. L. "*Venus Vituperator:* Ovid, Marie de France, and *Fin'Amors.*" *Classical and Modern Literature* 13 (1993): 283–95.

Stegmüller, Friedrich. *Repertorium Biblicum Medii Aevi.* 11 vols. Madrid: Consejo superior de investigaciones científicas / Instituto Francisco Suárez, 1950–80.

Stein, Robert M. "Desire, Social Reproduction, and Marie's *Guigemar.*" In Maréchal, *In Quest of Marie de France.* Pp. 280–94.

Steinle, Eric M. "Anti-Narcissus: Guillaume de Lorris as a Reader of Ovid." *Classical and Modern Literature* 6 (1986): 251–59.

Stillinger, Thomas C. *The Song of Troilus: Lyric Authority in the Medieval Book.* Philadelphia: University of Pennsylvania Press, 1992.

Stock, Brian. "The Self and Literary Experience in Late Antiquity and the Middle Ages." *New Literary History* 25 (1994): 839–52.

Stone, Gregory B. "Dante's Averroistic Hermeneutics (On 'Meaning' in the *Vita nuova*)." *Dante Studies* 112 (1994): 133–59.

Strubel, Armand. *Guillaume de Lorris, Jean de Meun: Le Roman de la Rose.* Études littéraires 4. Paris: Presses universitaires de France, 1984.

Stump, Eleonore. "Augustine on free will." In *The Cambridge Companion to Augustine*, ed. Eleonore Stump and Norman Kretzmann. Cambridge: Cambridge University Press, 2001. Pp. 124–47.

Sturm-Maddox, Sara. "Transformations of Courtly Love Poetry: *Vita Nuova* and *Canzoniere.*" In *The Expansion and Transformations of Courtly Literature*, ed. Nathaniel B. Smith and Joseph T. Snow. Athens: University of Georgia Press, 1980. Pp. 128–40.

Tarrant, Richard J. "Ovid and Ancient Literary History." In Hardie, *The Cambridge Companion to Ovid.* Pp. 13–33.

Thonnard, François-Joseph. "La notion de concupiscence en philosophie augustinienne." *Recherches Augustiniennes* 3 (1965): 59–105.

Thut, Martin. "Narcisse versus Pygmalion: Une lecture de Roman de la Rose." *Vox Romanica* 41 (1982): 104–133.

Took, J. F. *Dante, Lyric Poet and Philosopher: An Introduction to the Minor Works.* Oxford: Clarendon, 1990.

Tudor, A. P. "The Religious Symbolism in the 'Reliquary of Love' in *Laustic.*" *French Studies Bulletin* 46 (1993): 1–3.

Uitti, Karl D. " 'Cele[qui] doit estre Rose clamee' (*Rose*, vv. 40–44): Guillaume's Intentionality." In *Rethinking the "Romance of the Rose."* Pp. 39–64.

Vance, Eugene. *Mervelous Signals: Poetics and Sign Theory in the Middle Ages.* Lincoln: University of Nebraska Press, 1986.

Vlastos, Gregory. *Platonic Studies.* Princeton: Princeton University Press, 1981.

Volk, Katharina. *The Poetics of Latin Didactic: Lucretius, Vergil, Ovid, Manilius.* Oxford: Oxford University Press, 2002.

Ward, John O. and Neville Chiavaroli. "The Young Heloise and Latin Rhetoric: Some Preliminary Comments on the 'Lost' Love Letters and Their Significance." In Wheeler, *Listening to Heloise.* Pp. 33–119.

Watson, Patricia. "Ovid and Cultus: Ars Amatoria 3.113–28." *TAPA* 112 (1982): 237–44.

Welliver, Warman. *Dante in Hell: The "De vulgari eloquentia."* Ravenna: Longo, 1981.

Wetherbee, Winthrop. "Literary works." In *The Cambridge Companion to Abelard,* ed. Jeffrey E. Brower and Kevin Guilfoy. Cambridge: Cambridge University Press, 2004. Pp. 45–64.

———. *Platonism and Poetry in the Twelfth Century: The Literary Influence of the School of Chartres.* Princeton: Princeton University Press, 1972.

Whalen, Logan E. "A Medieval Book Burning: *Object d'art* as Narrative Device in the Lai of *Guigemar.*" *Neophilologus* 80 (1996): 205–211.

Wheeler, Bonnie, ed. *Listening to Heloise: The Voice of a Twelfth-Century Woman.* New York: St. Martin's Press, 2000.

Wheelock, James T. S. "A Function of the *Amore* Figure in the *Vita Nuova.*" *Romanic Review* 68 (1977): 276–86.

Wilkinson, L. P. *Ovid Surveyed.* Cambridge: Cambridge University Press, 1962.

Wilson, Katharina and Glenda McLeod. "Textual Strategies in the Abelard/Heloise Correspondence." In Wheeler, *Listening to Heloise.* Pp. 121–42.

Wood, Chauncey. *The Elements of Chaucer's "Troilus."* Durham, NC: Duke University Press, 1984.

Zeitlin, Froma. "Reflections on Erotic Desire in Archaic and Classical Greece." In Porter, *Constructions of the Classical Body.* Pp. 50–76.

Zizek, Slavoj. *The Sublime Object of Ideology.* London: Verso, 1989.

Zumthor, Paul. *Essai de poétique médiévale.* Paris: Seuil, 1972.

INDEX

Abelard, Peter, 10–11, 12, 59–84, 166–67, 177n1, 179n25, 180n30, 180n37
  Ethica, 71, 77
  Rule, 78, 81, 82–83
  Theologia, 71
  Theologia christiana, 68, 181n50
  Theologia 'scholarum,' 181n50
Accessus ad auctores, 88, 183n10
Aelred of Rievaulx, 113, 172n17
Ahern, Charles F., 56, 57, 176n6, 177n44
Ailes, M. J., 179n21
Alan of Lille, 63, 179n20
Allen, Peter, 41, 110, 176n10, 185n22
Ambrose, Saint, 2, 171n4, 173n1
Andreas Capellanus, 5–6, 6–7, 111, 114–115, 123, 144, 172n18, 172n19, 178n12, 186n33, 189n46, 191n72, 191n74
Angiolieri, Cecco, 126, 127
Aquinas, Saint Thomas, 4–5, 6, 7, 171n6, 172n11, 172n12, 172n25
Aristotle, 4, 6, 7, 17, 36, 113, 115, 171n1, 172n11, 172n12, 172n24, 191n5
Arnaut Daniel, 1–2, 171n3
Augustine, Saint, 5, 7, 10, 11, 50, 58, 59, 75, 155, 165, 168, 172n15, 172n23, 173n4
  Confessions, 10–11, 13–37, 175n28, 175n42; and Lamentations 150–52, 158

De civitate Dei (The City of God), 14–15, 172n14, 173n5, 173n6, 173n8, 174n10
De doctrina christiana, 172n9, 190n60
De libero arbitrio, 20
De musica, 29, 175n39
De trinitate, 20
  and Abelard, 60, 72–73, 78, 82
  and Marie de France, 86, 99–100
  and *Roman de la Rose*, 107, 116, 124
  and *Troilus and Criseyde*, 147, 149
  and *Vita nuova*, 125, 140
Averroes, 191n5

Baldwin, Anna, 181n61
Barolini, Teodolinda, 126–27, 138, 187n2, 187n12, 189n48, 190n57
Barrow, Julia, 182n68
  See also Burnett, Charles, and Luscombe, David
Baswell, Christopher, 175n37
Baudri of Bourgueil, 63, 179n19
Baumgarten, Emmanuèle, 185n14
Bede, 192n14
Beebee, Thomas O., 179n25
Bernardus Silvestris, 27, 175n37, 175n38
Besserman, Lawrence, 148, 191n2
Blamires, Alcuin, 179n16, 181n57, 182n73
Bloch, Howard R., 8, 85, 102, 173n28, 183n2, 183n21, 184n38
Blodgett, E. D., 52, 177n36
Bloomfield, Morton W., 192n26

Ovid—*continued*
  Tristia, 57, 151, 175n42, 176n1: and
    Abelard, 64–67, 68, 69, 79; and
    Marie de France, 85–103; and
    Roman de la Rose, 106,
    107–113, 114, 120, 124,
    167–68, 185n20; and *Troilus
    and Criseyde*, 147–49, 168; and
    Vita nuova, 133, 135, 136, 137,
    140, 142–43

Parè, Gèrard, 117, 186n40
Paschasius Radbertus, 152–55, 192n13,
    192n14, 192n16, 192n17,
    192n18, 192n20, 192n21
Paul, Saint, 13, 30, 35, 36, 68, 74
Paupert, Anne, 183n25
Pelen, Marc M., 113, 186n28
Pellegrino, Michel, 174n23
Percy, William A.
  See Johnson, Warren
Peripetetics, 14
Peter the Venerable, 73, 181n54
Petrarch, 59, 60, 75–76, 77, 78, 82
Piccone, Michelangelo, 189n47
Pickens, Rupert T., 183n2
Col, Pierre, 106
Plato, 5, 7, 17, 36
Platonists, 15
Plé, Albert, 171n6
plenitude, 10, 11, 14, 20, 36–37, 39,
    52–53, 68–69, 73, 90, 94, 99,
    117, 151, 155, 158–59, 161, 164,
    166–67, 168, 183n19
Poirion, Daniel, 184n7, 185n15,
    185n17
Pompey, 62
Prior, Sandra Pierson, 98, 183n27
Priscian, 85
Propertius, 39, 49–50
Psalms, 20, 74, 152–53, 172n15,
    173n7

Rabanus Maurus, 152, 192n22
Ragland-Sullivan, Ellie, 173n27

Regelado, Nancy Freeman, 106, 114,
    184n2, 184n5, 185n11, 186n31
Ribard, Jacques, 183n24
Rist, John M., 173n7
Robertson, D. W., Jr., 180n48
Robertson, Howard S., 183n28
Roman de la Rose, 6, 9, 11, 12, 105–24,
    128, 148, 163, 167, 168, 180n34,
    185n16
  See also Guillaume de Lorris; Jean de
    Meun
Roscelin de Compiègne, 62
Rougemont, Denis de, 8
Roush, Sherry, 126, 187n8
Rule, Benedictine, 78
Rychner, Jean 87, 183n6

Schibanoff, Susan, 193n45
Schiesaro, Alessandro, 52, 177n38
Sedulius Scottus, 172n17
Segre, Cesare, 183n5
Seneca, 73
Shapiro, Marianne, 130, 188n31
Sharrock, Alison, 40, 45, 49, 56, 57,
    176n7, 177n23, 177n31, 177n45
Shaw, J. E., 190n52
Shippey, Thomas A., 101, 184n36
Shullman, J., 53, 177n40
Sigebert of Gembloux, 181n56
Singer, Irving, 8, 173n29
Singleton, Charles S., 140, 156, 157,
    171n1, 188n28, 190n53, 190n61,
    192n28, 193n32
Smalley, Beryl, 192n25
Solignac, Aimé, 15, 174n11
Sommariva, Grazia, 177n39
Song of Songs, 145, 152–54, 158,
    191n74, 192n15
Spitzer, Leo, 189n47
Stakel, Susan, 114, 186n32
Stapleton, M. L., 88, 183n11, 183n16
Stegmüller, Friedrich, 152, 192n12
Stein, Robert M., 183n2
Steinle, Eric M., 185n18
Stillinger, Thomas C., 187n6